WHEN HE'S AN ALPHA
The Olympus Pride Series, Book 2

SUZANNE WRIGHT

The characters and events portrayed in this book are fictitious. Any similarity to real persons, living or dead, is coincidental and not intended by the author.

Copyright © 2021 Suzanne Wright

All rights reserved. This book or any portion thereof may not be reproduced or used in any manner whatsoever without the express written permission of the publisher except for the use of brief quotations in a book review.

Cover design: J Wright

ISBN: 9798713765286

Imprint: Independently Published

For the Hard Rock Hotel. The vacations I've had there ... Ah, good times.

CHAPTER ONE

God, this was going to absolutely *suck ass*. In her opinion, the only thing shittier than breaking things off with a guy you cared for was knowing that said guy wouldn't give a measly fuck. Which was why Havana Ramos really wished she lived in a world where ending a fling by text message wasn't considered distasteful.

If Tate Devereaux wasn't both her landlord and a male who she respected, she might have ignored her annoying morals and done this from the comfort of her sofa. Instead, she was currently walking along the street that led to the cozy little cul-de-sac where he lived. She would give him the courtesy of a face-to-face talk, and she would pretend not to be upset when all he did was shrug and tell her to enjoy the rest of her day.

This really shouldn't be so hard. Casual relationships were supposed to be simple, fun, and easy to walk away from. But she'd found that they could be the messiest of all relationships. It was just far too easy for lines to get blurred and hearts to get bruised. There were just so many dos and don'ts that she found it hard to keep up. And the golden rule? *Do not get attached.*

Well, she broke the fucker, didn't she?

Generally, she wasn't afraid to break rules. It was sort of fun. But *this* particular rule was not made to be broken.

If she thought there was a chance the fling could evolve into something more, she'd stick around and see if anything came of it. But after earlier overhearing the words that Tate exchanged with his brother, she knew it was time to cut her losses and walk away.

Maybe it was better that Tate wouldn't care. It meant she didn't have to worry that he'd evict her out of spite. The apartment she shared with one of her closest friends wasn't anything special, but it was pure gold for lone shifters like Havana. Living in a complex owned by the Alpha male of a strong pride gave her an element of protection.

It was only six months ago that Tate replaced his father as Alpha, but he'd already earned a reputation as a man who shouldn't be fucked with. People rarely tangled with his kind anyway.

The full-blooded animals of his kind were referred to as Pallas' cats, but shifters stuck with "pallas cats." These feline shifters were moody, mercurial, and preloaded with an "I couldn't give a rat's ass" vibe. If someone pissed them off, they'd attack without hesitation and savagely tear into their prey with a demonic ferocity. Considering pallas cats were, pound for pound, one of the strongest breeds of shifter, they could do a whole lot of damage—despite not being much bigger than a housecat when in their weirdly cute animal form. In sum, they were crazy.

Havana's kind weren't exactly beings of pure light either. Devil shifters were bigger than the full-blooded animals of their kind, Tasmanian devils, and had long ago solidified their spot in the archives of terror with their notoriously bad tempers, blood-curdling shrieks, absolute fearlessness, and habit of feasting on the dead. In her opinion, they were simply too awesome not to exist.

Shifter society wasn't terribly fond of Havana's kind, so she'd known when she made inquiries about the vacant apartment that there was a chance she'd be turned away. But Tate hadn't even commented on it. Then again, they'd both been a little caught up in their immediate sexual chemistry that had fairly crackled in the air. That day, he'd watched her closely as he gave her a tour of the apartment, a carnal promise in his eyes that made her skin prickle.

Snaring the attention of such a powerful Alpha had been something of a thrill. It was also a stroke to her ego, which had taken a pounding when she learned that her on-and-off-bed-buddy was now in a serious relationship. Dieter had flitted in and out of her world like a directionless butterfly for a year. She'd hoped there'd come a day when he'd be ready to commit. But when that day *did* come, Havana hadn't been the woman he'd committed to.

When Tate made his move and was very clear that all he wanted was casual sex—no obligations, no romance, no expectations, no emotional investment—that had sounded good to her. Generally, she didn't get involved with Alphas. She'd known too many who abused their power, bullied those they were supposed to protect, and sought to control people through fear ... much like her old Alpha. Which was why she'd researched Tate before applying to rent the apartment.

She'd learned that he wasn't one of those assholes who was drunk on power or who exercised control in a domineering way. He didn't dish out orders while ruling from his metaphorical throne, lazily leaving his Beta to oversee matters. Tate was *all up* in the pride's business—a constant, visible, active presence that wasn't afraid to get his hands dirty and stood between his pride and the world like a shield. So her wariness of Alphas hadn't held her back from accepting his offer.

Over the past four months, they'd gone separately about their daily lives—worked, ate, relaxed, slept—and then hooked up for sex a few times a week. They were not *part* of each other's lives: she wasn't "his," even though they were exclusive.

Still, she was acquainted with many of his pride mates since she shopped at the pride-owned stores she was currently walking past—all of which were close to her complex. As such, she knew he'd made no secret of their fling. He'd made it publicly clear that she was off-limits. But he'd never formally introduced her to his family or ever taken her out on dates.

Although they only met up at either her apartment or his house, it wasn't a wham-bam-thank-you-ma'am kind of thing. They also hung out, ate dinner, enjoyed some light conversation, and sometimes even watched a movie. He never made her feel used or disrespected. He was always *totally* focused on her and very much present in the moment.

And the sex? It was off-the-charts hot. Like all natural-born alphas, Havana could be pretty demanding in the bedroom and didn't give up control easily. It wasn't about sexual games. Testing her bedpartner was a primal drive inside every alpha female. It was instinctual to put up a fight, test the male's strength, and make him work for control.

Tate was a very dominant man. He expressed that dominance and need for control during sex, so he hadn't been bothered by her refusal to submit easily—in fact, he'd seemed to like the challenge. So, yeah, they were a good match in bed.

She'd enjoyed the fling for what it was. For a while. Recently, she found herself lamenting that he had no interest in getting to know her. It had started to hurt that he didn't ask her personal questions or for her to elaborate on any information she volunteered. It had also started to bother her that he only ever contacted her when he was interested in hooking up—other than that, it was radio silence.

She wasn't actually upset with *him*, just with the situation. Because, really, she only had herself to blame for *again* falling for a guy who couldn't give her what she wanted.

She knew from his pride mates that some of his ex-bed buddies had agreed to his terms in the hope that he'd eventually commit. But Havana hadn't walked into their arrangement thinking that it would be a steppingstone to a real relationship. She'd honestly thought she could enjoy a brief fling and not cross any emotional lines.

Well she'd failed. Spectacularly.

And her pathetic hopes that the fling might blossom had died a quick death right in the middle of her stairwell earlier when Tate and his brother had been fitting a new door lock on another level, and they'd had no idea she overheard them …

"*You and Havana look good together, Tate. You two have had a thing going for just over four months now, yeah?*"

"*Yeah.*"

"*That's a long time for you. Is it heading into semi-serious territory?*"

"*No.*"

"*Maybe you should consider making it a little serious and seeing if it goes anywhere. You're thirty-two years old; you ain't getting any younger.*"

"*Not interested in a real relationship, Luke. You know that. So does Havana. We're just having a bit of fun, and that's all we're gonna have.*"

She swallowed hard at the memory. Really, she should have guessed it was coming. A Dead End road sign had fallen over practically in front of her this morning.

Her first thought was, "*Well, fuck.*"

Her second thought was, "*Is that what Tate and I have, a dead-end relationship?*" And she'd concluded that, as much as she wished differently, they in fact did. The universe had kindly given her a reminder that this was going nowhere.

Yeah, she believed in signs. She heeded them. They'd never led her wrong.

Her inner animal wasn't so happy that Havana intended to make a graceful exit from the fling. The devil was fussy and relatively antisocial, but she liked Tate; liked that he was so self-possessed and unapologetically masculine. She was in something of a funk right now.

Havana felt like indulging in a good sulk, too, but she had no right. She'd known from the very beginning that she and Tate weren't building anything.

She'd also known, courtesy of his pride mates, that a woman he once tried imprinting on had completely fucked him over. That had been three years ago. He'd kept his relationships short and casual ever since—his usual cut-off date was two months. But he'd let his fling with Havana continue for longer, and she'd stupidly read a little too much into that. She shouldn't have, considering he'd been very clear that there'd be no happy ending. There was no sense in whining about it now—not even in her head.

As she skirted the corner of the street and turned into the cul-de-sac, her stomach rolled. Which she totally ignored, because this had to be done. Approaching his house, she noticed two of his enforcers lingering near the building on guard. She said a quick hello to each of them as she walked up Tate's front yard and onto his porch.

Pulling up her mental bootstraps, she jabbed the doorbell. It seemed like forever before the door swung open. Her pulse spiked as rich inky blue eyes landed on her—it was easy to see the killer instinct there. It was also easy to melt right into a puddle of hot to trot goo. What else was a girl to do when presented with so much male deliciousness?

Tall and powerfully built, Tate Devereaux was the definition of rugged with the merciless slash to his full mouth, the harshly masculine lines of his face, and the fine layer of stubble that dusted his square jaw. His short hair was dark as pitch and sleek as a cat's fur. Intricate tattoos were inked on his arms, chest, and back, accentuating the muscles there. And there was a *lot* of honed, roped muscle to be seen on that body.

Even without the subtle yet potent alpha vibes that spilled from him, there would be *no* missing that Tate was a leader down to the bone. He projected an innate authority and supreme self-assurance that commanded attention. There'd be *no* steamrolling this guy. Tate was a man who decided his own path. He didn't follow the rules; he made his own, all the while exuding a calm surety that he'd get what he wanted one way or another.

Basically, he made all her sexual bells ring-a-ding-ding. Loud. With feeling.

One corner of his mouth kicked up slightly. "Hey," he greeted simply.

Damn, *that voice*. It was deep. Low. Gravelly. Uber-sexy. It also dripped with the power that was a basic part of his character.

"You didn't call to say you were coming," he said, but it wasn't an admonishment.

Havana hadn't called because he would no doubt have assumed she was interested in hooking up tonight. She hadn't wanted to mislead him.

She walked in as he stepped aside to let her pass. The door had no sooner closed behind her than Tate pulled her flush against him, making her stomach flip. Her nerve endings sprung to life and her blood went hot. Her body clearly wasn't on board with her "it's time to walk away" plan.

He buried his face in her neck. "Your scent makes my mouth water."

His own scent had a similar effect on her. Right then, it rose between them. *Dark chocolate mint, rich coffee beans, and warm worn leather.* It never failed to stir up her hormones—they were so easy for him, the traitors.

Sliding his hand up her outer thigh, he scraped his teeth over her pulse. "I'm glad you came."

Doing her best to ignore the way her body lit up for him, she splayed her fingers on the center of his chest and said, "We need to talk." They also needed to stop this now before she gave into the temptation to indulge in a bout of goodbye sex.

He lashed her earlobe with his tongue. "We do?" It was a careless question.

"It's important, Tate." She pushed hard against his chest. "Really, we have to talk," she said firmly.

He very slowly backed up, his gaze flitting over her face. "About what?"

She opened her mouth, but no words came out. God, it should be simple to end something that hadn't really begun. Especially when it had never been fated to last long.

Part of her was tempted to make some bullshit excuse for why she'd turned up and just give him more time, but that would be dumb. She *needed* to walk away now. It was the right thing to do. They were wasting each other's time by dragging out something that had no future.

Ignoring the knots in her gut, Havana lifted her chin. She'd make this quick, painless, and civil. "I wanted to do this face-to-face. I'm pretty sure you'll agree with me on this. Still, it's awkward for me to be the one to say it out loud, but one of us needs to. I had fun and everything, Tate, but I think it's time we each went our own way."

Seconds ticked by as he simply stared at her. Then his brows snapped together, and a low growl rumbled out of him. "The fuck? What brought this on, Havana? Last night, you were moaning beneath me, asking me to take you harder. Before you left, we made plans to get together next weekend. Now you're telling me we need to go our own way?"

She double-blinked, sincerely surprised that he gave a rat's ass. "Yes, it's time we did. Take care of yourself, okay?"

She turned, intending to leave. His arm shot out, slamming his palm on the wall beside her head, acting as a barrier. She didn't turn back to face him. She just stared at his arm, grinding her teeth as anger-filled alpha vibes *radiated* from him—they whipped at her skin and settled heavy on her bones.

He took a prowling step closer, swallowing up the small distance between them, and put his mouth to her ear. "I've been inside that pussy more times than I can count. Now you're telling me I no longer have any rights to it. You can at least explain why."

"Look—"

"You met someone else? Is that what this is?"

Frowning, she twisted to face him, forcing him to edge back and lower his arm. "What? *No.*"

"So what am I missing? What happened between last night and right now that made you want to walk away?" He squinted. "Did someone say something to you? Has one of my pride mates got their panties in a twist because their Alpha's involved with a loner?"

"If any of them had a problem with you and I sleeping together, they didn't make me aware of it."

"Then why do this?"

"Like I said, it's just time that we each went our own way."

He moved his face closer to hers. "You didn't seem to feel that way last night when you were coming all over my cock."

She damned her cheeks for heating. The sex between them was amazing, sure, but that was all they had. And telling him how much that hurt her wasn't anywhere on her annual schedule. She wasn't going to put herself out there and make herself vulnerable only to have him tell her what she already knew—he wouldn't give her more.

Besides, knowing Tate, he'd feel shitty that she was hurting. She didn't want that. He was a good guy who'd walked a very fine line, careful never to make her feel used without leading her into thinking their relationship was anything other than casual.

"Answer me, Havana. What the fuck brought this on? Why are you telling me we're done?"

Every instinct she had bristled at the sheer *demand* in his voice; at the utter expectation of a response, like he held authority over her. She narrowed her eyes. "Oh, how very vehement you sound. I get that you're an Alpha, but you're not *my* Alpha. Now quit looming over me. *I don't like it.*"

"Then tell me what I want to know."

"I already did."

"It was a half-assed answer. I want to know the rest."

"There's nothing more *to* know." She rubbed at her temple. "God, why are you making this difficult?"

"Difficult?"

"Yes. You weren't supposed to care. This wasn't supposed to bother you. I don't know why it does. I don't get why you're pushing me on this."

"If I'd suddenly turned around and declared that you and I were done, you wouldn't have wondered why?"

"No. Because you were clear from the beginning that this fling would have a quick expiry date. I would have thought you'd have ended it before now. You didn't, but you *would* have some time soon. You wouldn't have lost any sleep over it; wouldn't have considered it a big deal. You'd have easily moved on with your life … because I'd never actually been part of it, had I? I'd just hovered on the edges of it—you wouldn't allow anything else."

Tate ground his teeth, silently conceding that she was right. He hadn't pulled her into his world, hadn't offered her a place in it, hadn't marked her as his. So he shouldn't feel like he was losing something. Something important.

When Havana first declared they needed to "go their own way," it had taken a few seconds for her words to sink in. Then anger had *exploded* in his gut, and a cord of something that was strangely akin to panic had twined tight around his lungs—that cord was still there, making his chest twinge with every breath. Her declaration thrust his cat into the throe of a hissing, snarling fit of fury, and the feline showed no signs of getting his shit together.

His cat usually never gave a damn when a woman chose to walk away. The animal tired of females fast. He usually began to withdraw after a month or two—he'd been that way since Ashlynn pissed all over them three years ago.

Similarly, Tate never much cared if a woman ended a fling. Purely because, due to his cat's habit of withdrawing from relationships, Tate was careful not to choose females who held too much appeal for him. But as everything in him rebelled at the thought of Havana walking away, he realized he hadn't succeeded at holding her at a distance. More, he'd gotten far too comfortable in their relationship, shallow though it was.

He also realized that his cat had been more invested in the fling than Tate had originally thought. The feline's interest in Havana hadn't yet waned. But the cat *would* pull away from her eventually ... and there'd be nothing Tate could do to stop it.

Some of the women from his past had only been bluffing when they proclaimed it was "over." They'd said it in an effort to spur Tate into offering them more, which had never worked. But he could see that Havana wasn't playing that game. She meant what she said. She was ready to scrape him off.

It shouldn't have bothered him. In fact, Tate should have been able to nod and wish her well. He should have been able to agree that the fling had run its course.

He *shouldn't* have been thinking about caging her against the wall, stripping her naked, and fucking her into changing her mind.

Tate silently cursed, knowing he had no one to blame but himself. He'd never felt such elemental, explosive chemistry with another female—it had sparked to life the moment he laid eyes on Havana. He'd known all the way down to his gut that it would be a bad idea to touch her; that she wouldn't be easy to walk away from. But he'd taken the risk because he'd wanted her so fucking badly.

He'd thought a few weeks in her bed would be enough to work off the insanely carnal need she roused in him. Four months later, he was *still* fucking ravenous for her. But then, what red-blooded male wouldn't be?

There was something very ... arresting about Havana. It was in the way she held herself with such regal grace. She always looked fearless. In command. Comfortable in her own skin. Haughty in a way that would challenge any male to try to win her attention.

More, she shimmered with a feminine alpha energy that seemed to light her up from within. It glittered in those exotic, almond bluish-gray eyes that were framed with thick dark lashes. Persian eyes, he thought.

Long and feathered, her hair fell in sleek maple brown ripples down her back. He loved to run his hands through it, especially when eating at that fantasy mouth. Loved to stroke and lick all her soft golden-brown skin and explore her wicked curves. And, fuck, those smooth toned legs felt insanely good wrapped around him. All of her felt good. Felt *right*.

And now she was telling him he no longer had the right to touch her, taste her, be inside her.

Tate felt his nostrils flare. This whole thing had come out of left-field, and he didn't know what to make of it.

She'd said that none of his pride mates had expressed any disapproval over her involvement with him, but Havana wasn't the type to name and shame. There were a few ambitious females in his pride who were gunning to be Alpha female. They tried flirting with him on occasion, and they weren't pleased by his disinterest. One or more of them could have felt threatened by Havana and decided to act on it.

Not that trying to scare her off would have worked—his little devil wasn't easily intimidated. But if they'd made several comments, she might have gotten tired of dealing with it, might have felt that an emotionless fling wasn't worth the hassle. Unlike those other females, she had no aspirations to rule alongside him—he would have sensed it if she had. He was used to having people around who wanted something from him.

Tate had always known he'd one day take over the pride. He hadn't wanted to be *given* the position by his father, though. He'd wanted to earn it. So he'd worked his way up from enforcer to Beta, mastering every skill necessary to lead. Because it had been common knowledge among the pride that he'd one day rule, people had been trying to climb up his ass for years.

Women often strove to please him, telling him what they thought he wanted to hear, reluctant to disappoint him. Not because they gave much of a shit about him, but because they wanted the prize at the end of the tunnel—to become Alpha female.

Havana, however, didn't want anything from him. She didn't even seem particularly impressed by his role. She didn't take his crap, give him his own way all the time, or relentlessly try to impress him. Hell, she didn't even *address* him like he was an Alpha. When they were together, he was just Tate to her. She didn't see his status, she saw *him*.

There were few people Tate felt able to lower his guard around. Havana was one of them. She made him feel at ease. Calm. Unjudged. It enabled him to switch off and relax.

She also didn't try pushing his boundaries. She just let the situation be. Let *him* be. She made an effort to get to know him, but she never asked anything too personal. She didn't sulk if he dodged a particular question—she just gave him a haughty eye roll that was *all* alpha and never failed to make his dick twitch.

She wasn't afraid to challenge him, especially not in the bedroom. She put up a resistance and made him work for the right to take control. So there was a lot of biting and scratching, though they were both careful not to draw blood or leave permanent marks. He'd never admit out loud that he'd almost branded her once. Well, twice. Maybe even several times.

To put it simply, Havana Ramos was his equal. She accepted and understood him in a way that only another natural-born alpha could. And he liked her a fuck of a lot. So he really wasn't down with her plan for them to each go their own goddamn way.

She exhaled heavily. "I'm going to head home."

"Not until you tell me why you want to walk away from me."

"For God's sake, Tate, can you not just drop it?" She thrust a hand into her hair, and her inner animal momentarily glared out at him through her eyes. Given the devil's temper, he wouldn't be surprised if she shifted and tried to bite his face off.

The smaller a breed of shifter, the more likely he was to avoid it—and there was a very good reason for that. Smaller breeds not only tended to be ten times more ferocious, it was as if mother nature gave them some utterly cool defenses to compensate for their size.

Take devil shifters: their bones were tough as steel. They had the bite force of a giant piranha. They possessed an immense strength that was out of proportion to their size. And the odor they released from their anal glands could make even a skunk think, "Fuck, no."

Devils were disliked by some but respected by all. Because you had to respect that a creature the size of a small dog with an oversized head could burst your skull like a goddamn piñata.

One thing Tate liked about devils was that they weren't unpredictable. They were very consistent creatures, so you knew exactly where you stood with them. More to the point, you knew that if you pissed them off, they'd shift into small, furry canisters of pure rage that would happily rip the skin from your bones. So, yeah, there was really no such thing as giving an angry devil shifter *too* much personal space. Still, he wasn't going to do as she requested and "drop this." It was too important.

"Is this an ego thing?" she asked. "You like to be the one who decides when it's over?"

"This has nothing to do with ego. This is a simple case of me wanting you to stop dancing around my questions. One thing I like about you, Havana, is that you're a straight-shooter. You say it how it is. Right now, though, all your shutters are down. I can't imagine what could possibly be going on up here"—he gently tapped her temple— "that you'd feel you couldn't tell me."

"Since when have you *ever* cared about what goes on inside my head? You never ask about anything—not my past, not my opinions, not my likes or dislikes, nothing. In that sense, you barely know me."

"Bullshit. I might not know your origins, your favorite color, or how you came to be a loner, but I know you." He hadn't asked her questions about herself, but he'd paid attention. Watched her. Studied her. Filed little things away in his head. He knew plenty about her.

You couldn't fit Havana in a box. She was short-tempered yet the calm in the storm. Caring yet not tactile. Friendly yet not social. Frank yet guarded. Impulsive yet not a slave to her impulses. She was a practical person but whimsical enough to believe in "signs." She wasn't a girly girl but also wasn't a tomboy. She was just … her. A quirky and intriguing mix of tough and vulnerable.

"And you know me," he added.

"Not well. You kept a metaphorical ocean between us."

A muscle in his cheek ticked. "There's a reason I keep a distance from—"

"You don't need to explain yourself," she instantly assured him. "Really. You have every right to insist on boundaries. That's not wrong. I'm just making the point that I never got to properly know you, that's all. Look, I'm making the right decision for us both here. We fooled around for over four months. It's not wise to continue something that isn't going anywhere. That's how people's expectations get muddled. That's how they get hurt."

She wasn't wrong. She also wasn't telling him the complete truth. "Maybe that's part of the reason you're declaring you're done, but there's more to this."

She flicked her gaze upward. "You know, I'm beginning to think that nothing I say will be enough to justify my decision to you. Also, it's kind of narcissistic of you to feel like there needs to be a *major* reason why a girl would choose to walk away from you. Sometimes, people just want to leave dead-end relationships. They just want to move on."

Pain knifed through his gut. A pain that was unexpected. Dangerous. "And you just want to move on?"

"Yes, I do. Because it really is best for both of us." She let out a long breath. "I don't want us to part on a bad note. You're a good guy. And I had fun."

"Yet, you're done."

She gave him a wan smile. "This was always going to end. I'm just making it happen sooner rather than later."

Tate shook his head. He wasn't ready for this to be over. What they had might not be deep or serious, but it was good. He didn't want to give her up yet. "Baby—"

"Don't, Tate. Don't do that. Just let this be. It truly is better to do this now," she added, her voice going thick with emotion. But then she took a step back, and a mask of indifference slipped over her face.

The sudden distance in her eyes raised his hackles and made his cat snarl. She was a mere foot away, but there might as well have been a goddamn abyss between them. She suddenly seemed so utterly out of reach on every level. So completely inaccessible. He could feel her slipping through his fingers like water.

The cord of panic around his lungs tightened until it hurt to breathe. The urge to bite her, brand her, bubbled up out of nowhere and surged through him with such strength that he reached for her, intending to clamp his teeth around her pulse.

The fuck?

Shaken, Tate lowered his arm and backed up.

"See you around." Then she was gone, and the door closed behind her.

He scrubbed a hand down his face, cursing beneath his breath. He wanted to do as his raging cat demanded—track her down, haul her back, and make her think twice about walking away from him again. But Tate stayed where he was. He let her go. He had no business going after her because, really, what the fuck did he have to give her?

Nothing. Not a goddamn thing.

CHAPTER TWO

Pausing in sweeping the shiny floor of the indoor basketball court, Havana sighed at her friends. Her head was pounding, so she didn't appreciate the echoing sounds of the ball bouncing, sneakers squeaking on the floor, or the curses and grunts. "Could you two both stop goofing around and help me tidy up so we can shut the place down?"

Bailey stilled, her face all innocence. "We were just checking that the ball wasn't deflating. Turns out it's fine."

"Now how about that," Havana said dryly. "Go retract the bleachers into the walls, please." She looked at Aspen. "Could you put the rest of the sports equipment back? And could you maybe find the little beanbag I saw your bearcat run off with earlier? I know she hid it somewhere." Why bearcat shifters stole and stashed objects—most of which they couldn't possibly have a use for—Havana didn't know. The full-blooded animals of their kind, which humans referred to as red pandas, didn't appear to do it.

"Will do," replied Aspen, idly plucking at the dark choppy layers in her long, angled bob. The tall, curvy female then strode off in that catwalk-haughty way she had.

"Thank you." Havana turned back to sweeping the floor. For years they'd worked at the rec center, which was exclusive to lone shifters. As sad as it was, loners were often targeted, so it was a dangerous lifestyle. The rec center was a safe place where they could relax, have fun, and meet others in their situation. It made them feel less alone. It gave them somewhere to "belong," even if only for a few hours a day.

The center had saved Havana. She'd been living on the streets when a regular here had coaxed her into checking the place out. The owner and manager, Corbin, had offered her a place to stay at his large house, which was a foster home of sorts for homeless lone shifter children.

Aspen had already been living there when Havana arrived. Bailey came along a year later. The three of them were different breeds of shifter, but they'd become so close they were like sisters.

They considered themselves a miniature yet unofficial clan of sorts. Their co-worker and close friend, Camden, kind of loitered on the edges of it. They all lived in the same building. Bailey was Havana's roommate while Aspen and Camden lived in the neighboring apartment.

It wasn't always easy for loners to find accommodation. There was a lot of prejudice against them from both shifters and humans alike. Plus, Havana had to conceal that she was a shifter if the landlord was human—devils hadn't yet come out of the shifter closet. Many species hadn't, including Tate's kind. *Ugh*. She tried her best not to think about him, but her thoughts often circled back to him.

A week had gone by since she broke things off. She hadn't heard or seen anything of him during those seven days. But then, she hadn't thought he would. Sure, he hadn't liked that she'd ended the fling, but she'd bet that was only because he would have preferred to be in control of *when* it ended—Alpha males were all about control.

The first thing she'd done after leaving his house was text Aspen and Bailey, asking them to meet her at a local bar so Havana could get blitzed. They'd drank shots, trash-talked male shifters, and contemplated calling Tate to inform him that he was a fuckface—something they thankfully hadn't done, because she'd have been mortified when sober. They'd topped off the evening by fighting with some bitchy jackals who apparently had an issue with loners. All in all, it hadn't been a bad night.

Done sweeping, Havana blew out an upward breath, making her bangs lift. She'd worked extra shifts at the center over the past week, hoping to ease her devil's annoyance. The animal was in a super foul mood.

It wasn't until Havana stalked out of Tate's house that she realized her devil had expected him to ask Havana to stay. The devil had believed he'd offer Havana more; that he wanted her bad enough to overcome whatever commitment issues he had. When he'd instead let her go, he'd pissed the devil off to such an extent that she'd slammed a mental door on him. She'd been in a huff ever since, and Havana couldn't seem to snap her out of it.

The devil hadn't reacted quite as dramatically when Dieter got all cozy with an eagle shifter, nor had she seemed surprised. Maybe the devil hadn't expected him to commit. Really, Havana shouldn't have hoped for it either, given that Dieter disliked the lone shifter lifestyle and wanted to join a flock.

He'd been born to an eagle shifter couple who were loners, so he'd never known anything different. He wanted that sense of belonging that came with being part of a flock. He had this grand notion that his life would be a bed of roses if he was ever accepted into one. He didn't understand why Havana liked being a loner.

Unlike him, she hadn't been a loner all her life. She'd once been part of a devil shifter clan. Contrary to what Dieter believed, being part of something didn't always give you a sense of "belonging." The members didn't always look out for their own. Didn't always take care of you. Sometimes they even took *from* you … leaving you all alone in the world.

The heavy door swung open, making the hinges creak. She turned to see Corbin walk inside. The grizzly had opened the center many years ago in memory of his younger sister, Celine. Their parents had been lone shifters, so there'd been no one to take in Corbin and Celine when said parents died in a house fire. The children ended up living on the streets, and poor Celine later died a terrible death at the hands of a hyena clan. Corbin tried to help others in the way no one had helped him or his sister. He was gruff on the outside but gooey on the inside.

He'd taken many loners under his wing over the years, giving them whatever support he could, providing jobs for them at the center, and helping them find safe accommodation—sometimes at the local homeless shelter for lone shifters. He was seriously ace, in her opinion.

"Almost done in here?" he asked.

Havana smiled. "I think so, yeah, we—*Bailey, get off the maintenance trolley.*" The weirdo was balancing on it while spinning in circles. Havana didn't know if it was a black mamba thing or a Bailey thing, but the female had a seriously short attention span. Bailey's mind switched context fast and often, so she had a habit of blurting out questions that were usually unrelated to whatever was happening around her. Most people found it kind of endearing.

Bailey pouted, which somehow looked cute. "Fine, fine." She hopped off the trolley and flicked her sleek hair—which she'd recently dyed a striking silver that suited her perfectly—over her shoulder. She was a pretty thing with her deep-set eyes, oval face, and the high cheekbones any female would envy. It was clear she had some Asian ancestry.

Mambas possessed the same notoriously bad temper as devil shifters and often picked fights purely for shits and giggles. But people tended to assume that Bailey wasn't as fierce and feisty as her inner snake. Mostly because she looked so sweet and innocent. Yeah, she really wasn't.

With her default unimpressed expression, Aspen looked aloof and disinterested in people. Yeah, she absolutely was. But that was a bearcat thing. They gave zero fucks about what went on outside their own little world—they didn't like to complicate their lives.

What bearcats *really* didn't like was to be cuddled. But because they were so adorable, it was often the first thing people tried to do. In truth, that cuteness was a weapon—it suckered you in, made you move closer, made you think you were safe. But there would be no snugglefest from these cantankerous creatures who had uber-sharp teeth and a chomping power that could crush bone.

Honestly, Havana was no more a fan of cuddles than bearcats were ... which was why she tended to snarl if anyone tried hugging her. She'd always been that way, according to her late mother.

Corbin folded his arms. "I was hoping to speak with the three of you."

Feeling a lecture coming on, Havana asked, "About what?"

He tilted his head. "You really can't guess?"

Aspen arched her brows. "We have to guess? Ooh, this could take a while." She hummed. "You want to chew a chunk out of our asses for shoving dead sardines down the seat tube of Jackson's bike? If so, I'm not apologizing. He *totally* deserved it for cheating on Bailey—and with Ginny, of all people."

"Limped-dick motherfucker," Bailey muttered.

"No, it's not about that," said Corbin. "I agree he had it coming, although the stench was disgusting, so I'd ask that you pick a different mode of revenge in future."

"Okay, so what did you want to talk about?" Havana narrowed her eyes. "Is this about us putting Creepy Stan up for sale on Gregslist?"

Corbin shook his head. "No."

"Trying to buy an otter when we were smashed?" asked Havana.

"No."

Bailey clicked her fingers. "Ooh, baptizing Hoe Bag in the pool?"

His lips thinned. "Her name is Ginny. And I wouldn't call holding her head under the water until she almost drowns a baptism."

Bailey shrugged. "*She* was praying."

Corbin sighed. "I don't want to talk about her either."

"Then what?" asked Havana.

He folded his arms. "Oh, maybe I was curious about the barfight you had with three jackals last weekend."

"Ah," was all Havana said.

He looked at Bailey. "I heard you drew first blood by slapping one of them so hard you split her lip."

"I didn't like the way she was looking at me," said Bailey.

His eyes slid back to Havana. "You're usually the voice of reason when Bailey tries to start shit. But instead of calming things down, you went head-to-head with the second jackal."

Havana shrugged one shoulder. "I didn't like the way she spoke to me."

His gaze moved to Aspen. "And you decided to go at the third jackal with a stiletto blade, despite her trying to break up the fight."

"I didn't like the way she smelled," said Aspen.

Bailey nodded at Aspen. "She *did* smell weird, didn't she? Like wet clothes that had been left in the washing machine too long. It was just ... ew."

Corbin rubbed his forehead. "I don't know why I ever expect to hear rational answers from any of you."

The door opened again. A tall, broad-shouldered figure of pure gorgeousness stalked inside. *Camden.* He and Aspen had been close friends since before Havana and Bailey arrived at the center. There were a lot of shadows in the tiger shifter's eyes—eyes that often had a cold, reptilian quality to them that made her devil's fur stand on end. Not that the animal feared him, she just sensed that there was something missing in him. Or perhaps it had just been snuffed out.

Whatever the case, he could be so emotionally unreactive that it was *eerie.* Havana had never heard him laugh. He rarely smiled, and it was even rarer that he raised his voice or lost his cool. But when it came to Aspen, well, he was different. He didn't linger on the edge of her world as he did with others, he was smack bam in the middle of it.

At one time, he'd seemed to view Havana and Bailey as interlopers and hadn't wanted them around. Havana had made it clear that she didn't wish to take Aspen from him, she wanted him to be part of their unofficial clan. He'd settled on hearing that, but he'd never become a true part of it.

He treated Havana and Bailey like family, but in a distant-cousin-who-tolerates-you-as-best-he-can kind of way. The bearcat was probably the only living being he truly gave a shit about. Which was no doubt why his boyfriend didn't much like her. In fact, none of the tiger's past partners—male or female—had liked her, as if they felt threatened by their close friendship.

Sidling up to Aspen, he casually draped his arm over her shoulders. "Ready to go home yet?"

"Yes," replied the bearcat. "I'm having a serious craving for mac and cheese right now."

"I can accommodate that." Camden looked at Corbin. "The fitness rooms are all locked up."

Corbin gave a satisfied nod.

"I think we should order takeout, Havana," said Bailey. "I'm not feeling in the mood to cook. Are you?"

Aspen frowned at the mamba. "You don't cook, you nuke meals in your microwave."

Bailey shrugged. "Same thing."

"No, it really isn't," said Aspen. She slid her eyes to Corbin. "Just to let you know, a few of the kids are hoping you'll organize another camping trip."

"I don't suppose you and Camden will help out again if I do, will you?" asked Corbin. "You're both experienced campers. I heard you saw a bear last time."

"We never actually saw it," said Aspen. "We just heard it shuffling around outside the tent, making weird noises. For a moment there, I thought, 'Well, the zombie apocalypse has officially started.'"

Corbin set his fists on his hips. "You heard movement outside your tent, and your first thought wasn't, 'Oh, must be an animal'? It was, 'Shit, zombie'?

Really?"

"Z-Day *is* coming. We have to be ready."

Corbin sighed. "If you say so. Now let's lock this place up."

Bailey lifted her finger. "Gotta grab my stuff from my locker first."

"I'll wait for you in the car," Havana told her.

Outside, Camden guided Aspen to his vehicle in the parking lot. Havana headed straight for her own car, flicking through the notifications on her cell phone. And she pretended she wasn't hoping to see a message or missed call from Tate.

Nearing her car, she unlocked it with the key fob but didn't hop in—she was busy deleting the shit-mail from the inbox of her email account. That done, she pocketed her phone and reached for the door handle. Feeling a sharp prick on her lower leg, she went to slap at the spot, hoping to squash the damn mosquito. But then there were two more sharp stings in quick succession—one on her thigh, and one on her arm. She glanced down and muttered a curse as she saw *three darts*. What in the everloving fuck?

Snapping her head up, she turned and—*there*. A mean-looking asshole was standing near a large van, holding a tranquilizer gun. He met her gaze, his mouth gaping open as he no doubt wondered why the darts were having no effect.

Anger washed through Havana and her devil, who let out a furious snarl. Havana charged at the bastard, sprinting across the lot. His eyes widened. He fired again, hitting her dead center in the chest, but she kept on coming. He bit out a loud curse.

With a surge of good ole devil strength, she yanked the gun out of his grip and slammed the butt of the weapon on his head, dazing him. Wicked fast, she flipped the gun around and shot him twice in the neck. His hand fluttered at his throat as he tried pulling—

The driver's door swung open and a huge hulking male jumped out of the van. She fired, but no darts came out. *Fuck*. She tossed the weapon at his head, but he jerked aside, dodging it.

He slammed his meaty fist into her jaw, making her head whip to the side. She twisted her body with a hiss and snapped out her leg, delivering a pitiless bladder shot that made him grunt and stagger back into the door he'd left open.

Lunging forward, she lashed out and raked her uber sharp claws down his face and—

"Havana!"

The sound of footsteps thundering along the ground made the bastard curse. He leapt into the vehicle, and then it disappeared with a squeal of tires. Corbin and Camden pursued it, yelling at the driver, who hadn't even closed the door yet.

Bailey and Aspen came straight to Havana, their eyes wide.

"You okay?" asked the bearcat.

"Fine," replied Havana, plucking the darts out of her body. She rubbed at her jaw. "That fucker has a punch on him. He was a wild dog shifter. I haven't come across one of those in a while."

Bailey planted her hands on her hips. "What the *hell* was all that about?"

"I don't know." Havana looked down at the shooter, who'd slid to the ground at some point and was out cold. *Cougar,* she sensed. "But maybe he can tell us when he wakes up."

Sitting on the chair in front of the shooter, Havana smiled as he started to come around. They'd taken him to the storage basement within the rec center, stripped him naked, and then securely bound him to a sturdy chair. "Hi, welcome back."

His eyelids lazily fluttered open. It was another minute before reality seemed to hit him. And then he went stiff as a board. He probably would have shifted if she hadn't made the bindings so tight—the zip ties would cut right into him if he tried it.

"I know it must be somewhat disconcerting to wake up and find yourself naked and tied to a chair while surrounded by five pissed-the-fuck-off shifters. But as you're responsible for the pissed-the-fuck-off part, I figure you realize this is *totally* your fault and all."

His eyes darted around the basement, no doubt seeking exits. There was only one. Corbin was currently standing at the base of the steps in front of it, calm as you please. He'd agreed to take a backseat and let Havana lead. He knew about her old "side job." It was the same job Bailey, Aspen, and Camden had had once upon a time.

"Now, you probably already know that my name is Havana Ramos." She gave their captive an encouraging smile. "Why don't you tell me yours?"

The cougar held her gaze, his own glimmering with defiance.

Havana sighed. "Aspen, be a dear and give the kitty a temporary name. It would be rude to just refer to him as 'Asshole.'"

Leaning against the wall near Camden, Aspen paused in filing her nails to study the cougar. "He looks like a Bogart to me."

"Really?" Bailey tossed a mint into her mouth as she sidled up to Havana. "I would have said Chauncey. Or Hyman. It's an honest to God's boys name, I swear."

"And the perfect name for a pussy, which is exactly what we have here," said Aspen before going back to her nails.

"Then Hyman it is," said Havana. Turning back to him, she held up the phone that she'd dug out of his pocket earlier. "We're going to need your PIN, Hyman."

He swallowed as his eyes once more danced around the room. "9587."

"Thank you." Havana entered the PIN. The screen flickered, and the phone let out a weird bleeping sound. Then the screen went utterly black. She pressed button after button, but nothing happened.

"What's wrong?" asked Bailey, peering down at the phone.

"It clapped out." Havana narrowed her eyes on the fucker in front of her, who was looking rather pleased with himself. "Let me guess, you gave me the wrong PIN so it would set off some sort of tripwire that wiped the phone clean."

He only smirked.

"Oh, you're thinking that makes you clever." Havana shook her head sadly. "No, Hyman, it makes you stupid. Like *really* stupid. Because now the only way we can get answers about who you are, why you came, and who was with you earlier ... is by making you tell us. You might not enjoy that part."

He snorted.

Aspen pushed away from the wall and slowly came closer. "You know what? I think he doesn't believe we'll harm him. To be fair, most of the people we've 'harmed' made that mistake. They just saw some harmless-looking loners and completely underestimated us. Which, incidentally, is how we landed our old job. Our ex-boss knew people would overlook us, and that suited him."

Bailey arched a brow at the cougar. "Would you like to know what our old job was?"

The dumb shit rolled his eyes.

"I'll take that as a no," said Havana. "All right, we won't bore you with details you have no interest in. But *you* will tell *me* why you came for me tonight. Really, I don't think it's unreasonable of me to want to know why you shot me four times."

A line formed between his brows.

"You're wondering why the tranqs didn't knock me out," she sensed. "Devils are immune to those sort of drugs—we don't advertise that, of course. Why make it easy for those who'd get the silly idea to target us? People like you, for example. Now, tell me why you came for me."

He notched up his chin and stared at her.

Havana sighed. "Bailey."

The other female shifted in a flash. The slender mamba slithered out of the puddle of clothes, a stunning gunmetal gray with oblique dark bars down her sides.

Hyman's eyes went wide. He tried inching backwards and twisted within the confines of the ropes that were wrapped around him. But the chair didn't budge, and the binds didn't loosen.

The mamba raised three parts of her body off the floor, spread her narrow neck-flap, opened her inky-black mouth, and let out a furious hiss that sounded like a damn pressure cooker.

"Last chance, Hyman," said Havana. "Why did you come for me?"

His panicked gaze shot back to Havana. He opened his mouth but then just as quickly snapped it shut.

She sighed. "All right, if that's how you want it …" She nodded at the snake.

The mamba struck lightning fast, biting his thigh.

He jolted, letting out a small cry of pain. "*Fuck*."

Havana lightly scratched her cheek. "I'd say you probably have somewhere between 120 and 150mg of venom pumping through your bloodstream right now. Not enough to kill a shifter, but enough to put you through a world of misery."

His breaths coming quick and fast, he stared down at the punctures wounds in what looked to be disbelief.

"You're no doubt feeling a tingling sensation near the bite wound. The other symptoms will set in pretty fast. Your eyelids will get all droopy, and you'll get a metallic taste in your mouth. There'll also be blurry vision, vertigo, puking, severe stomach cramps, and more—I'll let some of them be a surprise for you.

"It'll all go on for, oh, about fifteen hours. But your body will recover, the effects of the venom will wear off, and you'll be back to normal. Then we can talk again. Yay. Of course, you could decide to stick with the whole telling me nothing plan. Bailey won't mind biting you a second time. Or a third. Or even a fourth. She's awesome that way. So you might want to think about that before you decide to be stubborn again. It won't go well for you."

He gaped at Havana, as if stunned.

"You really should have shown more interest when my friend tried warning you about our old job," said Havana. "If you had, she would have told you that we used to work for the Movement."

His face blanched.

"Yes, yes, the group only deals with human anti-shifter extremists. Members are defenders of our kind. A national treasure, even. So shifters have no need to fear them. *But*, as I can see you're considering, it would never be wise to piss off an ex-member. Because we have no qualms about using all the dangerous skills we learned. And we're no strangers to making someone suffer. If I'm honest, I've actually missed it."

Aspen put a hand to her chest. "Thank God. I thought it was just me."

Havana rose from her seat. "Well, Hyman, I'll leave you to enjoy your evening. But I'll see you again in the morning, bright and early."

Bailey shifted back to her human form and pulled on her clothes. "I'm still in the mood for takeout, you?" she asked Havana.

"Takeout works for me."

CHAPTER THREE

"You're not listening to me, are you?"

Snapping out of his thoughts, Tate blinked at his father. "Not really, no."

Leaning back in the dining chair, Vinnie sighed. "I figured as much when I asked if you'd ever consider fucking a goat and you actually nodded."

Tate snickered. His father was a damn nut, which was something he hid well. Vinnie was also good at hiding his calculated nature. He knew how to come across as approachable, easygoing, and happy to help. In truth, he was as cunning as they came and could cause a riot in heaven itself.

Lifting his mug of coffee from the table, Tate took a sip. "I zoned out because you were rambling about minor shit rather than telling me why you turned up here at the crack of dawn."

"You consider your brother having his carotid artery nicked in a fight 'minor?'"

"I'm thinking of it as Karma, since he nicked mine when I was twelve." Tate had the scar on his throat to prove it. Before reaching adulthood, he and Luke had treated each other as mortal enemies merely because pallas kits didn't get along with siblings who were too close in age. "I told him that very same thing when he reported the incident to me twenty minutes ago. Besides, it's not like our healer didn't fix him up."

"I noticed he and Farrell have made themselves comfortable in your living room," said Vinnie. "Have you gotten used to having bodyguards yet?"

"No. And I don't like it much." When he was at home, Tate often sent them on errands just to get some alone time. As the prior Beta, he used to *be* a bodyguard. He and Luke had shadowed their father pretty much wherever Vinnie went.

After Tate ascended, he'd promoted his brother from Head Enforcer to

Beta, knowing the position would fit him. Luke was a natural-born alpha but had zero wish to lead a pride. Plus, there was far too much anger in him, and far too little patience for politics. Vinnie had slipped into an advisory role, too action-oriented to retire from active duty. The pride had adjusted just fine to the change of leadership, as had their allies and contacts.

It hadn't seemed like such a dramatic change for Tate, because Vinnie hadn't abruptly stepped down. He'd subtly begun to pull back little by little and tone down his assertiveness, which stirred Tate's natural take-charge instincts and made him automatically push forward with each step Vinnie took back.

The biggest change for Tate was moving to the cul-de-sac. He'd only ever lived in apartments before now. But his father had recommended he live in a separate building from the rest of the pride or they'd be knocking on his door every two minutes with simple queries. Vinnie hadn't been wrong, so Tate had moved out.

His father had also been right in predicting that being Alpha would suit Tate. He'd fully settled into the role. It fit him well. It also fulfilled his cat, who'd been angling to take over for years.

What saddened Tate was that it shouldn't have been a case of Vinnie retiring alone. It should have been a case of *the Alpha pair* retiring. But Tate's mother had died many years ago. He couldn't call up a clear mental image of her face anymore.

Shifters didn't always survive the breaking of the mating bond. The mating bond was special in that it could bind two people in a metaphysical way that fed every bit of their soul. But if a shifter lost their true mate and that bond thereby snapped, they also lost a huge part of themselves.

"Before we get into what I want to speak with you about," began Vinnie, "tell me why you've been in a perpetual pissed-off state over the past week."

Tate rubbed the bridge of his nose. "I've just got shit on my mind."

"Would that shit be related to the pretty little devil shifter you were seeing?"

Tate narrowed his eyes at the "were." He hadn't yet made it public that his fling with Havana was over. "Who told you I was no longer seeing her?"

"It was a guess based on your sour mood. Am I right?"

Tate merely gave a curt nod, not wanting to discuss it.

"By the way you're grinding your teeth, I'm sensing you're not happy about it."

Tate just gave a nonchalant shrug, though he felt anything *but* nonchalant. The truth was ... he missed her. He'd never gotten involved with a female like Havana before. Someone who intrigued, tempted, and challenged both man and feline in equal measures. Which was no doubt why his cat missed her, too. She could hold their attention in a way that no other female ever had, not even the one they'd almost imprinted on.

Tate did his best not to think about Havana, but many times he'd found himself wondering where she was, what she was doing, who she was doing it with. She cropped up in his thoughts far too often, especially at night. He couldn't even jack off without her appearing in his mind's eye, so then he'd end up coming to memories of the times he'd had her beneath him. He hadn't taken another female to his bed as it wouldn't have been fair to them when his mind was on Havana.

Okay, that was a barefaced fucking lie. He hadn't taken another female to his bed because he didn't *want* another female. He wanted Havana.

He still couldn't quite believe he'd almost marked her. The urge had come out of nowhere and crawled all over him. More disturbing, it hadn't left him. He felt it everywhere. It was like a hum in his blood. A pounding in his veins. A craving in his gut. An itch he couldn't reach, because it seemed to be *beneath* his flesh.

The disconcerting urge hadn't lessened with time. If anything, it seemed to have intensified. He would have questioned if she could be his true mate if the impulse to brand her had stemmed from possessiveness. But it was more of a need to dominate, to force her to submit to his wants and not leave his side until he was good and ready. Which meant he had no business leaving any such mark on her.

His cat, being a mostly selfish creature, didn't agree. The feline wanted to find her. No, *hunt* her. Catch her. But Tate knew his cat wouldn't wish to keep her, and therein lay the problem.

"Walking away is definitely the right thing to do if a relationship doesn't have a future," said Vinnie. "You'll find your true mate eventually, or someone who you care for enough to take as a mate. Havana will do the same. I once read that loners tend to have more luck finding their true mates—probably because they often travel. A beautiful woman like her won't struggle to find a man."

Jealousy swirled in his belly, and Tate had to bite back a growl. He tossed his father an impatient look. "Stop trying to bait me. It pisses me off."

"Most things do lately." Vinnie sobered. "And, completely off the subject of Havana, my news is *definitely* not going to improve your mood any."

Even as Tate's shoulders bunched with tension, he said, "Go on."

Vinnie leaned forward and rested his clasped hands on the table. "Priscilla called me earlier. Apparently, Ashlynn wishes to return to the pride."

Shock slammed into Tate, making his thoughts go blank for just a moment. His cat peeled back his upper lip—the feline hadn't yet forgiven their ex-partner. "Why is it that Priscilla never came to me with this?"

"It's not because she struggles to accept that *you're* now Alpha, if that's your concern. She's been a friend of mine for years. She's worried you'll turn down Ashlynn's request, so she came to me for advice on how best to handle the situation. I offered to act as a medium purely because I would rather you heard this from me than from Priscilla. According to her, Ashlynn simply believes it's time she came home but fears she won't be welcome."

She'd never be *welcome* to Tate—too much shit had happened between them. And who wanted to be around their ex when said ex had fucked them over? But he'd always known she'd return sooner or later. Whereas the news once would have riled him, it now did no more than irritate him. She no longer had any real power over his emotions. "I'll call Priscilla and inform her that Ashlynn can return."

Vinnie frowned. "You want her back here?"

"No. But nor do I feel any great need to keep her away. She's no one to me."

"You and Ashlynn were a couple for over twelve months. The stirrings of imprinting were there. You suffered greatly after those minor threads broke."

He had, yeah. And it had killed what Tate felt for her. Back then, he'd been so sure he loved her that he'd also been open to imprinting on her, even though it meant forsaking his true mate. The decision had been simpler for Ashlynn. She'd known for a long time who her true mate was; she'd known she couldn't have him.

She'd been just twelve-years-old when she *felt* that one of their pride mates, Koby—a man fifteen-years her senior—was her true-mate. She hadn't wasted a moment in declaring it to him. Freaked out, Koby had insisted she was wrong. He'd later imprinted on the female he was dating, Gita.

It had devastated Ashlynn, but she'd ploughed through, determined to build a life without Koby. She'd claimed she wanted to build that life with Tate. But when Gita later died, Ashlynn had told Tate that she needed to be with Koby. Not just to rally around him and help him overcome his loss, but to eventually make him accept that Ashlynn was meant for him.

At first, Tate had been too shocked to connect with her declaration. She'd made promises to him when they first got together. She'd vowed that he wasn't second best. She'd sworn that she had let Koby go, too angry at him to consider claiming him anyway.

She'd lied.

Once the shock wore off, a freezing-cold burn had spread through his body and iced his blood, numbing him to everything, shrouding him in apathy. He hadn't raged, ranted, or even talked it out with anyone. Instead, he'd thrown himself into the Beta role and allowed his friends and family to distract him. Tate hadn't been willing to let the breakup eat him whole. He hadn't been willing to spend even a moment's time grieving the loss of a person who'd already wasted a year of his life.

People had watched him closely, expecting him to unravel. But he hadn't. Not even when, a month after he moved out of her apartment, the imprinting threads snapped. It had felt like drowning. Drowning in pain, emotion, nausea, exhaustion—waves of which had hit him at random times and pulled him under. But he'd always resurfaced, and the nightmare eventually ended.

When the numbness finally wore off, some anger had crept in. He couldn't blame her for wanting her true mate, but Tate was pissed that she'd made him so many empty promises. He'd let that anger go for his own sake, though. There was no sense in clinging to that kind of dark emotion.

"You don't think it would be hard for you to have her around?" asked Vinnie.

"No," replied Tate. "She's part of my past—a regrettable part. That's it."

"And what if she wants you two to try again?"

"It won't happen. If I wanted her back, I could have had her back." Four months after they separated, she'd turned up at his old apartment, begging him to take her back. He'd instantly suspected what he later learned—Koby had refused to accept her. More, the grieving male had claimed he'd never want her.

Tate felt pity for her now, but back then he'd felt only anger that she'd think so little of him as to ask that he take her back after all she'd done … like he should so easily forgive her betrayal and, moreover, be content with being second best. Well, he wasn't. So he'd turned her away, and she'd hauled ass out of the pride the day after that.

"Does she know Koby switched to his brother's pride?" Tate asked, because it was possible that she was returning to try to again claim the man.

"According to Priscilla, yes, Ashlynn knows and has apparently given up on him." Vinnie twisted his mouth. "You're so sure that you've really moved on from her? You built walls after she left. You haven't been as open to trusting women since then. You've never allowed yourself to really connect with anyone. Maybe you still feel something for her."

Neither Tate nor his cat were so trusting these days, but … "I moved past what happened. It's neither here nor there to me if she comes back." He felt nothing for her now. Not even a twinge of emotion. There was nothing *to* feel. As if his system had purged itself of her in every sense of the word.

Vinnie pursed his lips. "All right. But if you're truly over the woman, you need to stop letting what happened affect how you live your life. You're giving your past too much power over your present and future—that's never going to end well. You'll just keep sabotaging your own happiness."

Tate frowned. "I'm not doing that."

"Aren't you?" Vinnie softly challenged. "You seemed happy enough with the devil shifter. Yet, you walked away from her."

"She was the one who walked away."

"Oh, I see. Well, I can't say I blame her, considering the relationship wasn't going anywhere. She's done the best thing for both of you."

Yeah, so she'd claimed. But "the best thing" didn't *feel* best. And Tate didn't believe it was the only reason she walked away. No, there was more to it than that, and he didn't think it was unreasonable of him to have wanted the full truth.

"I'll let Koby know Ashlynn's coming back, just in case he wishes to come and see her," said Vinnie. "But it's unlikely he will. Even if he *has* come to believe that she's his true mate, I can't envision him wanting to do anything about it. Gita was his world and there's no replacing a woman who touches you that deeply. Having experienced a fully formed imprint bond, he may not be able to truly mate again. The soul generally doesn't choose to go there twice."

Some people claimed they'd heard of instances where widowed shifters could mate again, but Tate believed they were bullshit. After all, if the rumors *were* true, they'd come complete with names and specific details to give grieving shifters hope. "Do you wish you could bond with another female?"

"No," replied Vinnie without hesitation. "No one could ever replace Gaia for me. There's no room in my head or heart for anyone else, and there isn't enough of me left to give anyway. I'm not a full person without her, and I don't wish I was. Because the parts of me she took with her when she died were all hers to take."

Tate swallowed. He couldn't relate to that level of pain. Ashlynn had wounded him, but the loss of her hadn't marked his soul, hadn't left him with a gaping hole that nothing would ever fill.

He and his father talked for a few more minutes before Vinnie left. Tate then headed into the living room. On the sofa, both Luke and Farrell slid their gazes from the widescreen TV to Tate.

"What was that about?" Luke asked.

Tate sighed. "Ashlynn wants to come back to the pride."

His brother's lips parted. "You are shitting me."

"No, I'm not."

Luke cursed. "She has some fucking nerve." Studying Tate's face closely, he narrowed his eyes. "You're going to let her, aren't you?"

"I don't have a real reason not to. Do I *want* to see her again? No. Do I care if I do? No. I'm not holding a candle for her."

"I know that. And I know you've let your anger at her go, but *I* haven't."

"Jessie won't be happy she's coming back," said Farrell, referring to his pregnant mate. "She and Ashlynn had a huge falling out when Jessie refused to support her leaving you for Koby. Ashlynn shut out pretty much everyone who disagreed with her decision."

"There'll probably be several people who won't be happy to see her again," Luke predicted. "Not just because she hurt you, but because she showed so little respect for Koby's grief and Gita's memory. I mean, who comes onto a grieving man? He was an absolute *mess* when Gita died. The last thing he needed right then was Ashlynn insisting they were fated to be."

"I can't blame her for wanting her mate," began Farrell, "but she should have been more interested in comforting him than in snapping him up. Jessie said that Ashlynn just wasn't rational where Koby was concerned."

That was something Tate had realized far too late. "I need to call Priscilla and inform her that her daughter can return. Then I want to hit the bakery."

Farrell smiled. "You're giving me a chance to check on Jessie. I appreciate it, Tate. I don't like her working so hard when she's so far along in her pregnancy, but there's no getting her to stay at home."

"People will get word to you if she's overdoing it or needs to go home," Tate reminded him.

Many of the pride worked at the pride-owned stores and lived in either the cul-de-sac or one of the two nearby apartment buildings—all of which were also pride-owned. Pallas cats didn't claim territories but often grouped together for protection in such a way.

There weren't just Olympus Pride members working at the local stores. Some of the employees were human and even lone shifters ... And *now* he was back to thinking about Havana again. Well if she'd given him straight answers, he wouldn't think about her half as much.

Maybe he'd been right to suspect that there was another man. She'd keep it quiet to protect him from Tate, who would pummel the bastard into the ground for touching his woman. Well ... Havana hadn't been his woman *as such*, but she'd certainly been off-limits.

"You okay, bro?" asked Luke. "You're looking mighty fierce over there with that scowl."

"I'm fine." He made a quick call to Priscilla and then headed to the bakery with Luke and Farrell. After scoffing down a Danish and finishing his coffee, he left the shop ... and found himself heading in the opposite direction than he'd intended. And he knew exactly where his feet were taking him.

Havana knocked on Bailey's bedroom door. "If you're not done in twenty minutes, I'm leaving without your skinny ass!" she yelled, hoping to be heard over the loud music coming from inside the room.

"I'll be two minutes, heifer!" the mamba bellowed.

Havana snorted. Bailey always left everything until the last minute. Still, she was rarely ever late for work. But this was no ordinary morning, since they were leaving early so that they could spend a little time with Hyman before the rec center opened. With any luck, he'd be in a much chattier mood now that he knew his captors weren't as harmless as they looked, thanks to their previous career.

The Movement had formed to deal with radical, violent humans who'd maintained that shifters should be disallowed to mate with humans, confined to their territory, electronically chipped, restricted to having one child per couple, and placed on a registry like goddamn sex offenders. Moreover, the extremists had no issue with attacking and bombing shifters in an attempt to cull the population.

The Movement handled the extremists— countering their attacks, assassinating the big cheeses, wiping out entire factions. In sum, the group fought violence with violence.

The Movement often recruited unmated lone shifters, because these were people who could fly under the radar more easily than non-loners. Havana, Aspen, Bailey, and Camden had lived quiet, simple lives working at the center, but behind the scenes, they'd done plenty of jobs for the Movement.

The group had trained them in everything from combat to interrogation techniques. They'd given them a purpose, paid them well, and treated them like family. Then eight years later, they'd let them go, encouraging them to live lives free of missions. Aside from the key players, members were only allowed to work eight years of service. The group wasn't willing to allow anyone to sacrifice a life with their mate to deal with bigoted assholes.

Only Corbin knew about their past work for the Movement. The group was careful to keep the names of their members, particularly the key players, secret. Sadly, there were shifters who'd sell those names to extremists or human law enforcement for the right price.

Crossing her fingers that Bailey wouldn't be late, Havana returned to the kitchen and poured more coffee into her mug. She'd only taken one sip when there was a knock at the front door. That had to be Aspen and Camden— the bearcat had texted to say they wanted to be present for the next "talk" with Hyman.

Havana placed her cup on the counter and crossed to the door. She glanced through the peephole out of habit, and her body stiffened while her devil hissed. *Tate.*

A flare of excitement buzzed through Havana's veins. A flare she quickly stomped on. He'd be here as her landlord, nothing more. Unless … he hadn't heard about what happened last night, had he? If so, he was nosy enough to pry, and he'd be all *Grr, you're under my protection, why didn't you call me, grr?* It seemed unlikely that news of it had reached him, though.

Bracing herself for the impact of his full-on raw masculinity, Havana opened the door. Her stomach flipped as their eyes locked. She wasn't perversely glad to see him. She wasn't. Nu-uh.

Oh, how she bullshitted herself at times.

His gaze glittered with heat as it travelled the length of her, making her pulse quicken and her hormones clumsily trip all over themselves. Standing a few feet behind him, Luke and Farrell watched her closely.

"Can I come in?" Tate finally asked.

She should say no. She should turn him away. But that would be weak and cowardly. She could handle being around him. She'd *have* to learn to handle it, considering he was her landlord.

Havana slowly stepped to the side to allow him to pass. He told his bodyguards to wait in the hallway and then entered her apartment. Her devil snarled as he boldly walked into her living area like it was his own. Hmm, it would appear that the animal wasn't going to forgive him any time soon.

Havana followed him, only stopping when she reached the edge of the fluffy rug. She *loved* to watch him walk. Loved how his long legs covered the ground with an unhurried, confident stride. All that predatory elegance and animalistic sexuality was hot as holy hell.

Tate sank onto the black leather sofa and draped his arms over the back of it. He glanced around, sweeping his gaze over the butterscotch walls, the cherry oak furniture, the abstract artwork, and the leather armchair.

He followed the path of his hand as he slid it over the arm of the sofa. She wondered if he was remembering the time that he bent her over it and savagely hammered into her. If the heated glance he shot her was anything to go by, the answer was yes.

His gaze briefly flitted to the large corner bookcase. "I'm not sure why a person would need that many books."

"You can never have too many books—everyone knows that." She tipped her head to the side. "Why are you here?"

His broody, super-intense eyes drilled into her so boldly it almost made her squirm. Almost. She was made of sterner stuff.

He swiped his tongue over his front teeth. "We need to talk."

"We did that last weekend."

"Not really. You said your piece, danced around my questions, and then you left."

Well, yeah. Her devil flexed her claws, wanting him gone. Havana opened her mouth, intending to ask him to leave, but then she thought better of it. Tate had a one-track mind—he never conceded, never gave up, never backed down. The quickest way to get him out of her apartment would be to just let him talk. "All right. Say whatever you came to say."

His eyes bore into hers, as if he was desperate to see *inside* her head. "I've been racking my brain trying to figure out what made you want to walk away all of a sudden. Your decision came out of nowhere, and I want to know what really led to it."

No one could ever say he wasn't tenacious, could they? "I honestly don't get why you can't drop this. You only ever meant for the fling to be temporary, so I don't see an issue here."

"The issue is that you're not being upfront with me." He pushed to his feet, making her heart thud in her chest. He leisurely stalked toward her, all smolder and danger and dominant male energy, only halting when there were mere inches between their bodies. Sexual tension crackled in the air, making the hairs on her nape stand on end and her body get all tingly and stuff. Gah, she should *not* have let him in.

"Is there someone else?"

The oh so casual question made her nape prickle. "I already told you there isn't. It's just time to go our separate ways."

"Why? What we had was good."

"What we had was *sex*. A fling. It was no different from the others you've had in the past."

His jaw hardened. "It was different." The admission seemed torn out of him.

"How?"

"It was exclusive, for one thing. I didn't demand exclusivity from my past casual partners. I didn't give a whisper of a shit if they slept with other men. I also never fucked any of them in my bed—only you. So yeah, Havana, it was different."

Oh. Well. Okay. She hadn't known that. Determined not to be moved by it, she shrugged one shoulder and said, "I was still only a plaything to you."

"Plaything?" he echoed, dropping his voice a few octaves. "You liked it when I played with you. Liked it when I used you. Tasted you. Pinned you down. Fucked you however I wanted to fuck you." He brushed his mouth over hers. "But you were never just a plaything to me."

As need rose sharp and fast inside her, Havana clenched her fists so tight she felt her nails dig into her palms. She knew she should shove him away, but it was hard to be sensible when so much sexual tension pulsed in the air.

He moved his mouth to her ear. "Do you remember the first night I had you? I slammed you against my front door the moment I closed it. I would have taken you right there in my hallway ... but you weren't going to make it easy for me. You ran, you struggled, you fought. But then you yielded, and I took you on my dining table with your legs hooked over my shoulders. Fucked you so deep and raw you screamed for me. I've never come that hard in my life. Not until I had you the next time. And the next time. And the next time."

She squeezed her eyes shut. She was easily seduced by words and he knew it. Knew her "trigger words," so to speak. Knew exactly what buttons to push.

He breezed his thumb over her lower lip—it was such a soft touch, and yet she felt it in her core. "You remember, don't you?"

"Sort of." She let out a shaky breath as his big hands possessively spanned her waist. "Tate."

Humming, Tate buried his face in her neck and breathed her in, letting her luscious scent fill him up. He'd missed it. "Just your scent alone makes my dick hard." There was nothing subtle or delicate about that staggeringly irresistible blend of cherry blossom, rich jasmine, and fresh lotus flower. And when it was spiced with arousal just as it was right then, that scent could bring him to his knees.

He ground his teeth as the impulse to mark her began to pulse in his chest like an aching wound, becoming more of a *need* than an urge. Tate refused to answer it. Leaving a mark of possession was one thing. Marking someone as an exertion of dominance was a whole other thing. He'd never do that to Havana.

Wanting to feel more of her, he snaked his hand down her stomach, heading for her pussy. But her fingers curled tight around his wrist and stilled his hand.

"Don't," she said.

"Don't what, baby? Don't touch you? Don't taste you? Don't give us what we both want?" He caught her earlobe with his teeth and gave it a light nip. "Tell me it doesn't feel good when I'm inside you. Tell me you haven't missed it."

Keeping a tight hold on his wrist, she placed his hand at his side. "You need to step back." Her voice cracked.

"I don't think you want me to." He trailed his finger down one side of her face. *So soft.* Her pupils were dilated, her cheeks were flushed, and her breathing wasn't quite steady. Still, she looked him directly in the eye, bold and sure. His cat loved that. "I also don't think you really wanted to end things between us. Everything was fine. *You* were fine. Then something changed."

"Nothing changed, Tate. Things were exactly as they'd been from day one—simple, shallow. That was how you wanted it. And hey, that's fine. But you couldn't have honestly thought I'd be okay with you keeping one foot out the door and using me to amuse yourself until your true mate came along."

He felt his jaw go hard. "It wasn't like that."

"Sure it was. Look, I can understand if you're sick of jumping from bed to bed. If you want to stick with one female while you wait for your mate, fine. I just won't be that female."

"I'm not as desperate to find my true mate as you seem to think."

"Whether or not you're *desperate* to find her isn't relevant. The fact is that, ultimately, you'll want to one day bond with her."

It wasn't a "fact" at all. Unlike many shifters, Tate had never felt driven to find his mate. Many people saw it as their main purpose, but he often wondered if binding your soul to that of another was really worth the bother.

He'd never forget the fear he'd felt all those years ago watching his father—a man so strong and resilient and robust—begin to crumble at the breaking of the mating bond. Tate had never seen him like that before. Vulnerable. Fragile. Broken.

Vinnie had later told him it was like a slow death, like crawling through hell and then having to repeat the experience over and over. Vinnie would never have suffered that way if Gaia hadn't been murdered by a shifter who'd turned rogue. And why had he turned rogue? Because he'd lost his mate, and the snapping of the true-mate bond had caused him to lose all sense of rationality.

Part of the reason Tate had been open to imprinting was that he'd never viewed true-mate bonds as shiny, sparkly things. But the shitstorm with Ashlynn proved that there was no avenue of mating that didn't have the potential to result in a total clusterfuck. Neither avenue appealed to him all that much.

Tate snapped out of his thoughts when the music coming from Bailey's room abruptly switched off.

Havana stepped away from him. "You should go. Bailey and I need to be somewhere."

"I'm not going anywhere until I get the answer I came for. Tell me the truth, Havana."

"I did."

"No, you told me a partial truth. I want the rest." His peripheral vision picked up Bailey entering the living area.

"There's nothing more to tell you," said Havana. "Really."

Bullshit. "What you're saying doesn't add up."

"Well, the cougar will hopefully fill in the blanks," said Bailey.

Tate blinked. "Cougar?"

Bailey nodded. "The shooter. He's a cougar. You coming along to meet him?"

Tate went perfectly still, and his cat's ears pricked up. "What do you mean 'shooter?' What shooter?"

A sheepish expression came over Bailey's face. She looked at Havana. "That's not what you guys were talking about, huh?"

Havana shook her head. "No."

"Oops," said the mamba. "I figured you were telling him what happened, what with us being under his protection and all."

"One of you got shot?" asked Tate, his stomach hardening. "Who? Tell me."

Bailey raised her hands. "Easy there, big guy. There were no bullets, only tranqs. And they don't work on devils, so she was fine."

Anger whipped through Tate. His cat hissed long and loud, slicing out his claws. Clenching his jaw, Tate took a prowling step closer to Havana. "Someone shot you with tranqs?" The quiet question dripped with red-hot fury. "When? Who?"

Havana scratched her nape. "Look, Tate, we have to go—"

"Don't blow me off. Not now. Not about this. As Bailey rightly pointed out, you're under my protection just like every other tenant in this building."

"You know, the 'I'm an Alpha, fear my wrath and do my bidding' tone really doesn't work on me."

Well aware of that, he dragged in a steadying breath and made an effort to speak calmly. "Havana, I promised you'd be protected. I keep my word. I'm asking you not to make me break it. That's exactly what you'll do if you keep me from helping you." He paused. "Who shot you, and when did it happen?"

She sighed. "Last night. We don't know his name yet."

"We call him Hyman," Bailey helpfully chimed in.

Tate's nostrils flared. "And neither of you thought to tell me about this? Don't say it's not my business. Every tenant in this building is my business. An attack on any of them is an insult to me. I want to know exactly what happened."

Havana gave him one of those alpha eye rolls, like he was being a dramatic man-child she couldn't help but pity. "There's really not much to tell until we get the cougar to talk. He shot me with tranqs in the parking lot outside the rec center. I snatched his gun and used it on him. His buddy jumped out of a van, and we had ourselves a brief struggle. He hightailed it out of there when Aspen, Bailey, Camden, and Corbin came rushing over. We … detained the cougar, asked him some questions. He wasn't very cooperative, so we decided to give him the night to think over whether he really wanted to continue playing it that way."

"What about his phone? Does he have one? Did you check it?"

"He gave me a false PIN that wiped the cell phone clean. I can't even make it switch back on. I withdrew his SIM card and put it in another phone, but it was blank."

"Did his friend hurt you during the struggle you were talking about?" The question was loaded with a promise of vengeance. "Don't lie to me, baby."

"Don't call me baby. He punched me. I kicked him in the bladder and clawed him. That's pretty much the extent of it." She sighed. "I should have seen it coming anyway."

He frowned. "What?"

"I heard the song *Tranquilizer* play twice yesterday—once on my car stereo, and once in the coffeehouse. Coincidence? I think not."

Tate just stared at her for a moment. "When you very first mentioned you believed in 'signs,' I didn't think you were being serious."

Her brow creased. "Why *wouldn't* I be serious? You don't believe that the universe occasionally gives us clues to help us along the way?"

"No, babe, I don't."

She shook her head, like he was hopeless. "Well, that's on you. I can't help you with that. Now I want to go speak to the cougar, so we need to wrap things up here."

"Where are you keeping him?"

"The basement of the rec center."

"I'll come with you. With any luck, I'll know who he is. Either way, I'll help you get his name out of him and anything else he knows."

"All right. There's a good chance he'll be pretty talkative."

Tate frowned. "Why do you say that?"

"Just a little feeling I have."

CHAPTER FOUR

Crossing to the entrance of the rec center, Havana smiled at Corbin, hoping that he wouldn't notice just how brittle that smile was. Sexual frustration plucked at her composure, and her body was still tingling in all sorts of places. More annoyingly, the source of said frustration was walking beside her with his bodyguards trailing behind him.

She'd considered fighting Tate on coming along, but he was right; he might be able to identify Hyman. The quicker she found out who this cougar was and what he wanted with her, the better she and her stressed-out devil would feel.

"Morning, Corbin," Havana greeted.

"It really is a fine one, isn't it?" Bailey smiled brightly. "Tate and his cats are here to meet our guest and help us work out what's going on."

Corbin tipped his chin at Tate. "Devereaux," he greeted politely, having met him through their mutual contacts from the local homeless shelter for loners.

Tate gave him a nod. "Good seeing you again, Corbin."

Once the grizzly had exchanged greetings with the others, Havana asked him, "Have you spoken to Hyman this morning?"

"Yes," replied Corbin, pushing open the center's front door. "His dignity was all over the basement floor, along with his vomit and shit and piss. It wasn't a pleasant sight. I have a feeling he'll be more cooperative today."

Tate frowned. "Vomit, shit, and piss?"

"My venom causes diarrhea and puking and lots of other wonderful stuff," Bailey explained as they all filed inside the building.

"Wait, you bit him?" Luke asked the mamba.

She nodded, sliding him an odd look—she often watched him warily, believing the Beta had a dark side. "We stripped him naked, tied him up, and then left him to suffer the effects of the venom all by his lonesome."

"After spending hours sitting in his own waste and *finally* escaping the pain, it's unlikely that he's going to want to go through it all over again," Aspen added.

Tate squinted. "And whose idea was it to go at him that way?"

"Havana's," Bailey told him.

Havana ignored the curious glance Tate cast her. This was another reason she hadn't wanted him to come. He was bound to notice that she was no stranger to interrogating people, and he might wonder why. Well, he'd just have to wonder.

As they walked through the center, Corbin spoke to Havana, "Keeping him tied to the chair, I dragged him out of the puddle of waste and then washed both our guest and the floor with the portable hose, but it still reeks down there. Just thought I'd warn you."

"No worries," said Havana. "Thanks for cleaning him up. Couldn't have been a fun job."

"He whined like a bitch the whole time, like I was washing him with acid," Corbin grumbled.

Havana led the way as they descended the basement steps. Sure enough, the scents of bile, ammonia, shit, and pure shame laced the air. It took everything she had not to balk. Her devil shook her head as if to shake off the potency of the smells.

Havana gave their captive a winning smile. Pale, tremoring, and clearly dehydrated, he was looking more than a little worse for wear. "Morning, Hyman. I heard you made quite a mess of yourself during the night." She flapped her hand. "Don't worry, there's no need for you to go through all that again. Unless, of course, it's what you want."

Havana held up the bottle of water she'd brought with her, and he swallowed with an audible click of his tongue. She unscrewed the cap and removed it. "Tip your head back." He did so, and she carefully poured some water down his throat. "You may have noticed the newbies. They're from the Olympus Pride. The one coming toward you is Tate Devereaux, the Alpha, in case you don't recognize him."

Fear flickered in Hyman's eyes.

Tate sidled up to her and glared down at the cougar. "I'm also Havana's landlord, and I'm naturally pretty pissed that someone would target a female who's under my protection. What's your name?"

The cougar swallowed and then coughed. "Rupert Merchant," he replied, his voice hoarse.

Havana smiled again. "It sure is a pleasure to meet you, Rupert."

"I prefer Hyman—just sayin'," Bailey interjected.

"I admit, it does have a certain ring to it." Havana dragged over a stool and sat down in front of him. "Are you part of a cougar pride, Rupert?"

He gave a lethargic shake of the head. "Loner."

"I see. Well, as you can imagine, I'm awfully curious as to why you shot me with tranqs last night. Maybe you could clear that up for me."

He licked his lower lip and briefly averted his gaze.

"Or Bailey can bite you again. That's always an option. Look, this can go one of two ways. You can answer our questions and then die. Or you can piss around, relive the experience you had last night, and then we'll talk again once the venom has worn off. Either way, we're not going to stop questioning you until we get our answers." She paused. "Why did you come for me?"

He was silent for a long moment. "It … it was just a job."

"A job?"

"I got a message on my cell. It had your name, address, car registration, and the address of where you work. I was to grab you and take you to the abandoned factory near the old lighthouse. Your car wasn't parked outside your building, so I came here, noticed your car in the lot, and I waited."

Unease pricked its way up Havana's spine, and her devil froze. "Someone texted you my details? Who?"

"Don't know. Never met the guy. He called me one day and said he'd heard good things about me from his associates; heard I'm a man who gets shit done and he'd like to have me on his payroll. I couldn't trace his call, he made it through a spoofing site. He always contacts me that way."

Tate folded his arms. "And what is it you do for him?"

Rupert hesitated. "It's always the same—he sends me a person's details and a location where I should take them. It's never the same location, and he's never the one waiting for me."

"Who is?" asked Tate.

"There are only ever two guys—they've never told me their names. They barely even talk to me, but I know from their voices that neither of them is the guy who calls me. When I arrive, they transfer whoever I've brought from my van to theirs."

And that would have been Havana's fate, Tate thought, grinding his teeth. Her devil shifter DNA was the only thing that had saved her. If it hadn't been for that, he'd have probably received a call at some point today to tell him that she was missing. The very idea made his cat lash out with his claws. "How do you contact this man who hired you?"

"I don't. He contacts me."

"And what does he want with these people you retrieve for him?"

"He never said. But they're always lone shifters. Sometimes women, sometimes men, sometimes children. Different breeds of shifter. Like he's picking people at random, or just wants a random selection of people."

Sometimes children. Anger bloated Tate's insides, but he kept it out of his tone as he asked, "And you have no idea why?"

"He never told me. And the guys who I deliver the loners to wouldn't tell me shit either."

"Describe these men for me," said Havana.

"They wore ski-masks. I never saw their faces. But I scented that they're jaguars."

Tate lifted his brow. "And the person who hired you? Is he a shifter?"

"I don't know—he never said, and I never asked."

"The jaguars didn't once say anything that would give you an idea of what their boss wanted all these loners for?" asked Havana, her tone purely conversational.

Tate noted that she sure was good at acting calm and non-judgmental even while she had to be pissed.

The cougar swallowed. "One time, when I was just about to drive away after dropping off a swan shifter, I had the window open and heard one guy say that the boss would definitely get 'top dollar' for the swan. I didn't hear all of the second guy's response, but I heard the words 'shame you and me can't bid at the auction.'"

Tate tensed. "Auction?"

"They also said something about 'the family' and 'kin' and 'patriarch.' Like … I don't know, like they were mafia or something."

Wariness stiffened Tate's muscles, and he exchanged a look with his brother.

"That's all I know," said Rupert. "It's all I wanted to know. If you know too much, you become a liability. I didn't want to get bumped off."

"And so you kept on delivering loners, knowing what their fate would be." What a fucking prince. "What about your partner who drove the van last night? What does he know?"

"No more than I do."

"What's his name, and where do we find him? *Rupert*," Tate pressed when he failed to answer.

The cougar's mouth tightened. "He's a *friend*."

"One who left you behind," Bailey cut in, doing a pirouette for some damn reason. "Is he worth going through another fifteen hours of venom-induced misery?"

Rupert winced and then muttered a low curse. "Sinclair," he eventually burst out. "His name is Sinclair Rodgers." Rupert reluctantly rattled off his address. "He won't be there. He'll have packed his shit and left by now."

"You think he'll be on the run?" Havana asked.

"He'd be stupid to hang around after we failed to deliver you," Rupert told her. "We messed up once before. The boss doesn't tolerate failure but gave us a second chance. We screwed that up."

"In that case, it's best not to give Sinclair more time to flee." Havana looked from Aspen to Camden. "Go check his apartment on the off-chance that he's still there. Be careful." The pair nodded and disappeared up the stairs.

"Go with them," Tate told Farrell, who instantly obeyed.

Havana turned back to Rupert. "Now, I want the names of all the people you were hired to kidnap. I also want the locations you were instructed to take the loners."

"Can I have some more water?"

"Names and dump sites," she pushed.

"I don't remember all of them. I can give you the ones I remember."

Havana typed every name and location into the notepad app on her phone.

Tate cocked his head, glaring at the cougar. "It didn't bother you to snatch all those people? You're a lone shifter yourself. Surely, that should have made you a little reluctant to take this job."

Rupert shrugged. "Being a loner is no breeze. Their lives were already fucked."

"My life isn't," said Havana, pocketing her phone, *so* pissed at this fucker she almost couldn't stand it. Loners were in enough danger from packs and clans etc. They didn't need additional danger coming from *other* lone shifters. The fact that he could kidnap *children* and not give a sliver of a fuck what happened to them ... he really did need to die. Slowly. Painfully. "In fact, I happen to like my life a lot. Who's to say that *they* weren't enjoying *their* lives until you delivered them to be auctioned off?"

"If I hadn't done the job, someone else would have," Rupert insisted. "And it's not like I *hurt* them. I'm just the delivery guy."

"*Were*, Rupert, you *were* the delivery guy." Havana stood upright. "After today, you won't be anything, because I don't intend for you to live to see the end of it."

Rupert notched up his chin. "Fine. Get it over with."

What, as if she'd give him a swift execution? He didn't deserve one. Havana would have enjoyed spending a few hours putting him through a tremendous amount of pain, but she couldn't handle the stench down here much longer. Plus, it was probably best not to make it clear to Tate that she had some experience with torture.

She didn't look away from the cougar as she said, "Bailey." Wicked fast, the female shifted. "I think three bites should do it."

He tensed as the mamba slithered out of the puddle of clothes. "No. *No*."

"Yes. *Yes*. Why you thought your death would be quick, I have no idea."

He glared at Havana. "I told you everything you wanted to know!"

Her face hardened. "You also kidnapped women, men, and children for some fucker to sell them. You didn't care that pretty much *anything* could happen to them after they were sold. You showed them no kindness or mercy. So why the fuck should we show any to you?"

And then Bailey's mamba struck, biting him three times in quick succession.

He cried out, struggling against his binds.

Havana sighed. "This is all on you, Rupert. You really should have made better life choices." She spun on her heel and faced Corbin. "I'll clean up whatever mess he makes after he takes his last breath."

The grizzly waved his hand. "Don't worry about that, I got it."

Once Bailey was back in her human form and fully dressed, they left the basement.

"So," began Bailey, "there's some guy out there holding auctions where he sells loners. Did I get that right? Is that actually happening?"

"Sounds like it," said Corbin, planting his fists on his hips. "What is the world goddamn coming to? And how the hell do we find out who's behind all this?"

Havana rubbed at her chin. "It would be helpful if Sinclair stuck around, but there's a good chance he's in the wind. Aspen will let us know soon enough. We need to ID the jaguars, but I don't see how we can."

Bailey bit her lower lip. "Someone somewhere has to have heard of these auctions, even if they're only rumors."

"I'll reach out to my allies and contacts," said Tate. "They might have heard something."

Havana nodded because, despite that working alongside him wouldn't be fun, she'd take whatever help she could get. She had a contact from the Movement who she could consult, but she didn't tell Tate that. "You know what Rupert meant by 'the family,' don't you?"

Tate twisted his mouth. "Possibly. There was a group of half shifters who called themselves that. They were led by a wolf hybrid named Gideon York."

"I've heard of them," said Corbin. "They're all dead."

"Most would agree that you're right on that," said Tate. "But some think Gideon is alive."

"Okay, *I* haven't heard of him," declared Havana. "Who is he?"

Tate folded his arms. "Gideon's mother was human and his father was a wolf shifter. Gideon didn't have an easy time in his pack. He couldn't shift. Many saw him being latent as a weakness, but anyone who hurt him would later suffer in some way. Skinned animals would be dumped in their bedrooms. Their family pets would turn up dead. Their cabins would be set on fire. In one case, a kid got his foot caught in a bear trap that had been taken from the perimeter of pack territory and dumped in his backyard. No one could prove Gideon was responsible, but most believed he was.

"When he turned eighteen, his Alpha asked him to move off of pack territory. He didn't kick Gideon *out* of the pack, just asked him to relocate. Fast forward four years, and Gideon began a pack of his own that would welcome any shifter, no matter the breed, so long as they were only *half* shifter. They called themselves a family, not a pack. They didn't have pack mates, they had kin. They didn't have an Alpha, they had a family patriarch—Gideon. And they massacred his pack—including his parents, twelve-year-old brother, and nine-year-old sister. No one was spared."

"Jesus," Havana breathed.

"The deceased Alpha's relatives believed Gideon was to blame, so they went to Gideon's compound to challenge him," said Tate. "But the patriarch wouldn't open the gates, so the pack bypassed the fence and set fire to the compound in the hope of making everyone exit. How the rest plays out often depends on who's telling the story. The most common version is that Gideon killed his kin and then himself rather than face the wolves. But some believe he murdered the majority of his kin and then escaped with the few he allowed to live."

"Why would they think that's a possibility?" asked Havana.

"Because when the fire was put out and the wolves walked through the wreckage, they discovered a bolt hole. The bodies were so badly burned that no one could be sure if Gideon was among the corpses."

"If he had a bolt hole, why not take everyone with him?"

"Gideon wasn't really interested in building a 'family.' He'd wanted an army that would follow him blindly and aid him in getting revenge on his pack. He'd keep you around while you were of use, but if that changed, he'd eliminate you in an instant. His kin had served their purpose.

"Considering the pack would have hunted him, it would have suited Gideon if people believed he was dead. Some say he went underground; that he now does business via whatever select few people know he's alive. It's believed that most of his underlings often don't even realize who their orders really come from."

Havana licked the edges of her teeth. "Assuming he is alive, would he be someone who'd auction off loners?"

"I'd say so, yes," replied Tate. "He hated shifters—not simply because of the trouble he had with his pack, but because he resented them for being able to shift when he couldn't. It was said that he even detested his inner wolf for never surfacing."

"Given what he did to his biological family and pack," Luke began, "I'd say he'd think nothing of trafficking strangers. He was never right in the head. Maybe because of his upbringing, or maybe because his wolf never surfaced—that can make a person and their inner animal unstable.

"Given the terminology the jaguars used, I'd say that he's alive and running this show. Finding him won't be easy. Some of the wolves who burned down the compound searched for him for years, wanting to be sure he was dead. They never found him."

"The two jaguars must be his 'kin,'" said Bailey. "They'll know where he is. They're our ticket to finding him."

"I hope your contacts can help, Tate," said Havana. "We have to do what we can to stop the next auction before it starts."

"Why did you ask the cougar where he delivered each of the loners?" Corbin asked her.

"It's possible that the location of the ... auction house, for lack of a better term ... is somewhere reasonably close to the drop-off points," said Havana. "They were all in this city, so it stands to reason that the auction house is also here."

"In my opinion, Vana, there's no sense in checking out the abandoned factory where Rupert and his buddy were supposed to dump you," said Bailey. "There's no way the jaguars hung around overnight waiting for them."

"I agree," said Tate. He looked at Havana. "If there's a specific reason why each of the loners are selected for auction, someone else may come for you. Be careful. Stay on high alert. Don't go anywhere alone."

"I have no plans to make it easy for anyone to grab me," said Havana.

Tate gave a satisfied nod. "I'll go make some calls and find out what I can. I'll pass on whatever I learn."

Havana inclined her head in thanks. "Appreciate it."

"I'll see you out," Corbin told him.

Tate gave her one last, long look she couldn't quite decipher. Then he, Luke, and Corbin walked away.

Havana turned to Bailey. "I'm going to call Cesário," she told her, referring to their ex-boss. "Although I believe Gideon York is behind this, I have to consider that the anti-shifter extremists could be connected to the auction—they would *happily* traffic shifters. If such a thing has been happening, Cesário will have heard about it.

"While I talk to him, call Dawn at the homeless shelter. Make her aware of the situation so she can warn the loners she's housing to be careful. Also, give her the names of the loners that Rupert snatched in the past and ask if she's heard of any of them. I'll text them to you now." Havana quickly did so.

"Your message just came through," said Bailey, tapping the screen of her phone with her thumbs. "If I can't get through to Dawn, I'll call one of the volunteers like Madisyn or Makenna. Tell Cessy I said hi."

Havana sighed. "He hates it when you call him that."

"I know." Bailey walked away, putting her cell to her ear.

Havana found her ex-boss's number in her list of contacts. She'd spoken to him once or twice since she retired. Neither she, Bailey, Aspen, or Camden *would* have retired so soon if it hadn't been compulsory.

Some people had originally thought that the Movement would only make matters worse. On the contrary, the group handled the extremists so well that not only had the factions lost a truck load of support from humans, the rate of their attacks had dramatically lowered. Due to that and the work of PR shifter groups, humans and shifters co-existed much more peacefully nowadays. Still, the extremists would never really go away, so there was a chance they were connected to the auctions. Which was why she needed to speak with Cesário.

The phone rang three times before he answered. "Haven't heard from you in a while, Ramos," he said, his voice curt and gruff.

She smiled. "Hello to you too, Cesário. I'm well, thanks."

"Then why're you bothering me?"

She wasn't fooled by that put-out tone. He was a big softie deep down where it counted. Deep, deep, *deep* down. "I just wondered if you'd heard any rumors about anti-shifter extremists selling loners at auction."

"Extremists? No. But I've heard whispers that such auctions occur. Why?"

She told him about good ole Rupert.

"Jesus, Ramos, can you not just live a quiet life? It was kind of the point of you retiring."

"I felt like spicing things up a little. These auctions *could* be run by extremists."

"If so, they're keeping their connection to the auctions so quiet that even the Movement is unaware of it, which makes it unlikely—we're on top of their every move."

"Okay. Tell me about the 'whispers' you heard."

"It's rumored that someone's been auctioning off lone shifters every four months for the past year. Some say the auctioneer's human. Others believe he's a hybrid. No one wants to believe he's *full* shifter, because no one wants to think our own kind would betray us that way. Whoever this person is, they're as cruel as they come. You know, something similar did happen before with a black bear shifter."

"Seriously?"

"Yeah. He was pissed at being shunned by his clan, so he kidnapped a bunch and auctioned them off. He took bids online, and he made a shit-ton of money before his clan tracked him and shut down the operation. They killed the bastard, so you can be sure he hasn't gone back to his old ways."

"But someone could have been inspired by it."

"They could've. His clan mates also managed to find the bears he'd sold at auction. I'd like to say the buyers were all extremists, but our intel made it clear that the extremists weren't even aware of the auctions."

"Then who were the buyers?"

"Some were humans who wanted shifters as test subjects. One buyer was a human who wanted a child shifter as a pet; they kept him in a fucking cage. A few were shifters, though. One wanted some bears for his illegal fighting pit; another wanted one for their brothel; another wanted a sow as a sex slave."

She curled her upper lip, disgusted. "So, basically, there are all sorts of shitty reasons why someone would buy another living being at auction. And that means I can't make any assumptions about who might be bidding on the loners."

"Is Corbin aware of what's happening?" Cesário and the grizzly were old friends. Corbin allowed him to check out the rec center for potential recruits because he believed it was good for loners to have a job, direction, and purpose.

"He knows. He sat in on the interrogation. So did my landlord, Tate Devereaux. He's going to use his contacts to help."

"Ah, the Olympus Pride's new Alpha. I've heard many things about him—all positive. He and his father are good people to have on your side. That pride will help you get to the bottom of all this shit sooner rather than later."

"You ever heard of Gideon York?"

"Oh, I've heard of him. He was a bad apple if ever there was one. Why?"

"Rupert Merchant said the jaguars talked about 'the family,' 'patriarch,' and 'kin.' We're thinking Gideon might very well be alive."

Cesário sighed. "I'd like to think the twisted fuck is dead, but if there was one thing Gideon was good at, it was surviving. Yeah, he could have got out of his compound. And yeah, he could be running these auctions. He used to traffic guns and drugs when at the compound. I can see him easily making the jump to trafficking people."

Havana nodded. "If you hear any news regarding the auctions, I'd appreciate it if you'd point me in the right direction. I'm not asking you to get involved or throw any manpower my way. I know the Movement's purpose is to deal with *extremists*, not wayward shifters. The minute the group starts targeting anyone other than extremists, they become assassins and lose credibility as defenders. I'd never ask you to misuse any of the resources you have. Just let me know if you hear anything."

"That I can and will definitely do. And you're right; pursuing our own kind isn't the purpose of the Movement. I don't want to have to personally step the fuck in, so you'd better not get dead, Ramos. It will seriously piss me off."

She felt her lips tip up. "It will piss me off even more."

He grunted. "Keep me updated."

"Will do. By the way, Bailey says hi."

He huffed. "She hasn't gotten herself killed yet? Now that surprises me."

"I'll let her know you miss her."

"Yeah, you do that."

Still seething, Tate stalked through the antique store and jogged up the stairs to the apartment above it. He, his parents, and siblings had all lived there at one time. It was now only occupied by Vinnie and Tate's youngest brother, Damian.

Vinnie's mother, Ingrid, managed the store. She willfully ignored that her son smuggled money through many of the antiques—something he often did for anti-shifter extremists, who had no clue that Vinnie was a shifter. He then passed on that info to members of the Movement.

As Tate strode into the living room, Vinnie looked up from where he was sitting on the sectional sofa reading something on his phone. The older man frowned. "What dumb fucker put that look on your face?"

"A sick son of a bitch who thinks it's acceptable to have loners drugged, kidnapped, and then put up for auction," replied Tate.

Vinnie blinked. "Say that again."

Instead, Tate explained, "A cougar tried to drug and kidnap Havana last night." Too restless to sit, he stood in front of the fireplace as he brought his father up to speed. Sitting in the armchair, Luke occasionally tossed in pieces of information.

Puffing out a breath, Vinnie rested his phone on the coffee table. "Jesus."

"Fucked up, isn't it? I'll reach out to our contacts. I'm not optimistic that they'll know where Gideon is, or if they'll have any info about the auctions—they'd surely have otherwise put a stop to them."

Vinnie nodded. "You should give Maddie a call and warn her that the people at the homeless shelter could be in danger, just in case Havana hasn't yet done so. How long did it take to get the cougar to confess it all?"

"Not long. He was pretty cooperative."

"How many bones did you need to break before he became so cooperative?"

"None. He was chatty because he wasn't eager to go through another fifteen hours of horror, apparently."

Vinnie's head jerked back. "Who tortured him for fifteen hours?"

"Bailey's mamba bit him," said Luke. "And then they all left him to suffer overnight. Havana waltzed into that basement earlier as polite and pleasant as a kindergarten teacher. She didn't push him to talk. Just gave him the option of answering her questions honestly or being bitten again."

As Tate had watched her interrogate Rupert, he'd gotten the feeling that it wasn't her first rodeo. She'd been too steady and confident, too sure of her technique. And she hadn't had a single measly issue with letting the bastard die hard, as if it wasn't the first time that she'd had to make such a decision.

"Where's the cougar now?" asked Vinnie.

"Still in the basement, dying a slow and painful death after Bailey's mamba bit him three more times. Havana's orders," said Tate.

Humor lit Vinnie's eyes. "Devils are seriously unforgiving, aren't they?"

He studied Tate closely. "I take it you'll be working with her on this."

"Of course. She's my tenant and under my direct protection. Plus, I have an entire building of loners who could be future targets if I don't get this operation shut down. But I would have involved myself in any case, because this shit's just plain wrong."

"Oh, I'm sure it has *nothing* to do with the none too small fact that you like her a lot more than you're comfortable with," Luke mocked.

Tate only narrowed his eyes.

"I suspected your fling with her was over," Luke added. "But I was hoping I was wrong."

"Were you now?"

"I like her. I like her for you. If you want my opinion—"

"I don't; never do."

"—you should have given a relationship with Havana a chance. Or would your cat have objected? Because if so, you were right to let her go. But if he'd have been interested in exploring something with her, you were dumb not to at least be open to the idea. And if you want to know what I think—"

"I don't; never do."

"—she'd have been willing to try a relationship with you. It really is a shame that we'll never know if it would have worked out between the two of you. You're thinking this is none of my business, and you're right. I'll say no more on the subject. But I'm always gonna think you were a fool to let her go."

"And I'm always gonna wonder where you got the insane idea that I give a rat's ass what you think about anything."

Luke snickered. "Be an asshole all you want—I know you love me. You might have tried to kill me several times when we were kids, but you didn't actually do it. Remember the night when I was twelve and you shoved a sock in my mouth and then tried to suffocate me with your pillow? It nearly worked, but then you stopped. You let me live. That's love."

Tate frowned. "I stopped because you let out a moist-sounding fart that stunk like rotten eggs and almost knocked me sick."

Luke's brow furrowed as his gaze turned inward. "Oh yeah, I forgot about that."

"And I wouldn't have tried to kill you that night if you hadn't tossed my birthday cake out the window like it was a goddamn frisbee."

"That was an accident."

Vinnie exhaled heavily and raised his hands. "Let's cut our trip down memory lane short, shall we, boys?"

Tate grunted and rolled back his shoulders. "Yeah, lets," he said, pulling out his phone. He had a lot of calls to make and, to his frustration, very little optimism that those calls would gain him the answers he needed.

CHAPTER FIVE

A few hours later, Tate jabbed the "up" button on the elevator. He threw his brother a sideways scowl. "Stop smirking."

"It's hard not to when I can see how much you're struggling to keep your distance from Havana," said Luke.

"I'm not struggling."

"Then why are we at her building?"

"I need to give her an update."

"And it had to be done in person?"

Well no, but … "It's a good excuse to subtly check on her. I'm not just worried about her physical safety. It has to be a mind fuck to know that someone intended to sell you at a goddamn auction like you're an antique dresser."

"True. She seemed okay earlier, though."

"That could have been a simple case of shock. Now that she's had time for everything to sink in, she might be freaking the hell out." Havana generally wasn't the type to freak out, but Tate wanted to be utterly sure she was fine.

A *ping* proceeded the opening of the elevator doors. After he and his brother stepped inside, Tate pressed the button for her floor. And, that quickly, his body began to hum with anticipation—it was an automatic physiological reflex after months of coming here to see her. As if his system had come to associate the short upward journey to her floor with a dark carnal pleasure that he just couldn't imagine ever experiencing with someone else.

It was like she'd made some sort of mark on him. One he couldn't see but could feel. One that kept pulling him back to her again and again.

The elevator soon came to a smooth stop. As he and Luke walked along the corridor, Tate noticed Havana stood in the doorway of her apartment up ahead, chatting with one of the other tenants.

The older woman gave him a deferential nod before sighing. "Oh, this business with the auction is just horrible, isn't it?"

"It is," replied Tate. "But it'll be dealt with. In the meantime, be careful."

"Oh, I will. Trust me." She gave Havana a pointed look. "You take care now."

"You, too," said Havana.

With a little wave, the woman walked away.

Havana's eyes met his, and Tate felt the electric snap of attraction in his blood. Those bluish-gray eyes flared, telling him she'd felt it too, but she blanked her expression fast.

To his consternation, the drive to brand her hadn't yet dimmed. It was still like a live wire inside him, and he had no idea how to shut it off. He just knew he had no intention of answering that drive. He wouldn't force a mark on her just to make some kind of point, no matter how much his system pushed at him to do so.

"I'm hoping you came because you have amazing news to deliver," she said, stepping back to allow him to enter. "Like that one of your contacts knows where Gideon is."

Tate took three steps into the apartment before he admitted, "Unfortunately, I don't yet have that info. Most of them believe he's dead, but not all. They're still looking into the situation with the auctions and—" He cut off as a mamba launched its entire body at the adorable bearcat sitting on the rug. The bearcat let out a yowl, and then the two were wrestling and rolling around on the living room floor. Lounging on the sofa, Camden only sighed.

Havana crossed to the animals. "For God's sake," she snapped. "Are you really not bored of this at all?"

The animals easily broke apart, so it was clearly a play-fight. The bearcat sat up, cute as a button, and scratched at her ear. The snake raised her head and flicked out her tongue.

"We're supposed to be watching a movie, so could you please go shift and put on some clothes?" Havana asked them.

The animals cast Tate and Luke a brief look before each heading to a pile of clothes. But then the bearcat's long, ringed tail lashed out and whipped the mamba. The snake hissed and coiled to strike.

"No, I'm done with this," Havana declared. "Go. Shift. Now."

Tate's body tightened at the dominant, no-nonsense way she took control. He'd seen her do it with her friends more than once. Watching her own her strength and step into her unofficial Alpha role was always a turn-on.

The animals both shot her a put-out "you're no fun" look. It was as the bearcat turned that Tate noticed two puncture wounds on her back.

"Looks like the snake bit her," he warned.

Havana waved that away. "She'll be fine. Bearcat shifters have a peptide that can neutralize any snake venom."

He blinked. "Really?"

"Yep. And don't think Bailey's mamba doesn't take *full* advantage of that and bite the bearcat whenever she feels like it." Havana walked into the kitchen.

Signaling for his brother to remain in the living area, Tate trailed after her. He found her standing at the counter, where bags of various snacks had been laid out. "Farrell told me that Sinclair wasn't at his apartment."

Her nose wrinkled. "He was long gone by the time Aspen, Camden, and your Head Enforcer arrived. Apparently, it was too much to hope that there'd be something at Sinclair's place that would give us any clues as to where he might have gone or who hired him."

"Farrell couldn't find any photos there, so we don't have a clue what Sinclair looks like." Tate propped his hip against the counter. "My allies and contacts have been debriefed about everything. Only a few had heard a rumor about the auctions, but they weren't convinced it was true until now. Unfortunately, none had info on Sinclair. There's no record of him anywhere, so he either destroyed his paper trail or he isn't using his real name. Many loners don't." He tilted his head. "Do you?"

She smiled. "Don't start asking personal questions unless you want some tossed your way."

He edged closer and persisted, "Is Havana Ramos your real name?"

"Is it true that you have no interest in ever mating?"

He frowned. "Where did you hear that?"

"You have a lot of gossipers in your pride. Some believe that little nugget of speculation is true; some don't."

Tate stared at her for a long moment, saying nothing. He really didn't want to get into all that shit about Ashlynn's betrayal and his mother's death, so he did what he often did when someone asked him a question that he wasn't comfortable answering. He didn't lie, he just changed the subject. "Luke spoke to Dawn on the phone about the names of the loners Rupert gave you."

Havana shot him a little smile but didn't call him on his failure to answer her. "Yes, she did."

"Luke also said Dawn claims one of the loners once stayed at her shelter."

Havana sighed, her face falling. "Yeah. Keziah Crompton. She's only fifteen. Dawn last saw her two weeks ago. She thought the girl just decided to leave—not all residents choose to stay long. I just hope she's alive and we can somehow find her."

Havana was surprised her hands didn't shake as she tore open a bag of chips and poured them into a bowl. Having Tate so close—inhaling his scent with her every breath, feeling his body heat radiate against her, listening to that sensual voice that could talk a girl to orgasm—was hard on her senses. It was tougher still when she could feel his eyes boring into her, watching her *too* closely.

She cast him a sharp look. "Enough with the staring."

"Stop being so beautiful, and I'll stop staring. Maybe. Probably not. I like looking at you. And since I just got a tiny peek of your neon pink bra strap, I'm wondering if you're wearing the matching panties. I recall peeling them off you on more than one occasion."

She was *not* touching that comment. "Anyway, I spread the word throughout the building that it's possible loners are being targeted. Corbin did the same at the rec center. Dawn is making the residents of the shelter aware of the situation."

"My pride mates will inform the loners who work for our pride to be careful."

"Aspen posted a warning on an online forum for lone shifters, asking them to pass it on. The news went viral pretty quickly."

"Good."

Once she'd poured all the snacks into bowls, she gathered the empty packets. "I found out today that a bear shifter once auctioned off some of his clan members after they shunned him."

Tate's brow furrowed. "Who told you that?"

"Someone I met at the rec center years ago," she replied vaguely, tossing the bags in the trash. "Anyway, the story goes that the bear took bids from people online."

Once she'd finished relaying the incident, Tate shook his head in disgust. "It's sickening to know there are people out there, human or shifter, who'd actually buy or sell others." He narrowed his eyes, his gaze speculative. "You handled the interrogation well."

She didn't let her expression alter. "Why, thank you."

"Why do I get the feeling it wasn't your first?"

"You'd have to ask yourself that—I can't answer it for you, Garfield."

His lips thinned. "Didn't we agree that you wouldn't call me that anymore?"

"No, you asked me not to. I didn't say I wouldn't." And it seemed a good way to divert him from his line of questioning.

He moved closer, boldly entering her space. Then he frowned. "Why is your devil so pissed at me?" he asked softly. "My cat senses it, he hates it. What did I do that upset her so much?" His gaze sharpened. "It wouldn't happen to be the very thing that made you decide to walk away, would it?"

She exhaled heavily. "God, Tate, you're like a goddamn bulldog." On the one hand, it was impossible to not admire that level of relentlessness. On the other hand, it was damn irritating.

"Just tell me what I did. I can't apologize or fix it if I don't know what I did."

She softened. It wasn't *his* fault that she'd been unable to keep her feelings out of their fling. He'd been nothing but honest with her from day one. "You didn't do anything. Really."

"Then why is she so mad at me?"

"She's a devil. She spends seventy percent of her day mad. Don't take it personally."

"Movie's ready!" Bailey shouted from the living area. "Where're the munchies?"

"On their way," Havana loudly replied, grabbing two bowls.

"I'll carry the others." Tate followed her into the living area and, like her, positioned the bowls on the coffee table. "What are we watching?"

Havana felt her stomach flip. "You want to stay for the movie?"

He shrugged. "Got nothing else to do."

"I'm up for it," said Luke.

Hell. The whole point of watching a movie with her girls was to relax and wind down. She couldn't do that so easily if Tate was here—her body was too aware of him, too attuned to his, too braced for his touch for her to settle and feel at ease.

It might not have been so bad if she could have sprawled in her favorite armchair, but Luke had already claimed it. And since Bailey was lounging in the other chair, that only left the sofa. Aspen and Camden had taken up one side of it, which meant Havana and Tate would have to squeeze on the other end. There'd be no keeping a reasonable distance from him.

She'd be lying if she said she actually wanted him to go, though. She'd missed him. Watching a movie with him wouldn't hurt. It wasn't like they were alone or anything.

"Just don't touch my popcorn," Aspen said to both Tate and his brother.

Luke held up his hands. "I already know that bearcats don't share food for shit."

Sinking into the sofa, Havana reminded him, "Pallas cats aren't much better."

"You're not wrong," said Tate, taking the spot beside her. He placed his phone and keys on the coffee table, as if to mark his territory in some way— it was an Alpha male thing, from what she'd observed. He then leaned back, the side of his body pressed against hers, and draped one arm on the back of the sofa behind her head.

"We're in the mood for a comedy, so we chose this," said Bailey, gesturing at the movie she'd selected on the streaming service.

Luke frowned. "You call *Halloween* a comedy?"

Bailey looked genuinely perplexed. "You don't find it funny?"

The Beta shook his head. "Can't say I do."

"Huh. Weird."

Sure enough, the three females laughed several times throughout the movie. Tate could honestly say he didn't know what they found so funny, but he was glad that Havana had relaxed beside him. Well, she wasn't *completely* relaxed. There was an undercurrent of restlessness radiating from her, just as there was from him—the chemistry between them was always running in the background, always keeping their systems on edge.

He didn't push his luck and give into the urge to play with her hair. Mostly because he didn't want to anger her devil any further—she wasn't going to welcome casual touches while so irritated with him. He had no clue what he'd done to upset her so much, and he couldn't understand why Havana wouldn't be upfront with him about it.

Once the movie was finally over and the table was cleared, Aspen and Camden said their goodnights and left. Bailey then traipsed off to her bedroom, looking sleepy.

As Havana walked Tate and Luke to the door, Tate signaled for his brother to wait outside the apartment and then turned to her, intending to again ask what her devil's problem with him was. But he hesitated when he saw that her face was all soft with fatigue. He didn't want to poke at her for answers when she'd finally relaxed. He wanted her to get some sleep so that her instincts remained sharp.

He pinned her gaze with his. "You'll be careful? Gideon probably won't seek to acquire you again—not now that you're on your guard. But it's best to be safe than sorry."

"I'll be careful. Always am." She rubbed at her brow, clearly exhausted.

Seeing her so tired made him want to nuzzle her, cosset her, tuck her in bed. But she wouldn't allow it. "Good," he said. "If something or someone doesn't seem right to you, if you feel like you're being watched or followed, you call me."

She pursed those lips he loved. "Sure."

That was a placatory answer if ever Tate had heard one. "This is serious, Havana."

"Oh, I'm well aware of that. And if I find myself in a situation that I'm not positive I can handle alone, I will reach out for help."

"But you won't reach out to me," he sensed.

She lifted her shoulders. "We're not together anymore. We never really were."

"You're still under—"

"Your protection, I know. Look, I've been taking care of myself for a long time. Believe it or not, I'm actually pretty good at it. No one who comes at me will find me an easy target."

"I can believe that. It's just ..." He closed the short space between them.

"I don't want anything to happen to you."

The soft admission touched Havana in places it had no business touching. A pang of longing hit her hard, making her chest squeeze. It was bad enough that her body pined for his. It made it ten times more difficult that her heart was equally involved. Her pulse jumped when he gently rested his hands on the sides of her head, spearing her with a look so intense her stomach fluttered. "Tate—"

"Ssh," he soothed, dropping his forehead to hers. He inhaled deeply, as if breathing her in.

Her devil rumbled a put-out sound and turned away from him, but Havana didn't move, letting herself have this small moment.

He lifted his head and pressed a kiss to her forehead. And then to her temple. And then to her cheek. His mouth grazed her ear as he gently squeezed the side of her neck. "Missed you," he gruffly whispered. And then he walked out.

The tension left Havana's body in a rush, and all she could do was lean against the door as she closed it. Jesus, the guy knew what buttons to push—buttons he'd just practically stomped on.

Missed you.

She wasn't going to let those words give her hope. No, she was done holding out for people. Done letting her dreams and fantasies play havoc with her good sense.

Hearing footfalls, Havana pushed away from the door and turned to see Bailey.

"You know, you could consider having one last night with him," said the mamba.

Havana frowned, sure she'd heard her wrong. "Say what?"

"Sometimes it can help to have one more night with an ex just to burn out old feelings. It's kind of like tying up loose ends, I guess. It gives me a sense of closure." Bailey shrugged. "It's just something for you to think about."

Havana scrubbed a hand down her face. The idea held too much appeal for all the wrong reasons. "I don't think it would give me closure. I think it would make it harder for me to move on."

"Going cold turkey doesn't always work out so well. Sometimes it's better to wean yourself off something."

"Maybe. I'll think about it. But not right now. I'm too tired, I need sleep." But with the terms "one last night," "burning out old feelings," and "sense of closure" floating around her head, it was a while before Havana finally drifted off.

Watching two little girls moving in sync on the dance pads, Havana smiled. The rec center's video arcade was pretty popular among the kids and teens. The walls were lined with various machines. There was everything from whack-a-mole and claw cranes to air hockey tables and zombie-killing games.

Glowing screens and neon lights cut through the dimly lit area. The smells of popcorn and other concession foods laced the air. So many sounds filled the large space—dings, bleeps, chimes, shouts, revving engines.

"Are you *sure* you don't want to stick close to home for a few weeks?" asked Madisyn, holding the stuffed toys her daughters had won before they'd headed for the dance pads. The pallas kits, Yasmin and Regan, were utterly adorable. They were always singing and laughing with each other. A fight often broke out between them at some point, though, and those fights were never pretty.

Havana replied, "If you think my going to the shelter would draw trouble to it or make the people there uneasy, I can skip going until they feel better about it." Madisyn worked at the homeless shelter for loners and had once been a loner herself before mating into the Mercury Pack, which was closely allied to the Olympus Pride. "But if not, I'd rather keep teaching the self-defense classes. The residents may need the techniques now more than ever."

"No one has expressed a problem with you being there," Makenna cut in. The she-wolf was Madisyn's co-worker and part of the Phoenix Pack. Tate's cousin, Mila, had mated a Phoenix wolf years ago, so the pride considered them allies, too. "The people who take your classes are worried *for* you, and they think it's awesome that you overpowered your attacker—it gives them confidence that the moves you teach can actually work."

"Then I'll keep teaching the classes," said Havana.

Madisyn gave her a grateful smile. "We appreciate it. Just so you know, I passed on the cougar's confession to my pack mates—they're going to see if they can locate Sinclair and Gideon. We want to find Keziah, like, *yesterday*. She's such a nice kid. Dawn feels bad that it never occurred to her that Keziah had been taken. But we'd all just assumed she didn't want to stay at the shelter."

"We keep telling Dawn she has no need to feel guilty," said Makenna. "But she's not hearing us. My pack intends to help, too—they're utterly pissed about this. I guess the reason Gideon is targeting loners is that it's unlikely any flocks or clans or whatever will go look for them or wish to retaliate."

"He's obviously comfortable in that belief, because otherwise he would have checked that I wasn't under anyone's protection," said Havana.

"I was thinking the same thing," said Aspen. "There's no way he'd have chosen to add you to his collection of loners if he'd known he'd be tangling with the Olympus Pride. I mean, I know he didn't give Rupert or Sinclair any info that could expose him, but Gideon had to know there was a chance they could have discovered *something*."

Havana nodded. "He's been careful so far, which is why he's managed to stay largely under the radar and convince a lot of people of his death. I can't envision such a careful person doing something as stupid as to, in a roundabout way, challenge a pride of pallas cats."

"Word about the auction is spreading far and wide," said Aspen. "So Gideon probably knows by now that either Rupert or Sinclair told you about it. He'll be on pins, wondering just how much you know."

Havana sure hoped so, because she liked the idea of him sweating and fretting. The bastard was going down, and whoever helped him with his auctions would go down with him. And *soon*. She'd make sure of it.

Corbin sidled up to her with a sigh. "We may have a problem. Nothing major, just a minor complication."

Havana frowned. "What's that?"

"Ginny's here," he replied.

Havana felt her nose wrinkle. "Yeah, I noticed." The female in question was slowly heading their way, and her devil thought it an excellent idea to vent her frustrations on the sly little bitch. If only there weren't so many kids around ...

"The issue is that Bailey noticed her, too." He tipped his chin at a nearby door marked "Staff" and added, "She disappeared in there. She hasn't come back out yet."

Aspen lifted her shoulders. "Maybe she's staying out of the way so that she won't be tempted to lunge and attack. It's mature, really."

"Our dear Bailey's not anyone's definition of mature," he said. "And I say that with affection."

Aspen gave him a look of disappointment. "You could try having a little more faith in her, you know."

He glanced away. "Maybe."

Havana and Aspen exchanged an amused look. He had every reason to be wary. Bailey *never* let shit go. Purely because she didn't want to.

Havana pasted an impersonal smile on her face as Ginny and her little crowd approached them.

"Hey, guys," said Ginny, her smile bright. "Oh, Havana, I heard about what happened the other night. I'm glad you're okay."

Although she looked the height of concern, Havana wasn't buying it. Still, she said, "Thanks."

Ginny let out a dramatic sigh. "It's just so awful. Do you think they'll come for *more* people who go to the center? Could they, like, have a problem with it or something?"

"I really don't know. But it would be stupid of them to come back here when we're all on the lookout for trouble."

Ginny absently scratched her left palm. "I guess so."

"Ooh, you're going to lose money," Makenna interjected.

Ginny blinked. "I'm, what?"

"An itchy left hand means you're going to lose money," Makenna patiently explained. "It's pretty common knowledge, sweetie."

Havana stifled a smile. The she-wolf was incredibly superstitious, bless her. Havana believed in signs, but that a simple act such as spilling salt could cause destruction? No.

Ginny shook her head and turned back to Havana. "Anyway, Corbin wasn't all that clear on how you managed to stop the kidnappers from taking you." It was more of a question than a comment.

"They were expecting an easy target," said Havana. "It's hard to take me off-guard."

"Same here. I'm *very* alert. But still—" Ginny stumbled back with a little squeal as Havana's arm shot out and she caught a mamba midair that had leapt from the top of a machine.

"It's unlikely that anyone else will be sent to take me or another loner from the center, Ginny—it's simply too risky," said Havana. Without even looking at the snake wriggling in her grip, she walked over to the staff room as she added, "Nonetheless, I'd advise you to be careful. Loners always should be, considering the dangers out there." Havana pulled open the door, tossed the hissing snake inside the room, and then shut the door. "And don't forget to let Corbin know if you see anything or anyone suspicious."

"I won't." Ginny straightened her tee and swallowed. "Um, yeah, we're going to go now." She quickly walked off, bumping into her friend whose drink consequently tipped up and spilled all over her. Then Ginny's handbag slid off her arm and crashed to the floor, scattering its contents—and there was a *lot* of them—all over the thin, dark carpet. She and her friends quickly scrambled to pick everything up.

"Where's my purse?" Ginny demanded. "Where is it? Where did it go?"

"I don't know," said the girl whose drink had spilled. "It might be under one of the machines or something."

Makenna shrugged at Ginny. "Told you you'd lose money."

Her lips thinning, Ginny continued to help her friends search for her purse.

Madisyn turned back to Havana. "Wow, you really are hard to take off-guard—I didn't even sense that the mamba was close by, and my instincts are super sharp."

Corbin sighed at Aspen. "And you said I should have more faith in Bailey. You knew she'd likely gone into that room to remove her clothes and shift, didn't you? Her snake probably used the air vent to get out."

"I'm guessing Bailey doesn't like that girl," said Makenna, her eyes on a whining Ginny, who was looking under the machines.

Aspen did a long, languid stretch. "Bailey's ex cheated on her with Ginny."

Madisyn winced. "Wronging a mamba seems … well, suicidal, really. Admittedly, *my* kind aren't very tolerant creatures. Still, I'd say pallas cats are a little less dramatic in the way we seek vengeance."

A nearby girly scream pierced the air.

"Why. Won't. You. Die?" yelled Regan, slamming her sister's head on a machine.

Yasmin swiped her claws at Regan. "I'm going to rip off your face!"

Makenna smiled at Madisyn. "A little less dramatic, Mads? Really?"

"That doesn't count," said Madisyn, her cheeks heating. "It's only because they're siblings who are close in age." She rushed over to her daughters and separated them.

Makenna chuckled. "I love those girls. Hey, Corbin, you still taking Dawn to the movies tonight?"

The grizzly frowned. "Why?"

Aspen laughed. "You always get so self-conscious and weird whenever anyone asks about you and Dawn. Don't worry, we've all agreed to pretend that we don't know how much you like her."

He only grunted.

Right then, Bailey casually walked out of the staff room and approached their group. "I'll swear you live to spoil my fun, Havana." She shot a haughty look at Ginny, who stalked off with her friends—Havana couldn't tell whether the girl had found her purse or simply given up searching for it.

Corbin put a hand on the mamba's shoulder. "Look, I know Jackson's betrayal stung, and I know it stung worse that he cheated on you with someone you so strongly dislike. But, considering you've punished her in several ways over the past month, could you not just let it go?"

Bailey flicked something off her tee. "Forgiveness is for losers."

"Neither Jackson nor Ginny are worth the emotional energy you're giving them right now," Corbin insisted. "You've made your point to both of them, and I'm pretty sure they regret crossing you. Take pity on them."

"Pity is for losers," said Bailey.

"Just leave it be, Corbin," Havana advised.

Madisyn returned and puffed out a breath. "Sorry about that. The girls are going to behave themselves now. Oh, hi, Camden." She smiled at the approaching male.

He merely nodded before passing Aspen a takeout cup. "Got you that vanilla shit you like."

Aspen's mouth curved as she took the latte. "Aw, thanks."

"Didn't you get us anything?" Bailey asked him.

"Thought about it," he said. "That was as far as I got."

Bailey shook her head. "Tigers are just rude."

He gently tapped Aspen's earlobe. "I'll see you at six."

The bearcat's brow furrowed. "You will?"

"We agreed we'd have dinner at the steakhouse tonight." He sighed, looking away. "How quickly she forgets me."

"I remembered," Aspen claimed. "I was just testing you."

He snorted. "Yeah, right."

"Die, Thing, die!" shouted Yasmin, throttling her sister.

Madisyn cursed. "This is *not* cool, kids! Not cool at all."

CHAPTER SIX

As a familiar female stepped out of the coffeehouse up ahead, Tate's cat bared a fang and sat up straight. Wearing a deer in the headlights look, Ashlynn froze. Tate had heard she'd returned last night, but this was the first he'd seen of her. If she was anyone else, he'd have paid her a brief visit to welcome her back to the pride, but she'd have sensed that the welcome was false—there seemed no point in insulting either his intelligence or hers.

She'd changed a little since he last saw her. She'd dyed her reddish-brown hair a bright blonde; it used to hang down her back but was now styled in a blunt bob. She was slimmer. More toned. Carried herself with more confidence. The piercings in her eyebrow and lower lip were a surprise, and both suited her.

She made a pretty picture, but his body didn't react whatsoever—not even to the alpha vibes she exuded. As Tate stared back at her, the only thing he felt was regret that he'd taken a chance on someone whose feelings for him had been fickle at best.

Tate sensed Luke and Farrell go on high alert behind him, ready to intervene at the slightest signal.

She swallowed and tried for a smile. "Hi, Tate."

He gave her a nod. "Ashlynn."

She said a quick hi to both Luke and Farrell, but neither responded. As her gaze slid back to Tate, her tongue flicked out to touch her lip ring. "How are you?"

"Good. You?"

"Better now that I'm home. I missed this place. Missed everyone. Congratulations on ascending to the Alpha position, by the way. I'm pleased for you."

He inclined his head slightly. Forcing himself to be diplomatic, he said, "I'm sure you'll settle in fine. If you have any issues, contact Luke." As Beta, his brother was the pride's go-to person when it came to minor problems.

"Wait," she said when Tate started to walk away. "I was planning to come see you at some point today. Um, I'd like to talk to you."

"About?"

"Not pride business. This is personal. Maybe we could have dinner later? There are things I'd like to say. Things I didn't get a chance to say after … what happened."

"We said all that needed to be said the night before you left."

She shot him a pained look. "I didn't *want* to leave. My mother said it would be best to give you some time. I knew I'd messed up and that you needed space. I still kept in touch. Or I tried to. You blocked my number and email address, you blocked me on social media, and you returned all my letters without even opening them."

"I didn't want them."

"I got that message." Sadness glimmered in her eyes. "I really am sorry, Tate. Sorry about everything. Sorry for letting you down and hurting you."

Letting him down? That was something of an understatement, but whatever. "You already apologized. Twice, actually." He'd gotten his first apology in the same breath that she announced they were over. He'd gotten another the night she begged him to take her back.

She licked her lips. "I regret that things didn't work out between us."

He shrugged. "It just wasn't meant to be." Tate looked beyond her and caught sight of Havana heading to the grocery store with Aspen. His pulse jumped, and his cat went from irritated to keyed-up in an instant.

As if she felt Tate's stare, Havana paused in the shop doorway and glanced around. Yeah, that was his girl—alert as any apex predator. Their gazes locked, and he'd swear his heart squeezed. Her eyes gleamed with … something. Something that made his cat purr. But then she looked from him to Ashlynn, her expression closed down, and she headed into the store with Aspen.

"Is everything okay?" Ashlynn followed his gaze.

An odd elemental urge to hunt and track began to beat in his blood. "I've got to go," he told Ashlynn, his gaze still on the shop.

"Could we maybe have that dinner I mentioned later today? There are things you need to know. How about we meet at the Steakhouse?"

She was truly living in a fictional world if she thought they were going to strike up some sort of friendship. "I'm not interested in having dinner with you. I'm not interested in talking with you about the past. I'm not interested in us being friends or hanging out."

"Please, Tate, one dinner. It's important. I gave you the space and time you evidently needed. Now I'm back."

"Yeah, you are. But I don't see how that has anything to do with me on a personal level. I'm your Alpha; you're a member of my pride—that's it."

"You won't make time for a woman you partially imprinted on?"

He felt his brows snap together. "You and I didn't imprint on each other at the fuck all." Thin threads of the bond had once existed in the air between them, connecting them in a small way, but those threads had never *formed* something. It was the difference between a roll of cotton and a T-shirt. The roll carried the potential to become something. The tee was a creation, formed from an endless amount of threads. "There was no bond. Only the potential of it. You know that. And now I really need to go."

"*One* dinner, Tate."

"Jesus, Ashlynn, let it go. It's not gonna happen."

Her eyes narrowed. "Is this because of that devil shifter you're fucking?" she asked, a sneer in her voice.

His cat rumbled a growl. "Careful, Ashlynn," warned Tate, his voice coated in a silky menace.

"You used to call me Ash. You used to always have time for me."

"Yeah, I made a lot of mistakes with you. I won't make them again." With that, he stalked off, the visceral urge to track Havana now beating faster in his blood. He didn't question it. Just followed it, egged on by his cat. So Tate wasn't at all pleased when a voice called out his name and delayed him.

Feeling Tate's gaze boring into her back, Havana stepped into the grocery store, ignoring the petty jealousy swirling in her belly. Women tried to talk and flirt with him all the time, but she hadn't let it bother her before because she'd known he had too much integrity to cheat or sleazily flirt back. But now that they were no longer seeing each other, there was no need for him to ignore any females who came onto him. And that bothered her *far* too much.

Of course, there was no saying that the mystery woman he was talking to outside was in fact making a move on him, but Havana's jealous streak still didn't like it. In fact, neither did her devil—she might not be feeling particularly warm to him right now, but she still didn't like the thought of him with another.

Well, she and Havana would just have to learn how to deal with it, wouldn't they? He'd inevitably find himself a new fuck-buddy at some point. And Havana would *not* wish all manner of diseases and allergies on the woman. Nope.

Havana grabbed a shopping cart while Aspen hooked a metal basket over her arm. There was a *whooshing* sound as the door behind them opened.

"Ah, Havana," said a voice in a thick Russian accent as a woman sidled up to them. "I heard about your attack, I told my James we must visit you, but here you are. You are fine, yes?"

Havana smiled at Tate's aunt, a female wolverine shifter who was mated to Vinnie's brother. Full of sass and attitude and tenacity, Valentina Devereaux was beyond awesome. Havana *totally* wanted to be her. "I'm good, thanks."

Valentina looked from her to Aspen. "This auction business sickens me."

"Same here," said the bearcat. "Although I hate that the bastards went after Havana, I'm glad they made a mistake."

"It was indeed mistake to target Havana. Tate is *furious*. He will see that these people pay."

Aspen stared at him through the window, her eyes narrowed. "Who's that woman he's talking to?"

Valentina's face clouded with annoyance. "His ex, Ashlynn. Do not worry that she is back, Havana. She is no competition. He is done with her."

Havana stilled. Wait, his *ex* was back? Her stomach sank.

Aspen's eyes cut to Valentina. "What happened between them?"

"Ordinarily, I would say that it is Tate's business and you must ask him. But he says little about her, and I do not want Havana worrying about it." Valentina's lips flattened. "I did not like that he took chance on Ashlynn. I sensed she pined for our old pride mate, Koby, who she claims is her true mate. But he had imprinted on another female, Gita. When Gita died, Ashlynn left Tate hoping she could finally have Koby. The imprinting threads snapped. It was very tough time for Tate."

Hell. Havana's heart literally ached for him right then. That woman out there had seriously put him through the ringer. "Did she mate with Koby?"

"No. He still did not want her. She asked Tate to take her back."

Aspen gaped. "She had the downright gall to ask him that?"

"Oh yes," confirmed Valentina. "When he rejected her, she left pride. No matter how much her family begged, she refused to come home. Cowardly, in my opinion. She is too weak to be natural-born alpha. I *despise* weakness. That was three years ago. Now, all of sudden, she has returned."

Havana's gut twisted. It was possible the skank had come back for Tate.

Havana looked out of the window just in time to see him sexily prowl toward the store with Luke and Farrell flanking him. But then the three males stopped as one of their pride mates jogged over to Tate. She also noticed that Ashlynn hadn't moved from her spot and was watching him *very* closely. Such a pretty name for a hoe bag.

If she *did* want him back, if she managed to earn his forgiveness, he might well take her back if he still cared for her. Which would be none of Havana's business, of course. He was free to do whatever he pleased with whoever he pleased. But, well, he deserved better. And Ashlynn deserved a punch in the tit. Both tits, even. A kick up the ass wouldn't go amiss either.

Valentina sniffed in Ashlynn's direction. "I blame her for how commitment shy he became." She looked at Havana. "But he has kept you in his life for over four months now. I am very hopeful that this means good things. I adore Tate. I want him to be happy. If she tries to come between you and him, do not let her. You and Tate make good couple."

Havana forced a wan smile. "Sorry to disappoint, but our fling is kind of over."

"What? Do not tell me that foolish cat ended it."

"He didn't end it. I did." Havana shrugged. "It wasn't going anywhere, so I walked."

"And he did not go after you?" Valentina made an exasperated sound. "That boy. He is like my son, Alex. Only learns his lessons hard way. Perhaps it is Devereaux trait that all males in family carry." She cupped Havana's cheek. "You keep chin up. He will see sense eventually. Tate is complex man, but not stupid. Now, I must go pass on a message to my pride mate. I will see you both again soon. Say hello to Bailey for me."

As the wolverine hurried away, Havana began to walk down the aisle with Aspen at her side, feeling down and deflated. "I think I'll get a pizza-to-go from here so that I don't have to cook tonight." She wasn't in the mood to do anything other than veg out in front of the TV and stuff junk food down her throat.

"I'll go order it for you before I pick up some things," said Aspen. "Hey, did you know the full story about Tate's ex?"

Havana shook her head. "He never spoke of her, and I never asked."

"Maybe the reason he has such razor-sharp boundaries is that he's trying to avoid ever triggering the imprinting process to start. I mean, if *you* felt the pain that came with the snapping of imprint threads, it'd make you reluctant to go down that road again, right?"

"Probably. But I really don't want to talk about Tate or his ex or anything else that has the potential to give me indigestion. I just want to get this grocery shopping done so I can head home and pig out."

"I'll go to the pizza counter, place your order, and wait for it to cook. I'm guessing you want the usual toppings."

"You guessed right, thanks."

"No thanks needed." Aspen disappeared.

Havana walked down several aisles, tossing various foods into the cart such as apples, oranges, bagels, cupcakes, potatoes, and meat trays. She liked shopping here. Unlike with human-owned stores, the fluorescent lighting wasn't quite so bright, and the background music wasn't loud, so the place was kinder to a shifter's enhanced senses. There was no lessening the strength of the food smells, but she didn't mind that; she liked inhaling the scents of cinnamon buns, fresh-baked bread, and citrus fruit.

Hearing her phone chime, she dug it out of her purse. *Dieter*. She blinked, surprised. Like Tate, he only contacted her when interested in hooking up. Huh. She answered, "Hello."

"Fuck, Havana, I only just heard about what happened," he burst out. "Why the hell didn't you call me?"

Havana's brows lifted. "Well, hello to you, too. Yes, it *has* been months since we last spoke. I'm doing great, thanks for asking."

He snorted. "Like I'm going to bother my ass with small talk when *you were almost kidnapped*. Jesus, I got the shock of my life when I heard about it."

"Yeah, the whole thing was quite a surprise for me, too."

"You're all right?"

"I'm fine. Really. What about you?"

"I *was* fine until I received that fucked-up news about you. I can't believe you didn't call me. We've been friends a while, Havana. You had to know I'd want to hear about this."

She wouldn't say they'd ever been *actual* friends. Just two people who were friend*ly* and occasionally hooked up. He'd never been a shoulder for her to cry on. Never shared his dreams or goals with her. Never been at her side through tough times. Well, whatever. "How're things with you and Tabitha?"

"They're fine, but don't think I'm letting you change the subject. If you have any more problems, if anything else happens, you pick up the phone and *call me*."

She almost snapped her teeth. It was pretty freaking irritating that both he and Tate—two guys who didn't want to make her a part of their lives—thought it reasonable to demand that she look to them for help. It was *slightly* different with Tate, considering she was officially under his protection, but still irritating.

"Dieter, you know better than to use that tone with me—it gets you nowhere."

He growled. "I'm just asking that you call me if more shit goes down."

"You're not asking, you're demanding. And I'm trying not to laugh because, yeah, you seem to think I'll bow to your whim."

"I just worry about you."

"You can worry without laying down laws I'll never follow." She carefully lowered a crate of eggs into the cart, balancing it on a box of cereal. "Now I have to go. Take care." Hands landed on the end of her cart. Her head snapped up. And she froze. Because right there was Tate, looking all delicious and sexy and self-possessed. He was also staring down at her, his eyes slightly narrowed.

"We're not done," Dieter insisted.

Oh, they were. "I'll talk to you again soon." Ignoring his protests, Havana rang off and returned her phone to her purse.

Her devil glared at Tate, her mood fouler than usual after seeing him with his ex. Havana might have been equally irritated if Valentina hadn't relayed the whole story. Ashlynn really *had* screwed him over. It was impossible not to feel bad for him.

"Who is Dieter?" he asked, his tone even.

She curled her hands around the cart handle. "An … acquaintance of sorts, I guess you could say."

"An acquaintance who knows you in the biblical sense?"

She thought about pointing out how that was absolutely not his business, but she'd just learned a fair bit of personal info about his past. She figured turnabout was fair play. "Yes."

A muscle in Tate's cheek ticked. "What did he want?"

"To know if I'm okay. What did your ex want?"

Tate frowned. "Who told you about her?"

"A few of your pride mates mentioned her over the past few months. Valentina pointed her out just now. She was under the impression that you and I still had a 'thing' going on, so she explained about your ex, not wanting me to worry that the girl was competition. And you didn't answer my question."

"You haven't really been answering mine properly lately, but I'll tell you anyway. She wanted to apologize for how things went down three years ago and then asked if we could have dinner. I said no."

"Have dinner?" Hmm, maybe Skank of the Century really *was* back for him.

"Yeah. She wants to talk. I don't."

Havana wasn't entirely convinced he was as disinterested in Ashlynn as he sounded. They had serious history, after all. He had to be at least a little curious to know what she had to say. "Okay. Now could you move, because I need to grab a few more things. Thank you," she said when he released the cart. But he didn't leave. He fell into step beside her as she pushed the cart round to the next aisle.

"What are you doing?" she asked him.

Glancing into her cart, he replied, "Wondering how hard it will be to convince you to share that chocolate trifle with me. We had fun with one of those once, didn't we? It tasted better when I was eating it off you."

She almost spluttered. This was *not* a conversation she wanted to have. And that was *not* a memory she wanted to revisit in the middle of a damn grocery store. "Don't you have Alpha stuff to do?"

"If someone needs me for something, they know how to reach me."

Alphas were often on call 24/7. It couldn't be easy, but she doubted Tate would ever find it something to complain about. He was a man of action. He seemed to thrive on it.

"Now, about that trifle …"

"You're not getting any of it," she said. "You want one, buy your own."

Aspen came into view, her basket full, holding a pizza box. "You done yet?"

"Almost. Just got to grab some milk." Havana nearly ran over something with her cart. Noticing what it was, she sighed. "Okay, now things are just getting weird."

Tate's brow furrowed. "Weird how?"

"Last night, I had a dream that I was trying to check into a motel, but it was closed. Earlier, a woman walked past me singing *Moonlight Motel* to herself. And look what we have here." Havana picked up the object off the floor. "A DVD of Bates Motel, season one."

He pursed his lips. "And you think all this means ... what?"

"I think the universe is trying to tell me something, but I can't figure out what. It clearly has something to do with motels, though."

He clamped his mouth shut, clearly fighting a smile. He looked at Aspen, as if expecting her to share his amusement. The bearcat only stared back at him.

"Wait, you both believe the universe is reaching out to you?" he asked.

"Not to *me*," said Aspen. "I believe it's reaching out to Havana. It often does. We just can't always work out what it's trying to communicate."

His gaze bounced from her to Havana. "Right. Well, whatever."

Havana huffed. "Fine. Don't believe us. Now, I have to finish my shopping." She gave him a breezy smile. "Later."

He didn't return the "later." He also didn't stalk off. He followed her to the refrigerator, whistling a merry tune.

Walking around the store with him was just ... odd. During their fling, they never went places together. They certainly hadn't done anything as mundane as shop for groceries together.

Reaching the fridge, Havana grabbed the bulky jug of milk, plonked it in her cart, and then headed to a checkout stand with Aspen. Havana cast him confused, sideways looks while he helped pile the groceries onto the conveyor belt.

Her devil, not liking his insistence on sticking close, urged Havana to smack him over the head with her prickly pineapple. The animal wasn't pleased that Havana resisted.

Havana paid no attention to his nosy pride mates, who were watching them curiously, seeming under the false impression that she and Tate had come shopping *together*. It would appear that he hadn't yet made it clear that he and Havana were over—especially since Valentina had been completely unaware of it.

He helped Havana bag the groceries and, by the time she'd paid and was ready to leave, he'd returned the cart. "I'll help," he said. Not an offer, a statement of intent. He grabbed a bunch of her bags before she could protest.

Outside, Luke and Farrell each took a bag from her, and then all three men stuck close as she and Aspen walked to their apartment building.

When they reached the main door, Havana tried to take the groceries from the guys. "I can carry them upstairs myself."

Tate smiled. "Can you? Clever girl." He held tight to them and, whistling that damn tune again, keyed in the entry code to unlock the door. He and his bodyguards then followed both her and Aspen into the building and up to Havana's apartment.

Although he agreed it likely wasn't necessary, Tate had Luke and Farrell do a walk-through of it to ensure there were no intruders. The three men then wordlessly helped her put away the groceries so that Aspen could return to her apartment to get ready for her dinner with Camden.

Once the task was complete, Tate politely dismissed his brother and Head Enforcer. The moment Havana heard the front door close behind them, the sexual hum in her blood went up a notch with the simple awareness that she and Tate were alone. A sudden tension thickened the air like sultry summer heat, so she knew that same awareness was having a similar effect on him.

"Where's Bailey?" he asked.

"She's working an extra shift at the rec center. Purely because the new guy's cute and she wants to get to know him." Havana opened the warm box to reveal her pizza.

Tate came closer. "Smells good. You can spare a slice, right? Come on, there's no way you'll eat all that. You were gonna put at least half of it in the fridge to have for lunch tomorrow."

That *had* been her intention. The trouble was that she often forgot there was cold pizza in the fridge and then ate something else for lunch, so it went to waste. "Fine. You can have a slice."

Of course, he grabbed the biggest one as soon as they settled at the dining table. And because she was a total sucker who was still feeling sorry for him after what his bitch of an ex put him through, she let him eat a few more slices. Before she knew it, the pizza had been demolished between the two of them.

Figuring it was now time to herd him out, she cleared her throat and gave him an easy smile. "Well, thanks for the assist. I didn't need it, but thanks anyway."

Tate almost smiled. It was a dismissal, pure and simple. He thought it rather cute that she believed he'd be so easily handled.

He lounged back in his chair, making it clear that he wasn't going anywhere just yet. His cat rumbled an irritable sound. The feline wanted to be closer to her. Wanted to win her still-distant devil's attention. "Tell me about Dieter." If it turned out that this guy from her past was sniffing around her, Tate would *not* be pleased at the fuck all.

"There's not much to tell. We occasionally hooked up before he began dating his current girlfriend." She tilted her head. "It must be hard for you to have your ex in the pride again."

"It isn't. She's of no interest to me now."

"Oookay."

He squinted. "You don't believe me?"

"I never said that. I'm just not so sure you're being honest with yourself about it."

"I strike you as a man who bullshits himself, baby?"

"Don't call me baby. And no, you don't. But not many shifters buy apartment buildings to house loners and then place them under his protection. I just can't help wondering if you did that for those strangers because you couldn't do it for Ashlynn. She left the pride, right? She was alone. Vulnerable. It couldn't have been easy for you to know that, even if she did hurt you."

"I can see why your thoughts have taken you down that route, but Ashlynn's nothing to do with why I bought this complex."

"Then why'd you do it?"

"I know through Madisyn just how hard it can be for lone shifters to find suitable and affordable accommodation. Especially when they have to worry about being too close to the territories of flocks and packs etc. Many beg her to let them live at the shelter because they're too afraid to go out into the world. It gave me the idea of providing a place purely for loners to live—call it my good deed for the decade. Almost every tenant in this building was sent to me by Madisyn."

"I see."

Tate watched her as she began to clear the table. "Do you? Or do you still doubt me?"

She lifted her shoulders. "I just can't see how you could have no interest in someone you once tried to imprint on—that's no small thing."

Tate pushed away from the table and crossed to her, liking how her pupils dilated and her heartbeat kicked up. His cat purred, straining to be closer to her. "Did I seem interested in her when you saw me talking to her earlier? Or did I seem more interested in you?"

"I didn't really take much notice. I only glanced your way for a second or two."

"But that highly perceptive brain of yours will have absorbed everything there was to see."

"In any case, we don't need to talk about her. I shouldn't have brought it up."

"In your position, I'd be wondering if you still had feelings for your ex, so I'm going to make sure you get that that's not the case here. She and I were together three years ago. The relationship didn't work out, and I don't wish that it had. Neither does my cat."

Havana *really* wished he'd drop the subject. It hurt to hear he'd once cared for someone so much he'd wanted to imprint on them, because it highlighted that he hadn't even come close to experiencing any such feelings for her.

The hurt annoyingly did *nothing* to douse the sparks of electric sexual tension that bounced from him to her. Nor did it make her hormones cease doing the damn foxtrot. It was impossible to stop her body from responding to him, apparently.

"She's part of my past—that's it," he added. "She's not important. I don't want her back. I want *you* back."

Havana rolled her eyes even as the claim made her stomach flutter. "What you want is a weekly hookup. There are plenty of women out there who I'm sure would be more than happy to be your new fuck buddy."

He edged further into her personal space. "I don't want other women. I want you. And don't make out like you were just a convenient body to me, Havana. What we had might not have been serious, but it wasn't cold or impersonal either."

"True. You never treated me with anything less than respect. But the fact is that I never meant anything to you."

His eyes briefly flared. "You meant something," he said, his voice low and soft and so damn intimate it made her pulse jump. "You still do."

"I don't buy that."

"You should. It's the truth. I've never lied to you before. Why would I start now?" He tucked a loose strand of her hair behind her ear and then gently flicked her lower lip with his finger. "Did you know I have a policy not to get involved with any of my tenants?"

She felt her brow pinch. Actually, no, she hadn't known that.

"It's not wise to mix business with pleasure, and I'm not in the habit of going against good sense." His warm, calloused hands loosely cuffed her wrists, his gaze glittering with *so much* heat and carnal promise. "But," he began, dropping his tone to bedroom territory, "I knew the second I first laid eyes on you that I was going to have to have you."

That soft, velvety rumble danced down her spine, hummed along her raw nerve endings, and tightened her nipples. Four months of them sleeping together had *trained* her body to respond to his "sex voice." And he goddamn knew it.

She swallowed. "Tate—"

"I knew there'd be no fighting it, and I sure as fuck didn't want to fight it. So I didn't bother trying." He slowly smoothed his hands up her arms, over her shoulders, up her neck and onto her face. His eyes dropped to her mouth, gleaming with unabashed hunger, and her heart started working overtime. If she let him kiss her, she'd be lost. Still, it was an honest to God's struggle not to lick her lips in invitation.

She didn't dare try to push him away, because she didn't trust that she actually *would* shove him backwards. She didn't trust that her hands wouldn't instead yank him closer. "You should go," she rasped.

"I don't want to go, baby," he whispered. "And I don't think you want me to either." He smoothed his thumb over her cheekbone. "I meant it when I said I missed you."

"You missed fucking me," she corrected.

"That, too." He dropped his forehead to hers. "Still miss the taste and feel of your pussy. So fucking sweet and tight. I liked knowing no one else could have it ... that only my mouth could taste it ... that only my hands could touch it ... that only my dick could fuck it. I was far more possessive of it than I had the right to be." He punched his hips forward, snuggling his cock—God, he was so hard—against her pussy. "Hmm, there it is. I can smell how wet it is for me." He moved his mouth to her ear. "I want it, Havana."

She hitched in a breath as he ground his cock against her, hitting her clit just right. Her nipples seemed to tighten even more, and her aching pussy spasmed. She grabbed onto the countertop behind her—it was her only anchor right then.

God help her, she wanted him inside her. There. Now. Hard and fast and rough.

But that would be bad. Right? She didn't know. She couldn't think. Couldn't reason. As if the intense chemistry in the air had made her brain shrivel up.

He skimmed his nose along the side of her face. "Let me have you." He lightly nipped her jaw. "Let me." It wasn't a plea. Wasn't even a request. It was an attempt to lure, cajole, entice. An invitation to sin and submit.

She shivered as he dipped his head and his breath fanned her hypersensitive neck. Without thinking, she tilted her head slightly to give him better access. A growl of approval rumbled its way up his chest.

He pressed kisses along her throat. "Let me give us what we both want, Havana."

She bit back a moan as he ground against her clit yet again. Hell, she was going to cave, and she knew it. There was only so much a girl could take.

If he'd tried bossing her into giving in, she could have resisted—even if only to be contrary. But he'd coaxed, seduced, charmed. She found that a lot harder to fight ... which he knew perfectly well, the tricky cat. And, honestly, she didn't want to fight it.

Maybe Bailey was right. Maybe if Havana took the time to burn out what she felt for him and work him out of her system, she'd get the closure she needed.

He lifted his head and slid his fingers into her hair. "I need this."

He wasn't alone in that. *One night*, she decided. She'd allow herself one last night with him, even though ... "It probably isn't a good idea." She let out a shaky breath as he lowered his face to hers, leaving their mouths mere inches apart.

"Tell me you don't want this. If you can say it and mean it, I'll step back. I will." So slowly it was agonizing, he lowered his face that *little* bit more ... until their mouths touched as he said, "Tell me you don't want it."

She couldn't. She didn't. And he seemed to take that for the surrender that it was.

CHAPTER SEVEN

Fisting her hair, Tate took her mouth and plunged his tongue inside. And there it was—that sweetly addictive taste that had set up a craving in him four months ago. He groaned, long and loud. Fuck if he hadn't missed it.

As need exploded between them, he used his grip on her hair to angle her head and sank his tongue deeper. The kiss was hot. Wet. Hungry. Urgent. He couldn't get enough.

He swore he could get fucking drunk on her taste—it made his head spin, just like her delectable scent that now perfumed the air laced with arousal. It made his inner feline frantic for her, like her scent was fucking catnip.

Tate growled low in his throat as she thrust her fingers through his hair and wildly scratched at his scalp. The sting made his rock-hard dick throb painfully. He roughly ground against her clit again and again, feeling the heat of her pussy through their jeans.

Neither of them had much control. They were both frantic and desperate, yanking at each other's clothes. Soon, both his tee and her blouse were gone. She curled one leg over his hip just as he cupped her breast and thumbed her nipple through the black lace of her bra.

Arching into his hand, she tore her lips free to take a breath. With a snarl, Tate claimed her mouth again, nowhere near done with it. He feasted. Devoured. Plundered.

He gave her taut nipple a pinch and slid his hand over her breast, up her chest, and then snaked it around her throat. Just as he'd expected, her body stilled. Her breath caught. And a throaty snarl poured out of her mouth into his.

She broke the kiss, clearly riled by his dominant hold. "Let. Go."

If he thought she genuinely didn't like it, he'd release her instantly. But this wasn't about likes or dislikes. This was a battle for dominance. Not a sexual game. It wasn't about kneeling, lowering your eyes, or obeying every order. This was something much more primal—an alpha female demanding that her male prove himself worthy of her and any ounce of submission she'd deign to give him. Both he and his cat intended to do just that.

So Tate flexed his hand around her throat, leaned all his body weight into her, and said simply, "No."

She scratched at his wrist hard enough to sting but didn't draw blood. "Let fucking go."

Tightening his grip on her hair, he instead snatched her head back and squeezed her throat. "Behave. Unless you want to get dry humped against this counter. I'm not opposed to that, but I'll be the only one who gets to come."

She shoved at his chest and kicked at him. He let her. She was strong enough to escape his hold if it was what she truly wanted. But this wasn't a test of his *physical* strength. She was pitting her will against his. So he didn't move an inch, didn't loosen his hold on her, didn't berate her, didn't lose his patience. He just stayed very still, outwaiting her, letting her know that he wouldn't be cowered.

She eventually ceased struggling, but there was no surrender in the act—her body was still tense, her muscles coiled to strike. As such, he didn't release her, but he slowly lifted her head by her hair. "That's better. Now ... open your jeans."

Her eyes flared.

"Do it."

"Can't," she bit out. "You're crushing me."

"I'll give your hands some room once they're heading in the right direction. Now *open your jeans*. I want to slide my finger into that pussy of yours." He was so attuned to her that he sensed her tense muscles slacken just a little.

She tried slipping her hands between their bodies. He pulled back his hips a few inches, giving her some room, and felt her fingers tackling her fly. A zipper lowered—

She lunged forward and latched her teeth on his throat, taking him off-guard. His cock went impossibly thicker, and his jaw ached with the need to return the bite. Hands shoved his chest hard enough to make him stagger backwards. Then she was gone from his hold and racing out of the kitchen. He should have seen that coming.

Her heart pounding and her devil urging her on, Havana rushed into the living area, conscious of him chasing—

Her breath whooshed out of her as an arm wrapped around her waist from behind and yanked her against a hard chest. "*Motherfucker.*"

Ignoring her struggles, the bastard wrestled her to the floor. He flipped her onto her back, yanked down her bra, and sucked her nipple into his mouth.

She inhaled sharply and clamped her hands around his shoulders. Jesus, that felt good. *Too* good. But she wasn't ready to give into him yet. She didn't shove him away, though, because it would hurt like a bitch while he was letting her feel the edge of his teeth on her nipple. Each rough suckle sent a spark of pleasure straight to her pussy.

Even as her devil snarled at his insistence on subduing and dominating her, she didn't want him to stop. It wasn't that she or Havana wanted to be ordered around or disciplined. They just wanted a male who knew what he was about in the bedroom; one who *owned* his strength in such a way that he could take control.

Havana wasn't ashamed of it. It was a natural part of her sexuality that she liked to explore and didn't bother to question. During the battle for dominance, she was the focus of his world, just as he was hers. There was no room for thoughts of anyone or anything else.

She never felt weak in the moment when she finally yielded. It wasn't an expression of weakness, it was a concession that he'd earned the right to take control—something she'd wanted him to do all along. And once he had it, he was on a *major* high. There was something empowering for her about being responsible for that high he was on. But neither of them would come to that point if he didn't earn it.

He slid his hand down her stomach and slipped it into her panties, unerringly finding her clit. She couldn't help but moan as he worked it hard—flicking, rubbing, pinching, and rolling the tip of his finger around it first one way then the other. Damn, the bastard was good.

"That's it, very good," he praised before latching onto her nipple again.

What, he thought she'd yielded this soon? *Pfft.* She scratched his nape hard enough to make him release her nipple with a snarl. Using a fancy defensive move, she flipped him over, leaped to her feet, and ran.

She didn't get far.

He tackled her again mere seconds later, sending them both to their knees. She swore as he then bent her upper body over the chair cushion and curved himself around her.

He growled into her ear, "I wasn't done." He palmed her breast and shoved his free hand into her panties. "Fucking take what I give you." Not in the least deterred by her struggles, he expertly played with her clit as he cupped and shaped her breast, pausing every now and then to pinch and tweak her nipple until it throbbed.

She tried to resist just sinking into the moment, she honestly did, but it was so goddamn hard. He knew her every weak spot. Knew her every hot button. Knew exactly what to whisper in her ear to ramp up the need racing through her.

She hissed. "You're a fucking dick."

Tate felt his mouth kick up into a smile. "Oh, I know that." He slid his hand deeper into her panties, slipped his finger through her slick folds, and dipped it inside her. She squirmed, trying to drive herself onto his finger, but he used the weight of his body to pin her in place. "You want my finger deeper, baby? Hmm? Then all you have to do is stop fighting."

She twisted her head and bit his jaw hard, which he could have ignored if her hand hadn't reached down and squeezed his balls through his jeans—it didn't hurt, but it did make him flinch backwards in surprise. Then she was gone again.

Fuck. He pursued her fast, snatched her off her feet, and tossed her over his shoulder. Her fists pounded his back as he stalked into her bedroom, where he then threw on the mattress so hard that she bounced. She probably would have lunged at him if he hadn't then collapsed on top of her and pinned her wrists above her head.

His poor baby writhed and cursed and growled in sheer exasperation. Tate transferred both her wrists to one of his hands and then snapped open his fly. He almost groaned in relief as his aching cock sprang free. He pulled her own fly wider open and, paying no attention to her struggles or insults, kissed and suckled on her throat while rubbing his cock against her clit through her panties. It wasn't long before her growls became moans and she went from squirming to arching into him.

He raked his teeth over her pulse, flirting with the relentless temptation to bite and mark—it never gave him any reprieve. But no, he couldn't do that to her.

His dick jerked when she let out a whimper loaded with so much hunger that she had to be literally hurting with the need to come. Hell, he could fucking relate. "Shh, I've got you," he soothed into her ear. "I can give you what you need. All you have to do is settle down for me. I can't taste your pussy if you don't."

She stilled, obviously intrigued by that idea.

He brought his face back to hers. Her eyes stared up at him, hazy with arousal and glinting with desperation. There was something else there. A hint of capitulation that pleased his cat. This wasn't a *full* surrender, though. More like she was going to let him have his way *for now* purely because it suited her.

Tate kissed his way between the valley of her breasts and down her stomach and then gripped the waistband of both her jeans and panties. He spread more hungry kisses along her navel as he ever so slowly began to tug down her jeans and panties, stopping when they hit mid-thigh, trapping her legs in place.

Ignoring her frown, he did a teasing foray at the soft, bald V of her thighs with his tongue. "Haven't tasted my pussy in over a week. I'm gonna enjoy this." He used his thumbs to spread open her slick folds, and then he lapped at her clit and slit.

She was going to kill him, Havana decided. She was. The asshole knew she hated the feeling of being restricted. Okay, that wasn't entirely true. She didn't hate it, she just hated that she liked it. In truth, being unable to move her legs—unable to spread them, or lift them, or expose more of her pussy to his mouth—inflamed her even more than it frustrated her.

She gasped as he wrapped his lips around her clit and suckled. Her eyelids fluttered closed. Damn if the man didn't have one talented mouth. She wanted more of it.

She squirmed. "My clothes. Get them off."

He lashed her clit with his tongue. "All right. On one condition."

Havana narrowed her eyes, and her devil went still. "What?"

"Once I've got you naked, you have to spread those thighs wide and offer me what I want."

In other words, he wanted another element of surrender from her. Not a surprise. She almost jumped as he gently scraped his teeth over the V of her thighs.

He inhaled deeply. "Not sure what I love more—your taste or your scent." He suckled on her clit again, not so gentle this time.

She palmed the back of his head and bucked toward his mouth, not whatsoever impressed when he stopped.

"Well, what'll it be? You want me to eat this pussy or not?"

She felt her nostrils flare. "Fine. I'll give you what you want. Then you give me what I want."

"Done." Tate stood, pulled off her shoes, and then ragged off what was left of her clothes. He also shed his own clothing.

She could only stare at the thick, long cock tapping his belly. He made a damn spectacular sight with the broad shoulders, roped muscle, sleek tanned skin, rock-hard abs, and solid thighs.

He flicked up an expectant brow. A growl of approval rattled his chest when she slowly spread her legs, offering herself. "That's it." He knelt on the bed, gripped her hips, yanked her pussy to his mouth, and then plunged his tongue inside her.

Havana fisted the bedsheets. "Oh, fuck." There was no teasing, no playing. He drove her hard and fast toward an orgasm—licking, probing, nipping, and feasting—but the bastard stopped just before she came. "Oh my God, *you are such an asshole!*"

Barely holding back a smile, Tate wiped his face on her stomach and then draped himself over her. "I don't want you coming until I'm in you." He palmed her ass and tilted her hips, loving how she clung to his back. She sucked in a sharp breath as he lodged the thick head of his cock inside her. But he didn't thrust forward, didn't give her more.

She pricked his back with her nails. "*Tate.*"

He lightly bit her earlobe. "What do you want, Havana? You have to tell me." Because he didn't want any recriminations. He didn't want her later accusing him of seducing her against her better judgement or some shit like that. But, being a little miffed that he hadn't once let her come, she didn't seem in the mood to be cooperative.

She licked her lips. "You," she replied simply, *stubbornly.*

Tate sank another inch of his dick inside her. "That's not a good enough answer. Too vague, as you well know." He lightly raked his teeth along her cheek. "What do you want?"

Her upper lip quivered. "Stop talking and just do it."

He closed his teeth warningly around her jaw. "Do what?"

"Get inside me."

"I already *am* inside you. If you want more of my dick, make me believe you want it."

She snarled. "Fuck this shit." She punched up her hips, aiming to impale herself on him, but he'd pre-empted her.

Tate reared back, pulling out of her, and slid off the mattress so that he stood at the foot of the bed. He flipped her over, gripped her ankles, and yanked her down the mattress until only the upper part of her body rested on it.

She fisted the sheets for purchase, but he clamped his fingers around her wrists and then pinned her hands behind her back, keeping them both trapped in one of his. He used the weight of his legs and hips to pin her lower body still so that no amount of squirming freed her.

"Let me up, you prick!" Havana stilled as he slowly slid two thick, calloused fingers inside her. The sensation was just ... God, she needed it. Needed more. Needed everything.

He swirled his fingers. "When I get my cock in you, I'm gonna fuck you so hard. Gonna take what I've been craving for over a goddamn week. And you're going to love it. You're going to love every second of it. But none of that's going to happen until *you tell me that you want it.*" He roughly pushed his fingers even deeper, shocking a gasp out of her. "So fucking say it."

She didn't bother struggling again—there'd be no moving, no bucking him off, no deterring him from having exactly what he wanted. He wasn't going to take her until she backed down. Even her devil recognized that. "I want it," she ceded, letting herself go pliant against the mattress. "I want you to fuck me."

He hummed in masculine satisfaction. "That wasn't so hard, was it?" He withdrew his fingers and replaced them with the broad tip of his cock. "Come when you're ready."

Dear God, he slammed home with such force that it knocked the breath from her lungs. Her inner muscles squeezed him tight, wrenching a groan out of him. "Fuck me," she rasped.

Keeping her hands pinned behind her back, he rode her hard, digging the fingers of his free hand into her hip. She felt the slap of his balls each time he drove forward. She would have reared back to meet his thrusts if she could have moved. But, in a display of pure male domination, he completely overpowered her. And she liked it. Wanted it. Had needed it from second one.

She came within minutes, but he didn't stop. He savagely fucked in and out of her, grunting and growling. She fought to free her hands for the hell of it, but he kept his grip tight around her wrists as he quite simply rutted on her.

"That's it, fight me." Tate slid his hand from her hip to her nape and used it to pin her down as he kept on powering into her. She bit out a harsh curse and struggled again. "You're not going anywhere until I'm done with you."

If Tate thought she wanted to be free, he'd release her hands. But she liked the struggle; liked it rough. Which was a real good thing, because Tate's control had left him the second her blazing hot pussy enveloped every inch of his dick. There was no way of getting that control back when his senses were swamped by her—her throaty moans, the scent of her arousal, the hot clasp of her inner muscles, the sight of her bent over the bed taking his cock.

He had so little self-discipline where she was concerned ... which was why he kept eying the back of her shoulder. He wanted the skin there gripped between his teeth. Wanted to bite down hard—not to exert his dominance, but to leave a mark of possession there. And it didn't help that his cat was pushing him to do it.

Cursing, Tate fucked her harder, surged deeper, took everything. He ground his teeth as his balls tightened and he felt the telling tingle at the base of his spine. Releasing her wrists, he grabbed a fistful of her hair, yanked her head back, and used his free hand to collar her throat. She didn't fight him that time. Didn't bristle or curse him ... because he'd earned the right to hold her that way. "Come for me one last time, Havana."

Her breath hitched. "I don't think I can."

"Yes, you can. You will." He squeezed her throat and hammered into her harder, faster. "Do it."

She sucked in a breath and then let out a raspy scream as her pussy spasmed and clamped down on his cock. Tate slammed into her again and again ... until finally his release rammed into him and dragged him under. He exploded, filling her with everything he had, growling as her inner muscles milked him. It was a good few seconds before he realized that he had the skin at the back of her shoulder gripped between his teeth. *Shit*.

Tate instantly released her flesh and collapsed forward on his elbows, all hollowed out. Still, he slowly and idly glided his cock in and out of her while they came down from their high, just as he always did. The whole time, he called himself all kinds of stupid for branding her. "About the mark—"

"It's fine, Tate," she slurred. "It'll heal."

His cat bared his teeth at the idea. "I still shouldn't have done it."

"Jeez, relax, will you? You're messing with my buzz here."

Tate snickered. "Wouldn't want to do that." Despite that she didn't seem all that bothered by it, he softly kissed the bite in apology. Honestly, though, he wasn't as sorry as he should have been.

Weirdly, the urge to mark her that had lived and breathed inside him for what felt like months wasn't yet gone, but it had lost its vehemence. It was now more like a subtle, background pulse in his gut.

Havana stirred slightly as she felt his dick slip out of her. She almost moaned in disappointment. He looped an arm around her waist and shuffled her up the bed so they could both lie flat. She remained on her stomach, her muscles all loose and lazy, her eyes closed.

He could be incredibly sweet and tactile after sex, so Havana wasn't surprised when Tate curled into her side and stroked her back, mapping and petting her. Utterly sated, her devil all but hummed in contentment.

He pressed his mouth to her shoulder as he smoothed his hand up her nape and thrust his fingers into her hair. Those fingers began a slow, firm massage that almost made her toes curl.

"Your wrists okay?" he asked, dabbing another kiss on her shoulder.

She opened her eyes, liking the languid look in his own. "You didn't hurt me."

He skimmed his fingertips over her hairline, behind her ear, and down to dance along the crook of her neck. "How's your devil doing?"

"Practically asleep."

Humming, he dragged his fingers down her spine and then gently stroked one globe of her ass. "Love your body. Especially that world-class ass." He carefully eased her onto her side and smoothed his hand over her hip, up her stomach, and palmed her full breast. "And these tits. Love fucking them." He lazily sipped from her mouth, his tongue barely flicking the tip of hers. It didn't matter whether his kisses were hard and urgent or soft and easy—they were always mind-melting.

Pulling back, he flitted his intent gaze over her face. He brushed her hair aside … as if he didn't want a single strand obstructing his view. "You look even more beautiful after you come," he said, his voice low. "Your eyes go all soft and dreamy, and your face gets all warm and flushed. Love that look."

A phone began to chime, slicing through the deliciously lazy atmosphere. Tate's phone.

He edged off the mattress, crossed to the foot of the bed, and snatched his jeans off the floor. He dug his cell out of his pocket and swiped his thumb over the screen. "Yeah?"

Even with her enhanced hearing, it was impossible for Havana to make out what his caller was saying—Tate no doubt kept the volume low on purpose so that no one could eavesdrop. She could tell it was a male voice, though.

Tate sighed. "I'll meet you there in five minutes. Call Bree or one of the other omegas. They'll help calm him." He ended the call and turned to her. "Got to go, babe. One of my pride mates is pitching a fit and causing a scene. Need to shut that shit down."

Havana remained exactly where she was as he dressed. She'd forgotten how it hurt to watch him drag on his clothes and leave. He never did it *immediately* after sex, but he never stayed long. She hadn't ever judged him for it—it was simply his way of ensuring that the boundaries remained clear. But it wasn't much fun for her.

She wondered if maybe he'd stop pushing her for sex now that she'd finally caved. It was possible that his ego had indeed been smarting after she ended their fling. Now that he was able to be the one who officially walked away, he might very well do so. Which would be for the best, so she'd suck it up. And eat ice cream. Lots and lots of ice cream.

Dressed, Tate leaned over and pressed a kiss to her hip ... then to her shoulder ... then to her forehead. "I'll talk to you tomorrow, yeah?"

She nodded and forced a smile. "Yeah."

His eyes narrowed and searched her own. "What's wrong?"

"Nothing." She cleared her throat and gave him what she hoped was a more authentic-looking smile. "So, I guess I'll see you again when we take the next step to put a stop to the auction."

His brows lifted slightly. "You thought tonight would be a one-off?" he asked, his tone carefully even. "That this was some sort of goodbye fuck?" He sat on the bed, rolled her onto her back, and planted a fist either side of her head. "I told you I want you back. I meant it."

She sighed. "Tate—"

"You can again claim it's time for us to each 'go our own way' if you want, but what's the point, Havana? Neither of us are ready for that."

God, she wished she could argue with that. But there was too much unfinished business between them. Too many feelings she hadn't yet burned out.

"You don't want me to stay away from you, Havana, and I sure as fuck don't have any wish to stay away, so why not just let things be?" He cupped the side of her face and swiped the pad of his thumb over her cheekbone. "I wish you'd tell me what I did to upset your devil and make you want to walk."

And now she was feeling like shit. "You didn't do anything."

"I did something, I just don't know what. Whatever it is, I'm sorry. I'd never purposely hurt you, Havana."

"I know you wouldn't." And she hated that she'd made him believe differently. So she admitted, "But you could. You have that power. And I don't like it."

He twisted his mouth. "Yeah, I reckon you could cut me just the same. I can't say I like it. But I'm not going to let it keep me away from you, and I'm not going to let you do it either." The hand framing one side of her face slid down to cup her chin. "Let's just explore and enjoy what we have while we have it."

"We did that for four months. You don't think it would be dumb to let this go on for longer, given that you're determined for things to stay uncomplicated?"

Tate lowered his face to hers. "I've got to tell you, babe, there'll be nothing uncomplicated about walking away from you." He took her mouth, sinking his tongue inside to stroke her own, then just as swiftly pulled back. He slid his nose against hers. "Tomorrow."

Watching him stalk out of her room, Havana rubbed at her forehead. By nature, she wasn't an indecisive person. She didn't second-guess herself. When she made a choice, she stuck to it. And if it turned out that the decision hadn't been wise, well, she just plain dealt with the consequences.

Right then, she was mentally fumbling. Did she think that ending their fling had been the wrong thing to do? No. Sort of. If your emotions were involved, it *was* better to cut your losses when a relationship wasn't going anywhere. But he was right; she wasn't ready for them to part ways.

Tate Devereaux had gotten under her skin, and she didn't see that she had any choice but to take the time to work him back out again. Which absolutely sucked balls.

Cursing, she slipped off the bed and grabbed a camisole and shorts from her dresser. It was time to do what she'd planned to do earlier—watch TV and pig out.

CHAPTER EIGHT

Having had a shit night's sleep, Havana stepped out of her bedroom the next morning feeling like death warmed up. She trudged into the living room, and the sight she stumbled upon made her sigh. It no doubt wasn't often that a person found a bearcat on the floor wrapped in a black mamba, especially when said bearcat was ramming the head of the hissing snake on the hardwood floor.

It wasn't an uncommon sight for Havana, but it rarely happened during the morning for two reasons. One, Aspen didn't usually come here so early. Two, Bailey was so focused on being ready on time that she didn't let her mamba out. But as they were all off work today, they could afford to be lazy and fool around. This, though? No. It was too early for this shit.

Havana planted her hands on her hips. "Seriously?" she barked, making both animals freeze. "You know the rules, people—no brawling before I've had at least *one* cup of coffee. So do my addled brain a favor and release. Each other. Now."

The animals parted, and then both females shifted.

Aspen threw Bailey a dirty look. "Your mamba is such a bitch. I'm surprised I don't have any cracked ribs."

Bailey sniffed, rubbing her head. "I'm equally surprised I don't have a cracked skull. Your bearcat is so damn moody."

"And yet, your snake constantly taunts her. Explain."

"You want, like, a rational explanation?"

"That would be good. Am I going to get one?"

"Depends what your personal definition of 'rational' is."

Aspen shook her head and pushed to her feet. "Forget it."

Massaging her aching temple, Havana headed to the kitchen. There, she prepped the coffee machine before switching it on. Soon enough, she was sitting at the table with breakfast and a mug of steaming hot coffee.

Fully dressed, Aspen hummed to herself as she entered the room. Stumbling to a halt, she said, "Uh-oh."

Bailey materialized behind her, also now dressed. Her eyes lit up when they locked on the table. "Ooh trifle—" She cut off, her face freezing. "You're eating trifle for breakfast. That is never good."

Aspen took the seat opposite Havana. "Okay, what's wrong?"

Havana shoveled another spoon of the chocolate dessert into her mouth. "I took Bailey's advice."

Aspen scrunched her face up. "You ... you took *advice* from Miss Logic is For Losers?"

Bailey frowned at the bearcat. "Not liking your tone."

"But you can't argue that your advice might not necessarily be good to heed, can you?" challenged Aspen.

Huffing, Bailey took a seat at the table. "Well, maybe not. But logic gets in the way sometimes. I don't like obstacles."

Aspen turned back to Havana. "What advice did she give you?"

Havana licked at her spoon. "To have one last round of sex with Tate so I could find some closure. I hoped it would work, so yesterday after dinner ..."

"You did the dirty." Aspen bit her lower lip. "I take it your hopes didn't come to fruition."

"No, they did not."

"Well that's a bummer." Bailey puffed out a breath. "But this doesn't sound like something that would send you into the trifle-for-breakfast-zone."

Havana sighed. "Tate wants to drag out the fling a little longer. And while I can't deny that he's right in claiming neither of us are truly ready to part ways, I can't give him what he wants. I just can't. I'll only get more and more attached. And, honestly, it hurts that the only thing he sees when he looks at me is someone worthy of a fling. If I keep sleeping with him, I'll end up hating us both. But getting rid of him hasn't been as simple as I thought."

Aspen twisted her mouth. "There is one sure-fire way to make him leave you alone."

Havana paused in bringing another spoonful of dessert to her mouth. "What?"

"Tell him the truth," replied Aspen. "Tell him you want more. If he's so against the concept, there's no way he'll stick around. In fact, he might even freak out."

Bailey nodded and pointed a finger at the bearcat. "That would definitely work, because he won't be able to argue that continuing with the fling would be harmless. He'll have to either step up to the plate or back the hell off."

"He's not going to offer me more," said Havana.

"Maybe not," said Aspen, her tone soft. "And I know it'll suck to hear him tell you he can't give you what you need, but the present situation also sucks. If you *really* want him to leave you alone and give you the space to move on, this is probably the only way to do it."

Bailey's shoulders slumped. "You know, Vana, I really do hate that the two guys you grew to care for don't want what you want."

"Same here." Havana sipped her coffee. "On the subject of said two guys, Dieter called yesterday. He heard about the attempted kidnapping. He insisted I call him if I have any further problems."

Bailey snorted. "He can't honestly think you'd turn to him for help after he chose another woman over you."

"To be fair, he has no idea that it hurt me."

Aspen rested her arms on the table. "I think Dieter cares about you in his way, Havana. But he doesn't want the lone shifter lifestyle, and he's had no luck getting a flock to accept him. He knows his best bet is to mate into one. I think Tate cares about you, too. I think he just isn't prepared to face it yet."

"I'm not so sure about that." Havana took another gulp of her drink. "And it's possible that he'll get back together with his ex."

Bailey blinked and straightened in her seat. "His ex?"

"Yep, she's back. Valentina—who says hi, by the way—told us a little about her yesterday. Her name's Ashlynn, but I often refer to her as 'the skank' in my head. She and Tate tried to imprint on each other, but it all went south." Havana relayed the story to the mamba.

Bailey folded her arms. "Do you think she's back for Tate, hoping he'll make her his Alpha female?"

"Maybe. She wanted to have dinner with him so they could 'talk.' He turned her down. He swears he has no interest in her."

"Do you believe him?" asked Aspen.

Havana hesitated. "He was pretty convincing. If he was lying, he was also lying to himself." She ate another spoonful of trifle.

Aspen drummed her fingers on the table. "So … are you going to tell him what you want?"

Havana's stomach rolled at the idea, but she couldn't deny that it made sense. Which was uber unfortunate. She put down her spoon. "Yeah. It'll be hard, and it'll be harder still to hear him tell me what I already know, which is that he can't give it to me. But it's probably the only guaranteed way to make him give me space. I can put my pride aside to get that."

Bailey pouted. "I hate that you're hurting."

"Me, too," said Aspen.

Havana saw something in their eyes that made her go still. "Don't even think about it."

Bailey rose to her feet. "It's gonna happen."

"I mean it, don't."

Aspen stood. "You're gonna have to suck it up."

"Do not hug—" Havana ground her teeth as both rounded the table and wrapped their arms around her. "You girls are such bitches."

The bearcat smiled. "We love you, too."

Bailey's nose wrinkled. "We do?"

Aspen lightly slapped the mamba over the head, which only made Bailey snicker.

Just as the girls released her, Havana's cell phone began to ring. She grabbed it from the table and sighed. *Tate*. "Speak of the devil ..." She swiped her thumb over the screen and answered, "Hello."

"Need you to meet me outside your building," he said. "If you're not dressed yet, do it fast."

She froze at the urgency in his tone. "Why?"

"One of my contacts just called," he said. "Someone tipped the guy off as to where Sinclair is. I'm guessing you'd like to come along while we nab him."

Oh, she most certainly would. "I'll be five minutes." Ending the call, Havana told the girls, "Tate knows where Sinclair is. You guys coming?"

"Absofuckinglutely," stated Aspen.

Bailey tipped her head toward the bearcat. "What she said."

Havana stood. "Then grab your shit. Let's go."

S tanding across the street from the single-story motel, Havana couldn't help but think it was a sad sight to behold. Dirty windowpanes. Peeling paint. Blackened bricks. A flickering vacancy sign with burned-out letters.

Trash littered the sidewalk and parking lot. Weeds sprouted through the cracks in the pavement. The surrounding trees were leafless and decayed.

The windows looked old and cloudy, but they wouldn't have provided a clear glimpse of Sinclair's room anyway, since the guy had pulled the curtains shut.

She looked at Tate. "Told you the universe was trying to clue me into something with the constant motel signs, didn't I?"

He frowned and went back to staring at the building.

People really needed to listen to her more often, in Havana's opinion.

"What's the plan?" Aspen asked no one in particular. "Are we knocking on the door or just barging in?"

"If we knock, we put him on alert," said Tate. "If we barge in, we can take him off-guard."

Alex rolled back his shoulders. "Then we barge in." The wolverine wasn't part of Tate's ranks, but Alex acted as an interrogator when needed.

Havana couldn't lie, she was disappointed that she wouldn't get to do much interrogating of her own—in fact, so was her inner devil. But Havana's main concern was getting some answers.

"Barging in works for me," said Vinnie.

Tate gently squeezed her wrist and shot her a "be careful" look. He'd been watching her closely, as if sensing that something was wrong, but he hadn't commented on it. "Let's move," he ordered.

Luke and Farrell flanked him as they all crossed to the motel. Even from outside the door to Sinclair's room, Havana could hear the TV blaring.

Tate snapped out his leg and booted the door open. They charged inside the room, ready to attack and defend. Then they skidded to a halt, and Havana's mouth dropped open. *Jesus.*

Sinclair was slouched in the bulky chair, his eyes wide and unseeing, his face and jaw slack … and a fucking bullet hole in his forehead.

"Hell," said Vinnie.

Tate's mouth went tight. "Someone else got to him first. Probably Gideon to cover his auction-related tracks." He swore, his nostrils flaring.

Luke circled the deceased shifter. "Single shot to the head. He was bound tight to the chair but not tortured, so I'd say he answered their questions without putting up any kind of resistance."

"He's been dead a few hours at least," said Alex.

Which was why it goddamn *reeked* in here. Both the coppery scent of blood and nauseating scent of death were heavy in the room, mingling with the cloying smells of urine, mold, and stale cigarette smoke. It made her devil's nose wrinkle in distaste.

"Do a quick check of the room, Farrell; see if there's anything interesting among his belongings," said Tate.

"Sure thing." Farrell then began rummaging through a small, wobbly dresser.

Tate checked Sinclair's pockets. "No cell phone. Whoever shot him probably took it in case there was anything incriminating on it."

"There's one here." Havana grabbed the phone beside the old TV and skimmed through the call log and messages. "There's nothing on it. No texts, no saved contacts, no history in the call log. It's gotta be a burner."

Bailey glanced at the phone. "It looks brand new. There are no scratches or smudges on the screen." She sighed. "On the plus side, you don't have to worry that Sinclair's going to attempt to finish the job he started and kidnap you."

Yeah, there was that. Havana inhaled, sifting through the various smells, but she couldn't pick up the scents of any people other than Sinclair and the shifters who'd accompanied her here. Any others seemed to have long since faded.

There might have been some trace of them if the other smells in the room hadn't been so pungent. Still, she asked, "Can anyone scent other shifters?"

The others shook their heads or muttered a negative … aside from Alex.

"There's the faintest trace of jaguar," said the wolverine. "But it's extremely faint."

"Jaguar," echoed Tate. "So Gideon sent his minions here." Tate might have felt some pity for the bastard if he hadn't been, well, a bastard.

Having done a search of the entire room, Farrell said, "He either had nothing incriminating in his possession, or it was taken from him."

They all stilled as the burner phone in Havana's hand began to ring.

Each and every cell in Tate's body went on high alert, and his inner cat tensed. He crossed to her and said, "Let me answer it. If it's someone hoping to speak with Sinclair, they might buy that I'm him. Everyone be very quiet." He took the phone and answered using the speakerphone option, "Yeah?"

"Who might I be talking to?" a cultured male voice asked. One Tate didn't recognize. He glanced at the others, noting that none of them appeared to recognize the voice.

"You're the one that called me," Tate pointed out.

"Yes, but I'm quite aware that my dear friend Sinclair is unable to answer. You must be one of the shifters who were seeking him. Excellent. I left a phone at the motel room hoping I could have a little talk with the people who are trying to push their way into my business. I was quite sure you'd come for Sinclair."

Tate's lips thinned as he quickly deduced, "*You* called in the tip. You led us to him."

"It seemed the easiest way to communicate with you that didn't involve a face-to-face meeting."

Galled that he'd been so easily manipulated, Tate bit back a curse and gestured for Luke and Farrell to canvas the area. For the caller to know that people had entered the room, either he or one of his minions was nearby.

"Who are you?" Tate asked his caller while Luke and Farrell headed into the bathroom where they'd no doubt use the rear window as an exit.

"A lot of my friends call me Abe," the unfamiliar voice replied.

"Abe," Tate repeated. "I didn't know that was a pet name for Gideon." Silence greeted the comment. Yeah, this fucker was Gideon York. And if he or his minions *were* nearby, it was possible that they had a gun trained on the building. Tate signaled Vinnie, Alex, and the females to move into the bathroom.

"Hmm, just what did Rupert tell you?"

Tate waited for the others to quietly enter the small, dingy bathroom before he joined them and replied, "Enough to know who you are, York."

"Gideon York is dead."

"You don't sound dead."

Another long silence. "I don't, do I?" Apparently, he was done with the pretense. "I feel it is important that we are all able to come to an understanding. I've come to learn a few things since Rupert and Sinclair failed me. It would seem that Miss Ramos is under the protection of Tate

Devereaux, Alpha of the Olympus Pride."

Tate's grip on the phone involuntarily tightened. He met her gaze—a gaze that had held a hint of sadness ever since she exited her complex earlier, which he didn't understand but fully intended to question her about later. "She is," Tate replied.

"Would I be right in assuming that *you* are Tate?" asked Gideon.

"You would."

"Excellent. I've never met a pallas cat, but I've heard plenty about your kind. I've also heard plenty about you—all good things, by the way. You might be feared, but you're also highly respected."

"Is that a fact?"

"Yes, it is. I'd like to offer my apologies to you. If I had known Miss Ramos was under your protection, I would not have sent people to acquire her."

Tate ground his teeth. "No, you'd have sent them to acquire another loner for you to auction off like they're fucking collector's items instead of living beings."

"It is merely business."

"It's fucking sick."

"There are plenty of people who would disagree with you. People will buy shifters for any number of reasons—to keep in their private zoos, to hunt and kill, to use for their personal pleasure, to run various experiments on."

Standing in the doorway of the bathroom, Tate poked his head out to keep an eye trained on the front door. "And none of that bothers you?"

"As I said, it is merely business. What my clients wish to do with whatever assets they purchase doesn't concern me."

"Assets?" Tate felt his nostrils flare. "They're people, not assets. I suppose you prey on loners because they're mostly unprotected. Well, it was pretty careless of you to have assumed your latest target was unprotected. You knew Havana's address, but you didn't think to check who owned her building. You made a mistake there, and you made the kind of enemies you absolutely do not fucking want." Pallas cats *always* made bad enemies, especially if you messed with someone who had value to them. And Havana, well, she meant something to both Tate and his cat.

"Yes, it was a mistake. One I have apologized for. I meant no insult to you. And if you and the other people who are hunting me agree to back off, I will not make any moves against you. Havana Ramos will be left alone, as will anyone else under your protection. Everyone can go back to their lives."

"And if we don't back off?" Because they absolutely wouldn't.

"You will force me to take any measures necessary to stop you. I won't make this offer again. If I were you, I would accept it. You have no way of locating me. You could try to trace this call, of course, but any time you spend investigating me will be wasted."

"Yeah? Then why are you so worried that we're working to locate you?" Tate challenged.

"I am not worried. I am merely … inconvenienced by how much lone shifters are now on their guard."

Tate snickered. "I don't believe you, York. I think you know it's only a matter of time before we find you. And I think you know just how bad you'll suffer once we do. We pallas cats like our vengeance. Your friend Rupert, yeah, he died hard. You'll die harder."

For a long moment, Gideon said nothing. "I take it we don't have an agreement. That is a shame. Especially for Miss Ramos." The line went dead.

"Well," began Havana, "we know now that Gideon really is alive."

"I don't think he expected us to associate him with—" Tate swore as bullets peppered the front of the building. He moved fast, sliding fully into the bathroom for cover, as windows smashed and the wooden front door splintered. Then there was the screech of tires.

Tate cursed again and rushed out of the building just in time to see a dark blue car disappear around a curve in the road. Hearing footsteps, he turned just as Luke and Farrell came running into view. "You both okay?" he asked.

Luke gave a curt nod. "Don't know where that car came from, but it wasn't around when we checked this side of the motel before."

"The driver must have parked somewhere close but out of sight," said Farrell.

Tate glanced back at the others, checking they were all fine, relieved when he saw no one—especially his father and Havana—was injured.

"Did anyone get the license plate number of the car?" asked Alex.

Everyone shook their heads.

Tate hissed. "That motherfucker led us here so he could make us an offer and let us see what happened to people like Sinclair who landed on his shit list. My contact specified that the tip was anonymous. I didn't wonder if it had been passed on by Gideon."

"What did he say?" asked Luke. "I missed most of the conversation."

"He pretty much confirmed that he's Gideon York, and he told me that he'd leave us be if we all backed off. He didn't like that I refused to fall in line."

"Do you think he would have shot at us even if we agreed to his deal?" asked Bailey.

"No," said Tate. "Killing a bunch of pallas cats wouldn't have changed anything—our pride would have continued to hunt him, and they'd have hunted him harder to avenge us. That's why he didn't start shooting the second we arrived. He was hoping we'd take the deal and leave him be."

"He was also probably hoping that shooting at the motel room would make us reconsider hunting him," mused Vinnie. "Otherwise, he'd have waited for us all to step out of the building. He didn't. He gave us one last warning so that we'd know he meant business."

Aspen looked at Havana. "You need to be careful. There was a slight sneer in his voice every time he said your name. My opinion? He blames you for everything that's gone wrong."

"I'd say the same." Bailey rubbed at one arm. "It was a good thing we hid in the bathroom, huh?"

"He probably figured we'd hide once we wondered just how he could know that anyone was in the motel room," Vinnie theorized. "I doubt he thought the bullets would truly kill anyone."

"People are peeking out the windows of the other rooms," said Aspen. "Someone might call the police."

Luke shook his head. "It's a shifter-only motel. They won't call the human authorities."

Because shifter business was shifter business. They had their own rules as to how they dealt with things.

"I say it's time we got out of here," declared Bailey.

"I couldn't agree more," said Tate, tossing the burner phone into the trash. "But first, I want to question the shifters here and see if anyone noticed people entering or exiting this room at some point today."

They learned that no one heard a gunshot, so the firearm used to kill Sinclair must have had a silencer attached. One person claimed to have seen four people approach the motel room, but he'd been too far away to view their faces. The witness hadn't thought to pay them any attention, because he'd assumed they were staying in the room.

On their way back to the large SUV, Tate slid his hand up Havana's back and cupped her nape. "Come back to my place."

She looked at him, her expression guarded. "Why?"

"I want to be alone with you."

She looked at the floor and then gave a slow nod. "Okay."

He squeezed her nape. "Okay."

A complete bag of nerves, Havana waited as Tate unlocked his front door. Her muscles felt all twitchy. There would be nothing smooth or easy about this conversation. Nothing simple or painless about putting herself out there when the only thing she'd get in return would be an "oh shit" look. But Aspen was right. Tate would back off if he knew that he'd otherwise mislead Havana into thinking he wanted a relationship. He was too good a guy to play with her like that.

Obviously intending to give them privacy, Luke and Farrell settled on the porch swing.

Tate opened his front door and gestured for her to enter first. She reluctantly stepped inside, feeling like she was walking to her doom, and allowed him to shepherd her into his living room. The space was both masculine and stylish—deep neutral tones, dark woods, tan leather, sturdy furniture, sleek and straight lines, simple detailing, no frills or accessories.

He came up behind her, slid his hands up her arms, and pressed a kiss to the side of her neck. "You've been very quiet. You okay?"

"No." She stepped away from him and turned to face him. Tight as a drum, she bit her lip, dredging up the courage to confess the truth.

He ate up the space between them in one stride and rested his hands on her shoulders. "Don't let what that bastard said play on your mind. He's not going to get to you."

"It's not about Gideon."

"Then what is it? Tell me."

She took a deep, preparatory breath. "You were right that I didn't give you the full reason why I decided we need to go our separate ways."

He cocked his head. "You gonna tell me the rest?"

"Yes. Just be warned that you're not going to like what you hear."

He backed her toward the sofa. "Then let's get comfortable while we have this conversation."

"That's not—" She cut off as she plopped onto the sofa.

Tate sat beside her, twisted his body to fully face her, and splayed his hand on her thigh. "Right, go on."

"First, I need to tell you about Dieter."

A line briefly formed between his brows. "All right."

"I've known him for a while. We never had a typical bed-buddy arrangement. We had a fling at first. Then he went traveling, so we ended it. He goes traveling a lot. And whenever he was both local and single, he'd turn up, looking to hook up. That went on for too long, but I let it, because I cared about him."

Realizing he'd involuntarily clenched her thigh, Tate relaxed his grip. He didn't want to know she'd cared about another man, and he wondered if it was truly a case of "past tense." His cat slowly paced, wary of where the conversation was going.

"I thought he *had* to care about me if he kept coming back again and again," she went on. "I thought maybe he just needed time before he was willing to offer me something more. But about six months ago, he gave that 'more' to someone else. I'm not mad at him for that. He didn't *purposely* hurt me—he didn't even know I cared about him. It still hurt, though. So when you proposed having a short, shallow fling where I wouldn't have to give anything of myself, it suited me."

"But you end your flings early now so that you don't make the mistakes with others that you made with Dieter," Tate assumed.

"How I wish that were the case. Maybe I'm just a glutton for punishment or something, but I made the same fuck up with you." A somewhat self-depreciating smile touched her mouth. "Yeah, I came to want more."

Tate could only stare at her, at a loss for what to say. Even his cat stilled in surprise.

"I could see that you didn't feel the same—one thing I can say for you, Tate, is that you never gave me mixed signals. I didn't misread them. I just took a chance and gave you some time because I'm *that* stupid." She swallowed. "I'm done being stupid."

He closed his eyes. "Havana—"

"You were right when you said I wasn't ready to walk away. I'm not. But I *have* to do it, Tate."

Cursing beneath his breath, Tate jumped to his feet and scrubbed a hand down his face. The same feeling he'd gotten when she first ended their fling came rushing back—the sensation of her slipping through his fingers, of him losing something important. The cord of panic returned, too, and wrapped tight around his lungs once again.

More, the drive to brand her came back in full-force. He felt it everywhere. It was an itch, an ache, a throb, and a burn all at once.

"That's why your devil is pissed at me," he realized. "She wants more as well, and she's mad that I haven't offered it."

Havana nodded and pushed to her feet. "I didn't want to tell you the full truth for two reasons. One, I didn't want to make you feel bad that I was hurting when it was absolutely not your fault. Two, I didn't want to hear you say aloud what I already know—you're not going to give me what I'm looking for. I didn't think I'd *have* to tell you everything. I didn't think you'd care when I ended it. I definitely didn't think you'd insist on dragging the fling out even longer. I can't do it, Tate. You understand, right? You get it?"

Yeah, he got it. But he didn't want to get it. Didn't want to admit she had every reason to walk away. "So, you want to end this because it's too casual for you. Does that mean you're looking to settle down with someone now?"

"No."

"Then why end something that works so well when all you'll do is walk right into *another* casual relationship?"

"I'm ending this because it's the right thing to do. It hurts that I don't mean anything to you—it shouldn't hurt, and I don't want it to hurt, but it does."

"I told you last night; you mean something to me. I'm not in the habit of saying shit I don't mean."

"Maybe I do mean something to you. But if so, I don't mean enough for it to make a difference to you." Her eyes glistened with tears he knew she was too proud to shed in front of him. "I'd be cheapening myself if I accepted so much less from you than what I need. I won't keep being your fuck-buddy, especially when I know you'll walk away from me the second you find your true mate. I'm no masochist."

He reached for her. "Havana …"

She shook her head, backing away. "Don't."

Undeterred, Tate pulled her close and held her tight, sliding his hand up her back. He pushed his face into her hair and breathed her in. She didn't hug him back, but she also didn't fight him. He curved his hand around her nape and spoke into her ear. "I don't want you to go."

"I have to," she whispered, fisting the sides of his tee.

They stayed there like that for long minutes, saying nothing. Meanwhile, his cat raged and snarled and *demanded* that Tate subdue her, which pissed Tate off because they might not be in this fucking situation if the feline didn't make it impossible for them to have a real relationship.

Havana released his tee. "I need to leave now."

Tate dropped his forehead to hers. "I never wanted to hurt you."

"I know you didn't," she said, her voice thick, as she gently pushed against his chest.

Tate tightened his hold. But only for a moment. Then he slowly lowered his arms. "I'll walk you home. Don't argue. I want to be sure you're safe."

She nodded.

His stomach heavy, Tate walked her to her complex while Luke and Farrell trailed behind them—silent sentries. Tate entered the security code into the keypad to unlock the front door. He didn't say a word. He couldn't even really get a proper handle on all that he was feeling.

She gave him a wobbly smile. "Take care of yourself, Tate." She rushed inside and closed the door behind her.

Tate swallowed and, ignoring the ache in his chest and the tantrum his cat was throwing, he turned to his brother and Head Enforcer. Ignoring Luke's "you just made a big mistake" look, he said, "Assign two enforcers to watch her. I want eyes on her at all times."

"It'll be done," Luke assured him.

Tate nodded. He couldn't have her, but he could at least keep her safe. As much as he hated it, his protection was all he had to give her.

CHAPTER NINE

"Someone's not a happy bunny," said Corbin.

Looking away from the two juveniles who were sparring in the ring of the rec center's gym, Havana asked, "Huh?"

Corbin tipped his chin toward someone behind her.

Glancing over her shoulder, she saw none other than Dieter bearing down on her, his face contorted into an almighty glower. Her devil rumbled an irritable sound and turned away, uninterested. Ordinarily, her pulse would quicken and her stomach would flip at the sight of him. Now? Nothing.

Oh, the guy was still as good-looking as ever—dark, burly, and broad-shouldered with one very fine ass. But this time, her body just didn't react. Which would have made her smile if it wasn't for that glower he was wearing.

Dieter stopped at the edge of her personal space, and his dark masculine scent—one that used to stir up her hormones but now had no effect on her—wafted her way, almost overriding the smells of leather, sweat, and the cool air wafting through the open window. He threw up his arms. "What the hell, Havana?"

She blinked. "Excuse me?"

"You haven't called." He said it like they usually had long-winded phone conversations every night.

"I haven't called?"

"I figured you'd keep me in the loop. I'm finding out from *others* that you tracked one of the guys who tried to kidnap you, that he'd been shot at a motel. And then there's all this shit about the auctioneer leading you to the dead guy and attempting to make deals. *All* of which happened a damn week ago, and I'm only hearing of it now."

If he'd only heard about it recently, he'd obviously been out of contact with his loner buddies—probably because he was hanging out with his girlfriend and her flock. Havana had kept everyone at the center updated, wanting them to understand that this was serious shit and that they shouldn't forget for a single moment that they needed to be on their guard.

"What difference does it make if you find out from me or someone else?" she asked. "The majority of loners learned of it through word of mouth."

Dieter's jaw tightened. "Yeah, but the majority aren't your friends. *We've* known each other a while."

"I've known a lot of *them* for a while, having worked here for a whole lot of years."

"All right, I'll rephrase. The majority of those loners aren't both your friends *and* people you shared your body with."

Corbin cleared his throat and scratched his nape. "Yeah, I'll be in the corner helping the fox with the punchbag." He walked away.

She began, "Dieter, I get that you're concerned—"

"And yet, no calls."

Bristling at his tone, she lifted a brow. "Do *you* make *me* aware of everything that goes on in your life? Do you give me personal updates? Do you text me little anecdotes? No. Not now, and not in the past. I heard from you when you wanted to fuck—that was it."

"And now that I'm in a relationship, you're shutting me out?"

"Shutting you out of what? You don't seem to be getting the point. We were *never* people who kept in contact and shared details of each other's lives, no matter how serious our personal shit was. But even if we were, I'd have eased up on that to make sure Tabitha didn't get the wrong idea or feel uncomfortable."

"While I appreciate that, I'd still rather you keep me in the loop, but you don't seem to think I'm worthy of your time. Yet, you'll work alongside a pallas cat you were sleeping with. Oh yeah, I heard just now that you and your landlord were kind of cozy at one time. Heard he even has a couple of his enforcers guarding you, even though you two aren't an item anymore."

The enforcers had introduced themselves as Deke and Isaiah, and they'd announced that they'd be tailing her for a while. She hadn't objected, because having extra sets of eyes was never a bad thing. Plus, it would have meant talking to Tate. She'd completely avoided contacting him in the past week, and he'd given her that same courtesy. While she appreciated it, she also missed the shit out of him. And she often stupidly found herself wondering if he'd been spending any time with Ashlynn.

Dieter puffed out a long breath, making a visible effort to calm down. "I'm sorry I'm snapping at you. I just … This shit is fucked up, Havana. I don't want to one day get a call telling me you're dead. I'm worried about you."

"Don't be. I'm no easy target."

"And you have the pallas cat's protection, I know," he clipped. "Can I rely on you to call me if you need help, or is the cat gonna be the one you reach out to?"

"His name is Tate. And you don't have to say 'cat' in the same tone as you would 'cannibal.'"

"I don't like any species of feline shifter. You know that. *Especially* not pallas cats.

I won't point out all the reasons they're best to be avoided—you already know them, so it confuses the shit out of me that you got involved with one of those crazies."

"Like my kind are in a position to judge other species of shifter for being slightly insane. Devils aren't the most mentally balanced of creatures either."

Dieter grunted.

"Now you need to butt out of my sex life—who I sleep with isn't your business. And unless you want my foot lodged up your ass, quit snapping at me."

Wincing, he thrust a hand through his hair. "My insides seize up when you use that alpha tone on me. Look, I'm sorry, I shouldn't have jumped down your throat. Like I said, I just worry about you. But, having not seen you in months, I could have at least said hello first."

"Uh, yeah, most definitely."

"Let's start over. Hey, Havana, good to see you." He hugged her. "I've missed you."

She hugged him back, happy to find that, hey, she hadn't actually missed him. More, having him so close didn't stir her body in the slightest. "No, you haven't. You've been having *way* too much fun with Tabitha."

He chuckled. "Plenty of fun," he agreed. "That doesn't mean I didn't miss my devil."

Irritated, her inner animal chuffed at the possession in his tone.

Dieter broke the hug. "I have to go meet my girl, so I can't stay. Do me a favor and just keep me updated on what's happening. Or have Corbin do it."

Havana nodded, thinking she'd most definitely ask Corbin to pass on the info. "Okay."

He squeezed her shoulder. "Thank you. Stay safe, and take care of yourself."

"I will." Havana watched him walk away and, for the first time in a very long while, it didn't hurt to see him leave. A sense of peace stole over her as she realized that, huh, she was truly over the man. Which was not only fantastically awesome, it reminded her that although she might be hurting over Tate now, it *would* eventually pass.

Ignoring the little voice in her head warning her not to be so sure of that, Havana turned back to the juveniles in the ring just in time to see the shorter kid knock the other boy to the floor with a punch to the jaw. The taller kid shook off whatever daze he was in, pushed to his feet, and touched gloves with his opponent. *Good.*

A lot of people came to the rec center's gym to learn everything from simple self-defense to more sophisticated martial arts techniques. Even now, it was crowded. Some beat on heavy punching bags while others practiced moves, worked out, shadow-boxed, or hit the pads. The music playing was barely audible over the sounds of trainers barking instructions, fists smashing against leather, people grunting and cursing, and the whirr of skipping ropes.

Anyone was welcome to spar, but not for the purpose of hurting others. It was about applying what you'd been taught from the trainers, learning where you needed to improve, and learning how to fight with *controlled* anger.

"Aspen, wait!"

Hearing Bailey's voice, Havana turned to see Aspen striding toward her, her face like thunder, her eyes on the ring.

"I'm next," Aspen announced. She slipped through the ropes and jumped into the ring. Rolling back her shoulders, she paced and glanced at the females close by, challenging them with her gaze alone.

Yeah, sometimes people also used the ring to vent their frustrations—Corbin allowed it *providing* no one aimed to injure their opponent. And it appeared that Aspen was looking to do some venting.

"What's going on?" Havana asked Bailey as the mamba materialized beside her.

"Camden's boyfriend, Randy, just got in her face talking shit and telling her she'd better find a new apartment soon because *he'd* be moving in with Camden," replied Bailey. "Which I highly doubt. Anyway, our girl just stared at him and then walked away like he wasn't worth her time. It was clear she wanted to lamp him, though."

"Asshole," Havana uttered. "Where is he now?"

"He left in a strop when he didn't get the reaction he wanted. If Camden was gay instead of bi, I doubt any of his boyfriends would have felt so weird about how close he is to Aspen."

"He might be bi, but he seems to be more drawn to men. He hasn't been with a woman in *years.*"

"*Or* there's only one woman he wants, but he won't take the chance of messing up their friendship. Come on, we've *all* sensed a low hum of sexual chemistry simmering between them. Maybe they both want what neither is willing to risk losing their friendship for. Don't say Aspen would tell us if she cared for him *that way.* She wouldn't. She'd hold it in and try to ignore it. It's hard to voice that you want something if you're convinced you won't ever have it." Bailey gave Havana a meaningful look. "You know that well."

Havana sighed. "Yes, I do. And you're right, she'd say nothing."

It was hard to be sure what Camden felt for Aspen. His possessiveness toward her was almost child-like, sort of like a kid who didn't want to share his best friend. She mattered to him when very few things did.

Havana was certain of one thing—he'd have a hard time when Aspen found her mate. That kind of bond would make Camden feel threatened, even if what he did feel for her was platonic.

Havana cut her gaze back to the ring. "Oh, someone's decided to take on Aspen."

Bailey winced. "Fair play to them. That woman's a black bear, right?"

"Yep. And I'm guessing she thinks that, being taller and broader, she has the upper hand."

Bailey snickered. "Aspen will wipe the floor with her."

That was *exactly* what Aspen did. She punched, kicked, weaved, dodged, and tossed her opponent around the ring like the sow was a goddamn ragdoll. Done, Aspen left the ring, her face a study in serenity.

"Feel better?" Havana asked her.

The bearcat smiled. "Yeah. Hey, you two up for going to see a movie this weekend?"

"Sure."

"I'm game," said Bailey.

"Super. Well, see you later." Aspen gave them a little wave and walked off.

Havana looked at Bailey. "I envy her ability to *literally* work off her emotions until she's right back to cool and composed."

"It's like her superpower." Bailey grinned, adding, "Mine is to cause bloodshed and mayhem."

"Only you would be so proud of it."

Bailey's face suddenly brightened considerably, and she did a little clap. "Ho, ho, ho, Ginny's back. How exciting."

Havana threw her a pained look. "Bailey, maybe you could skip tormenting her this one time."

"I *could*." Bailey skipped toward Ginny.

Shaking her head, Havana turned back to the ring.

Walking down the stairs from his father's apartment to the shop floor, Tate briefly waved at Ingrid, who was deep in conversation with some customers. He was making his way down one of the slim aisles when a familiar female walked through the front door. Tate cursed beneath his breath, and his cat snapped his teeth.

"You really should have refused to allow her to return to our pride," Luke muttered, standing close behind him with Farrell.

"If I'd known she planned to be a pain in my ass, I would've," said Tate.

Ashlynn made a beeline for him. "I've been looking for you." She did a double-take at the sight of a rather creepy looking doll sitting on a wooden cabinet on their left. The shop sold everything from oil paintings and statues to tribal masks and china cups. Some items were featured on display tables while others hung on walls or were positioned around the store.

She swiftly switched her attention back to Tate. "I was hoping I'd find you here." She studied his face and bit her lower lip. "You're still mad."

"What do you think?" he clipped, keeping his voice low so as not to draw the attention of Ingrid's customers. They were at the other side of the shop, but there wasn't much noise to override voices—only the ticking of clocks and the very old song playing low in the background.

"Tate—"

"I've made it clear that I want nothing to do with you. Yet, you showed up at my home last night wearing nothing but a coat and a pair of high heels." She'd seemed sincerely shocked when Tate turned her away, which he absolutely did not get.

She winced, her cheeks heating. "Not my finest moment. I cringe every time I think about it. Look, I'd had a few drinks—"

"I'm not interested in why you did it. The fact is that it never should have happened, and it had better not happen again."

"I just wanted us to talk."

"You often show up at people's homes naked to 'talk?'"

Her blush deepened. "No. I was fully dressed last time I went to your house, remember? You wouldn't let me in then either."

"I can't understand why that surprises you. I've given you no reason whatsoever to think I'd welcome you into my home. Being turned away the first time didn't make you reluctant to try again?"

"No, because we *need* to talk."

"I told you before, I'm not interested in having any such 'talk.' It's not a complicated concept."

She took a steadying breath. "Look, you have every right to be so furious with me for leaving you—"

"I'm not furious. I was once, but not now. I can see why you chose to go to Koby. It's not something I'd have done if the situation was reversed, because I'd made a commitment to you. But I do understand why you went to him. There was no sense in holding onto my anger, so I let it go. That said, I have no inclination to 'talk' with you, have dinner with you, or anything else."

"You have no idea how much I regret what I did," she said, her expression one of distress. "I wasn't thinking clearly, Tate. I just heard that he was in pain and all alone. Every primal instinct I had pushed me to go to him. It was like a compulsion. It fogged my mind. I acted purely on instinct, not on good sense."

"It doesn't matter anymore. It hasn't mattered for a long time."

"You loved me. You could love me again."

"You killed whatever I felt for you. And, in doing so, you killed the possibility of me *ever* feeling those things for you again."

Her face fell. "You don't know that. Not for sure. We could get back what we had."

His brows snapped together. "Why would I *want* it back?"

"We were good together."

"And then we weren't. You asked me to move out. I gave you what you wanted. I left, I didn't interfere when you went to Koby. Now it's your turn to give me what I want—stay out of my face, get on with your life, and leave me to live mine in peace."

He skirted around her, stalked out of the shop … and almost crashed into his sister, which almost led to his bodyguards crashing into him.

Elle rocked back on her heels. "Whoa, bro, what's the rush? You okay?"

Tate flexed his fingers. "Yeah." He heard the doorbell chime behind him. Ashlynn's scent reached him just as Elle's face hardened.

His sister's gaze tracked Ashlynn as the woman hurried away. "Is the bitch bothering you?"

"You could say that," he replied, ushering his sister to the side so she wouldn't be jostled by pedestrians. "I don't remember her having selective hearing, but she seems to have it now."

"It's not that she's hearing only what she wants to hear," said Luke. "She's keeping up the pressure because she's *determined* to hear what she wants to hear, which is that you'll take her back."

"That'll never happen," said Tate.

"We know that," Elle assured him. "Most of the pride knows that. Some are hoping you'll give her another shot, though *heaven* knows why. It would be the last thing she deserves." Elle cocked her head. "You look tired, bro."

He *was* tired. Tired of dealing with Ashlynn. Tired of his efforts to find Gideon York getting him nowhere. Tired of being unable to unearth any info about the auctions. More, he was tired of fighting the urge to go see a certain devil shifter. "I've got a lot going on right now."

"You also look sexually frustrated—it's written all over you. I'd point out that many of the single females in our pride would be more than happen to help you out with that, but I don't think I'm wrong in sensing that the only female you want to sexually tangle with right now is Havana. You talked to her lately?"

His chest squeezed just hearing her name. He couldn't go a single day without thinking of her. The seemingly relentless urge to brand her was still his constant companion. Sometimes, it rode him so hard he almost shook with it. And the idea that she was somewhere out there trying to move on from him … yeah, he just hated it, even though he knew this was the way it had to be.

The time they'd spent apart hadn't eased his cat's obsession with her. The feline was pissed at Tate. Although Havana was the one who ended the fling, his cat wasn't upset with her at all. No, the feline didn't find it an excuse as to why Tate wouldn't go to her, because the cat knew him inside out; knew that Tate never let anyone else dictate his actions. The way his cat saw it, *Tate* was the one keeping him away from what he wanted most.

Maybe her now being strictly off-limits was what kept the feline so fascinated with her. Whatever the case, Tate was having no luck forcing his cat to move the fuck on. But since Tate himself wasn't doing much better at that, he wasn't in a position to judge.

"No, I haven't," he finally replied. "She wants what I can't give her, so …"

"Would it really be so bad to give it to her?"

No, it wouldn't. Tate wasn't keen on relationships, but he liked Havana enough that he'd be interested in seeing if they could build something good. The problem was … "My cat would hurt her. Not physically, but emotionally."

"Maybe. Maybe not. This could be the one time he truly is interested in a female on more than one level."

Tate snorted. "I've had that thought several times with other women, Elle. It was never the case then. I can't risk that it isn't the case now, because I've already hurt Havana without meaning to. I won't do something *knowing* I could hurt her again."

"So you've cut contact with her?"

"Yes."

"And how's that working out for you?"

It wasn't working for him at all. He missed her voice, her smile, her scent, her laugh. And he couldn't get the last memory he had of her out of his mind—the sad look on her face as she'd told him to take care of himself before heading into her apartment building. *Fuck*. He'd done that. He'd made her feel that way. He'd put that look there. The knowledge gutted him.

Luke put a hand on Tate's shoulder. "So your plan is to grow old and die alone?"

Tate blinked. "What?"

"If this is going to be your knee-jerk response to women wanting more from you, how do you ever expect to eventually commit to one?" asked Luke. "If you're waiting for your true mate, fine, but there's no saying you'll recognize her instantly. Oh look, there's Damian."

Tate tipped his chin at their youngest brother, who was walking along the opposite side of the street with a friend. Damian waved at them.

Elle perched a hand on her hip. "Look at him strolling around like he's a normal person and not the son of Satan. He blends well—I'll give him that."

Tate sighed. "Do you think you'll ever reach a mental place where you no longer feel compelled to brand our baby brother the Antichrist?"

She raised her hands. "I'm just calling the situation as I see it. But hey, if you want to convince yourself that Damian is a mere mortal, feel free to do so. I won't live in denial, Tate. Not even for you. His destiny is to bring forth the apocalypse and destroy us all. And I'm not gonna keep quiet about it."

"Yeah, I've noticed. I guess it's a good thing Damian loves you despite that."

"He's incapable of love. He feels only hatred and a thirst to kill."

Tate shook his head, at a loss. "If you say so."

"I do. Now go wind down, relax, and shake off everything that has you so angry."

There was really only one thing that would relax him right now. Only one thing that would help ease the restlessness plaguing him. But he wouldn't do it. Wouldn't seek Havana out. But even as he told himself that, he headed right for her building.

CHAPTER TEN

Havana yanked open the door of the industrial washing machine and crouched beside it. The laundromat facilities located in the basement of her complex were pretty decent. She most appreciated the ceiling fan—it could get seriously stuffy and hot in a room full of dryers. The basement was brightly lit to compensate for the small windows, despite shifters seeing well in the dark. Her devil, however, didn't like it down there. Didn't like the too-strong smells of detergent, softener, bleach, and hot metal.

She'd gotten home from the rec center an hour ago and, leaving Bailey and Aspen to catch up on the newest episode of a show they were addicted to, had headed to the basement.

It was empty of people, but there was plenty of noise. The whirring of the ceiling fans, the glugging and slurping of the washing machines, the clacking of zippers against the metal drum of the dryers.

Having transferred her clothes from the laundry basket into the machine, Havana added detergent powder and fabric softener. She'd just finished inserting quarters into the slot when she heard the squeak of hinges behind her. Havana switched on the machine and then glanced over her shoulder. She tensed.

Tate.

He looked as goddamn tempting as always, especially in that navy tee that stretched tight across his taut chest and showed off the badass tattoos on his arms. Her body instantly went into meltdown, and that all-too-familiar sexual chemistry flickered to life.

Oh, help.

Knowing there could only be one reason he'd sought her out, she turned to fully face him. "You have news about the jaguars or Gideon?"

"No, not yet." He took another fluid step into the room. "I went to your apartment. You weren't there. Camden said he saw you head to the elevator with a laundry basket, so I figured I'd find you here. How've you been?"

Havana hesitated, taken aback by the everyday question he'd casually thrown at her ... like they engaged in regular chit-chat all the time. "Good."

He gave a slow nod. "Glad to hear it."

Glad to hear it? She rinsed the granules of detergent from her fingers in the stainless-steel sink, dried her hands with paper towels, and then tossed the now-wet towels into the trash. "If you don't have intel to pass on, why are you here?"

His brow flicked up. "I need a reason to come see you?"

"Well, yeah, since we're not sleeping together anymore."

"That doesn't mean we can't be friends."

Havana did a slow blink. "Friends?" He had to be kidding.

"Why not?"

No, he wasn't kidding, she realized. She cocked her head, wondering if he understood what a kick in the teeth for her it was to hear him offer her *friendship*. "You want that? Really?"

"What I really want is to fuck you so hard and long you scream until your throat's raw, but you already know that." Tate cursed softly and raised his hands. "I'm not here to try to convince you to back down. I just ... I wanted to see you. Is that so bad?"

Her heart squeezed. "It's not bad, but you still shouldn't be here." Really, she hadn't expected to see him for a while. She'd thought he'd be absolutely intent on giving her space purely out of fear that he'd otherwise give her mixed signals.

He *had* to know he'd make it harder for her to move on if he showed up whenever he felt like it. Did that not matter to him at all?

"Come have coffee with me."

Her brow creased. "What?"

"The café doesn't shut for another hour. We can grab a drink. Sit. Talk."

"Talk about what?"

He shrugged. "General things."

"You're not serious."

"It's just coffee, Havana."

"Just coffee," she echoed, an edge to her voice. "You say that like it's nothing. Harmless, even. Yet, you never took me for coffee before. Never took me anywhere other than to your house. So it's not quite 'nothing' in your book, or we'd have done it at least once in the past."

"But as you reminded me, we're not sleeping together anymore, so our old boundaries don't apply."

Oh, he had some front. She hadn't once asked him to give her more; she'd respected that he couldn't, and she'd walked away without dishing out any blame. Could he not give her this one thing and just keep his distance for a while?

Apparently not.

The only reason Havana didn't chew a chunk out of his ass was that she didn't want to prolong this conversation. She just wanted him to go.

She took a long breath—a movement that physically hurt, since her ribs felt so damn tight. "Maybe someday in the future we can build a friendship and meet up for coffee or whatever on occasion, but that's not going to happen right now. I need some space from you. We'll still work together on tracking Gideon and putting a stop to the auctions, of course," she added quickly.

"You're telling me we can't be friends?"

"I'm not trying to be a bitch, I'm not striking out at you. I'm just being honest. It wouldn't be enough for me right now, Tate." And it burned that it would be enough for him; that he thought he could so easily keep things platonic.

He clenched his jaw. "Isn't it better than nothing at all?"

"It will be at some point, but not yet. Like I said, I need some space from you for a while. So unless the subject matter is Gideon, his jaguars, the auctions, or a landlord-thing, I don't want you to call or text or visit."

Tate felt his chest tighten. He knew he should leave her be—he couldn't give her what she wanted, and she clearly wasn't going to settle for anything less. Plus, giving her some breathing room to move on would be best for them both. Especially since it was impossible for him to be around her without wanting to be deep inside her body. But everything in him, including his cat, rebelled at the idea of granting her request.

She'd always been like a damn magnet to him. It was like she dragged him into her orbit. Initially, it had been purely on a physical level. But that changed when he got to know her. It was like she spoke to something inside him. He couldn't really explain it. There was no battling or ignoring that kind of pull. It haunted you. Incited you. Badgered you. So there'd be nothing simple about staying away from her. There never had been—hence why he stood right in front of her.

His eyes lowered to the pulse in her neck—it was beating fast and hard. He wanted to nuzzle that neck. Wanted to draw her luscious scent into his lungs and drown in it. Wanted to bite down hard and leave a mark. None of which he'd do.

He just needed to see her. Touch her. Smell her. He hadn't really expected her to agree to the "friends" thing, but it had been worth a shot if it meant he didn't have to keep his distance from her.

His cat purred, happy to see her, wanting to be closer to her. Granting the feline what he wanted, Tate inched forward, glad when she didn't step back. "Haven't you missed me just a little?"

"It doesn't really matter either way, does it?"

"It matters to me."

"Then no, I haven't missed you."

Sensing it was a barefaced lie, he felt his mouth twitch. "I see. I guess it's a good thing I have thick skin, or that might have wounded me." Unable to stand this close without touching her, he stroked his knuckles down the column of her throat. He raked his eyes over her face, taking in every curve and freckle—he had them all memorized. "You're so beautiful you sometimes take my breath away, you know."

She gave him a wary look. "Tate."

"Especially your eyes. They grab hold of a person by the throat." He loved staring into them when she came.

She licked her lower lip. "Look, I have a few errands to run, so ..."

Loosely fisting the ponytail that hung over her shoulder, he let the silky mass slide through his hand. "If you want the truth, I don't think that us being friends would be enough for me either. But can't we try?"

"In the future, yes. Just not right now."

Tate ever so slowly nodded, but not a single cell in his body was in agreement. He didn't want to be a figure that hovered on the periphery of her world—a mere landlord, a casual acquaintance who had no right to touch her. How the fuck could he ever sit and engage in small-talk with her, like he didn't know every inch of her body? Like he didn't miss what they'd once had? Like she meant nothing to him?

Needing to touch her again—and it *was* a need, one he was absolutely shit at fighting—he danced the tips of his fingers down one side of her face. "Never should have pursued you. Not when I suspected that letting you go wouldn't be so simple. But I had to have you. I needed to know if sex between us would be as good as my gut and my cock told me it would be." He lowered his mouth an inch. "It was better."

Like that, the air between them thickened and crackled ... as if memories of their time together charged the atmosphere. His cock, already hard and heavy, throbbed against his zipper.

She swallowed, and her eyes flared with need. "How's Ashlynn?" she asked, and he knew she'd done it in an attempt to break the spell between them. It didn't work.

"I couldn't give a damn. Neither should you." He cupped one side of her neck and breezed his thumb over the delicate line of her jaw. "I dreamed about you a few nights ago. I dreamed I had you beneath me, your hair spread all over my pillow, while I moved in and out of you. There was a bite mark on your neck that was weeping blood." He'd liked the sight of it a little too much both during his dream and after. "I woke up hard as a fucking steel spike. Jerked off to the thought of pounding in your pussy until you screamed." And he'd kept in his mind's eye that little detail of her wearing his mark the whole time.

She closed her eyes, as if to block out his words. "It's not fair of you to do this."

He lowered his forehead to hers. "I know." But he couldn't stop himself. "You have to go."

"Need one taste of you first. Just one." He was so starved for her he almost groaned at the mere thought of tasting her again.

She let out a ragged breath. "Not a good idea."

He framed her face with his hands and pressed a soft kiss to first one eyelid then the other. The electric sexual tension amplified and purred against his skin. He feathered his lips over her face, dabbing gentle, barely-there kisses everywhere but her mouth.

She didn't once open her eyes, but her breathing picked up. So did his. When her fingers dug into his arms, he thought she'd try to tug them away. She didn't.

"One taste," he whispered against her mouth, his lips nibbling hers, so fucking hungry for her he was surprised he didn't shake with it. "Open for me, baby. I need this." He suckled on her lower lip. "Op—" He blinked as she shoved him hard, sending him skidding back a few feet.

Condemning herself for being so damn weak when it came to this male, Havana pointed a shaking finger at him. "You don't get to do this."

His nostrils flared. "Havana—"

"You gave me up. I was the one to end the fling, yes, but you soon learned why. Did you offer me what I needed? No. You wanted things to go back to the way they were. And when you realized that wasn't going to happen, you took me home and then walked away. So you don't get to come here and pull this shit."

"I didn't walk away because you *don't* matter. I did it because you *do* matter. I'm doing what's best for you."

"Bull*shit*. When it comes to us, you've only ever done what's best for you. It was best for you to have boundaries, so we had them. It was best for you to have nothing more than casual, so you tried to talk me into changing my mind when I ended it. And now you're here, tossing me crumbs from your table, so I'll struggle to forget you and move forward. That is *definitely* not best for me. But it's what you want, so you did it."

He stalked to her, his eyes hard. "It's not like that. You've got things twisted in your head, and maybe that's on me, since I am pretty selfish when it comes to you—I won't deny that. But I'm not bullshitting you about this, Havana. I don't know how to give you more without hurting you."

She threw up her arms. "I don't know what that means."

"My cat ... he's obsessed with you. But he does that—focuses all his energy onto one female, gets all wrapped up in her—then he later pulls away from her out of goddamn nowhere. He's done it ever since Ashlynn."

Thrown, Havana could only stare at him.

"There were times he was so infatuated with a woman that I thought he'd finally gotten over his shit," Tate went on, looking so tired all of a sudden. "But I was wrong every time. I don't know what he's looking for in a partner, but he never fucking finds it. So then he withdraws, leaving women confused and hurt. Shallow flings with firm boundaries are just simpler. Nobody has any expectations. Nobody gets hurt. There are no recriminations when I'm forced to walk away."

Havana wished he hadn't told her, because she didn't want to "understand." She wanted to hold onto her anger so that it would drown out the hurt. But how could she not feel bad for both Tate and his cat? "Sounds like your feline has commitment issues. Or he withdraws to protect himself from further hurt. It would be understandable if he just didn't want to put himself out there again."

Havana would be just as averse to relationships if the situation was reversed. Her devil? Well, she'd probably rage about it for the rest of her days. "Why didn't you tell me sooner about your cat's struggles?"

Tate lifted a brow. "Would you admit your devil's failings to others?"

No, because she was as protective of the devil as the animal was of Havana. Predators didn't admit to weaknesses. In which case it was no small thing that he'd opened up to her about this.

Havana rubbed at her chest. Right then, she truly ached for both Tate and his cat. All they'd done was love and commit themselves so fully to a woman that they'd thrown themselves wide open to the concept of imprinting. In return, that woman had tossed it all back in their faces. They hadn't deserved that.

She frowned as a thought struck her. "I know your ex screwed you both, but it's possible he's holding back from other women because he nevertheless wants her back."

His cat's face scrunched up, and Tate couldn't help but snicker. "Trust me when I say that he has no lingering feelings for her. He just can't forgive or get past her betrayal. He refuses to let it go."

"Pallas cats can sure hold a grudge." She sighed, her shoulders drooping. "I get why you stick to casual now. I'd probably do the same thing, in your shoes. I appreciate you sharing all that with me. I know it couldn't have been easy. I won't repeat it to anyone."

"I know you won't." Tate trusted her completely, but he couldn't be so sure his cat had the same faith in her. He took a slow step closer. "I wish I met you before Ashlynn fucked up my cat's ability to trust."

"It might not be that he can't trust another female. It might be that he's just not willing to try."

"True. I can't be sure either way." He tilted his head. "Still pissed at me?"

She let out a heavy exhale. "No. Like I said, I understand now why you stick to casual flings. But the friends-thing still isn't going to happen for a while. Turning up here to 'visit' me … it isn't fair to me, Tate, and you know it. You know you can't do this again."

His shoulders tensed. "Babe—"

"I've never asked you for anything. Not even for a real relationship, despite how much I wanted one with you. I respected your wish to stick with casual. I didn't condemn you for it, didn't bitch about it. But I need something from you now."

He ground his teeth, because he knew what was coming. "Havana, it's not—"

"I need you to give me as much space as you reasonably can so I can move on. That's all, Tate. You can at least give me that, can't you?"

"You truly believe you'll be able to see me as nothing more than your landlord? You really think it'll be that easy for you to just cut me out of your life?"

Havana gave him a sad smile. "You were never really in it, were you, Tate?"

The door creaked open, and Bailey entered. She came to a sudden halt, her eyes widening. "Oh, um … I can go, if you guys are in the middle of something."

"No, stay," said Havana, glad of the interruption. The conversation needed to end *yesterday*. "Tate's leaving now." He didn't move, though. Seconds of tense silence ticked by as he speared her with that unbearably intense gaze. The silence grated on her raw nerves.

Finally, he sighed, and his expression morphed into one of resignation. She'd finally gotten through to him; she could see it. But it was a bittersweet victory, because it meant they'd be virtual strangers from now on.

"You know where I am if you need me," said Tate, his voice devoid of emotion. He gave Bailey a curt nod and then left.

As the door shut behind him, Havana swallowed hard, her stomach sinking. Hot tears stung the backs of her eyes. She wouldn't cry. She wouldn't.

Bailey arched her brows. "What just happened here?"

"I finally made him hear me," replied Havana. "But not before he tried coaxing 'one last kiss' out of me." She'd almost given in. Almost allowed herself that luxury. Which wouldn't have stopped at a kiss—she knew that as sure as she knew her own name. In no time at all, he'd have had her pinned against the wall drilling his cock into her. And part of her lamented that she hadn't just let it happen.

"It could be that absence is making his heart grow fonder," Bailey suggested.

"It's making his dick grow harder, that's about it." She nearly jumped as one of the machines buzzed having reached the end of its cycle. Damn, the bastard had left her a wreck.

"Don't be so sure about that. I'm not. Hey, I'm surprised your devil didn't surface and claw his face for pushing you."

Havana's brows met as she realized something. "Actually, she's not as miffed with him as she once was, not even after all the crap that happened just now." She still had that mental door firmly closed, though.

"Really?"

"Really. I mean, she wasn't exactly *pleased* to see him, but she didn't snarl or anything. She just watched him closely."

Bailey grinned. "Ah, she's impressed by his persistence. She likes that it hasn't been so easy to send him on his way."

"I guess," said Havana. "I suppose it's soothing her wounded ego."

"He's also proving himself to be strong, tenacious, and highly focused on you—she'll like all that. She'll even respect it."

Havana lifted one shoulder. "Maybe."

"You do realize that if he wins her over and you keep turning him away, she'll go from being 'off' with him to being annoyed with you, right?"

Actually, no, Havana hadn't thought of that. "It won't happen. I got through to him just now. He won't be back unless it's to discuss a landlord issue or something related to the auction business."

"Aren't you even a *little* smug that he struggles so much to stay away from you? *I* would be."

"Not smug, but it does make me feel a tiny bit better about the entire situation. It's not a good thing, though, because I need space from him. I've made that clear."

"Don't expect it to make much of a difference. You've made a lot of things 'clear' to Tate since you chose to walk away. It hasn't stopped him from coming back to you again and again. Face it, he's hooked. He just hasn't accepted it yet."

"Can't say I agree with you on that. In any case, I'm done talking about him. Why did you come looking for me? Is something wrong?"

"No, I was coming to let you know that Elle called and invited you, me, and Aspen to hang with her and Bree at the Tavern on Saturday night."

The Tavern, a bar-slash-restaurant-slash-pool hall, was the pride's local hangout. "What did you say?"

"I said I'd talk to you and Aspen and then get back to her. Aspen's up for it. I'm *all* for a night out, although I prefer our usual bar near Enigma. But if we go far from home, we make it easier for Gideon's goons to get near you. I'm not good with that. Plus, the Tavern is cool. And hanging out with pallas cats is always fun. Also, I like Elle and Bree. We had a blast with them last time."

Havana smiled at the memory. Elle was a hoot, and Bree—who was both the primary omega and Alex's mate—was probably the only person who had the ability to keep Elle out of trouble.

Havana's smile dimmed as something occurred to her. "Tate might not like me hanging with his sister. I mean, I don't think I'd like it if my ex bed-buddy hung out with my family—that being you and Aspen."

"I don't think Tate would begrudge you having fun with his sister. He'd probably like it, since it'll mean you have backup if you need it while out."

True. And Havana really could do with a night out. "All right, we'll hit the Tavern with Elle and Bree on Saturday."

"Awesome. By the way, don't rush back upstairs. Take your time down here."

"Why?"

Bailey pulled a face. "Well, Aspen's animal and mine got into another brawl. My mamba bit her a few times. The bearcat got pissed and offloaded her anal glands on my snake, the dirty bitch. Don't worry, Aspen dug out that special bleach you bought and scrubbed the floor to get rid of the stench, but it's still just a *little* smelly up there."

Havana shook her head, sighing. "Your mamba started the brawl, didn't she?" It was more of an accusation than a question.

"Hey, the bearcat grabbed my snake and lashed her around like she was a goddamn rodeo whip."

"Before or after your mamba bit her?"

"Before."

"I'll rephrase. Before or after your mamba *first* bit her?"

"Oh, after."

Havana briefly flicked her gaze upward. "Is there any chance at all that maybe one day your snake will stop taunting Aspen's bearcat purely for the sake of it?"

"You've asked me this question dozens of times before, and you always seem so surprised when I say no."

CHAPTER ELEVEN

She was going to end up punching the bitch. Seriously. There was no way this night wouldn't end in a barfight. But Havana had never had an issue with those. She found them sort of cathartic.

She'd been at the Tavern for a few hours now. She, her girls, Elle, and Bree had claimed one of the burgundy leather cushioned booths. Throughout the evening, they'd drank shots and cocktails while also munching on the complimentary bowl of nuts that Elle had swiped from the long bar.

The scents of beer, leather, oiled wood, and hot and spicy foods were heavy in the air. *Too* heavy for her devil's liking, but she was fussy that way.

The place was crowded, as usual. Filled with the sounds of laughter, chatter, glasses clinking, balls shuttling into pool table pockets, slot machines bleeping and pinging, and music blasting from the widescreen TVs that often featured sports games. Waiters and waitresses walked around delivering food platters, taking orders, and collecting empty glasses or bottles.

A comedian had recently finished his act, so the stage was now empty. The Tavern often provided entertainment, especially karaoke, live bands, or hypnotists.

The night had been great thus far. It hadn't been possible for Havana to wind down, though. Not when she was acutely conscious that Tate was on the opposite side of the space playing pool. When their eyes first locked, a hollow ache began to build in her chest. At the same time, though, she'd felt a strange sense of ... she couldn't describe it. It wasn't quite pleasure, but it was close. Like a small shot of adrenaline. Like when you tasted chocolate after having given it up for a long while. It was comforting and only made you want more.

She'd quickly looked away and had spent the rest of the evening trying her best to ignore his presence. But it was kind of impossible to ignore six-feet-plus of pure Alpha male hotness. She found her eyes occasionally straying his way. Every time they accidentally collided with his, it was like a jolt of electricity struck her body. Bleh.

He hadn't approached her, hadn't tried to speak to her, hadn't even so much as tipped his chin her way. She didn't get the sense that he was being rude. No, he was simply giving her what she asked for—space.

As she'd requested, he hadn't texted or called her or sought her out since that day they spoke in the basement of her building. It relieved her.

It also devastated her. But it was for the best.

Moving on from Dieter hadn't been anywhere near this hard. Given that all she and Tate had had was a fling, it *shouldn't* have been this hard. And her hormones shouldn't be doing the fandango just because he was in the same damn space.

Plus, it didn't help that fucking *Ashlynn* sat at a table not far from him. The skank had no compunction about pinning Havana with hard, steady stares. That was when she wasn't busy trying to make Tate notice her, flipping her hair and laughing overly loud with her friends, Eva and Aimee—two pallas cats who'd always been somewhat curt with Havana.

So far, she'd ignored the trio's behavior. Purely because it was fun to silently communicate that Ashlynn's attempt to intimidate her wasn't successful. But there was really only so long Havana could tolerate this crap. Her inner bullshit meter went off because in truth, yeah, she could *absolutely* tolerate it—she was good at ignoring such pettiness. She simply didn't want to keep ignoring it, and her animal certainly hoped she wouldn't.

Elle set her half-empty glass on a coaster. "So, a devil, a bearcat, and a mamba formed a clan."

"I feel a joke coming on," said Havana.

"It's just such an odd mix."

Bree tipped her head to the side. "Your animals don't struggle to get along or anything?"

"My bearcat has little patience for Bailey's mamba," said Aspen. "But that's only because the snake deliberately pisses her off for shits and giggles. Bailey and her serpent do *lots* of things for shits and giggles."

Elle looked at Bailey. "Your mamba doesn't bother Havana's devil?"

"No, she sees Havana as her Alpha," replied Bailey. "My mamba challenged her in the beginning, but the devil whooped her ass. You should seriously never get in a devil's face, no matter if they're in their human form or animal form."

Aspen nodded. "They're freakishly strong, and their bones are *super* tough. That's why Corbin won't let her spar for fun at the center."

Havana sniffed. "I still say it's an unreasonable rule."

"You broke one guy's jaw with a bitch slap," Aspen pointed out.

"He shouldn't have laughed when I got in the ring ... as if he was so sure he'd wipe the floor with me." Cocky bastard. "He should have known better. It's not like devils are mistaken for harmless. Which is why landlords are often rather disinclined to accept me as a tenant."

"Did Tate seem put off by it?" asked Elle.

Havana licked her lower lip, her stomach hardening—something it did each time the redhead mentioned her brother, which was often. "No. He didn't seem fazed at all."

"Little fazes Tate," said Elle. "He's always been like that. I'm kind of bummed that you two broke up. I got a little excited when he didn't seem interested in extracting himself from whatever you two had going on. I thought that just maybe Ashlynn's betrayal hadn't fucked him or his cat up too badly. And you seemed to make him happy. I want him to be happy."

"I don't think I necessarily made him *happy*, Elle. I just made him come really, really hard."

A chuckle burst out of Elle. "God, Havana, I like you. I really do." She sipped her drink. "You suit him so well. Ashlynn didn't. Not really. There was just something missing from their relationship. I feel bad for her on one level, because it has to be hard to have your true mate reject you, and watching him imprint on another female had to be just as hard. But she hurt my brother, so for that alone I'd hate her even if she was an angel sent directly from heaven."

"On the subject of Ashlynn," began Aspen, "I might just *explode* if she doesn't stop glaring at you, Vana. When she's not trying to kill you with her eyes, she's striving to get Tate's attention. Which isn't working. He's too focused on you. That's probably *why* you're repeatedly finding yourself on the receiving end of her glare."

Probably. Havana's devil kept letting out eerie little growls, done with the skank.

"She's going to pick a fight at some point—maybe tonight, maybe some other time," Aspen predicted.

Bailey looked at Havana. "Want me to bite her?"

It was tempting, but Havana wanted to have some fun with her. It would be a good stress-reliever, if nothing else. "Not right now."

"We can have her thrown out if you want," Elle offered.

Bailey frowned. "You wouldn't rather watch that bitch get her ass handed to her by Havana?"

Elle's entire face lit up. "I'd *totally* be up for that. But I don't want your night to end on a bad note."

Aspen snickered. "For us, ending the evening with a barfight is a common and much-loved practice. Tradition, even."

"I gotta warn you that Ashlynn won't be easy to take on," said Bree. "She's a strong alpha, and she's very well trained in combat."

Pleased, Havana said, "Even better. It's far less fun to beat someone who's hopeless at defending themselves. As Aspen said, she may not issue the challenge tonight, but it'll come at some point."

If they were anywhere else, Havana might have struck first. But she had more respect for the pallas cats than to start shit in their hangout. She'd defend herself, but she wouldn't pick a fight here. Which disappointed her devil, and since the animal's mood was becoming a little too precarious, Havana decided to change the subject. "On a cheerier note ... I'm jealous that you have Valentina Devereaux for a mother-in-law, Bree. I think she's plain awesome."

The pallas cat grinned. "I agree. You can't not adore her. I love working with her and her mate, James. They argue over the craziest stuff."

Bailey leaned toward Bree. "What's it like being mated to a wolverine? I heard they don't make easy mates."

"Oh, they don't," Bree confirmed. "He hates being away from me. And I mean *hates* it. He'd be sitting right at this booth if I hadn't made it clear that we wanted privacy for girl talk. So he settled over there with Tate, sulking. Wolverines are more protective and possessive than most shifters. It makes me crazy at times, but he's worth every moment."

Elle smiled. "It's so cute how devoted Alex is to her. Especially because he pretty much despises a large percentage of the remaining population."

"You imprinted on each other, right?" Havana asked Bree.

"We did, thank God." Bree blew out a relieved breath. "I was worried it wouldn't happen for us. The imprinting process is a powerful thing, even in its earliest stages. I can't imagine how hard it must have been for Tate when the threads of it snapped. I admire him for ploughing through that."

Havana tilted her head. "Why do I feel like you guys keep purposefully going back to the subject of Tate?" Seriously, Elle and Bree had done it over a dozen times.

Elle gave a sheepish look. "Fine," she said with a sigh. "Bree and I really want you and Tate to make another go of things. I know *you* want more than a fling—he told me. And I think he wants that too; he's just holding back for what he believes is a good reason, but I don't think he'll manage that for much longer. I get that you want to move on, but I'm asking that you not write him off just yet."

"You didn't see what he was like this past week, Havana," Bree cut in. "It was obvious that being away from you doesn't work well for him. Like *at all*."

Elle nodded. "I truly think he'll make the jump at some point and offer you what you want, Havana. My big fear is that, by then, you'll have decided it's too little too late."

"You can tell us that it's not our business if you want," said Bree. "You'd be right, it's not. But we both worry about Tate. And we want what's best for him—we think that's you."

Havana put down her glass. "I can't fault you for caring enough about him to want to intervene. But I don't believe he'll offer me anything. Even if I had the slightest hope that he would, I wouldn't be able to exist in a frame of mind where I was open to the idea, because it would only later eviscerate me if I had to watch him commit to someone else."

"I get it," said Elle, her smile weak. "I guess it wasn't fair of us to ask that of you. I'm sorry."

"Don't be," said Havana. "I'm glad he has people looking out for him."

"My Alex was hesitant to try a relationship with me," said Bree. "He held back for *years*; look where we are now. I understand why you can't let yourself hope that Tate will step up to the plate, but I'm not going to give up hope. Especially since he's been eye-fucking you pretty much since the moment he walked through the door."

Aspen looked at Havana. "*I'm* getting hot under the collar just watching him shoot you those darkly carnal looks, so I can't imagine what they're doing to you."

Oh, they made Havana feel a lot of things. Hot. Nervous. Turned-on. Hunted. But also annoyed, because he didn't have the right to eye-fuck her like that anymore.

Bailey shook her head in wonder. "Why do so many supremely hot guys seem to have weird-ass exes who're set on being a pain in the ass?"

"You *are* one of those weird-ass exes," said Havana.

Bailey raised her index finger. "Only if the guys have wronged me, so it doesn't count. Tate has done *shit* to Ashlynn, but she's clearly intent on being a problem."

Aspen flicked a hand. "If Havana doesn't take care of her, the zombies will."

Havana sighed. "There is not going to be a zombie apocalypse."

"I hear you say that, but I also once heard you say you'd never get involved with an Alpha," said Aspen. "Look what happened there."

"That's vastly different from—" Cutting herself off, Havana gave her head a quick shake. "You know what, let's just move on."

They all chatted a little more about inconsequential stuff, laughing and joking and ordering more drinks.

"I need to use the bathroom," Aspen announced at one point.

Not prepared to allow her friend to go alone, Havana stood. "I'll come with you." She looked down at Bailey, who seemed deep in thought. "You all right?" Havana asked, tapping the mamba's shoulder.

Bailey blinked up at her. "Huh? Oh, yeah. I was just wondering if caterpillars actually know what's gonna happen when they build a cocoon for themselves, or if they're later like 'whoa, what's with the wings and shit?'"

Havana felt her brows inch up slightly. "Um, sorry, can't help you with that. You coming to the restroom with us?"

"Sure," said Bailey.

Ignoring the gazes of both Tate and Ashlynn, Havana went to the restroom with her girls. They quickly did their business and then headed back to their booth. Well, Bailey sort of danced her way there while Aspen followed, wolf-whistling. Havana was only a few feet away from the booth when an unwelcome figure slid in front of her. Her devil snarled and jumped to her feet.

"Nice top," said Ashlynn, a brittle smile on her face.

Havana's mouth curved. "Thanks."

"It goes well with your heels."

"I'd have to agree." Noticing that her girls were on guard, Havana subtly signaled for them not to intervene. She could deal with this heifer just fine.

"I just wanted to say, well, I heard all about the auctions. God, it's hard to believe that kind of thing goes on. There are some seriously messed-up people out there. It's *awful* that they went after you, but at least it brought the terrible business to the attention of my pride. We Olympus cats won't let this go, what with you being one of Tate's tenants. If someone's under his protection, he takes it very seriously."

"Yes, I learned that fast," said Havana, keenly aware that the level of chatter in the space had dramatically lowered. Only the blasting music kept her and Ashlynn's words from being clear to all those trying to eavesdrop.

"I'm Ashlynn, by the way." Her false smile shrunk. "But I'm guessing you already know that. Elle no doubt told you plenty about me. I'll bet none of it was good."

"I have to admit, no, it wasn't good."

"You probably don't think much of me. You'll have heard what went down between me and Tate. He thinks I lied to him, but I meant my promises when I made them. I just couldn't keep them."

"You could've. You chose not to."

Ashlynn's face hardened. "Have you found your true mate yet?"

"Not that I'm aware of."

"The feeling you get when it hits you that they're yours ... it's indescribable. There's this compulsion to be around them. It's so hard to fight. I managed it while Koby was mated to another. But knowing he was in such pain after her death ... I couldn't ignore that."

"Again, you could've. You chose not to. No one put a gun to your head and forced you to leave Tate. You made the decision to do that, and you made it all on your own."

Ashlynn's eyes flared. "It's easy for you to say that because you haven't found your true mate. But I suppose you're right. I owe you an apology really, don't I?"

Havana frowned. "Do you?"

"A few of my pride mates are of the opinion that you care for Tate. If things had been different, he may have tried a relationship with you. But he didn't, because what I did hurt him so much that he literally closed himself off. So it's kind of my fault that you don't have the man you care for. And for that, I'm sorry." She gave Havana a sympathetic smile. "Don't feel bad for falling for someone you can't have. Women fall for Tate all the time, thinking he'll grow to care for them. He's easy to love, but his love isn't easy to win. It never was."

God, this woman sure was a rambler. "Good of you to own your shit, I guess."

"I made mistakes, and I know what I lost. I intend to win him back."

Havana lifted a brow, and her devil narrowed her eyes. "You think you have a shot?"

"Yes, I do. Once he's got used to me being around again, he'll settle. He'll let me in when he's ready. It gave me hope when I heard he broke things off with you. He might not have acknowledged it to himself yet, but he did that because I'm back and he knows it's time to break any ties he has with other women."

Havana held back a snort and gave her a bright smile. "Then it would seem that things will work out for you just fine."

"I want your assurance that you'll keep your distance from Tate. He and I need time to find our way back to each other. I don't want you or anyone else getting in the way of that."

Havana supposed she should be flattered that the woman felt so threatened by her. "Well, I can't give you what you want, seeing as he and I are working alongside each other to tackle the auction situation."

"But, other than that, you can keep your distance. So I'd like your assurance that you'll do exactly that."

Havana twisted her mouth. "Maybe if you hadn't spent the night sending me death glares, I'd be inclined to give you what you want. In the name of sisterhood and all. Then again, maybe not, because I simply don't like you. Personally, I think Tate had a lucky escape when you left him."

Ashlynn's face went hard as stone. "Careful how you speak to me. I am not someone you want to fuck with. Don't make me embarrass you in front of all these people."

"Embarrass me?"

"I have no issue with throwing down right here, right now."

Havana smiled, and her devil would have grinned wickedly if she could've. "What a coincidence. Neither do I."

Elle clamped her hand around Tate's arm and said, "No, you have to stay out of it."

Tate's mouth tightened. Every cell of his body demanded he stop the brawl before it could start. He didn't want Ashlynn even so much as *breathing* Havana's air, let alone touching her. "I'm Ashlynn's Alpha, this place belongs to our pride—"

"And a single word from you would make Ashlynn back off, yes, but you'll make Havana look weak if you intervene."

Yeah, so Elle kept saying each time he made a move to wade in. She wasn't wrong. Although Tate didn't want to undermine Havana's strength, he also didn't want to see her hurt. Ashlynn could be a vicious little scrapper, and she liked to sharpen her claws on people's faces. He liked Havana's face just as it was.

Deke and Isaiah, who were waiting for the slightest signal from Tate to leap into the fray, looked just as eager to do so.

"I have every right to intervene," Tate persisted. "Havana's under my protection, and the person confronting her is one of my cats."

"Which doesn't change that your interference would reflect badly on Havana."

"Still, it might be best if he *does* step in, Elle," Luke interjected. "Ashlynn's a tough fighter, and she can be—"

Havana slammed her palm into Ashlynn's chest so hard it sent her flying backwards. Ashlynn crashed into the brick wall, causing some of the sports paraphernalia to fall to the floor with her.

Everyone stilled, including Tate's cat. Because Havana had done that with a single shove. And she hadn't used herculean effort. She'd done it with a casual strength and such lightning-fast speed that all Tate could do was stare. It was one thing to *know* that devils were phenomenally strong. It was a whole other thing to see them demonstrate that power.

Ashlynn righted herself, her face a mask of sheer rage. "*Bitch.*" Throwing out alpha vibes in an effort to oppress Havana—which was fucking cheating, really—Ashlynn charged at her. Tate's stomach went hard, and his inner cat let out an enraged growl.

Havana grabbed the nearest chair and held it with all four legs directly pointed at Ashlynn—who, in her fury, stupidly fucking crashed into it.

She stumbled back with a loud wince of pain that morphed into a long hiss. "Fucking fight me!" Ashlynn demanded, planting her feet.

Shrugging, Havana lay the chair down flat on the floor, the legs facing *her* this time.

Ashlynn lunged. She didn't get far. Because Havana slammed her heel on one leg of the chair, making the top of it rear up and catch Ashlynn right on the chin.

Looking dazed, Ashlynn spat out blood. She glared at Havana, her nostrils flaring. "You'll regret that." She shifted. Her feline launched out of the puddle of clothes and hurled herself at Havana. Which might have been a good move … except that, in the meantime, Aspen had handed Havana a stool leg—he hadn't even noticed the bearcat *break* a stool.

Havana swung the wooden leg and whacked the feline like she was no more than a fucking baseball—and she did it with such force that the cat flew backwards and smacked into the wall hard enough to make Tate wince. The cat landed limply on the floor, out cold. And Havana, well, she dipped her hand into the complimentary bowl of pretzels that sat on a nearby table and tossed one into her mouth, casual as you please.

Nobody moved, no doubt as shocked as Tate. It was not often you saw a pallas cat get their ass handed to them. He couldn't even say that Havana had really *fought* Ashlynn. His little devil had done no more than toy with her, and she'd done it with no emotion. It was an insult. A message that Havana found her nothing more than a pest. Tate blew out a breath because, yeah, Havana's mercilessness went right to his cock. His inner cat fucking loved it.

The fact that she'd done this right in front of Ashlynn's pride mates, not giving a damn that they might retaliate, wouldn't anger the Olympus cats. No, like Tate, they respected that level of strength and fearlessness. Well, except for maybe Ashlynn's friends, who'd now recovered from their shock.

Gaping, Eva glared at Havana. "Fucking whore." Eva made a move toward her, her claws out. But then a black mamba dropped from the ceiling and wrapped tight around Eva's throat. Hissing, the mamba bit her face. Eva screamed and staggered.

A furious Aimee didn't take more than one aggressive step in Havana's direction before Aspen effortlessly tackled her to the floor and smacked a three-legged stool over her head, knocking the feline unconscious.

Havana crossed to Ashlynn's cat and carefully lifted her. Tate thought she might throw her at the table or something, but she didn't. She nodded at Aspen, who then grabbed a chair while Havana climbed the steps that led to the stage. Once the bearcat had positioned the chair in the center of the platform, Havana laid the pallas cat on the wooden seat. Bailey, who'd at some point shifted back to her human form and slipped on her dress, skipped over and tucked a colorful cocktail umbrella into the thick fur on the cat's neck.

Havana nodded, seemingly pleased. The three females then strolled off the stage. And Tate got it. Havana wanted Ashlynn to wake and find herself right there like that where everyone—including many of her pride mates—could see her. The feline would *never* live it down. Especially since people quickly began snapping pictures with their cell phones.

"Now that is *cold*," said Luke, his tone one of approval.

It was, and Tate couldn't help the grin that curved his mouth. His cat was pretty much head over heels for the delightfully vicious devil at this moment.

The bartender, Gerard, plonked three shots of tequila on the bar. "Drink up, girls. They're on the house." Yeah, he wasn't a fan of Ashlynn.

Tate made a beeline for Havana, who pinned him with a look that said he was supposed to be keeping his distance, but he ignored it. He wasn't going to slink away. He needed to check that she was okay.

Resisting the urge to pull her close and kiss her, he asked, "You all right?"

She knocked back her shot, her eyes alight with energy. "Never better."

"What did she say to you?"

"A few things, really. The gist of it? She's going to win you back, and she wants my vow that I'll stay out of the way. When I wasn't so inclined to make any such vows, she threatened to 'throw down.' Personally, I think she wanted to embarrass me in front of you."

"So you made a fool of her instead."

"And it was fun," Bailey cut in, smiling.

"It was just as entertaining to watch," said Bree, who'd gathered around them with Elle, Luke, Deke, and Isaiah.

Elle frowned at the mamba. "I didn't even notice you disappear, let alone shift forms."

Bailey shrugged. "Serpents are sneaky that way."

"Eva's *really* suffering from that bite of yours," said Bree.

"My mamba didn't inject much venom in her. Just enough to put the bitch out of commission." Bailey cast a brief look at Ashlynn's unconscious cat. "Do you guys think that will be the end of it?"

"No," Luke and Elle said at once.

The mamba grinned. "Awesome."

When Havana and her girls announced that they were leaving, Tate insisted on escorting them to their building. His guards walked in front while Havana's guards covered their rear.

Aspen and Bailey disappeared inside the complex, but Havana lingered near the main door; Tate could see the question in her eyes.

"No, I'm not pissed that you sort-of-fought with one of my cats," he said. "Ashlynn started it."

"I attacked first," Havana pointed out.

"Because she provoked you into doing so. Don't worry about her or her friends. I'll make sure they don't think to retaliate."

"I'm not worried about them," she said.

"I'm sorry that Ashlynn fucked with you tonight. I never wanted my past to touch you that way."

"It wasn't your fault, and it's not for you to apologize. Look, I could have defused the situation—I'm pretty good at that. I've *had* to be, because Bailey stirs shit so damn easily. But I didn't try to calm things down tonight. I *wanted* to take Ashlynn on. I wanted to send a message she couldn't fail to understand. So I did. None of what happened is on you."

"It still pisses me off that she put you in that position. There won't be a repeat of it. I'll make sure of it."

"Okay," she said, though she didn't look so convinced that he could stop

Ashlynn from ... well, being Ashlynn.

"You're sure you're all right?" he asked and, yeah, okay he was just dragging things out now. He didn't want to go. Didn't want to leave her again.

"I'm certain. Night, Tate."

He fisted his hand against the drive to reach out and touch her. She wouldn't welcome his touch, and he had to get used to it. "Night, Havana."

Once she was safely inside the building, Tate crossed to Luke, Farrell, and Havana's guards. "I need to deal with Ashlynn, Eva, and Aimee. But I don't think I could do it diplomatically right now."

Luke nodded. "You're too pissed on Havana's behalf. You wouldn't be able to speak to them as their Alpha. You'd be doing it as someone who cares for the person they targeted."

"I recommend you give them tonight to sweat over it, Tate," said Farrell. "Deal with them tomorrow when your head's clearer and your cat's calmer."

Tate rolled back his shoulders. "I noticed Ashlynn glaring at Havana, but I didn't call her on it because Havana didn't seem to care, and I didn't think that things would escalate."

"Same here," said Luke. "It never even occurred to me that Ashlynn would be stupid enough to confront someone who's under your protection, let alone threaten to throw down. I think she did it in the hope that she could somehow diminish Havana in your eyes."

Looking at Tate, Deke twisted his mouth. "Ashlynn has either underestimated Havana's ... value to you, or she's *over*estimated her own value to you."

Tate mulled over that for a moment. "It's probably a little of both. So far, nothing I've said or done has convinced Ashlynn that I don't want her back. I couldn't have been clearer, but she's not listening to me. She's certain I'm just too angry to admit that I want her and that I just need time. Which makes me think she's had it in her head for a while that she and I would reconcile eventually. Her belief is too set in stone."

"I agree," said Luke. "She didn't cut contact with you when she left the pride. She tried sending you messages and letters. That tells us she never really let you go."

"Maybe convincing herself you'd one day be hers again was the only way she could get through having been rejected by both Koby *and* you—two men she thought of as mates," Farrell suggested. "You wouldn't have rejected her if she hadn't fucked up in the first place, I know, but it still must have been hard for her to take."

"Whatever the case, I'm done dealing with her shit," Tate declared. "I'll summon her, Eva, and Aimee to my house tomorrow and speak to them individually. And I'll do my best to drum into Ashlynn's brain that there'll never again be an 'us,' even if it means being cruel just to make her let it go."

"She might hightail it out of the pride again," said Isaiah.

"Can't say I'd care much if she did, despite her being one of my cats," said Tate. "She didn't just fuck with Havana tonight, although that's enough to make me furious. By disregarding that Havana is under my protection, Ashlynn disrespected *me*. And by pulling that shit in our pride's hangout and metaphorically pissing all over their doorstep, she let down our entire pride. She's either one of us, or she's not. Tomorrow, she'll have to decide how it's going to be. If she has any sense in her head, she'll come to my house with a sincere apology and a promise that there won't be a repeat of what happened tonight."

Luke pulled a face. "I'm not optimistic that she will."

Tate sighed. "No, neither am I."

CHAPTER TWELVE

Assuring everyone that she'd be back again next week, Havana said her goodbyes to the residents of the shelter, who then began to filter out of the room. Puffing out a breath, she headed to the corner of the large space, where she'd dumped her gym bag.

Dawn crossed to her, smiling. "Thanks for this, Havana. I know you've got a lot going on right now, so I really appreciate you keeping up with the classes."

"It's no problem. Like I told Madisyn and Makenna, the people here may need them now more than they ever did," said Havana, hooking the straps of her bag over her shoulder.

Dawn's smile dimmed. "I asked Keziah to join your classes and learn some self-defense techniques, but she didn't want to. Maybe if she had, maybe if I made this sort of thing compulsory—"

"Dawn, it's not your fault that she was taken."

The cougar nodded, but there was no real agreement in the act. "I'm still hoping and praying that she's found. I dread to think what could be happening to her right this very second." Her eyes teared up, which plain freaked Havana out.

"No crying. Please. I'm not good at comforting people. Plus, Corbin will be able to tell you were crying when he picks you up for your date later, and then he'll get all cranky about it."

Dawn's lips curled on one side. "He's very sweet."

Hearing a child giggle, Havana looked to see a small, redheaded little girl stroking Aspen's bearcat while clinging tight to a ratty, plush cheetah toy.

Dawn put a hand to her chest. "That's the first time I've heard Rayna laugh since she arrived here two weeks ago. She's nervous all the time; never leaves her mother's side." Dawn tipped her chin toward the woman chatting with a juvenile.

Aspen had noticed that little Rayna was a bag of nerves, so she'd shifted into her animal form in the hope of putting her at ease. Aspen might be an ultra badass, but she was a softie when it came to kids.

"I must admit, I wasn't so sure the bearcat would let Rayna close," Dawn added. "They generally don't like to be touched."

"Bearcats would never harm a child," said Havana. "But adults? They're fair game."

"Then let's hope those two do the smart thing and steer clear of her." Dawn gestured at the young men creeping closer to the bearcat, looking at her like she was the most adorable thing they'd ever seen.

Havana almost rolled her eyes. People always wore that look whenever they got a glimpse of the bearcat. Apart from Tate. But then, he knew from his own kind that cuteness could also mean viciousness.

"I take it Aspen insisted on coming along to watch over you."

Havana nodded. "Yep."

"I'm surprised Bailey didn't come with you as well."

"She tried. I said that only *one* could come with me, and I allowed it purely to put both their minds at rest. So Bailey is back at the center. I'm not an easy target, and I have two pallas cats following me everywhere to guard me. They're parked in the lot outside."

Havana had wondered if they'd complain about guarding her since she'd tumbled all over their pride mate's shit last night at the Tavern. But they either didn't care or simply wouldn't dream of questioning Tate's orders.

"It brings Corbin comfort to know that you're so closely watched," said Dawn. "He's worried about you. We all are."

"*Ow!*"

Havana sighed on seeing that one of the males who'd been edging toward the bearcat now had the animal literally hanging from his hand, her teeth clamped around it. Havana gave her a sharp look. "Let him go. Now."

The bearcat shot her a disgruntled look but did as asked. She then climbed Havana's body as if she were a damn tree.

The guy gaped down at the bleeding puncture wounds on his hand and then stared wide-eyed at the bearcat now clinging to Havana's shoulders. "She mangled my hand."

Havana snorted. "Of course she did. She's a bearcat. You touched her."

"Really, Sean, you should have known better," said Dawn, shaking her head.

He shrugged, sheepish. "She's just so cute and sweet. Or, at least, I *thought* she was sweet."

Giggling, Rayna reached up and petted the bearcat's foot. "I have to go now. My momma's calling me. Bye!" She used her plush toy's paw to wave and then skipped away.

Havana glanced over her shoulder at the bearcat. "Shift. We gotta go."

In no time at all, Aspen was back in her human form and fully dressed.

"Thanks again for coming," said Dawn, patting Havana's arm. "And Aspen, thanks for allowing Rayna to play with your animal."

"Not a problem," said Aspen.

Havana raised a brow at the cougar. "Same time next week?"

Dawn smiled. "That would be great."

Outside the shelter, Havana squinted as the harsh glare of the sunlight stung her eyes.

"Damn, it's hot," said Aspen. "I think I might go sit on our rooftop when we get home and just lounge in the sun. You up for it?"

"Sure, why not?"

Walking through the parking lot, Havana waved at the two pallas cats who were leaning against their car. They simply nodded in response.

Just then, Aspen's phone began to ring. She checked her phone screen, grimaced slightly, and then pocketed her cell without answering it.

"Who's that?" asked Havana.

"Camden."

"You're not going to take the call?"

"Not when he's only gonna yell at me again for not telling him that Randy got in my face at the center."

"You had to know that *someone* would tell him. I mean, he *works* at the center."

"I was fine with him knowing, but I wasn't going to be the one who tattled. I don't want to come between him and his partners, even if I don't like said partners."

"I guess I can understand that." Knowing her friend wouldn't want to talk about it further, Havana said, "I'm thinking of cooking spaghetti and meatballs tonight."

Aspen's brows lifted slightly. "Ooh, can I wangle myself an invite?"

"I don't see why not, so long as your bearcat and Bailey's mamba don't—" She cut off as the pallas cats yelled something from the other side of the lot while hurrying toward her. Havana tensed, realizing Deke was shouting "Get down!" and Isaiah was bellowing "Duck!"

She was about to drop when a crack of thunder split the air. She flinched as a red-hot impact sank into her throat, causing an *explosion* of pain.

Time seemed to slow down as Havana swayed. She smelled blood. Felt warm liquid on her neck. Would have reached up to prod the liquid if her limbs didn't suddenly feel like noodles.

There were more cracks of thunder. Hot pain punched into her stomach, and then into her shoulder. *Fuck.* A gray blur gathered around the edges of her vision, and her devil went insane.

Just as Havana's knees gave out, she heard Aspen's panicked curse, the screeching of tires, and the pounding of heavy footsteps.

Havana slumped to the ground, choking on ... something.

"Stay awake, Havana!" screeched Aspen. "Stay a-fucking-wake!"

She couldn't. She could feel herself fading. She could feel a strange darkness creeping over her until there was just ... nothing.

Seated at his dining table, Tate glared at the female opposite him. Ashlynn sat with her back straight, her body rigid, and her eyes hard as stone. Probably because he'd just calmly but coldly reamed her up first one side then the other—and he'd done it in front of both Luke and Farrell, hence the embarrassed flush on her cheeks.

Still furious about the scene at the Tavern last night, Tate had already called in first Eva and then Aimee—both of whom had apologized before he spoke a single word—to give them a verbal smackdown. There'd been no instant apology from Ashlynn. She'd strolled into the room with her chin up and her shoulders squared.

"I can't believe you're pissed at *me* for what happened," she said.

"You instigated the whole thing. It was bad enough that you had so little respect for the pride as to start a fight in our own damn hangout. That the person you targeted was under my protection only made it worse. It meant she should have also been under *your* protection."

"She struck first," Ashlynn defended.

"Yeah, devils tend to do that. You knew that when you provoked her," Tate accused. "You were counting on it so that she'd later get the blame for whatever occurred."

Generally, pallas cats didn't pick fights. They didn't bother you so long as you didn't bother them. So it might have been easy for people to believe that Havana *had* been the one to start that shit if Ashlynn hadn't spent hours shooting her challenging glares.

"You were looking for a fight," Tate added. "And when Havana didn't give you one, you took it to the next level and confronted her."

"No, I just wanted to chat with her. That's all. I heard about the Gideon situation, I reassured her that our pride would take care of it and that you'd take it seriously. If I'd been her, I'd have wanted that reassurance. I was being *nice*."

Tate exchanged a look of disbelief with Luke, who was leaning against the countertop shaking his head. Beside the Beta, Farrell rolled his eyes.

"When I introduced myself, I could tell by the look on her face that she'd heard of me." Ashlynn's eyes briefly lowered. "I guessed she'd heard some highly negative things, which she confirmed. We talked a little about you. She's bitter that you don't care for her. She blamed me for you being so closed off *and* for you ending the fling, claiming it wouldn't have happened if I hadn't come home. She thinks you got rid of her for me. She said a lot of snarky things and then challenged me to a fight. I tried to reason with her, but she wouldn't listen. I'm sorry that this happened at the Tavern, but I can't apologize for not backing down. I'm not a person who'd walk away from a challenge."

"Maybe you should have made an exception last night, because she quite clearly overpowered you."

Ashlynn jerked her chin up. "She only won the fight because, hesitant to have a brawl in my pride's hangout, I didn't use my full strength."

Tate snorted. "It wasn't a fight. She didn't even injure you. She *played* with you. And then she topped it all off by humiliating you while you were unconscious." His cat still thought the whole thing was fucking awesome. Tate agreed.

The twin flags of red staining Ashlynn's cheeks darkened. "All I did was try to *talk* to her. I don't even know how things deteriorated so fast."

"Maybe she didn't appreciate you trying to get Tate's attention by embarrassing her," suggested Luke. "It seems clear to me that you wanted to weaken her in his eyes so that he'd lose interest in her, only it didn't work out that way."

"I know you're angry with me for hurting your brother in the past, Luke, but I think it's unfair of you to side with a female who isn't even one of us," said Ashlynn, prim and haughty. She looked at Tate. "You're not even giving me the benefit of the doubt. You're just pinning the blame on me."

"Because you *are* to blame," Tate stated. "Almost every word you've spoken here was a lie."

"It was not! I'm telling you, *she* wanted the confrontation. She was sure you'd dumped her for me, and she resented me for it."

Tate leaned forward. "Havana would have no reason to blame you for my ending the fling, because I *didn't* end it. She did."

Ashlynn's face went slack. She rallied fast. "That's not what she said when—"

"Let me be very clear," said Tate, his voice dripping with frost. "I don't care how embarrassed you are by how last night ended for you. You will not retaliate. You will not contact her—not even to apologize. I don't want you talking to her. *She* won't want you talking to her. She doesn't exist for you. Understand me?"

Ashlynn's eyes narrowed to slits, and her upper lip curled back. "If she matters so much to you, why haven't you let her past those walls of yours? Huh? Tell me that."

His cat bristled, and Tate straightened in his seat. "I let you return to our pride, but I can just as easily throw you back out. I don't owe you any explanations for *anything*. Very few people have earned the right to question my choices—you're not one of them. All you are to me is a member of my pride. But the behavior you displayed last night makes me wonder if you truly consider yourself one of us."

She frowned. "Of course I consider myself a member."

"Really? What you did wasn't fair or loyal to your pride mates. You let them down. You let yourself down. You sparked conflict and violence in the place we go to wind down; a place we hold celebrations and so is, therefore, special to many. You didn't care that your behavior could taint that. You cheapened yourself in their eyes and mine.

"Maybe being alone for three years made you forget how being part of a pride works. We support each other. Protect each other. Respect each other. We work together as a community of sorts. If you don't feel that you can do that, you are free to leave."

"You wouldn't care if I left?" she asked, her voice small. "You wouldn't care if I was alone again?"

"Not in the way you want me to. I don't say that to be cruel. I say it because you're not hearing me when I say *I don't want you*. Nothing you could say or do would change that. Nothing. Forget about pointlessly trying to win me back. Concentrate on being a productive member of the pride. The alternative? You leave. If you need time to think about what you want, take it. In the meantime, keep your head down if you know what's good for you. Now get the fuck out of here, and do not bother Havana Ramos again in any way, shape, or form."

Ashlynn's eyes sparkled like chips of broken glass. "Yes, Alpha," she said through gritted teeth.

Tate sharply tipped his chin toward the door.

She pushed to her feet and stalked out of the room with her head held high. Moments later, he heard the front door slam shut.

Farrell took a seat at the table. "That girl has some nerve. I think you got through to her, though. She heard you loud and clear when you said you're not interested in rekindling your relationship with her."

"Agreed," said Luke. "But I wouldn't be surprised if she later managed to convince herself that you only said these things in anger. She always seemed so confident that she could change your mind, though I have no clue why."

Tate sighed. "It was always her biggest weakness."

"What?" asked Luke.

"She gets tunnel vision when she wants something—doesn't see anything but the end goal, so she doesn't properly see the other aspects of the situation." It was no doubt why she'd tried pursuing a grieving Koby. "She doesn't acknowledge the hurdles, which means she never manages to overcome them and just doesn't know when to stop."

"If she doesn't learn to get past that, she won't make a good Alpha for whatever pride she one day leads," said Luke. "It sure as shit won't be ours."

"Too right it won't." Tate's phone began to chime. He fished it out of his pocket and saw that the caller was Deke. Tate answered, "Yeah?"

"Stay calm," said Deke. "Havana's fine, but … she was shot outside the shelter just now."

Tate's entire body went tight as shock slammed into him. His mind went utterly blank, as if unable to fully process what he'd heard. "What?"

"It was a drive-by shooting," Deke went on. "We got her inside the shelter. There's a healer here who fixed her up."

Tate fisted his hand as panic and fury set in. He let out a stream of vicious curses. "Put her on the phone," he ordered, needing to hear her voice.

"I can't, man. She's out."

Tate tightened his grip on the cell. "You said she was *okay*."

"She is, but she took three bullets—one to the stomach, one to the shoulder, and one to the throat. She lost a lot of blood. She's sleeping it off in Dawn's office."

Three bullets. Tate squeezed his eyes shut and abruptly pushed out of his chair, making it skid backwards. "*Fuck.*" She could have died. Probably would have choked on her own damn blood if a healer hadn't been so close. It was a minor miracle that she was alive.

"What's going on?" asked Luke.

Tate didn't answer. Didn't want to say aloud what he'd heard. Didn't know if he could speak the words without losing it.

His cat hissed and clawed at him, wanting him to move, move, move and *get to her*. And the internal battle that Tate had been waging against the urge to brand her just … ignited. It became a rampant storm inside him that whirled and whirled and whirled. It then abruptly swept outward, smashing his mental shields into nothing. Like that, a primal knowledge hit him so hard it almost made his knees give out.

He took a shuddering breath as several emotions rose up out of nowhere and thundered through him. Satisfaction. Certainty. Pride. Possessiveness. For months, he'd subconsciously prevented that primal knowledge from sinking in. Right then, he didn't fight it. He let it take hold. Let himself accept it. Havana Ramos was his true mate.

He understood now why he'd felt so driven to mark her. He'd been right in thinking that it hadn't been about claiming her. No, not even his subconscious would urge him to force a claiming bite on her. It was something else.

He'd involuntarily buried the realization that she was his true mate, keeping it trapped behind a mental wall. But the day she'd told him it was time that they went their own way, that wall had fractured. And the knowledge that she was his had been battering at the wall ever since—driving him to keep her close by whatever means necessary, even if it meant forcing his brand on her.

Not even the joy he felt at accepting the truth could push the anger from his system. His mate had been shot and, worse, he hadn't been there for her.

"Seriously, Tate, what's going on?" Luke persisted.

"Drive-by shooting," Tate told him, his voice guttural, surprised he could speak at all when fury clogged his airways. "Havana was shot."

"Mother of *fuck*," spat Luke.

Tate clenched his hand tighter around his cell. "Tell me you got the bastard who did it, Deke."

"Wish I could," replied the enforcer. "We were more worried about getting Havana help. The bullet that hit her throat nicked an artery. The shelter has cameras; they might have caught a decent glimpse of the shooter."

Nicked an artery.

Tate's cat hissed out a long breath. *Fuck.* He stalked out of the room, intent on reaching her. "I'll be right there. Don't leave her side, Deke. You watch her *every* fucking second, you hear me?"

"I hear you. I won't move from her side," Deke promised.

Tate rang off and pocketed his phone.

"Hold up, me and Farrell are coming with you," Luke called out.

Tate said nothing. He didn't care who came along, providing he reached her *fast*. Outside, Luke slid into the driver's seat of the SUV while Farrell rode shotgun. Eager to get to his mate, Tate would have insisted on driving if he was in a fit state to do so. He was close to losing his shit, and having his cat turn into a ball of fury inside him wasn't helping. So he simply hopped into the rear passenger seat and snapped out, "Drive."

"I know anger is riding you but lock it down," said Luke. "She's fine."

Tate gritted his teeth, his fists clenched. "She took three bullets."

"But she survived."

That wasn't the fucking point, because … "*She took three bullets.*" And he hadn't been there. Hadn't been able to help her. She could have died.

"And you'll make sure whoever is responsible pays for that. Take a breath, lock down the anger, and tell your cat to calm his ass down. You have to have a clear head for this, Tate. That's what she needs from you right now."

She'd needed a lot of things from Tate, but he'd given her none of them. He'd let her down and, in doing so, hurt her. He wouldn't do that again.

D rifting in that state that wasn't quite "awake" yet wasn't quite "asleep," Havana frowned when her inner devil nudged her, pushing her to snap out of it. Havana didn't want to. She was so tired, and her body just felt so heavy. Plus, it was hard to think past the thick fog in her mind.

A muffled cacophony of voices seemed very far away. Still, she could decipher a few of them. Bailey. Aspen. Dawn. Corbin. Tate.

Tate. His rumbly voice pierced right through the fog and caused her system to jumpstart—just his presence could do that.

She mentally scrambled, trying to work out why her devil was in a snit and why she felt so *drained*.

Her eyes weakly fluttered open. The world was on a tilt. Without lifting her head, she took in the office desk, the black leather chair, the framed pictures on the wall. She knew this room. It was Dawn's office. And Havana was currently lying on Dawn's sofa, she realized.

"It *had* to have been Gideon," said Aspen, her voice coming from Havana's left. "I'm not saying he pulled the trigger, I'm just saying he was behind this."

"Definitely," agreed Bailey, who seemed to be sitting on Havana's right. "There's no one else who'd target her this way."

"She's awake," said Tate.

A pair of jean-clad legs entered Havana's line of sight. Then Tate crouched in front of her and brushed her hair away from her face. Even though her body had all the enthusiasm of a wilting plant, her pulse nonetheless jumped.

"Hey," he said, his voice surprisingly soft given that his inky blue eyes were two swirling storms of anger. There was something … different about the way he looked at her. His gaze was more intense than ever before. More piercing. More intimate. But she couldn't quite reason it out.

"You're fine," he went on, lightly dancing his fingertips over her scalp. "Bullets are gone. Your wounds are healed."

Havana touched her throat. *The cracks of thunder. The hot punches of pain.* "I was shot?"

He nodded, his jaw tight. "It was a drive-by—the bastards were there and gone in an instant. Aspen and my enforcers carried you in here. A resident healed you, thank Christ."

Havana did a slow blink, struggling to absorb Tate's words. "A drive-by? Really?"

He nodded, his eyes blazing. "You were shot in the throat, shoulder, and stomach." The words sounded torn out of him.

Motherfucker. She ground her teeth, wanting nothing more than to pound Gideon into the goddamn ground because, seriously, who else would be behind this?

"You feel okay?" asked Bailey.

Havana sluggishly sat upright. "Just wiped. And monumentally pissed." She didn't need anyone to tell her she was lucky to be alive. That she'd come *so close* to dying just like that … it was a head wrecker.

Aspen scooted closer to her. "It all happened so fast I almost couldn't process it. You scared the *shit* out of me when you blacked out."

Havana frowned. "You have blood on you. They shot you, too?"

"No, genius, the blood's yours. It's all over you as well."

Havana looked down. Ugh. Her tee did in fact boast huge crimson red stains. How ultra-special. It wasn't the first time she'd taken a bullet, thanks to her old job, but she'd never been shot in the throat before. She hadn't ever needed the aid of a healer to save her life.

A muscle in Tate's cheek flexed as he skimmed his fingertips over her throat. "The bullet hit an artery." The alpha vibes radiating from him were almost electric with fury. Every man there appeared just as pissed. The tension in the air was unbearably thick. It was too much angry-dominant-male in one space, really.

"Aspen and the boys were so frantic to get you to safety that they rightfully didn't pursue the car," Tate went on, taking Havana's hands in his. "But we're about to watch the video feed from the outdoor cameras. Dawn's accessing it on her laptop now."

"It's almost ready to view." Dawn gave her a tremulous smile, standing at the edge of her desk, her fingers poised above the keys of her laptop. "I'm so glad you're okay, hon. I have to admit, you gave me quite a scare."

"With any luck, we'll see the face of whoever fired the gun," Tate added. "Then I can kill him."

"I kind of want in on that." Havana had plans to make the asshole suffer.

"Yeah, I thought you might," said Tate.

"We *all* want in on it," Aspen chimed in. "Even Corbin, who's scowling at you like you peed all over his shoes."

"You took ten years off my life, Havana," Corbin grumbled, as if she'd jumped into the line of fire for the sheer fun of it. "Bailey near lost her damn mind, so it's a wonder she drove us both here without wrapping the car around a freaking tree."

Bailey made a *pfft* sound. "Says the man who kept nagging, 'Can't you go any faster?'"

"And we're ready," said Dawn, setting the laptop on the coffee table, the screen facing the sofa. "I rewound the footage to the time Havana left the building, and I've brought up footage from both camera one, which is aimed at the street, and also camera four, which points at the parking lot. There's no audio, by the way."

Everyone gathered close to watch the two perspectives playing. The camera system was evidently good quality. The view wasn't in the slightest bit grainy as a black Charger with blacked-out windows drove down the street, slowing as it reached the shelter. The front passenger window lowered, and the barrel of a gun poked out of it.

Havana's stomach pitched as she glanced to camera four's view and saw her body jolt. She swayed and then dropped to her knees while the car sped away. Watching the screen, her devil let out an eerie growl.

Beside her, Tate bit out a harsh curse. "Replay the footage from camera one, Dawn. This time, zoom in on the Charger. I want the license plate number, and I want a clear image of that fucker's face. The angle's just right. I caught a quick glimpse of him just now."

Havana joined the others in leaning forward as the footage replayed. Dawn paused it and zoomed in, allowing them to read the license plate. Then she zoomed in even more, and Havana found herself looking right at her motherfucking shooter. Well, sort of. He was wearing a balaclava, but she could see those piercing, ice-blue eyes clear as day.

"He just *had* to cover his face, didn't he?" grumbled Luke. "I can't see the driver from that angle."

"He probably wore a balaclava too," said Farrell.

Aspen bit her lip. "Although it's not the same car that was at the motel, it could be the same shooter. Maybe even the same driver. They're either the jaguars or lone shifters, since Gideon likes to use loners to do his dirty work."

"I don't think they're Gideon's jaguars," said Havana. "I think they're cheetahs."

Everyone glanced at her.

"Why cheetahs?" asked Tate. "You think you recognize the shooter?"

"No, but … well, it's weird. This morning, I watched a clip on the news about a full-blooded cheetah who attacked a zookeeper. Later on, I saw a guy wearing a cap that had a cheetah's head on it. And then I met a little girl here today who has a plush cheetah toy."

Bailey nodded. "Then our boy has gotta be a cheetah."

Tate raised a hand, his gaze on Havana. "You're honestly basing your belief that the shooter's a cheetah on the simple fact that, three times today, a cheetah somehow featured in it?"

"Well it makes sense," said Havana.

Aspen hummed. "I'd have to agree."

Tate gave a quick shake of his head. "Right. Well, whatever."

Havana looked at Dawn. "I'd really like to thank the person who saved my life today."

"I'll take you to her." Dawn worried her lower lip. "I shouldn't have asked you to keep teaching the classes."

"Don't take on the weight of this," said Havana. "If they hadn't targeted me outside here, they'd have done it somewhere else, and there might not have been a healer close by like there was today."

"She's right," Corbin told the cougar. "The blame's not yours."

"Havana, you need to be careful from here on out," said Bailey. "Whoever was in that Charger either followed you here or knew where you'd be."

"No one followed her," Deke asserted, speaking for the first time. "We'd have clocked them."

"Then someone knows my routine," said Havana, her stomach churning.

"Now's the time to change it," Tate told her. "Take a different route to and from work. Switch up your schedule. And don't go too far from home."

"I'd already planned to take those measures," said Havana. Although it would gall her to restrict herself, she knew it was best to stay close to the Olympus Pride so that she had their backup—especially since she could very well need the help of a healer again at some point; the pride had two.

"We should leave. First, I'll call River and see if he can find out who that Charger is registered to," said Tate, referring to his pride mate who was also a police officer. "It might take him a little time, because he hasn't started his shift at the station yet."

Havana pushed to her feet. "While you make your call, I'm going to thank the woman who saved my life."

Afterward, they all exited the building. As Bailey hurried to her car with Corbin, Tate whispered something to Luke and Farrell, who then said their goodbyes and crossed to an SUV. Tate and Aspen stayed exceptionally close to Havana as she made a beeline for her car.

She swallowed on noticing the bloodstain on the ground. *Her* blood. She also noticed that Tate snarled at it, clenching his jaw so hard it had to ache.

"I'll drive," he declared. "I don't want you girls alone."

Havana frowned. "Shouldn't you be with your bodyguards?"

"They're going to drive in front of us. Deke and Isaiah will cover our rear."

"There's no need to—"

"Give me peace of mind. I can't stop seeing the image of you collapsing to your knees with three fucking bullets in your body," he said, looking sincerely tortured. "I need to be with you right now."

Havana told herself to not be moved by his fear for her but, yeah, it didn't work.

"Oh, take pity on him and hand him the keys," said Aspen, sliding into the rear of the vehicle.

Too tired to argue with him *and* uncomfortable with standing out in the open after having been shot, Havana tossed him the keys. "All right. Have at it."

His face went soft with approval. "That's my girl." He hopped into the driver's seat.

Instead of riding shotgun, Havana slipped into the back of the car with Aspen. Maybe it was cowardly to not want to sit close to him, but whatever.

Tate was clicking on his seatbelt when his phone started to ring. He bucked up his hips, pulled his phone out of his pocket, and looked at the screen. He frowned and answered, "Yeah?" His body went absolutely rigid. He tapped the screen with his thumb, and then the sound of a voice filled the car.

"Did you get my message?"

Havana felt her eyes widen. *Gideon.*

"What message would that be?" asked Tate, his tone admirably calm given that he looked anything but.

"Don't tell me you haven't heard yet." Gideon tutted. "I suppose you'll find out soon."

"Why not just tell me about this message, since you're on the line?"

"I heard that the beautiful Miss Ramos visited a homeless shelter today."

Tate's free hand fisted. "She did."

"Have you spoken to her since then?"

"Why do you ask?"

"It's just that I heard there was a shooting in that area earlier and, well, you can never be too careful. You might want to be certain she's alive and well."

Tate glanced over his shoulder and held the phone closer to her. "Havana, Gideon wants to know if you're alive and well?"

"Oh, I'm both, thanks," she said.

Tate faced forward again. "Does that answer your question, Gideon?"

There was a long beat of silence. "I don't know who that was, but I know it wasn't Havana Ramos," said Gideon.

Tate licked his front teeth. "Now, the trouble with drive-by shootings? The guy holding the gun can't linger to make sure the deed has been done. So he misses if certain things happen. Like if the victim is taken to a healer fast enough to save their life. There'll be no one to help *you* when I get my hands on you, Gideon," Tate added, his voice deepening. "I will find out where you are. Then? Then you're dead." He rang off and hissed out a breath. "Son of a bitch called to gloat."

"That guy *so* needs to meet a truly horrific demise," said Aspen.

Tate switched on the engine. "On that we agree."

CHAPTER THIRTEEN

Gripping the steering wheel a little too hard, Tate battled to keep a lock on the rage that churned in his belly. He'd been close to finding a small element of calm, but then fucking Gideon had called and wiped it away. The only thing keeping Tate sane right then was the woman sitting in the back of the car—his mate.

He kept sneaking glances at her in the rearview mirror as he drove, *needing* to drink her in, seeking to remind himself that she was right there. Breathing. Safe.

Even pale from blood loss, she didn't look the slightest bit weak. Tired, maybe. But not delicate or fragile. Her inner strength always shined through—that light never dimmed. Even so, the need to coddle and cosset and soothe her was like a living thing inside him. He probably needed that more than she did.

He wanted to take her to his house. Wanted Havana in his lair, where he could keep a close watch over her, where she could have peace and quiet to relax. But he didn't bother to say as much, because he knew she wouldn't agree to it. She didn't yet know that things had changed for him. Plus, Aspen and Bailey would want her close for a short while—there was no way they wouldn't follow her if she went elsewhere.

His cat bared a fang at Tate, in a funk because the man wouldn't take her to their domain. The animal was an elemental creature; he had no interest in the delicacies of the situation. He wanted Havana safe, and he believed the safest place she could be was his territory. He hadn't yet shaken off the panic he'd felt on hearing she'd been hurt.

Now that Tate had faced the truth of who Havana was to him, he knew he didn't have to worry that his feline would ever withdraw from her. His cat would never give her up. Not for anything. He'd kill for her, lay down his life for her, strive to make her happy, but never let her go.

Tate realized something else, too. His cat hadn't pulled away from other females because he had commitment issues, he'd done it because he wanted only one woman—his true mate; the only female he'd ever trust to never betray him.

Tate wondered how she would react to his upcoming declaration that they were mates. She clearly hadn't sensed it, or she'd have stated it at some point. Something was blocking the frequency of the bond on her end. It might not be easy to convince her that they were true mates, but he wouldn't stop stating his case until she at least admitted he could possibly be right.

Again, he glanced at both his passengers via the rearview mirror. You would think that, given what had just happened, they'd be a wreck. Havana had almost died, and Aspen had been forced to have a front seat to the drive-by. But neither were curled up in protective postures or staring into space, lost in their thoughts. Both were sitting upright, as alert and sober as marines.

He'd expected Havana to have had at least a small freak out on hearing she'd almost died. But when she'd woken at the shelter earlier and he'd told her what happened, she hadn't paled or panicked or gone into shock. She'd taken his news with a little *too* much composure. He couldn't help but get the feeling that it wasn't the first time she'd taken a bullet.

There were many things he didn't know about Havana ... because he'd never asked. It wasn't that he'd been disinterested. She'd intrigued him from day one, and he'd had hundreds of questions on the tip of his tongue. He'd wanted to know her better. He'd wanted to know what made her tick, how she became a loner, and where she came from. Each time she'd volunteered a hint of information, it had taken everything he'd had not to ask her to elaborate. He'd held back for good reason, but it hadn't been easy.

He wouldn't have to hold back from now on. He could ask whatever he wanted to ask. He could share with her whatever she wanted to know. He'd know her better than anyone else ever would, and vice versa—that was how it was with mates.

Finally nearing his destination, Tate again looked at the females via the rearview mirror. "I'm going to pull up outside the entrance of the complex so you can both head straight inside. I don't want you standing out in the open for longer than necessary. Gideon probably won't strike again today, but it pays to be cautious. Once you're both safely inside, I'll park the car and follow you in. Got it?"

Havana locked eyes with Aspen, who briefly frowned at her. He'd swear those girls could have entire conversations with eye-contact alone.

Both females met his gaze via the mirror and nodded.

Minutes later, he waited at the curb while they exited the vehicle and disappeared into the building. Tate then whipped the car into Havana's usual parking space. Slipping out of the vehicle, he scanned his surroundings—

including every rooftop—but saw nothing untoward.

He quickly spoke with Deke and Isaiah, making it clear that Havana needed to be escorted to and from her vehicle until all the bullshit had blown over. He also then dismissed them, Luke, and Farrell, since he'd be staying with Havana tonight. She might fight Tate on it, but he'd make sure he got his way in that. He didn't add that she was his true mate, since it wouldn't be fair to do so until he'd first had the much-needed conversation with her.

After giving Vinnie a quick call to relay what had happened, Tate headed to Havana's apartment. She opened the front door, looking … harried. He heard the raised voices of Camden and Aspen, so he could hazard a guess as to what had put that look on Havana's face.

"Hey," she greeted simply. "Thanks for parking the car." Her eyes dropped to the key fob he was holding. She held out her hand, palm up.

He placed the fob in her hand while carefully pushing his way inside the apartment, forcing her to shuffle backwards. "I'm still waiting on word about the license plate number. I'll no doubt receive a call from River any minute now," he said, knowing she'd be less likely to try to throw him out if she thought that having him close was the best way to get the info fast.

"Good," she said. "I want to know who these bastards are and, more importantly, *where* they are."

Walking into the living area, Tate looked at the two squabbling shifters, not happy that such a scene was playing out right in front of a clearly fatigued Havana. She didn't need this right now. "What's going on?" he asked her.

"Well … Camden tried calling Aspen just before the drive-by. She didn't answer. He's of the opinion that if she *had*, he would have heard the shot and could have 'done something.' Which, of course, is incorrect—he was too far away to help. Nonetheless, he's furious with her. I think it just spooked him that one or more of the bullets could have hit *her*."

Aspen's gaze shifted to the ceiling. "God, Camden, will you just *let it go?*"

The tiger blinked. "Let it go?"

"It's not like you could have reached through the phone and blocked the bullets or anything," she snapped. "So what does it really matter that I didn't take your call?"

"You didn't take *any* of my calls."

"I was kind of busy trying to stop Havana from bleeding out!"

"Yeah, I get that. But you could have called me afterwards. You didn't."

"I sent you a text on my way home," she reminded him.

"Oh yeah, I remember it. '*Havana got shot. Talk later.*' That made me feel a *whole* lot better."

"Then why are you whining?"

"Woman, I was being sarcastic."

The bearcat raised her hands. "Look, I really think you need to just chill."

"Chill?" he echoed in a cold whisper. "All that blood on your tee could have been *your* blood, Aspen. Did you think of that? The bullets could have missed Havana and hit *you*."

"I would rather they had. Watching my honorary sister almost die was not fun. Are you planning to at least tell her that you're glad she's okay?"

He cast Havana an aloof sideways glance. "Well, obviously, I'm glad. She knows that already."

Havana snickered, unoffended that the only thing he was truly glad of was that the bullets hadn't hit *Aspen*. Havana was just as glad of that. "Your heartfelt concern is so warming, Camden. Now, I realize you got a scare, but you need to stop with the yelling. What happened, well, happened. There's no changing it. And you don't truly want to yell at Aspen. What you *really* want to do is give her a hug and tell her you're relieved that she's fine."

Havana turned to Tate and said, "I'm going to take a shower and pull on fresh clothes, I'm sick of smelling my own blood. If you want to head home and just text me whatever River tells you, that's fine. But if you want to wait here, there's plenty of food in the kitchen."

With that, she padded to her room, still feeling a little off, thanks to the blood loss. Inside, she closed the door. Or tried to. It met some sort of resistance, and then Tate slipped into the room. Her heart jumped. "What are you—"

"Shh, I need to hold you a second." He palmed her nape, curled his free arm around her, and buried his face in her neck.

Her eyes fell closed. God, he was so warm and solid and *there*. He wasn't just holding her. It was more like he was trying to soak up the feel of her. And, because she kind of needed this too, she rested her palms on the twin columns of his back.

She'd push him away in a minute and order him out of the room. She truly would. For now, she'd let herself have this moment.

She could *feel* that his anger hadn't yet subsided, but he'd locked it down. For her. So that she wouldn't have to deal with his fury on top of her own. There was something very warming about that.

Her devil didn't lean into him but nor did she object to his hold, despite that the animal ordinarily didn't like to be fussed over or touched when in such a foul mood.

"I've needed to do this since the second I arrived at the shelter and saw you out cold on the sofa," he said against her neck. "Watching the footage of what happened ... fuck."

Fuck indeed. It certainly hadn't been one of the highlights of her year.

"I'll never get it out of my head. Never. If there hadn't been a healer at the shelter ..." His arm tightened around her. "I thought having my enforcers follow you would be enough to keep you safe."

"They tried to warn me. They helped Aspen get me inside. I'm grateful they were there."

Pulling back, Tate stared down at her, and the lines of his face smoothed out ... as if the sight of her relaxed him somehow. "We'll get that fucker. Gideon and anyone else connected to the auction."

"I know." Because nothing else was acceptable to her or her devil. She tried stepping back, but he didn't release her. "I really need to go shower. You're welcome to wait in the kitchen or living—"

"Don't," he said, his voice low. "Don't try to send me away. You've held your shit together well, and maybe you're truly not shaken by what happened earlier. But I still don't want you to be alone right now."

In truth, Havana *was* a little shaken. Not because she'd been shot, but because she'd almost died. It had all happened so damn fast that she hadn't really processed that she'd been shot—the darkness swallowed her before she had the chance to realize that she was going to die. And it didn't help to know that danger still lurked in the shadows and could again reach for her at any moment. Still ... "I won't fall apart."

"It wouldn't make you weak if you did. And although you probably won't have an emotional crash, I'd still rather you weren't alone. I want you to know you have someone here with you. I want you to feel as safe as you possibly can."

Havana could see he meant it. He wasn't just spouting whatever might make her agree to let him stay. He was genuinely concerned and wanted to be close by. It was important to him that she didn't feel unsteady or alone. And it galled her that it touched her, just as it galled her that he *did* make her feel safe—he always had.

If he'd tried to boss her into letting him stay, she could have stood firm against it. She could have ordered him out without a qualm. But whenever this big, strong, badass Alpha male went all sweet on her ... her defenses just went *poof*. "Look, I get that—"

"No, you don't get what's happening here. Not yet. But you will once we've talked. That can wait until after you've showered."

"Once we've talked? Talked about what?"

His fingertips dug into her nape as he massaged the muscle there. "There's a lot I need to explain. A lot you need to know."

"So tell me."

"I'll lay it all out for you once you've done what you're desperate to do, which is to wash the day away. What I have to say can wait."

"Just tell me this: is it something bad?"

He traced the shell of her ear with his finger. "No, nothing bad. Things have changed for me. In a good way. I swear, I'll explain everything soon. First, shower."

Havana crushed the hope that tried to blossom in her stomach. She wasn't going to let her thoughts run away with her. She knew better than to allow that.

She also knew better than to let him hang out in her bedroom. This was not him giving her space. But she didn't want to throw him out. She wanted to hear what he had to say. If she sent him away, she'd spend the rest of the day wondering what he would have said.

Havana sighed. "All right. Wait here." She kicked off her shoes and padded into the en suite bathroom ... and realized he was following her.

She turned, about to order him out. But the words got trapped in her throat when he whipped off his shirt. *Damn*, the guy had muscle to burn. And, Jesus, those abs were just perfection. Then there was the spectacularly defined V of his hips ...

He was far hotter than any man had a right to be. She didn't think the sheer impact of all that deliciousness would ever ease up. Not ever.

She was so busy ogling him that she didn't snap out of it until he gathered the edges of her stained tee. She gripped his arms, thinking it would *not* be good for them to be naked together. "Wait, you—"

"I'm not going to try to fuck you. I just want to take care of you. Let me," he said, his voice low—an order couched as a request. He slowly peeled off her tee and dropped it on the floor. And although she told herself she should put a stop to this, she didn't protest when he removed the rest of her clothes, or when he finished undressing. Nor did she protest when he herded her into the shower, soaped her down, and washed her hair.

He was so careful with her. Tender, even. Each touch was so soothing and reverent it made her throat burn.

Once they were out of the shower, he looped a towel around his waist and then wrapped another around Havana. He gently patted her dry with the soft, plush towel. There was nothing sensual or provocative about it, but her hormones were still a hot mess. Knowing, *feeling*, he was hard only made her so much more *aware* of his every touch, his every breath, his every move.

When he ushered her into the bedroom, she expected him to try his luck getting her into bed—which would have gotten him booted out of the room. He didn't try anything, though. He pulled on his clothes while she dragged on underwear, a racerback tank, and yoga pants. He then sat her between his thighs on the end of the bed and carefully brushed the tangles out of her wet hair. It was ... nice. Relaxing. Intimate. And utterly out of character for him.

They'd showered together before, but he'd never ... ministered to her like that. Never made her the center of his entire focus as he washed and dried her. Her devil kind of liked it, but the ever-moody animal still gave him the stink eye just because.

Placing her brush on the bed, he snaked his arms around her waist and tucked his chin in the crook of her neck. "You good?"

"I'm good."

"Hungry?"

A little, but ... "You said there are things you need to explain to me."

"Right." He lifted her, spun her to face him, and set her on his lap to straddle him—all of which he did with a casual strength that made her toes curl. He smoothed his hand up her arm, over the curve of her shoulder, and up to her neck. "Could have lost you today. You're thinking you're not mine *to* lose." Still cupping her neck, he tugged her face closer to his. "You're wrong."

Tensing, Havana frowned. "What?"

"When I heard you'd been shot, it rocked me. Sent my inner world fucking spiraling. My emotions were all over the place, and my mind was a mess. Then my mental shields came crashing down, and I had to admit to myself what I'd been consciously unable to face until now. You're my mate, Havana."

She did a slow blink, unsure she'd heard him right. "You're … I don't … Wait, what?"

He stroked his hand over her hair. "You're my mate. My true mate. My everything."

She tilted her head, studying him closely. "You don't *look* high."

His mouth twitched. "That would be because I'm not."

"Tate, you aren't thinking clearly. Maybe this whole drive-by thing sent your overprotective nature into overdrive—"

"Yeah, it did. I haven't felt rage like that in a long time. I forgot how much it chokes you. How it squeezes your chest and rips at your insides. It fucked with my head for a while. I might have found some calm, but I'm feeling pretty hyper-protective right now."

"And when that wears off—"

"I'll still be telling you that I *know* we're mates," he finished.

Her heart beating like crazy, Havana shook her head. "You're not thinking clearly. You're … I don't know, I don't get why you'd think we're mates." And yet, the words felt … *right*, somehow.

"I don't think it, I know it." Tate smoothed a hand up her back. He could understand why she was confused and conflicted, but for him, it was the opposite. He'd been restless for days, but he felt calmer now that he'd faced the truth. Everything seemed a lot clearer when she was there. Like she eased the chaos in his mind. "I told you my mother was killed by a rogue shifter, right?"

She double-blinked. "Yes."

"He went rogue because he lost his true mate. And when I watched my dad almost waste away right in front of me because he lost his own, I couldn't help but ask myself if true-mate bonds were worth the pain and destruction they cause when they snap. Then, after the clusterfuck with Ashlynn, I was in no rush to try imprinting again."

"You loved her," said Havana, her voice quiet.

"I thought I did back then. I thought we had a future. I was wrong on both counts. Just as I was wrong to believe she loved me. She couldn't have, considering all the promises she made meant nothing. Feeling the imprint threads snap ... It was a nightmare. Waves of pain or strong emotions would strike me at random times. There were headaches and short periods of depression. It was like being on an emotional seesaw.

"In sum, all my issues about mating blocked the frequency of our bond."

"And now, just like that, you're no longer so averse to finding your mate?" she asked, clearly skeptical.

"It was the bond I was reluctant to accept, not you. Never you. Once I realized that you're mine, my hang ups just lost their power. Because I would rather have you and take the chance that it could all go wrong than give you up again—I don't have it in me to do it a second time."

Havana felt those words worm their way inside her and burrow deep. When he'd said he wanted to talk, she hadn't imagined he'd claim they were mates. She didn't feel the tug of the mating bond. And although that didn't mean he was wrong, it also made her reluctant to believe he was right, despite his claim seeming to settle something inside her.

"I wish it hadn't taken you getting shot to open my eyes. What happened today ... the thought that I'd fucked around, wasted time, and could have lost you before I'd even had the chance to claim you ... it was the kick in the gut I needed but wish I hadn't had, because I hate that you almost died." He snaked his arms around her. "I failed you by letting my issues jam our bond. I won't let you down like that again."

She swallowed. "How is your cat feeling about all this?"

"He's on the same page as me. He wants no one but you. Before, I couldn't have guaranteed he'd always feel that way, which was why I gave you up. But now that I know you and I are mates, I can tell you for certain he'll never let you go." His arms contracted around her. "And neither will I."

They both stilled when his cell began to ring.

Tate fished it out of his pocket. "I need to take this," he told her. He swiped his thumb over the screen and said, "Tell me you have good news, River." His eyes went hard, and his jaw clenched. "Shit. ... Yeah ... All right, gotta go ... Later." He rang off.

"It wasn't good news," she guessed.

"No, it wasn't. The license plate number didn't match the vehicle. I don't know if the driver or shooter stole the plate, but it didn't belong to the Charger."

She groaned, exasperated. "Would it really be too much to ask that the universe send *dumb* criminals our way who struggle to cover their tracks?"

"I'd rather no criminals were sent our way." Tate brushed her bangs out of her face. "The bastards are gonna pay, Havana. No one harms what's mine and lives."

There was that "mine" word again. There was so much feeling in it, so much conviction. And she'd be lying if she said that she didn't like hearing him say it. But she had to be honest with him, even knowing it might slice at his ego. "Tate, I don't say this to hurt you, but … I don't feel the pull of the bond, I'm sorry." She thought he'd frown or scowl or curse. Instead, his expression softened.

"I already know that, baby. I can't exactly judge you for that—I didn't feel it myself until a few hours ago. I'm a lot of things, Havana, but I'm not delusional. I *know* you're mine. Every cell of my body is screaming it at me. Do you think I'd lie about that?"

"No. I just … I don't know, it's hard to process what you're saying." She felt blindsided, and her thoughts were all jumbled.

"What does your devil think?"

"She's doing a lot of haughty sniffing—it's kind of her thing. When I ended our fling, she thought you'd protest and offer me more. But you let me go, and she sort of slammed a mental door on you."

His eyes sharpened. "Ah, I see. Then I need to make her re-open it. I need to win back her trust and prove myself to her." He slid his hands into her wet hair. "She probably feels a little betrayed that I was once open to imprinting on another female. Do you?"

It *hurt*, but it had happened long before Havana walked into his life, so he hadn't exactly betrayed her. But she realized then that a small elemental part of her *did* actually feel betrayed. Which made no sense. Unless he was right. "You truly, honestly, definitely believe that we're mates?"

"With everything in me." He dabbed a feather-light kiss on her mouth. "I wouldn't say it if I wasn't absolutely certain. It's okay that you're not so sure—I'm sure enough for both of us. That I promise you."

Looking into his eyes and hearing the utter sincerity in his voice, it was impossible not to believe him. Did that mean he was right in his belief? No. But he certainly thought he was. And, given the almost primal way her entire being seemed to respond to his assertion, she was starting to think that just maybe he had reason to be so certain.

"I almost marked you that day you ended the fling, you know. I could feel you slipping away from me, and I hated it. The urge to bite you just bubbled up. It hasn't left me. Look, I'm not declaring that I need to claim you straight off. I don't want to claim you until you know all the way down to your soul that I'm yours. Otherwise, it wouldn't mean what it *should* mean to you. If you and your devil need time to see the truth, I'll give it to you. I can be patient. But I don't plan to leave your side much—you should know that now. Don't ask me to give you space. That I can't do. It would go against everything in me. Especially right now, while danger is shadowing you. So don't ask that of me, baby. I'll give you anything but that." He breezed his fingertip over her lower lip and then dropped his hand. "Tell me something. If you discovered I was right and that we're mates, would you be disappointed?"

She shook her head. "No. It's not that I don't *want* us to be mates. I just can't sense the bond."

"I suspect the mental door your devil closed is partly responsible for that. You must have a few issues of your own or you might have sensed the bond before she closed that door. We'll work out whatever's blocking the frequency in time. For now, we build on what we have. I'll do my best to win over your devil."

His latter comment made her devil narrow her eyes, but she didn't bark or chuff or put up a protest. Still, she clearly wouldn't make it easy for him. She'd make him work for it. Which she surely wouldn't bother to do if she didn't recognize him as *hers*.

"At least admit it's possible that we're mates, Havana."

She pulled in a deep breath. "It's possible." Why else would his assertion feel *right*? Why else would it settle and satisfy some elemental part of her?

Plenty of other things pointed to it being true—their elemental attraction, how hard it had been for her to walk away from him, how he had a way of making her feel safe, how strongly her devil had reacted to his failure to offer her more. And then there was the sense of betrayal that sat in the pit of her stomach at the knowledge that he'd almost mated with another.

"More than possible," she added. "Probable, even."

"Probable?" he echoed, a note of hope in his voice.

"Yes. I mean, I found it hard to believe initially—you threw me off-guard, and I already had so much going on in my head. But the more I think about it, the more it makes sense. And when I hear you say it, it … I don't know, it just calms me in some way. Plus, my devil isn't protesting, which is a telling point. I just can't say it with all certainty, because I don't feel the presence of the bond."

"Yet," he said. "You will in time. For now, it's enough that you're fully open to the idea." He paused. "You'll give me the chance to earn your devil's trust? You'll let us build on what we have?"

Havana sank her teeth into her lower lip. It was hard to reach for something you wanted so much when you didn't feel sure to your bones that it was yours *to* reach for. But every instinct she had insisted he *was* hers, and her gut had never led her wrong before. She didn't think it was leading her wrong now either. "I can agree to that."

Tate studied her face for a long moment. One corner of his mouth lifted, and he hugged her tight. "If we hadn't been true mates, I still would have come to you at some point and offered you more. I couldn't have made you any promises, but I'd have agreed to try 'more' and see where it went. You probably would have decided not to take a chance on my cat, given his history of withdrawing from women. But I'd have asked anyway."

"I would have taken the chance." If for no other reason than that she'd have always wondered what could have been if she hadn't.

His inky blue eyes warmed. "Yeah?"

She gave a slow nod. "Yeah."

"Even knowing we could have crashed and burned?"

"You and your cat are worth the risk."

CHAPTER FOURTEEN

You and your cat are worth the risk.

Framing her face with his hands, Tate pulled her closer and pressed his forehead to hers. "Baby." Fuck, she was killing him. *Killing* him.

He lowered his mouth to hers, intending to only feather his lips against her own in a soft, barely-there kiss. But the moment their lips met, his entire system seemed to jolt. A shudder went through him, and there was no way to stop himself from taking that mouth he'd missed.

He swept his tongue inside and groaned. *God, that fucking taste.* It had always acted as his own personal aphrodisiac, just like her scent … and now he knew why.

Tate growled low in his throat and kissed her harder. They both caught fire in an instant. Greedy and frantic, they moaned, clutched, squeezed, grinded.

The drugging scent of her need fueled the fire that blazed within him and all but inebriated his cat. Naked. Tate needed her naked. Needed her wet and ready to take him, because he *had* to be inside her.

He whipped off her tank with a snarl. "The bra. Take it off." Fisting the back of his tee, he yanked it over his head and tossed it on the floor. He let her stand long enough to shove down her panties and yoga pants. Then he yanked her back on his lap and once again ravaged her mouth.

This wasn't about battling for dominance. This wasn't a pitting of wills. This was about sealing a deal while reconnecting on the most basic level.

Banding his arm around her, he lifted her onto her knees and slid one finger inside her. Hot and slick, those tight inner muscles squeezed his finger. "Ride it."

Ignoring how her pussy contracted at the sheer authority in his voice, Havana fucked herself on his finger, not possessing a single qualm about taking exactly what she needed. The whole time, he whispered encouragements and left suckling little kisses all over her neck. And when he curved that thick finger just right, she almost burst out of her skin.

With a desperate moan, she dropped her hands to his waist and snapped open his fly, letting his rock-hard dick bound free. "Want you in me."

He didn't make her wait. He lifted her, positioned her just right, and planted her on his cock.

She froze, her breath catching in her throat with the pleasure/pain of being abruptly stuffed full. "Holy shit," she rasped.

His eyes glittering, he raised her again and then roughly impaled her on his dick once more. "Fuck me, baby." He hissed as she began to ride him hard. "Yeah, that's it, use my cock to get yourself off."

It wouldn't take long for her to come. A delicious tension was already coiling low in her stomach, making her desperate for more, rougher, faster.

Tate growled as she started slamming herself even harder on his dick. He filled his hands with her breasts, wanting to feel the round, firm mounds bounce in his grip. She really did have phenomenal tits. He wanted to bite them. Fuck them. Come all over them.

He pinched her nipple just right. She arched, and her head fell back. Not having that, Tate fisted one hand in her hair and tugged her head back up. "No. I want your eyes on mine when you come." He also wanted to punch his hips up to meet each thrust; to drive into her until she screamed for him. But he got off big time on watching his mate take herself there, so the latter could wait.

His gut clenched when she made this distinctive, telling little moan just as her pussy warmed, tightened, and quaked around him. "Christ."

A flush swept up her body. Her eyes widened. Her breath caught. Her pussy spasmed. And then she was coming. He used his grip on her hair to keep her head up so he could watch her orgasm take her; so he could watch as her eyes went blind, her swollen lips parted, and her brow creased like the pleasure was so good it was almost painful.

"Fuck, yeah." Keeping his cock snug inside her, Tate stood, turned, and dropped the upper half of her body on the bed. Gripping her ass tight, he pounded into her, wanting to bury himself so deep inside her she'd choke on him.

"Oh God, don't stop." Havana curved her legs around him and gripped the bedsheet. Every savage thrust hit her *so deep* as he fucked her hard, his pace far faster than hers. Oh, and then he adjusted his angle, finding a decadently sensitive spot inside her. She fisted the bedsheet tighter. *Holy shit, holy shit, holy shit.*

"Again," he bit out, finding her clit with his thumb. "I want you to come for me again."

Well, he'd get what he wanted, because she was already close. And as that very adept thumb rolled, pressed, flicked, and rubbed, the pressure inside her built and built and built.

He bent over her, his glittering eyes snaring hers. "One day, I'm going to leave a permanent brand on you, so the world knows you're mine. Until then …" He sank his teeth into the crook of her neck.

She sucked in a breath as pleasure *tore* through her in violent waves, bowing her back. He closed his mouth over hers, swallowing her scream, and growled as he slammed harder, faster. Then he exploded.

Havana melted into the mattress, her body shaking, her lungs burning for air. Tate collapsed on top of her, catching his weight on his forearms. For long moments, they just stayed there like that, trying to catch their breath as he slowly glided his cock in and out of her

He kissed the stinging bite mark on her neck and hummed. "Your scent gets so much sweeter after you come. Makes my cat want to lick you all up. I'll be the one doing the licking, though—it's part of my plans for later."

She drifted her fingertips over the sleek skin of his back. "Later?"

Lifting his head, he stared down at her, his eyes languid and lazy. "Yes, later. I'm staying here tonight."

She flicked up a brow. "While I have no issue with that, I have an issue with the 'don't argue with me' tone." So did her devil, but the animal was currently too out-of-it to do more than toss him a frown. "However, as you just gave me a momentous orgasm and I'm feeling all warm and tingly, I'll let it go. It's best if you don't pull out that tone again, though, 'kay?"

His mouth quirked. "Momentous orgasm?"

"That's all you got from what I just said?"

Holding back a chuckle, Tate kissed her. He could be overbearing without giving it much thought—not to be an asshole, but because it was literally in his nature to dominate and take control. He liked that she had no issues with putting him in his place. "Funny … you like the 'don't argue with me' tone when I'm using it in bed."

She narrowed her eyes. "No, I really don't."

He smiled. "Oh, you really do. I'll prove it later." Unable to resist, he dropped his mouth to hers and nipped her lower lip. He'd mark that tonight. He'd leave an imprint of his teeth on it, just as he had on her neck.

He swept his thumb over the brand near her pulse. The bite wasn't deep, but it wouldn't heal quickly. She'd wear it for at least a day or two—something that immensely pleased both him and his cat. The feline was currently rubbing up against her, letting out a satisfied, throaty purr.

Tate gave her one last kiss and then carefully pulled his softening cock out of her. He shuffled them both further up the bed, just as he had last time he was here. Laying on his side facing her, he combed his fingers through her damp hair. "I'm pissed at myself for taking so long to consciously sense who you are to me."

"Most shifters struggle with that. *I'm* struggling with it. So don't be mad at yourself."

"Can't help it. My cat's mad at me for it as well."

She bit the inside of her cheek. "Can you be sure he won't withdraw from me at some point?"

His cat pulled a cranky face, unhappy that she'd doubt his commitment to her. "Yes, I can. What happened with Ashlynn gave him trust issues. The only woman he felt able to trust after that was his true mate—I see that now. That's why he pulled back from the others. He was looking for you. You're the only one he's willing to commit to. I'm one hundred percent certain he'll all but cleave himself to you."

She twisted her mouth. "When you first told me how angry he is with her, I thought he might still care for her; that maybe he's clinging to his anger over her betrayal to drown out other feelings he … why are you laughing?"

His shoulders shaking, Tate squeezed her neck. "My cat just jerked back in horror. Babe, trust me when I say he feels nothing for her. To my cat, she isn't worthy of him or me." Tate's eyes danced. "He *loved* watching you play with her at the Tavern."

Havana sniffed. "She had that coming."

"Oh, she did." Tate dragged his hand down her back and palmed her ass, his touch nothing short of possessive. His. She was all his. And he'd very nearly committed to another woman. He silently thanked the universe for ensuring it never came to pass. "I know it has to hurt that I almost imprinted on her. But please don't see it as I chose her over you. It wasn't like that."

"You were choosing an imprint bond over a true-mate bond, I get it. I don't *like* that you did it, but I get why. And, given what happened to your mom and how that hurt your dad, I can understand how hard it must have been for you to push past all your hang-ups about true-mate bonds to be here with me right now, so I can't really be mad at you."

She was the fucking shit. Seriously. And he'd spend his life making it up to her that he'd almost let his issues keep them apart. He pressed a soft kiss to that mouth he loved. "Thank you for understanding."

She idly danced her fingers up his chest. "So … you haven't been spending time with Ashlynn recently?"

Tate could see that she was wary of the answer. It hadn't occurred to him that she'd worry about such a thing. "Not willingly."

Her brows dipped. "What does that mean?"

He sighed. "She turned up at my house twice. The first time, she came with dinner and wine. The second time, she came dressed in only a coat and high heels—she flashed me right there on my doorstep. I turned her away both times, obviously."

Havana gaped. "She honestly turned up mostly naked?"

"Yeah." Tate tugged her closer and breathed in more of her scent. "Look, I don't want to talk anymore about her—she's not important. But I won't lie to you. I won't hold back. Not anymore. So if you want to know the rest, I'll give it to you. But be sure you want to hear it."

"I want to hear it."

Yeah, Tate had figured she would. In her shoes, he'd have wanted all the facts just the same. "She seems to have it in her head that we can get back what we had, but I can't imagine why. I told her to fuck off when she came back to me right after Koby rejected her. She tried to contact me several times while she was away from the pride. I blocked her number, and I blocked her on social media. I returned all her letters—unopened."

"I didn't realize she'd tried contacting you while living as a loner. What did she say?"

"I didn't read her messages or emails. I figure they were either apologies or a repeat of the text she'd sent just before she left saying that she loved me and always would. In short, I made it clear I wanted nothing to do with her back then."

Pausing, Tate slid his hand up Havana's arm. "I made that clear *again* when she came home and asked for us to have dinner and talk. And earlier today I once again made an effort to drum into her brain that I have no interest in her. I was pretty harsh about it. She was mad as hell, so she might have now decided I'm not worth the bother."

Thinking on all he'd told her, Havana blew out a breath. The skank sure was a piece of work. "I still can't quite believe she's actually pursued you. I mean, I can understand *why* she'd want you back—you're hot, you're a good guy, and you're fearless enough to get rid of spiders—most girls don't like doing that."

Tate's brows lifted, and the corner of his mouth kicked up.

"But it's bad enough that she broke her promises and left you for another guy. To then pester you for years rather than let you find peace ... that makes it worse. And for her to then expect you to welcome her home and agree to give the relationship another try ... Wow. Just wow. How is it that you almost imprinted on this woman?"

"I don't mean to paint her as a one-dimensional bitch. She's not a terrible person. She's a good daughter. A protective older sister. A loyal friend. She helped her grandmother nurse her human grandfather when he developed dementia, which was hard on all of them. Although she was devastated that Koby chose Gita over her, Ashlynn was never anything but kind to her. She even physically defended Gita once from a falcon shifter at a club. Ashlynn wasn't resentful or bitter toward Koby. She told me she could never begrudge him happiness, even if she had to watch his relationship play out in front of her."

Tate twined a strand of Havana's hair around his finger. "But the thing with Ashlynn is that all her bad traits surface whenever she's not getting her own way. If she wants something, she'll go for it without even considering all the facts surrounding the situation. She didn't even give Koby time to grieve Gita before she made a move on him—she just expects to get what she wants. And when she doesn't get it, she can't make her peace with the situation and let it go. She becomes more determined than before to have it. If that means betraying or hurting others, she'll do it."

"She can only see the end goal."

He nodded. "Whenever she doesn't seem to be getting closer to that goal, she turns resentful and defensive. Not because she's an awful person, but because she hates that she failed. She can't admit to having a weakness. So she projects all the blame onto others. It's more of a self-defense mechanism than anything else, but it's a destructive one, and others get caught up in her drama."

"Well, she was dumb not to appreciate what she had in you. She should have held tight."

"I'm glad she didn't. I'm glad she broke things off, or there's a chance I wouldn't have you now."

Sensing that he meant every word, Havana frowned. "But you went through the whole imprint-threads-nightmare."

"I'm still glad she fucked up. I'd rather have you. And I do." As if to punctuate that, he kissed her soft and long and sweet. And then her stomach rumbled. He smiled. "I need to get you fed. You didn't have lunch, and your body needs to recover from the blood loss."

She pursed her lips. "I could eat."

"Then we eat."

Soon enough, they were dressed and entering the living area. Neither Aspen nor Camden had left. He was sitting on the sofa, *glaring* at Aspen … who was pointedly ignoring him. Havana rolled her eyes and asked, "Is Bailey home yet?"

Aspen smiled. "Yeah, she's in her room putting her phone on charge." Her eyes dropped to Havana's neck. "My, my, my, that's quite a bite. I take it you two kissed, made-up, and decided to give 'more' a chance."

"No," said Tate, sliding an arm around Havana's shoulders. "More like we kissed, made-up, and agreed that we're true mates."

Aspen's jaw dropped. "Seriously?"

"Seriously," he replied.

Her gaze cut back to Havana's neck. "But that's not a claiming bite."

"I can't feel the pull of the bond," grumbled Havana.

"Yet," said Tate. "*I* feel it—that's enough for now."

Aspen stood. "Well, congrats, guys. I mean, I know you haven't officially claimed each other. But it's a big deal that you *found* each other—that in and of itself is worth a 'congrats.'"

"It is, so thank you," said Havana, stiffly accepting a hug from the bearcat. When it went on a little too long, Havana struggled. "Okay, you can let go now."

"Do I have to?"

"Yes, dork."

Snickering, Aspen stepped back.

"Real pleased for you both," Camden said, his eyes dancing from Havana to Tate. "It's about time we had some good news around here."

"News?" echoed Bailey, strolling into the room. "What news? We have news on the license plate number?"

"Take a look at Havana's neck," said Aspen, grinning.

Bailey did, and her brows lifted. "Well, now."

"It gets better," Aspen told her. "Tate says he feels the pull of a mating bond."

Bailey gaped. "Really? That's *awesome*. Wait, you don't feel it yet, Vana?"

"It would seem that something on my end is blocking its frequency," said Havana, folding her arms, knowing she sounded sulky and not feeling all that apologetic about it. "I'll figure out what it is eventually."

Bailey gave a little clap. "I'm so happy for you."

Havana threw up her hand when Bailey moved toward her, her arms open wide. "I already had to deal with a hug from Aspen. I don't need another."

"Suck it up, sister."

Havana sighed as the mamba's arms wrapped around her.

"I'm feeling left out," said Aspen, diving on them both and hugging them tight. "Ah, that's better. Don't you think so, Vana?"

Havana felt her upper lip curl. "What I *think* is that if you both don't stop with this shit, *I will cut you*."

Bailey pouted. "But we're cold."

Havana effortlessly shoved them both backwards, making them grin like loons. Hoping to distract them from drowning her in more hugs, she said, "Tate *does* have some news about the license plate number. Sadly, it didn't belong to the Charger."

Aspen frowned. "Really? Shit."

Bailey's shoulders sagged. "Gideon wasn't wrong in what he said over the phone at the motel—finding him won't be easy." She slid her gaze to Tate. "Aspen told me he called you earlier, smug because he thought Havana was dead." The mamba licked her front teeth. "I really hope you're not planning to kill him quickly, because he needs to suffer a little before he croaks."

"No quick death for him. You'll get your pound of flesh. We all will." Tate guided Havana into the kitchen. "Anything in particular you feel like eating?"

Startled by the question, she blinked. "You don't have to make—"

"I want to feed you, relax you, take care of you, so let me."

He thought she'd argue? Not likely. She hummed. "Grilled cheese sandwiches would be good."

He gestured at the dining table. "Then sit. I'll make them."

Brushing her teeth the next morning, Havana watched through the mirror as Tate entered the bathroom and came up behind her. His eyes followed the path of his hands as he snaked them under her long tee and shaped her bare ass. He was already washed, dressed, and ready to face the world. She hadn't expected him to be one of those people who could enviably roll out of bed looking fresh as a daisy right after waking.

Well, he hadn't rolled *straight* out of bed. First, he'd woken her with his finger on her clit and then fucked her from behind while they lay on their sides.

He'd never stayed over before, just as she'd never spent a full night at his house. But last night he'd curved his body around hers, pulled her close, and told her to sleep well before drifting off. And she'd honestly never slept better in her life. She'd felt settled. Safe. Home.

Tate met her gaze through the mirror. "Never seen a better ass than yours," he said, giving it a brief squeeze. "Looks even hotter now that it has my brand on it."

She sent him a mock scowl, spat out the toothpaste, and rinsed her mouth. "I'm thinking you went a little overboard with the whole branding thing." He'd bitten her in too many places to count.

"Just making up for lost time. You wouldn't believe how many times I almost bit you in the past."

She'd had to fight the same urge during their fling. And although he would have welcomed it, she hadn't branded him last night. Mostly because she didn't trust that she wouldn't bite or claw him hard enough to draw blood and mark him permanently—that wouldn't be fair to him when she hadn't given him the go-ahead to do the same. Plus, she wasn't sure how his cat would react to being marked. Considering the many issues he had, the animal may need things to go slowly.

"Well it's a good thing I wasn't planning to do any sunbathing in a bikini," she said. "I'm covered in so many bites even another shifter would raise their brows."

Tate smiled, feeling utterly unrepentant. He *liked* having her all marked up. Liked that she'd look in the mirror, see those brands, and remember she was his. Liked that others would see them and understand she was taken. "Yeah, they probably would." His little devil huffed and returned her toothbrush to the holder. "Breakfast," he said.

She nodded. "Breakfast. I'm thinking pancakes."

"Works for me."

In the kitchen, Bailey was prepping the coffee machine in her pjs. "Morning," she mumbled. "Who wants coffee?"

He and his devil placed their orders before Havana got to work on breakfast. He didn't know what it said about him that he found it unexpectedly hot to watch her cook. Her movements were quick, efficient, purposeful. There were rarely any wasted movements with Havana; she didn't fidget, tap her foot, or even get distracted by her playful shit-talk with Bailey.

Soon enough, she was setting a stack of pancakes on the table. The three of them immediately dug in.

Tate sipped at his coffee, his eyes on Havana. Now seemed as good a time as any to broach the matter playing on his mind. "I'm going to ask a few things of you that you're probably not going to like."

"You want to step up the security measures around me," she guessed, trickling syrup over her pancakes. She didn't say it with annoyance, which seemed like a good sign. Alphas generally didn't react well to having others surround them with protection, him included—it was reflexive, really, but he needed her to push past that.

"Firstly, I don't want you going anywhere alone, no matter how short the journey will be," said Tate. "You can kick ass, yes, but no one is invincible. If you hadn't had Aspen and my enforcers with you yesterday, we might not be sitting here now." And that fucked with his head far too much.

She ran her tongue over the edges of her teeth. "I can agree to that," she said, begrudgingly.

Some of the tension seeped from Tate's shoulders. "Secondly, I'd like you to either ride with Deke and Isaiah *or* borrow one of my pride's vehicles until this is over." Oh, now that made her go still. "They all have bulletproof glass," he quickly added.

"They do?" asked Bailey.

"My father dabbles in organized crime," he reminded the mamba, "so he has enemies." Tate looked back at Havana. "Maybe asking this of you is me being overcautious, but it's also sensible. It's always better to be safe than sorry."

Bailey flicked her a look. "Bullet in the throat," she muttered beneath her breath.

Havana sighed, her shoulders drooping. She couldn't deny that it made good sense. But she really, really wanted to, because it galled every alpha instinct that she had to have someone try to wrap her up in cotton wool. "I'll borrow one of your pride's cars." She had no reason to distrust his enforcers, but she didn't know them well enough to be comfortable with them chauffeuring her around.

Tate gave a slow nod. "Lastly, Deke and Isaiah are no longer simply going to follow you in their car. They'll also shadow you on foot and stick close at all times, whether you're at work, in a store, or—"

"That's not really necessary."

"Yeah, it is. Because while they're outside whatever building you're in, they can't be sure if you're safe *inside*."

Well ... true. But she didn't like the thought of two near-strangers tailing her every moment of the day.

"Gideon was cocky yesterday when he called," Tate reminded her. "You can imagine what he felt when he realized his plan had failed. He's going to want to rectify his mistake. Let's not give him the room to do so."

"Bullet to the throat," Bailey again muttered quietly.

Havana ground her teeth. He was right. She knew he was. And if Alphas as powerful as Tate had guards when they were out in public, there was no reason for her to bristle so much over having two enforcers hanging around her. Fine. She'd expected Tate to look all smug that he'd gotten his way, but he only looked relieved.

He squeezed her hand. "I know it's not easy for you to accept that level of protection, especially when you barely know my cats."

In truth, if it hadn't been for the drive-by yesterday, she might not have been so cooperative. "I don't fancy having another brush with death."

Once they'd eaten their breakfast and stacked the dishwasher, Tate headed into the bedroom to check in with Luke and his enforcers via phone.

Bailey sidled closer to her. "So ... I can see that Tate's happy you two are mates. You don't seem quite so content. What's wrong?"

"I'm not unhappy," said Havana. "I'm just annoyed that I can't sense the bond."

"Like he said, you will *in time*. Just so you know, I'm fucking thrilled for you."

"Well, thanks. Now go get dressed so we're not late for work."

"I won't be late." Bailey had just reached the kitchen doorway when someone knocked—no, *pounded*—on the front door. The mamba sighed. "Aspen's apparently in a mood."

"Then please don't poke at her."

"I can't help it," said Bailey, heading for the door.

Havana only rolled her eyes and took another sip of her coffee. She heard the creak of hinges.

"How did you get into the building?" Bailey asked their visitor, making Havana's brows snap together.

"Where is she?" a voice demanded. *Dieter.*

"She's in—hey, it's rude to shove people."

Havana entered the living area to see Bailey frowning at his back as he marched into the apartment like he had every right.

He made a beeline for Havana and yanked her to him, hugging her tight. "You okay?"

"I'm fine," she assured him.

"Corbin called me and told me what happened. I needed to see for myself that you were fully healed."

"I am," she said, stepping out of his embrace and putting space between them. "How did you get in the complex?"

"Someone had wedged the main door open so they could go back and forth with some furniture," he replied. "Now please tell me you have the name of the person who tried to kill you yesterday. Or even better, his severed head."

"I wish I could."

He cursed beneath his breath. "He needs to be found before he thinks to try it again. Shit, Havana, I can't believe you almost died." Dieter's gaze switched to something behind her, and then his entire body went tight.

Glancing over her shoulder, Havana watched as Tate slowly stalked into the living area. His unblinking stare was locked on the newcomer as his long legs covered the space with his usual animal grace. Then he was at her side, his arm brushing hers.

And now she felt awkward. Dieter wasn't her ex-boyfriend, but he was close enough to count. Tate knew that; he knew she'd once cared for this man. She didn't want him to think that those feelings still lived inside her, but if she touched Tate in reassurance, he might think she was trying to shove their relationship in Dieter's face to make the guy jealous or something.

"Everything all right, Havana?" Tate asked, his eyes still fixed on their visitor.

"Yeah, fine." She was about to make the introductions, but Dieter spoke before she had the chance.

"Who are you?" he asked Tate, his tone somewhat belligerent with a note of territorialism ... like that of a bratty juvenile who didn't like finding an unfamiliar guest in his home.

The male at her side didn't bristle. "Tate Devereaux, Havana's—"

"Landlord, right," Dieter finished, narrowing his eyes.

"Among other things." Tate flicked up a brow. "And you are?"

"Dieter," he replied simply. Like Tate would know who he was. Like Havana must talk about him all the time or something.

"Just Dieter?" asked Tate. "Like just Madonna, or just Cher?"

The eagle shifter's nostrils flared. "Dieter Lincoln. I thought your enforcers were supposed to be guarding Havana."

"They were," said Tate. "Hence why the shooter targeted her via drive-by. He no doubt figured it was his best bet of hurting her without being caught."

"Well, he was right, wasn't he?" Dieter snarked. "She took three bullets yesterday. Could've *died*."

"I'm aware of that," said Tate, his voice so carefully calm it raised the hairs on her nape. It must have had a similar effect on Dieter, because he seemed to resist the urge to toss more shitty comments at Tate. Wise decision.

"Ever since Tate realized there was a danger to me, he's been on top of this situation," said Havana. "You don't get to come here and point fingers at people who have been trying to keep me safe when you haven't done a single thing to help."

"Not because I don't care," said Dieter. "I was just—"

"With Tabitha. Which is where you should have been. All I'm saying is that you need to jump off your high horse."

"And *you* need to leave this place and lay low for a while. These people after you? They either know your routine, or they're having you followed—neither of those scenarios are comforting. You could move in with me until it's over. Or I can arrange for you to stay on my girl's territory for a while."

Havana stared at him. He couldn't *honestly* think either of those things would happen. "I don't have any intention of going into hiding."

"Swallow your damn pride. Being an alpha doesn't make you invincible. What happened yesterday should have taught you that lesson. Laying low is best and you know it. Jesus, Havana, surely you realize *you're lucky to be goddamn alive.*"

A growl rattled Tate's chest. "I get that your emotions are running high right now, but you need to watch your tone."

He'd taken the words right out of her mouth.

Dieter blinked. "What?"

"I don't like the way you're speaking to her," Tate went on, his face hard. "More, I don't like that you think you *can* talk to her that way. It stops. Now. And while we're on the subject of what I don't like, you can take a step back as well. I don't want you this close to her while you're angry."

Dieter's brows slid together. "You think I'd, what, hurt her?"

"Don't know. Don't know you. I just know I don't want anyone near my girl while they're in the mood you're in right now. Simple as that."

"Your girl? What does that mean? The fling's back on, is it?" Dieter asked, a sour note to his voice.

"I didn't say that."

His face flushing, Dieter glared at Havana. "Wait, you're *dating* this guy?" He asked it in the same tone someone would ask if she held satanic rituals in her basement. "For God's sake, he's your landlord. What, you want to lose your home? He'll evict you if it doesn't work out in the long-run. And it *won't*. From what I've heard about him, he's only interested in shallow relationships."

"That bite mark on her neck says different," said Bailey.

Dieter went utterly still. His eyes dropped to Havana's neck and darkened. "You let him mark you?" he asked, his tone so even she could almost miss the anger there.

Havana sighed. She'd never allowed Dieter to leave brands on her because she'd known they wouldn't have *meant* anything to him—they wouldn't have been marks of possession, they'd merely have been wounds he left in the heat of the moment.

Dieter shook his head. "I don't get any of this. *You* don't do commitment any more than *he* does."

She felt her head jerk back. "Where'd you get that idea?"

"In all the time I've known you, you've never been in a relationship. You like to keep things casual." He gestured from her to him. "Case in point."

"I don't have some kind of phobia of commitment. It just took me a while to find someone I wanted to commit to." Which had originally been Dieter, but she didn't say that. "Which is exactly what happened with you. Meeting Tabitha changed things and made you want more."

Dieter snapped his mouth shut. "And meeting this guy changed things for you, did it? Did you stop to wonder if meeting *you* changed anything for *him*? Because I don't buy that it did, or he'd have offered you 'more' straight off. He didn't. And did the fling progress to more? No. It ended. *Then* he comes back on the scene, and you two are dating. Sounds to me like he doesn't really know what he wants."

"Right, you're done here," declared Tate, officially through with this asshole. Just looking at him, *knowing* Havana once cared for the man, was hard as fuck. Hearing Dieter badmouth him and try to make her doubt his commitment to her ... it was tempting to sucker punch the piece of shit. His cat was all for it.

Dieter scowled. "Well, this isn't your home, so you don't get to tell me when I'm done here. Butt the fuck out."

"Dieter," groaned Bailey. "Don't be stupid. He could probably kill you with his thumb alone."

Havana raised her hands. "All right, let's move on from this, shall we? Dieter, I appreciate you coming to check on me. I really am fine. Thanks for stopping by."

His spine stiffened. "You want me to go? You're kicking me out?"

"I'm trying to prevent this situation from escalating," she said. "If you can calm down, you're welcome to stay. If you can't, you need to go and come back when you *are* calmer."

Dieter's eyes blazed. "For fuck's sake, Havana, how do you expect me to be calm when *you almost died*?"

A growl vibrated Tate's chest. "Didn't I warn you to watch your tone?"

Dieter's eyes flickered, but then his expression morphed into a cold glare. "How *I* talk to *my* friend is not your goddamn business."

Tate stepped right into his personal space. "Wrong," he said, his voice low and deep. "Havana's my business. How people *treat* her is my business.

And from what I can see, you're not that good of a friend."

"Now, hang on a—"

"All you've done since you walked in here is bitch at her for one thing or another. You talk to her like she *owes* you explanations, and then you act like a dick when you don't like what you hear. You're all about how *you* feel, not how *she* feels. So right now, I'm not liking you. Which means I'm not liking that you're anywhere near my mate."

All the bluster drained from Dieter in a rush. "What?"

"You heard me."

The eagle's gaze bounced from Tate to Havana. "You're not bonded."

"We will be."

Dieter looked at Havana, his face slack. "He's your mate?"

Tate didn't look away from the eagle, but he heard her reply, "Yes, I was hoping you'd be happy for me."

Dieter closed his eyes, but not in time to stop Tate from seeing the flash of pain in them. When those eyes opened again, they were blank.

"Just a few minutes ago," Tate began, "she gave you a choice—calm down or leave. Make that choice, or I'll make it for you. And I think you get that I'll have no issue with throwing your ass out of this apartment. Something tells me I might even enjoy it."

Dieter's gaze slid back to Havana, still utterly devoid of emotion. He parted his lips as if to speak, but then he clamped them shut and cleared his throat. "I'll talk to you again soon." He spun on his heel and left, closing the door behind him.

Bailey puffed out a long breath. "We should totally have him over more often." With that, she headed to her room, presumably to get dressed.

Tate turned to fully face Havana. "You okay?"

"Yeah," she replied, scratching her nape. "You?"

"I'm good." He looped an arm around her and drew her close. "He doesn't like that you've found your mate." In fact, Tate was thinking that the eagle might have offered Havana a relationship if she'd confessed to wanting more from him. Either that or seeing her with someone else simply hadn't been easy for the guy. Some could feel a little proprietary over people they'd slept with, even if it had been emotionless sex.

"I think he's just all wound up about the drive-by," she said.

Tate didn't think so. He'd seen the hurt in the eagle's eyes. "I wanted my family to be the first people I told about us being mates. Instead, it had to be *that* asshole."

"Think your family will be happy for you?"

He smiled. "Oh, yeah. They like you."

She smiled right back. "I like them. The rest of your pride might not be so pleased that your mate is a lone devil shifter, though."

Tate snorted. "After your display of mercilessness at the Tavern, they all think you're the shit. Pallas cats respect strength and viciousness—you know that." They'd be happy to have her as their Alpha female. He didn't say that, though, because he had no idea how she felt about running a pride and he didn't want to spoil the mood. They could discuss it later. Right then, all he really wanted to do was taste that mouth of hers again. So he did.

CHAPTER FIFTEEN

Standing in front of his fireplace, Tate glanced at each of his family members, who were spread around the room in various poses. Their wary expressions weren't a surprise. Tate had sent them each a text, asking them to meet him at his home—mysterious, yes, but he'd wanted to share his news with them all at once.

"Is everything all right?" asked Vinnie.

Tate nodded. "Better than all right."

A smile split his sister's lips. "Let me guess ... You got your act together and fixed things with Havana?"

"In a manner of speaking," said Tate. "She's my true mate."

A shocked silence momentarily fell over the room.

Elle gawked. "Seriously? How cool."

Ingrid clasped her hands together, her face a study in delight. She crossed right to Tate, pulled him into a hug, and smacked a kiss to his cheek. "This is just *fabulous*. Darlin', I'm so happy for you. Havana's my kind of girl—strong, fierce, protective of the people in her circle. Many of the males in our pride will be jealous as hell that you snapped her up."

"I suspected she was your mate when you almost went ape-shit yesterday after hearing she'd been shot," Luke said to him, his mouth curved. "I hoped I was right. It's about time you and your cat settled down."

"My thoughts exactly." Vinnie stood and slapped Tate's back. "Congratulations, son. I'm pleased for you."

"Same here," said Damian, smiling. "Havana's hot as hell." He raised his hands when Tate narrowed his eyes. "So I'm told," Damian quickly added.

"Where's your claiming bite?" asked Luke.

"We haven't gotten around to claiming each other yet," said Tate. "She can't feel the bond. She's not denying that it's there—her gut is telling her we are mates."

Elle drummed her fingers on her thigh. "What do you think is blocking the frequency?"

Tate shrugged. "I'm not sure yet, but I suspect the fact that her devil slammed a mental door on me has a lot to do with it. The animal was rightfully pissed when I gave Havana up."

"Ah," said Ingrid with a slow nod. "Well, you'll win the devil over in time. And your cat will help. You should let the animals run together and see if he can soften her up a little."

Tate had had the same thought. The devil might not be as upset with his feline as she was with him.

Vinnie tilted his head. "You know, Tate, I was worried you might never recognize your true mate. Don't think I didn't know how wary you were of true-mate bonds. You've clearly overcome that wariness now, which is good. But don't let it creep back in, son. Having a mate, being so intricately connected to her, is a beautiful thing. Let it happen. Don't fight it. You'll never regret it, not even for a single moment."

"I don't imagine that I will," said Tate.

"Good." Vinnie returned to his chair. "She'll make a strong Alpha female. Keeping a pride of pallas cats in line is no easy thing, but she'll manage it just fine. She's already an Alpha, in her way. Those girls of hers would follow her anywhere."

Tate nodded. "She thinks of them as family."

"She won't join the pride if Aspen and Bailey aren't also allowed to join. She'd feel as though she was abandoning them," Vinnie pointed out.

"I already know that, which is why I'm planning to offer them a place in the pride."

"I doubt any of our pride mates will object to it. We've all gotten to know Aspen and Bailey a little since they moved into your building. I've only heard people say good things about them. The three are a little on the crazy side, sure, but we pallas cats like crazy. Even Valentina likes them, and she's not easy to please."

"I personally think they're *great*," said Elle. "God, I'm so happy you've found your mate, Tate. We haven't had a lot to smile about recently. This news *rocks*."

"Agreed," said Luke. "So, Tate, how easy do you think it'll be to convince Havana to move at your pace? Because I just know you'd move her into your house today if you thought she'd be up for it."

Well of course he would. "It'll take time, but I can be patient. I know better than to put pressure on a female as dominant as Havana—it never works well."

Luke pursed his lips. "In other words, you'll act like there's no rush but do shit like gradually move her things to your place, center all your charm on her, and insert yourself into her life so that you're firmly under her skin. Like a tic."

Well, yeah, but Tate decided against admitting it. "If she wants to take things slow, we'll take it slow."

Elle snorted. "You are so full of it."

Vinnie lifted a brow at Tate. "I assume you have no problem with this news circulating amongst the pride."

Tate shook his head. "No problem at all." He was proud to be able to declare that Havana Ramos was his mate. And the more people who knew she was off-limits, the better.

"Good," said Vinnie. "Because your grandmother would have trouble not sharing it with *the world*."

Ingrid only rolled her eyes.

"Ashlynn's gonna shit a brick when she hears about this," said Damian, sounding positively delighted. "After all she's done, I'm kind of liking that idea."

"Me, too." Elle frowned at their youngest brother. "And I have to say I'm disappointed in you, Damian. Despite all the dark, destructive powers you possess, you never did anything to avenge Tate. Never put a hex on her. Never turned her into a toad. Never even gave her stomach poisoning. What kind of Antichrist are you?"

"One that exists only in your totally whacked head," Damian retorted.

Elle scowled. "Don't you try gaslighting me. And don't call me whacked."

"Don't call me the Antichrist."

"Do you prefer Beelzebub? Lucifer? Abaddon?"

"What I'd prefer is to have a sister who isn't neurotic or paranoid and doesn't have back flab."

Elle sucked in a breath. "I do *not* have back flab."

"Oh, you do, and that's no surprise. Your idea of a balanced diet is having a candy bar in each hand."

"Enough," Vinnie bit out. "You know, I had hopes that the arguments would cease now that you're both older, but those hopes are starting to die."

Elle *hmphed*. "As will we all when he unleashes his evil—"

"Oh my God," Damian burst out.

Elle snorted. "*He* ain't gonna help you, oh bringer of darkness."

Tate couldn't help but smile. His family was crazy. It was part of why he loved them.

Watching from the corner of the rec center's café as a male shifter loudly kicked up a fuss about the hot coffee that had been spilled all over his lap, Havana flicked a look at Bailey. "You realize that Corbin isn't going to buy that you 'accidentally' knocked over Randy's drink in passing, right?"

The mamba only shrugged, clearly enjoying the spectacle. "If the asshole hadn't acted like a total cock toward Aspen *again*, I wouldn't have felt the need to scald his dick. I hope he gets blisters. Big ones."

Aspen's grin was a little feral. "Bitch-slapping him earlier was fun but, yeah, this is *way* better."

Havana might have felt a little sympathy for Randy if he hadn't confronted Aspen for a second time, verbally blasting her for "fucking up" his relationship with Camden and calling her everything from a whore to a slut. Why Randy was surprised that Camden dumped him for fronting Aspen a few days back, Havana didn't know. It wasn't exactly a secret that the tiger never tolerated anyone even *trying* to upset Aspen. "Has Camden heard that Randy got all up in your shit again?"

"Not that I'm aware of," said Aspen.

"Maybe if you *personally* told Camden about this second stunt, the cranky tiger would stop sulking that you didn't tell him about the first," said Bailey.

Aspen frowned. "I'm no tattle-tale."

Hearing her cell ring, Havana pulled it out of her pocket. *Tate*. Just like that, her stomach fluttered. She answered, "Hey."

"Hey, baby," he said, his voice warm and deep and rumbly. "My family wants us all to get together at my place tonight to celebrate you and I finding each other. Ingrid was planning on cooking something special, but I know how much you love Chinese food, so I said we could all order a takeout if you're up for it?"

"Like I'd ever turn down Chinese food." And it warmed her that he'd pick that over a home-cooked meal.

"Invite your girls. Camden, too, if you'd like. I want both our families there."

She smiled, liking that he understood how important Aspen and Bailey were to her. Even Camden, despite his insistence on holding himself apart, mattered to her. "They'll be there." Mostly because they were too nosy to miss it.

"Good. Everyone is planning to turn up at seven."

That gave her a couple of hours to do laundry and stuff. "Seven works."

"I'm on my way to the center to pick you up. I shouldn't be more than ten minutes. And before you tell me you're quite capable of driving yourself home, I'm aware of that. I'm not doing this out of overprotectiveness. I'm doing it because I've been jonesing to see you all day."

She felt one side of her mouth hitch up. "All right. See you soon."

"Soon," he agreed. Then she had dead air.

"I'm guessing that was Tate," said Aspen. "Your face only goes all soft like that when you're talking to him."

Havana felt her brow furrow. "My face does not go soft. And yes, it was Tate. He wants me to invite you two and Camden to his house tonight. His family wants to celebrate that he and I found each other. We're doing that with Chinese takeout, because my man knows me well."

"Well I'll be there," said Bailey.

Aspen pulled her phone out of her pocket. "Me, too. I'll text Camden and check if he's up for it."

"Okay, good. Also, Tate's on his way to pick me up from work just because."

Bailey's eyes lit up. "That means I can drive home the car he gave you, right?"

"Loaned, he *loaned* it to me."

Bailey snorted. "If you don't think he'll try pushing you to keep it, you're dumb. Tate is an Alpha, Havana. That means his level of protectiveness toward you will be off the charts. He'll *need* to know that you're as safe as you can possibly be. You know that."

Aspen nodded. "My advice? Just roll with it, Vana. You're both natural-born alphas, which means you'll clash over certain stuff. Choose your battles wisely rather than butting heads with him all the time. You won't get him to compromise on matters of your safety—no mate ever would, especially not an Alpha."

"Pure truth," said Bailey. "And you have to admit that having bulletproof windows is just plain cool."

Havana folded her arms over her chest. "Hmm."

It wasn't long before he arrived at the center. Havana had expected him to text her once he pulled up outside, but he came right into the building and tracked her down, and then hauled her close right in front of God and everyone.

"Hey." He dipped his head and kissed her. "Hmm, needed that."

She smiled. "Always happy to be of service." She didn't fail to notice how many female eyes drifted his way. She could understand it. He was one of those people you just couldn't help but look at. That didn't mean she was good with them ogling him—especially when she was *right there*. It was just plain disrespectful.

She could be the bigger person and just ignore it. But even as she told herself that, she tossed some frowns at the oglers. They averted their gazes quick enough.

He slid his hand up her back. "You ready to go?"

"I am. Bailey's going to drive the car you loaned me back to the complex."

He interlinked his fingers with Havana's. "I figured she would."

After saying her goodbyes to Bailey and Aspen, Havana allowed Tate to lead her outside.

Opening the rear passenger door of the SUV, he said, "In you go, baby." Once she was inside, he slid in beside her while Luke took the front passenger seat. In the driver's seat, Farrell briefly greeted her as he switched on the engine.

Tate took her hand. "Come back to my place with me."

She pursed her lips. "Hmm, what's my incentive?"

"There'll be food. And sex. Lots and lots of sex."

"Then I'm in. Sounds better than laundry."

Tate smiled, satisfied. He wanted some time alone with her. Wanted some *uninterrupted* time with her. Wanted them to be at a place where people like Dieter wouldn't show up.

It wasn't long before they arrived at his house. As he planned to stay home the rest of the day, he politely dismissed Farrell. Luke didn't see the point of leaving, since he'd be attending the takeout celebratory meal, so the Beta opted for hanging out in the back yard.

When she and Tate were finally inside the house and he'd closed the door firmly shut behind them, his cat rumbled a contented sound, pleased to have her in his lair. Just the same, something in Tate relaxed. And not just because she'd be safe here. He'd always liked having her on his personal slice of territory, but he liked it a fuck of a lot more now that he'd finally acknowledged that she was his mate. It gave him a deep sense of peace that settled into every bone.

He liked that her scent would mark his things and linger after she left. Liked that he no longer had to worry about giving her mixed signals—he could touch her as much as he wanted, could ask her to spend the night in his bed, could pepper her with the many questions that had floated around his brain for months.

Right then, Tate *really* wanted to tumble her into bed, but he wrestled down the urge. It mattered to him that she felt comfortable here, and he worried that it would taint things for her that he'd only ever brought her here to hook up before now. He wanted her to see this place as her future home, and that meant making her *feel* at home. He doubted that burying himself inside her right this moment would be the best way to communicate that things were different now.

Walking up behind her, he slid his arms around her waist and rested his chin in the crook of her neck. "Beer? Water? Soda? Coffee?"

"A beer would be good."

He kissed her temple and then retrieved two beers from the fridge. After passing her one bottle, he took her hand, led her to the sofa, and sank onto the soft leather. His beer in one hand, he patted his thigh with the other. "Sit with me."

Careful not to spill her own drink, she straddled him and rested one hand on his chest.

He hummed, content that he had her right where he wanted her. He sipped from her mouth. Soft. Slow. Lazy. A deep, raw need stirred to life inside him and tightened his body, but he kept his hunger for her in check.

Later. He'd fuck her into oblivion later.

Despite being hard as a rock, he felt ... at ease. Everything about her both incited and settled him. Her incredibly soft skin, her luscious scent, her addictive taste, the way her body seemed to fit against his just right. She pleased every single one of his senses in the best way.

He tossed back a mouthful of beer and smoothed his hand up her back. "How was your day?" Watching her throat work as she took a swig of beer, he felt his gut clench.

"Good. Yours?"

"Fine. It's always destined to be a good day when you get to tell your family you've found your mate. Mine are very happy for us. They're confident you'll make a good Alpha female."

She tensed, her eyes widening.

He felt his mouth quirk. "When you accepted that we're mates, you hadn't considered that you'd naturally run the pride alongside me at some point."

"It all got a bit lost under the wave of info that's drifting around my brain," she admitted.

"It's not like being an Alpha will be new to you. You might not have an official clan, but it's close enough to count."

"Being the Alpha of three is a *lot* different from being the Alpha of a full-on pride."

"You can handle it." He rubbed her thigh. "Aspen and Bailey are of course welcome to join the pride. I know you'd never want to leave them behind, and I would never ask it of you. Do you think they will join?"

"Yes, though they might be a little leery. We've been loners a long time. They're not used to answering to anyone other than me."

"Camden is welcome to join as well, by the way." He tilted his head. "I've got to say, you don't look so enthusiastic about being part of my pride."

"It's nothing personal. It's just ..." She trailed off, sighing. "People assume that being a loner is terrible. For me, life was better *after* I became one."

"You had a bad experience with your childhood clan?"

"You could say that. The members didn't really support each other or work together. We weren't a unit. There were divides. There was no sense of belonging or kinship. Every family was out for themselves. And looking back, I can see that the Alpha male liked it that way. People are easier to control if they're not united."

Tate squeezed her hip. "I'm sorry you were born into such a shitty excuse for a clan, baby. My pride is nothing like that."

"I know. I've seen that for myself. I'm not saying I won't join your pride if we mate—"

"*When* we mate."

"When we mate," she corrected. "I just want you to understand why you shouldn't take it to heart that I won't jump for joy at the prospect of no longer being a loner."

Okay, he could see why she'd feel that way. He could also see that this could possibly jam the frequency of their bond if he didn't deal with it. He resolved right then that he'd ensure she got to know his family and pride mates better so that she'd feel more at ease with them. Hopefully that would dim her reluctance.

"Will you tell me more about your past?" he asked. "I'm hoping you trust me enough to share it with me. I want to know you. I want to know everything about you."

Havana almost smiled. How often had she wished he'd say that? Too many to count. Her body relaxed a little more into his. "I want you to know me, just as I want to know you. If you have any questions, just ask."

He knocked back more beer. "All right. Let's start with an easy question. Is your name really Havana Ramos?"

"Yes. You look surprised."

"A lot of loners change their names," he pointed out.

"Usually only those who are in hiding or get up to shady shit."

"True. Where are you from?"

"Vancouver. My father was Spanish. He transferred to my mother's clan in Canada after they mated. They met when she was vacationing in Spain." Just thinking of her parents made her chest ache like a bitch. She took another fast swig of her drink.

"You talk of them in the past tense," he noted, his voice low and soft. "What happened?"

She fingered his collar. "It's not a pretty story."

"It's *your* story. Which means I want to hear it. But we don't have to speak of it now if it's too hard for you."

Her stomach rolled at the thought of revisiting that time in her life. Setting it aside for a while sounded good to her. But how could she and Tate ever build anything if she didn't let him in? The answer was … they couldn't.

She took in a preparatory breath that was a lot shakier than she'd have liked. "Our Alpha was an asshole. Yasiel either didn't know the difference between leading and bullying, or he just didn't care. My older brother, Rolando, dated Yasiel's daughter, Neoma."

Thinking of Rolando made a sad smile pluck at Havana's mouth. He'd been an overly protective big brother. Oh, he'd teased and pushed her buttons at times like only a sibling would, but he'd never let anyone say a bad word to or about her. She'd adored and looked up to him.

"Neoma was a sweet girl," Havana went on. "Rolando fell hard for her. So when her father declared he was entering her into an arranged mating, Rolando was devastated. Neoma begged her mother to intervene, but the Alpha female rarely contradicted Yasiel. Rolando had been so sure she'd stand up for her daughter."

"But she didn't, did she?"

Havana shook her head. She'd always wondered if the rest of what happened could have been prevented if Neoma's mother had just spoken up for her only child. "Rolando tried convincing Yasiel to change his mind. But the Alpha didn't give a shit what my brother or Neoma wanted. He was determined to solidify his alliance with another clan, and he had no compunction about using Neoma to do so."

Tate rubbed her thigh. "Sad as it is, it's not an uncommon practice."

"No, it isn't. No one should ever be used as a bargaining chip. Neoma was *terrified* of the male she'd been promised to. He was like her father, only worse. Rolando was determined to save her, but Yasiel wouldn't budge. So … Rolando challenged him."

Tate's brows hitched up. "Your brother had a shitload of courage and honor."

"He did, but those traits didn't help him during the duel. Rolando was strong, but he was no alpha. Yasiel outmatched him in every way." As she'd watched it play out that night with the rest of the crowd, she'd flinched at every bite, scratch, and blow he'd received. His cries of pain had been like red-hot knives stabbing her chest. "Rolando submitted when it was clear he had no prayer of winning the duel. But Yasiel killed him anyway."

A thunderous expression twisted Tate's face. "The fuck?"

She understood his shock and outrage. If a shifter submitted during a duel, their opponent backed off—that was how it worked. Or how it *should* work. But, unlike her brother, Yasiel possessed no integrity. He'd wanted to punish Rolando for challenging him. He'd wanted to scare the rest of the clan into towing the line.

A muscle in his cheek ticking, Tate curved his hand around her nape and gave it a comforting squeeze. "You don't have to tell me anything else. I can guess the rest anyway. You and your parents abandoned the clan, but you tragically lost them at some point over the years," he said, his voice humming with anger.

She appreciated the "out" he'd offered, but she'd rather tell the full story now than revisit it later. "I wish it *had* happened that way. But it was so much worse than that. My dad, Manuel, was so furious and devastated in his grief, he attacked Yasiel the moment Rolando stopped breathing. Then it was a huge pile-on—enforcers jumped in to protect Yasiel, my relatives jumped in to defend my father and avenge my brother. My mother stayed with me, crying and yelling warnings at Manuel to duck or watch his back or move aside.

"It was just … chaos. Pure chaos." The air had stank of blood, anger, fear, and pain. She'd never forget the screams. Never. "Yasiel and his enforcers tore my father and extended family members apart right there in front of everyone."

Tate's eyes fell closed for a brief moment. He tugged her closer and slid his hand around to cup her face. "Baby," he said simply, the word laced with so much warmth and compassion it almost brought tears to her eyes.

Ignoring the ache in her throat, she went on, "Me and my mother were branded traitors and shunned. She tried to hold on, but she couldn't. I don't think it was just the breaking of the true-mate bond that ate at her strength. I think she was just so heartbroken. She died a few weeks later. Then I was alone."

He muttered a low curse. "How old were you?"

"Twelve."

His jaw hardened. "You were on your own at the age of twelve?"

She nodded and took a steadying swig of her beer. "I drifted for a while before ending up here. I was living on the streets when one of the regulars from the center found me and brought me to Corbin."

"Is your old Alpha still alive?"

"Probably. I considered going back there many times to kill him. But my devil was a mess after what he did. It was hard to get her to move forward. I worried that if I went back there even to avenge my family, it would undo all the work I'd done to help her heal." She inhaled deeply. "So now you know it all."

Rage beat in Tate's blood, but he kept it buried. She didn't need to be dealing with his anger right then. This wasn't about him. It was about *her*. Careful not to jostle her, he leaned forward and planted his beer on the coffee table. He did the same with her own bottle and then sank back into the sofa, keeping her flush against him, tucking her face against his throat.

Neither spoke a word as he skimmed his hands over her back, shoulders, and nape—soothing, comforting, gentling, and wishing he could absorb her grief.

It wrecked him to think she'd lost her entire family. Wrecked him that her brother, father, and several other relatives were slaughtered right in front of her. Worse, she'd not only then been disowned by the very people who should have protected her, she'd had to watch her mother die ... leaving her all alone.

Alone. At age *twelve*.

Tate tightened his grip on her nape. "I don't even know what to say." What *did* you say to someone who'd lost their entire family, especially in such a tragic fashion?

"You don't need to say anything. It happened a long time ago."

"That doesn't make your grief any less important. I know what it's like to lose a parent, but I didn't *see* my mother suffer the way you did your father and brother."

"That doesn't make it easier for you that you lost your mom than it does for me." Havana stroked his chest. "I'm sorry she was taken from you."

Tate pressed his mouth to her hair. "I watched my dad deteriorate after her death, so I do know how hard it was for you to watch your mother weaken."

"It takes a strong person to hold on after they lose their mate." Havana lifted her head. "My mother ... she loved me. She didn't want me to be alone. But she wasn't strong. I don't blame her for not holding on. I don't blame the bond for how it weakened her, either. It just ... it is what it is. And even if they'd been human, I don't think she'd have survived the loss of my dad. They were so wrapped up in each other, so completely woven into each other's being, that I honestly felt left out sometimes. Rolando once said the same thing."

"My parents were close and tight," said Tate, sliding his hand over her hair. "But not to the point that they made more time for themselves as a couple than they did for me and my siblings." And he really didn't like that her parents were very much the opposite, but he didn't say that. They were gone now. Criticizing their parenting would only upset her.

She shrugged. "I guess all couples are that little bit different. You don't need to be mad at them. They did love me and my brother, they just ..."

Loved each other more, she didn't say but Tate heard. And of course she'd sensed that he was unhappy with them—his mate was too observant.

As she rested her head on his chest and burrowed into him, he tightened his arms around her. "Never again, baby. You'll never be alone like that again, I swear it you." His cat squirmed to get closer to her, hating that she was hurting. The feline wanted to comfort and rub up against her, wanted to have time with her devil and give the animal that same comfort.

They stayed like that for a while, saying nothing.

Tate waited until she lifted her head again before he said, "My cat wants to officially meet your devil tonight. Would she be up for that?"

A slow smile curved Havana's mouth. "Yes. She'd like that."

He smiled right back. "Good. We eat takeout with our families first. Then we shift."

"Sounds like a plan."

The evening went well. The meal was rowdy, but in a good way. There was a lot of talking, laughing, and even some playful shit talk. The latter was mostly between Elle and Damian, which never failed to exasperate their father.

Each of Tate's relatives kissed Havana's cheek and hugged her, welcoming her into their family, making it clear that they believed she'd make a good Alpha for their pride. Bailey was pretty well behaved, all things considered. But she did watch Luke closely. Not with sexual interest, which was fortunate, since he'd been off the market for years—and for very good reason. Bailey observed him like he was a ticking bomb. The Beta often regarded the mamba through narrowed eyes but said little to her.

Camden appeared eager to leave, but he wasn't rude to anyone and didn't once try to hurry Aspen out of the house. Which meant the bearcat had probably warned him not to in advance.

Later, after they'd all demolished their meal and cleaned up their mess, people began to trickle out of the house until only Tate and Havana remained.

Tate palmed her ass. "Ready to let our animals out now?"

She hummed. "Sure."

He held out his hand, smiling when his mate took it without hesitation. He led her through the house and out into the backyard. A human would take one look at it and describe it as wild and neglected. Tall, weedy grass. Mossy, thick trees. Bulky, prickly shrubberies. Nonsensical-looking rockeries. It was an ideal playground for a pallas cat, though. Tate believed Havana's animal would like it just the same.

He turned to fully face her. "You shift first." He wanted to get a good look at her devil. Maybe even give her a few strokes, if she'd let him.

Havana's face scrunched up. "I don't think that's a good idea yet. She's too ... edgy."

"She doesn't quite trust that I won't hurt you again," he understood. "That's fair. I don't like it, but I get it." And he only had himself to blame.

"She just needs a little time."

"Then I'll give it to her." Tate shed his clothes, his blood heating as he watched Havana do the same. He had all kinds of plans for that body later. "Quick warning: my cat's probably going to rub himself all over you."

She let out a soft "of course he will" snort. "I consider myself warned."

Bones snapped and popped as Tate withdrew, giving his animal supremacy. Moments later, a pallas cat stood in Tate's place.

Havana smiled down at the feline as he shook his fur. She'd heard it said that pallas cats looked a lot like stuffed plush toys, and she could agree with that statement.

She could also agree that they were a combination of odd and cute. Tate's cat was no exception. He had small tufty ears, an abundance of rich long gray fur, black stripes across his cheeks, dark snow-leopard-like spots on his forehead, a bushy black-tipped tail that sported distinctive dark rings, and patches of white-cream fur on his throat, chin, and inner ears.

She knelt down. "Well, hey." His amber eyes—their pupils strangely round rather than vertical—locked with hers as he padded over to her, wearing every pallas cat's trademark cranky look.

He butted her knee, so she took the hint and stroked her fingers through his beautiful fur, admiring the white fluffy ends that made it look like his coat was topped with frost. Just as Tate had warned her that he would, the cat rubbed against her, leaving his scent all over her—purring the entire time.

When he was done scent-marking her, he pulled back and blinked up at her.

"Ah, you want to see my devil now. Okay." She gave control over to her inner animal, shifting forms in an instant.

The cat stepped forward and sniffed the devil, gently butting her nose with his. She haughtily lifted her chin, not easily charmed. He slowly circled her, sniffing and rubbing and chuffing.

She let her mouth gape open as she gave him a cautioning growl. Then she ran. He remained hot on her heels as they rushed through the grass, clambered over rocks, squeezed through gaps in the bushes, and skirted around trees.

They played for a while—pouncing, wrestling, rolling. Later, after lapping at the clean pond water, the pallas cat felt his human push for supremacy. The cat let out a disgruntled growl but didn't fight. He pulled back, allowing his human half to surface.

Tate stared down at the devil as she licked at her paw. She might be a vicious little thing, but he thought she was cute as hell. Like all devil shifters, she was thick and squat, though more in proportion than full-blooded Tasmanian devils. She had a large head, long claws, a tail roughly half the length of her body, and forelegs which were a little longer than her hind legs. Her fur was pure black, but she had a single white patch on her chest that he wanted to stroke.

He didn't dare touch her right then, though. Because as she locked her dark gaze with his, Tate could clearly sense what Havana had tried to tell him—the devil wasn't ready for that yet. She was still reserving judgment for now.

"I'll win back your trust," he promised her.

The animal only sniffed. Then bones popped and snapped, and Havana stood before him.

"Your devil's not going to make this easy for me, is she?"

Havana tilted her head, her eyes glinting with amusement. "Would you expect any different?"

"No, I guess not." He pulled her close and swept his hand down her back. "Stay with me tonight."

She slid her hands up his chest. "I'll expect you to make it worth my while."

He smiled and stroked her ass. "If you mean you want me to fuck you to sleep, I can do that."

"I really don't think you could, actually. I mean, I never fall asleep straight after sex."

"Hmm, I accept your challenge."

He also won.

CHAPTER SIXTEEN

While Tate played his fingers through her hair, Havana studied the dessert menu. She'd eaten at the pride-owned steakhouse with Aspen and Bailey a few times in the past—the food was good, especially the desserts. This was the first time that Tate had brought her here, though.

Over the past week, he'd taken her to various places—most of which were owned by his pride. One morning, he'd taken her for breakfast at the café. Another day, it had been lunch at the deli. Yesterday evening, he'd taken her to the ice cream parlor. They'd already made plans to go to the movie theater this weekend. It was as if he was intent on making a distinct effort to spend time with her *outside* of sex. Or maybe he saw it as making up for lost time, since they hadn't gone on actual dates during their fling.

Now, well, he was doing a good job of slotting himself into her life and ensuring he was commandeering as many hours of her day as he could. She hadn't really given much thought into what kind of mate Tate would be. If she'd had to guess, she would have said he'd be solid and steady and overprotective. Which he in fact was. But she wouldn't have guessed he'd be so … attentive.

It was little but touching things. Like always filling her tank with gas. Like keeping her favorite brand of coffee at his house. Like buying things for her to use while she was there—a replica of her toothbrush, a satin robe, her favorite snacks, her brands of shampoo and conditioner.

He'd also emptied one of his drawers "just in case" she wanted to stash her clothes into it rather than leave them in her overnight bag. His expression had been all "no pressure." So she'd used the drawer. And then he'd emptied another "just in case" she needed more room for her stuff. It was kind of cute that he thought she didn't know he was trying to move her into his house little by little.

He'd formally introduced her as his mate to pretty much every pride mate they brushed past, seemingly wanting Havana to get to know them and feel comfortable around them. They all appeared to be happy for him, and none had been rude or unwelcoming toward her.

He was always firing questions at her—some big, some small. But even more, he freely *shared* with her now. There was no holding back at all. No rules. No hesitations. No boundaries.

He was almost always touching her. Which should have felt uncomfortable because she wasn't all that tactile. But with him, it didn't bother her. It just felt right.

They'd let their animals run together a few more times. Her devil had softened toward his cat. She was beginning to soften toward Tate, too, but she didn't show it much—determined to make him work to prove himself worthy.

If he wasn't too busy throughout the day, he sometimes appeared at the center to see Havana at random times. She knew he regularly checked in with Deke and Isaiah—she often heard them talking to him via cell phone. Gideon hadn't struck again, but no one was getting complacent.

Aside from when she went to work, she never ventured far from home. She also never balked at Tate's hyper-strict security measures. The harder she made it for Gideon to get to her, the more agitated he'd become, and the more likely he'd be to make a mistake.

Tate splayed his hand on her thigh and squeezed. "Have you decided what you want yet, babe?"

She hummed. "I'm gonna go with the pecan pie."

Tate called over the waitress, who was one of his pride mates, and placed their orders.

Havana snapped the menu shut and slotted it back in its holder, accidentally jabbing him with her elbow. "Sorry. You know, you'd have more room if you sat on the other side of the table."

"I like looking at you, but I also like touching you. I can do more of that when sitting next to you than I can when I sit opposite you." His gaze dropped to her mouth, and then his lips were there, sipping from hers. "You taste better than anything here."

"Dude, you don't have to ply me with compliments—you'll get laid later for sure."

Tate chuckled, liking the back and forth they had. It felt easy. Comfortable. Intimate. "Good to know." He put his mouth to her ear and whispered, "If we weren't in a restaurant full of shifters, I'd be stroking your pussy with my finger right now. But I don't want them to know how you smell when you're desperate to come." He was far too possessive for that.

"Neither do I, so I appreciate your restraint."

He rubbed her thigh again. "So … has Aspen and/or Bailey told you if they'll join the pride, or are they still reluctant?" They'd asked to have a few days to think about it.

"I spoke with them about it again earlier. They said that if you and I mate, which will instantly make me a member of your pride, they'll join—*providing* they're allowed to continue working at the center."

"No one would expect them to stop working there. And there's no 'if' you and I mate. We *will* mate. It's only a matter of time. Which is why there's no reason you can't just officially join the pride now."

"Yes, you've made that clear before. On several occasions, in fact."

Okay, yeah, he'd mentioned it a few times. Maybe more than a few. "Because it makes sense."

She took his hand in hers. "I'm not going to rush any part of this relationship. You think your cat doesn't have commitment issues after all. But you could be wrong. I don't want to push any buttons for him. I don't want to make him feel pressured or as if things are moving too fast."

Realization dawned on Tate. "That's why you haven't branded me yet."

She nodded.

"He *wants* you to mark me. *I* want you to mark me." Neither Tate nor his feline liked that she held back on that. They'd wear her brand with pride.

"I don't want to risk spooking him. Plus, my devil needs time, too. She's lost some of her anger toward you, but she doesn't fully trust that you won't give me up again."

"That's not going to happen. Tell me you know that."

"I don't think you'll walk away again, because I understand all the issues surrounding your reasons for giving me up. She's too much of an elemental creature to process any of it."

He let out a long exhale. "I want to wear your mark. I want you living with me. I want you in my pride."

Havana had to stifle a laugh. "Well, aren't you cute?" And so very, very spoiled.

His brows snapped together. "Cute?"

"I get that you're used to people dancing to your tune, your Alpha-ness, but I'm not going to be one of those people—you know this already." Havana gave him a look that said he could pester her until he was blue in the face, but she wouldn't budge. She could see that he still wanted to push, though.

Well, of course he did.

Tate wasn't a man who let things stand in his way. He was used to getting what he wanted when he wanted it. And he always looked so endearingly perplexed when it didn't happen. It made her devil snort in amusement every time.

He sighed. "All right, fine."

She felt her lips twitch. "You can't say that through gritted teeth and think I'll truly believe you mean it, Garfield."

He tossed her a dark glower that promised retribution.

Just then, the waitress appeared and set down their desserts.

Havana thanked her and then picked up her spoon. Alone again with Tate, she cast him a brief sideways look. "Something bad is going to happen."

He frowned. "Why do you say that?"

"Okay, so can you hear the song that's playing right now?"

"Yeah. *Something Wicked This Way Comes*."

"Right. Well, as we were passing the café, I saw someone through the window reading a book with the same title. *And* I saw a poster in the bookstore advertising the Wicked musical. It said, 'Coming soon.'"

"Okay," he said carefully.

"The universe is warning us. The least you could do is acknowledge it."

"I'm acknowledging that, coincidentally, you came across the word 'wicked' in virtually the same context three times today."

Oh, he was beyond help. "If you want to ignore the signs, fine."

A smile playing around the edges of his mouth, he spooned some of his ice cream. "Does it come as a surprise to a lot of people that you're superstitious?"

Havana's head almost jerked back. "I'm not superstitious. I get why some people are—it helps them feel more in control of their lives, and if something goes wrong, they can blame it on a black cat that crossed their path or whatever. But they have to know it's impractical to view the world that way."

"And it's not impractical to believe that the universe sends out 'signs' to guide or warn us?"

She blinked. "Why would it be?"

Tate just shook his head. "No one would guess looking at you that you have this streak of whimsy in you. I kind of like it, even though I find it somewhat neurotic at times."

"Neurotic?"

"I say that with affection. I probably *shouldn't* find it cute, but I do. I don't know what that says about me."

Just then, the music changed. And Kylie Minogue's *Tell Tale Signs* began to play.

Havana grinned. He just sighed.

Once they'd finished their desserts and Tate had paid the bill—she'd wanted to go halves on it, but he'd insisted on paying—they left the restaurant. Standing on the sidewalk, she said hi to Luke and Farrell, who'd been waiting there the whole time.

Spotting Aspen and Bailey further along the street chatting to some Olympus cats, Havana smiled. The girls gave her a brief wave. Havana's smile faded as she caught side of Ashlynn on the opposite side of the street, holding hands with a male Havana hadn't before seen.

Ugh. This seemed to be Ashlynn's new thing. Parading males in front of Tate. She allegedly hadn't reacted well to hearing that he and Havana were mates. In fact, Ashlynn had apparently thrown a tantrum right in the middle of the pride's flower shop—ranting that Tate had to be mistaken; that he could do better; that Havana would never hold him.

The female hadn't confronted either he or Havana, though. She'd done nothing but smile at them each time they crossed paths—and she was always cozied up to a guy. Havana would love to think that Ashlynn had given up on Tate and was ready to move on. But anyone could see how often the bitch glimpsed at Tate, as if needing to witness his reaction to her touching another male ... just as she was doing right then.

"That girl is such a tool," said Havana.

Tate slid an arm around her shoulders and began leading her along the sidewalk toward his cul-de-sac. "Just ignore her. I do."

"Either she hasn't yet accepted that we're mates, or she simply doesn't consider it a deterrent to her plan to win you back. But then ... her own mate failed to claim her, didn't he? Maybe that would be enough for her to cease from viewing you as a lost cause."

"I honestly couldn't give a shit." Tate kissed her temple, breathing her in, wishing he could bottle up her scent, looking forward to it mixing with his own. "She doesn't matter. You matter. What we have and what we're building matters."

"Oh, I agree."

Tate frowned as a glint of metal caught his eye. Several things registered at once. A dark blue Charger cruising along the road. A window partially lowered. A face covered in a balaclava. *A gun aimed at Havana.*

"Fuck." Tate pushed her to the ground, taking cover behind a parked car, while Luke's body blanketed them both. Gunfire rang through the air. The vehicle shielding them jolted as bullets thudded into metal, windows smashed, and air hissed out of a tire. Then the fuckers were speeding away. Tate looked up to see the shooter firing at the enforcers that tried stopping the car—then it was gone.

Tate looked at Farrell. "Follow them!"

The Head Enforcer pulled his phone out of his pocket and shifted into his avian form. The bird shook off the torn clothing and took to the air in a flash, his talons clutching a cell phone.

Tate helped his mate to her feet, raking his gaze over her, his heart pounding like a fucking drum. "Baby, tell me you're okay."

"I'm fine, I'm fine, I'm not hit," she assured him, her eyes wide. "You good?"

"No, because those motherfucking fuckers came at you in my own backyard."

She put her hands on her hips. "Told you something bad was going to happen."

He just stared at her for a few seconds. Then he hauled her against him and hugged her tight, *needing* to feel her safe and warm and alive in his arms. Several of his pride mates crowded them, including Luke and Alex—both of whom looked ready to burn shit down.

"Oh my freaking good God, *what the hell?*" Aspen burst out as she and Bailey shouldered their way through the crowd. "Are you both okay?"

"We're okay," said Havana. "Though my heart is racing a mile a minute." She looked up at Tate. "Thank you for shoving me out of harm's way."

He kissed her forehead, not loosening his hold on her. His muscles hurt with the effort to hold back his cat—the feline wanted to shift, hunt, and kill.

"That was the same Charger from the drive-by," said Bailey, her eyes narrowed.

"I know," said Tate, his voice like gravel. "As soon as Farrell calls and tells us where those assholes stopped, I'll be heading their way."

"And I'll be going along with you," Havana announced. "No, Tate, don't argue. I know you want to stick me in your sock drawer where I'll be nice and safe, but no coddling. This shit has *everything* to do with me. I want in on it every step of the way. You wouldn't stay behind if our positions were reversed."

He opened his mouth to argue, even though he couldn't deny that she was right. But then he thought better of it. He had no chance of earning her devil's trust if he treated Havana like she didn't know her own strength or couldn't take care of herself. She was an alpha, and he had to treat her like one—especially since he planned on making her his Alpha female. "Fine. Let's get to the SUV. I want us to be ready to move in an instant."

Soon enough, a bunch of people were piling into the pride's seven-seater SUV. Luke slid into the driver's seat, Tate rode shotgun, Vinnie and Alex sat in the second row, and Havana settled on the rear passenger seats with Aspen and Bailey, who insisted on coming.

It wasn't easy to sit still when adrenaline and anticipation pumped through his veins. His cat was pacing, just as eager to get to the people who'd targeted his mate *yet again*.

It didn't take long for Tate's phone to start ringing. "Where are they, Farrell?" he answered.

Farrell rattled off an address. "They're both packing a bag, Tate. Looks like they're getting ready to run."

"Sit tight unless they try to leave before we get there. We're on our way." Tate ended the call and spoke the address out loud.

"Got it," said Luke, pulling out onto the road.

"Now I need to find out who lives there." Tate sent a text to River, asking for the details of whoever resided at the address. "According to Farrell, our boys are packing a bag. They probably don't want to hang around to tell their boss they failed him again."

"This was probably their chance to redeem themselves for failing Gideon once before," mused Alex.

"It'll be best not to interrogate them at their home," said Tate. "If Gideon decides to go looking for them and then realizes they're dead, he'll suspect we questioned and killed them. We don't want him to know that we're getting closer."

"I had that same thought," said Vinnie.

Tate turned to his brother. "If they haven't finished packing by the time we've arrived, do it for them and make it look like they bailed."

"Will do," said Luke.

Silence reigned right up until Tate received a text message from River. "The house is owned by a human who is currently renting it to both Malcolm Taggart and Vernon Clementine," said Tate. "They're humans, apparently. But they could be lone shifters posing as humans to their landlord. We'll soon find out."

After that, no one talked much throughout the drive. Everyone sat up straight as Luke parked the SUV in a somewhat shady neighborhood.

"The plan is simple," said Tate. "We apprehend them, tie them up, and bring them back to my dad's apartment for questioning." There was a spare room they used specifically for that purpose.

Tate twisted in his seat and skimmed his gaze over Havana and her girls. "You three stay here and keep watch over the SUV. We'll be back soon."

"Okay," the trio said in unison.

Tate blinked, surprised they hadn't insisted on coming along. Then again, the interrogation wouldn't be held here, so the women would only be missing out on watching Malcolm and Vernon get apprehended—it wouldn't exactly be entertaining.

Tate locked eyes with Havana. "Call us if anything happens out here that we need to be aware of," he said, so that they'd feel that they had something to do.

"Okay," they again said at once.

All right, now they were just being creepy.

"Let's get moving," said Tate.

As a group, he and his pride mates slipped out of the SUV. The street was empty, so no one saw them as they silently hurried over to Farrell, who stood in the gap that separated the house from its neighbor. Tate heard muffled voices coming from inside, but nothing else.

Noticing an open window at the side of the house, Tate headed right to it. He signaled at Vinnie and Farrell to cover the rear of the building and then gestured at Alex to watch the entrance. It was important to have every exit blocked, because the men were bound to run.

Tate and Luke stealthily climbed through the open window and then found themselves in a small dining room. They stood still for a moment, familiarizing themselves with their surroundings. The place was shabby. Peeling wallpaper. Sparse, worn furnishings. Stained carpet. The scents of dust, charred meat, mold, and …

"Cheetah," mouthed Luke, his nostrils flaring. He clamped his mouth shut, fighting a smile.

Yeah, cheetahs, just as Havana had predicted. Fuck, she would never let that go.

Footsteps hurried around upstairs. Someone was definitely in a rush. The only other sounds seemed to be coming from the living room—cursing, heavy breathing, a zipper shutting.

"Goddammit, Vern, hurry up!" yelled the shifter in the living room, who had to be Malcolm Taggart.

"Two minutes!" Vern bellowed.

Tate pointed from Luke to the ceiling, gesturing for his brother to handle the shifter upstairs. As Luke disappeared up the staircase, Tate headed for the living room.

The cheetah was standing in the middle of the small space, digging the heels of his palms into his eyes, muttering beneath his breath. The guy was so lost in his thoughts that it took him a few moments to sense that he wasn't alone.

Taggart's head snapped up. He froze. Then his eyes fell closed as he cursed. Shoving a hand through his tousled dirty blond hair, Taggart let out a shaky breath. "I think I can guess by the look on your face that paying you to walk away ain't going to work."

Clenching his fists, Tate moved to stand directly in front of him. "Good guess."

"What I did … it wasn't personal, all right," Taggart told him. "I just did what I was paid to do. I have no beef with you."

"You do now." Targeting Tate's mate was *very* personal to him.

The cheetah rubbed at his nape. "Look, I get that the loner is under your protection … although I didn't know that *at first*—not until the boss ripped me another asshole over the phone for failing to kill her. He said something about the Olympus Alpha being a smug fucker. I asked what he meant. He said the devil had your protection."

"She very much does."

"I didn't know that."

"But then you did, and you came after her again."

Taggart winced. "It was either I killed her for the boss, or I be killed *by* him. I chose me."

"And that was your mistake."

Taggart flew into motion, leaped onto the sofa, launched himself off the piece of furniture, and landed in the doorway. Fuck, bastard cheetahs were fast.

Tate pursued him as Taggart rocketed through the dining area toward the kitchen—

A mamba lunged out of nowhere and twined herself around the cheetah's leg. Her weight tripped him, making him fall to the floor. He kicked out, trying to shake off the mamba with absolutely no success.

A bearcat leapt off the bannister and landed hard on his back, making something crack. He twisted with a sharp cry, ramming his elbow into the animal. Snarling, she scuttled up his back and sank her teeth into his nape. He growled a sound of pain, but then he froze ... because a blood-curdling shriek came out of the shadowed hallway just before a goddamn devil raced toward him and clamped her jaws around the arm that had batted the bearcat.

Tate could only stare. This shit was ... yeah, he hadn't seen it coming. At all.

The females hadn't simply aimed to subdue and take Taggart down. They'd swarmed him and held tight to ensure he wouldn't let his inner cat surface. No shifter would change forms in this situation, because in that moment when a person transitioned from human to animal, they were extremely vulnerable.

Tate cleared his throat, amused. "Thank you, ladies. Your help was most appreciated. I'll take it from here."

Only once the three females had backed away did Tate roughly pull Taggart to his feet. A single uppercut knocked the fucker unconscious. Tate let out a loud whistle, signaling for his pride mates to come inside. And then a bullet fired upstairs.

Tate's heart jumped in his chest. "Luke!"

"I'm good," his brother called back. "Vernon, however, is not." Luke jogged down the stairs just as Vinnie, Alex, and Farrell raced into the house. "He and I had something of a struggle," Luke went on. "I didn't mean for the shot to be fatal, but he twisted at the last second. The bullet sank into his chest. He's a goner."

"At least we have this guy," said Alex, helping Tate bind an unconscious Taggart with zip ties. Meanwhile, the females shifted back to their human forms and returned to the SUV without a word.

Holding two duffels, Luke looked at Tate, his eyes smiling. "So ... your mate called it. They're cheetahs."

Tate threw him a dark look. "It would seem so. On another note ... I need to call some enforcers here to get rid of Vernon's body. One of them can also drive the Charger somewhere to help it look like the pair bailed." Once Tate had made the call, he turned to his Head Enforcer. "Farrell, I want you to stay local in your avian form just in case Gideon or some of his men turn up here looking for Taggart and Clementine. If they do, follow them and then report their location back to me."

Farrell nodded. "No problem."

After dumping Taggart in the trunk of the SUV, the men piled into the vehicle. They all turned to look at the three loners sitting on the rear passenger row. The females stared right back at them, utterly composed and completely casual ... like they'd been sitting there all along patiently waiting for the men to return.

Tate twisted his mouth. "All right." He faced forward and nodded at Luke, who then switched on the ignition.

"Told you they were cheetahs," said Havana.

Tate felt his lips thin. He didn't respond. But he did shoot his brother a scowl for chuckling like a fucking loon.

"You can't expect me to remain quiet and leave this to you and Alex," said Havana as they all stood outside the room within which their captive was being held. No one worried that he'd try to escape—they'd injected him with a serum that temporarily suppressed shifting.

"I wouldn't expect that of you, given that he fired the bullets that almost killed you," Tate assured her. He'd want to have his say, in her position. "I'm just saying that Alex and I will be leading the interrogation. I'm aware that you have skills in this area, though I have no idea where those skills come from." He intended to find out at some point. "Feel free to contribute. My father and Luke will do the same."

Havana, Aspen, and Bailey shared an odd look he couldn't quite decipher. Then Havana nodded and said, "Okay."

Tate narrowed his eyes. Because he was beginning to learn that her "okays" could be translated into, "You do your thing; I'll do mine." He sighed. "Babe—"

"No, I get that it's better for Taggart to have two people at most to focus on," said Havana. "I'll just contribute, like you said."

Tate sensed that she meant it. But he got the feeling that her contributions wouldn't be a mere question or two.

Luke materialized beside him. "Found this in the photo gallery on the guy's cell phone," he said, having earlier used Taggart's thumbprint to unlock the device while the cheetah was unconscious. "There's plenty more of them. They could prove useful."

"They could indeed." Tate took the cell. "Any exchange of text messages or emails between him and Gideon?"

"No," replied Luke. "But Taggart received calls from someone who could quite possibly be Gideon—all were made through a spoofing site. You can tell because the number of the caller comes up as gray rather than the clickable blue. Anyway, the most recent call was made last night."

So it could very well have been Gideon instructing Taggart to make a second attempt on Havana's life. "Now that he's conscious, let's go get some answers."

Tate entered the small box room first. The others slowly followed him inside. It was once Damian's room, but the kid now stayed in Tate's old bedroom. The walls had once been blue and covered in posters and decals. Now the walls were a plain white—no pictures, no posters, no mirrors, nothing. There was no furniture aside from two chairs, one of which Taggart was bound to, his eyes wide, the tendons in his neck bulging.

Whereas the room once smelled of Damian, dirty laundry, and teenage boy, it now reeked of cheetah and fear. The male's heartbeat thudded so loud and hard, it was a wonder the organ didn't burst out of his chest.

Tate's cat let out a pleased growl, liking that their captive was afraid. He should be. The cat had felt fear when he thought he might lose Havana. Now it was this asshole's turn.

The cheetah's breathing picked up as they all spread out and took up positions around the room. He cast Alex an exceptionally wary look. Well, no one wanted to anger a wolverine—those ferocious bastards fucking ate their prey, teeth and all.

Staring down at Taggart, Tate felt his hands clench and his back teeth lock. This piece of shit had tried to kill his mate. It was an honest to God's struggle not to slice open the bastard's throat. No, that death was too quick. Too painless. Tate had bigger plans for him.

Impatient by nature, his inner cat didn't want to wait. Didn't care to make the bastard sweat. He only wanted to surface and avenge Havana. But he did understand that it was important to get answers if they were to track down the bigger danger to her, so the cat stayed calm, his muscles bunched, his upper lip quivering to bare a fang.

Taggart's gaze snapped to something on the floor, and he jerked in his seat. "Fucking fuck."

It was only then that Tate noticed the black mamba slithering along the wooden planks. He looked at Havana, who gave him a reassuring smile and said, "It's fine, she won't bite."

She probably wouldn't unless ordered to by Havana, but Taggart didn't look so convinced of that. He was eyeing the serpent like it had come straight from the bowels of hell.

Exuding an air of cool that he absolutely did not feel, Tate grabbed the spare chair, twisted it, and then straddled it. "It's Malcolm, right?" He twisted his mouth. "I had an uncle named Malcolm. Distant uncle. He was an alcoholic. Compulsive gambler, too. Died in a car accident. Very sad."

"I thought his name was Mick," said Luke, his brow creasing.

Vinnie shook his head. "No, it was Malcolm. That man was his own worst enemy. He never knew what was best for him." Vinnie looked at the cheetah.

"I hope for your sake that we can't say the same about you."

"If he knew what was best for him, he wouldn't have shot Havana," said Tate, flexing his fingers.

Taggart swallowed. "I told you, I didn't know she was under your protection."

Like that made a single bit of difference to Tate or his cat. "Maybe you didn't *initially*. But it doesn't really matter either way. The fact is you *did* come after her. And so we came after you. Now, this boss of yours ... tell me about him."

"I don't know his name. He never gave it. He called me one day, said someone recommended me to him, and told me that he'd like to add me to his payroll. When he wants someone dead, he calls me."

Alex slipped his hands in his pockets. "And you make it happen, huh?"

Taggart forced a shrug, doing a poor imitation of nonchalant. "I do what I gotta do to survive."

"Bullshit," said Alex. "You chose the easy way. You could have done what the three loners here have done. You could have lived a normal life, worked a normal job, sought protection in other ways. You decided not to."

Tate tipped his head toward Havana. "You see that mark on her neck, Malcom? I put that there. Not just because I'm somewhat possessive, but because I like seeing my mate wear the imprint of my teeth on her skin."

Taggart's eyes widened, and the blood left his face. His legs tensed, as if he were getting ready to run. But no one had to point out that he wasn't going anywhere. "Look ... I didn't know she was yours, man."

"Doesn't matter if you did or you didn't," said Tate, his voice dangerous. "You pumped three bullets into her. Into *my mate*. That's not something a man like me would or could ever forgive." Tate still couldn't get the footage of the drive-by out of his head. He wasn't sure he ever would.

Taggart flinched as the mamba began to ever so slowly slither up his leg. "I told you, it wasn't personal."

"It was just a job, right. The shifter who tried kidnapping Havana told us that very same thing. Your boss sent him after her. He likes to sell loners at auction. Did you know that?" By the sheer shock on Taggart's face, the answer was no. "He's pissed because she apprehended her kidnapper and none of us will simply forget what happened."

"I didn't know he was doing that shit." Taggart flinched again as the mamba slid along his thigh toward his chest.

"I doubt it would have made much of a difference to you if you had. Now ... it seems your boss has jaguar shifters working for him. Do you know anything about that?"

Taggart's eyes sharpened. "Jaguars?"

Everything in Tate stood up and paid attention. "Tell me what you know." Because it was clear the asshole knew something.

The cheetah licked his lips. "What's in it for me if I tell you?"

"Simple." Tate held up the cheetah's phone, showing one of the photos Luke had found. "I won't hunt down and kill the woman you're all cozy with here."

Dread flashed across Taggart's face, but he quickly blanked his expression. "She's no one to me. I hardly know her."

Alex snorted. "You're not a very good liar, Mal."

The cheetah squeezed his eyes shut as the mamba put her head level to his. She flicked out her tongue, letting it touch the side of his face. "Can someone please get it off me?"

"She won't bite," Havana assured him, thoroughly enjoying his discomfort. She shrugged one shoulder, adding, "Well, not unless I tell her to." And after listening to him try to justify the fact that he'd tried to kill her *twice*, Havana was seriously tempted to signal for the mamba to strike. Her devil would rather take care of him herself.

Aspen's nose wrinkled. "Well, there was that time she bit a hyena without your say-so. You remember?"

Havana waved that away. "She was pissed that day."

"She's pissed today," said Aspen.

Havana slanted her head. "You make a valid point." She almost chuckled when Taggart swore beneath his breath, trembling.

He opened his eyes but didn't look at the snake, as if intent on pretending she wasn't there.

"We have shit to do, Malcom," said Havana. "We don't have time for you to deliberate on just how much the life of that woman in the photo means to you. Either she matters to you or she doesn't. But be aware that we *will* get the information out of you one way or another. You might as well willingly part with it and save her life in the process."

Sweat beading his upper lip, Taggart stared at her mate, a plea in his eyes. "I wouldn't have hurt the devil if I'd known she meant something to you."

"So you've said before," Tate told him. "I don't know why you keep repeating it."

"Apparently he thinks it'll be enough to make you let him go." Luke snickered. "Even if you could forgive him, Havana wouldn't. And, Mal, just one word from her will have that mamba sinking her fangs into you. Appeals are pointless."

"Utterly pointless," Tate agreed. "You're going to die tonight. It's going to hurt. A lot. And none of us will feel in the least bit bad about it, considering you not only shot Havana, you've been executing people for a while now. But if you tell me what you know about those jaguar shifters, I will not hunt down this woman in the photo—I swear that to you. I will leave her be and forget she exists. But if you *don't* tell us what we want to know, I will do to this woman what you did to mine—only I won't give her a quick death. No, she'll suffer. Hard. Maybe I'll even keep you alive so you can watch it happen. And you can explain to her that she wouldn't have had to go through that agony if you had just done the right thing by her."

Fear flickered across the cheetah's face. "Fuck."

Havana knew that, in reality, Tate would never hurt a woman. Knew he would never make one person pay for another person's actions. But Taggart clearly believed Tate meant what he said, which was what mattered.

Tate lifted a brow. "So, what's it gonna be?"

The cheetah briefly closed his eyes. "You swear you won't touch her or send anyone after her if I tell you what you want to know?"

"I swear it," Tate promised.

Taggart's head jerked when the mamba's tongue flicked his ear. He looked at Havana. "I'll talk, I will, just get her off me."

"But she looks so comfortable there," said Havana. "It would be a shame to disturb her. She gets cranky when disturbed. So cranky she can just … lunge and bite."

Taggart cursed again.

"Don't look at Havana," Tate told him. "You look right at me and start talking. The sooner you're done, the sooner the mamba will slither away."

Taggart took in a long breath. "I don't know much about the jaguars, really. But I saw them one night when I was at a casino—Ace in the Hole, a place near the docks. Three girls were singing on stage. They weren't very good, but one was hot as hell. Asian. A female jaguar. Long legs, big rack, purple streaks in her black hair. I bought her a drink after the show. We exchanged names. I told her she had a nice voice. She said I should tell her boss that because the old bastard had informed her that tonight's performance would be her last—he was hiring a new act or something. Then, two guys showed up. They were jaguars, too."

"Descriptions?" asked Alex.

Taggart reeled off quite detailed descriptions. Havana noted it all down on her cell phone's notepad app.

"What happened next?" Tate asked the cheetah.

"The one with the ponytail got pissed and territorial, he told me to stay away from her. I apologized and said I didn't know she was spoken for. He studied me hard, like he thought he might know my face from somewhere. Then he smiled and said, 'Malcolm Taggart.' He told me we had the same boss, said he'd heard good things about me from his boss and that I should keep doing a good job because it ain't wise to disappoint him."

Havana stilled, asking, "You know this jaguar's name?"

Taggart frowned thoughtfully. "When he got all possessive, the woman tried calming him down. She called him Enrique. I don't think they were tight. She looked kind of scared of him."

Tate tapped his fingers on the chair. "Did you catch the other jaguar's name?"

"No," replied Taggart. "He never said a word. Not one." He gulped, because the mamba chose that moment to curl up on his lap, her head perilously close to his inner thigh.

"What about the woman? We don't wish her harm," Tate quickly added when Taggart hesitated to answer. "We just need her name. We may need her help to find this Enrique."

The cheetah sighed. "Lola," he said, his voice low and defeated. "She introduced herself as Lola."

"Lola," Alex echoed. "Anything else you can tell us?"

Taggart shook his head. "That's all I got."

"So you don't have even the slightest clue who your boss might be?" asked Tate.

Again, Taggart shook his head. "Not one."

"I do," said Tate. "You've been taking directions from Gideon York."

Taggart's face went slack. "That guy is dead."

"No, the twisted fuck is just underground. And you've been serving a man who massacred an entire wolf pack and then killed most of his own loyal followers. Just thought you might be interested to know." Tate slowly got to his feet and casually pushed the chair aside. "You were very informative, Mal. I appreciate that, I do. I like it when people are cooperative. But not enough for me to go easy on you. And let's be honest, if someone did to your woman what you did to mine, you'd expect them to pay, wouldn't you?"

Taking a step toward the cheetah, Tate felt his hands ball up. "You'll pay for agreeing to kill my mate. You'll pay for putting those bullets in her body. You'll pay for almost taking her from me twice." Tate leaned forward and said quietly, "And then you'll pay all over again." He slammed his fist into the bastard's jaw.

CHAPTER SEVENTEEN

A while later, once their captive was well and truly dead, they fanned out around Vinnie's kitchen to discuss what they'd learned from good ole Malcolm Taggart. Tate leaned against the counter with his arm around Havana's shoulders, keeping her front pressed to his side and holding her arm around his waist. He needed the contact. Needed to breathe her in. Needed to have her close. His cat needed it. She seemed to sense that, because his not-so-tactile mate huddled into him without complaint.

Right then, Tate's composure was a precarious thing. Because he couldn't quite let go that he'd almost lost his mate. *Again.*

Taggart might no longer be breathing, but much of Tate's anger remained, making him tense and edgy. His muscles were so tight he was surprised they weren't cramping.

"I'll contact River and have him look into Lola," said Tate. "Even if she did lose her job, her address should be in the employee records—River can access them. If her address is shifter territory, we'll know what pride she belongs to. But it would be a fair assumption that she belongs to Gideon's family."

"There are only three local jaguar prides," said Luke. "We could quietly look into them and find out if any have a member named Lola."

Tate nodded. "Do it. I'll assign some cats to watch the casino for any signs of someone with Enrique and his friend's descriptions. They might be regulars."

"But if they only went to see Lola and she's no longer an employee there, they probably won't return," Alex speculated.

"It wouldn't hurt to have people stake-out the place just in case," said Vinnie.

"We could question the staff, but I don't think it would be wise," said Tate. "If they're friends of Enrique, they'll tell him we were there. I don't want Gideon to know we're close to finding him."

"He could cut and run," said Bailey. "He could kill whatever loners he's currently keeping captive for his auction."

Tate nodded. "And we can't risk that." He took in a long breath. "So, in sum, I'll have River look into Lola, enquire about the local jaguar prides, and assign some cats to watch the casino."

"I can take care of the latter two," Luke offered.

Tate inclined his head and then looked at Havana. "Do I want to know how you, Aspen, and Bailey got inside Taggart's house without being detected by any of us?"

"It wasn't that hard," said Havana, but she didn't elaborate.

Tate looked from Aspen to Bailey, who both steadily stared back at him. It was clear that he wasn't going to get answers from their corner. Doubting that pushing them on it would get him anywhere, he decided to let it go. For now.

They all talked a little more about Taggart, the jaguars, and Gideon before finally choosing to head out.

Tate was able to coax Havana into going home with him. As they walked along the street, they were stopped several times by his pride mates. Nosy as hell, each of the cats fished for information, but they were clearly also concerned about him and Havana. Tate kept the conversations short, uncomfortable with having his mate out in the open after yet another drive-by shooting, even though he knew it was unlikely that Gideon would have someone strike again so quickly.

Finally inside his house, Tate felt he could breathe easier. No one could get to her here. And even if someone went as far as to shoot at his windows, the bullets wouldn't break the bulletproof glass. She was safest here, on his territory, where he could protect her. Still, the tension didn't leave his body.

After he made the necessary calls related to the Gideon matter, Tate headed to the kitchen. He grabbed a beer for himself and poured Havana a glass of the wine he now stocked, knowing it was her preferred brand. They then settled on the sofa to watch TV. He lay on his back with her sprawled over him, her head resting on his chest. Needing skin-to-skin contact, he slipped one hand into her panties to palm her ass. He also snaked his free hand under her tee to drift his fingers over her back. But it was hard to relax when his brain kept playing the "if" game.

If he hadn't seen the barrel of the gun pointing out of the Charger's window, Havana might have been shot right in front of him.

If there hadn't been a car parked nearby for them to use as cover, Tate might not have been able to shield her from the bullets.

If they'd reacted even just a *little* bit slower, Havana might have been hit before she ducked out of range of the gun.

If Farrell hadn't been close by and able to follow the vehicle, they might never have found Taggart before he fled.

The whole thing had been a close fucking call, just like the last drive-by. Sheer luck had been on Havana's side both times. But if there was a third time, just maybe she wouldn't have that same luck. That thought made his throat burn. He couldn't lose her.

"Ow," she whined. "Claws."

Tate blinked and retracted his claws, realizing they'd been pricking the globe of her ass. He massaged the skin there. "Sorry, babe."

She lifted her head and rested her chin on his chest. "You need to stop brooding about whatever has you tense as a bow."

His cat puffed up in affront. "I don't brood."

"So says *every* dominant male shifter. In reality, you're all experts at it." She danced her fingertips along his collarbone. "Distract yourself. Think about something else."

"All right." Tate swept his hand up her back. "Maybe you can now tell me how you and your girls managed to not only sneak into Taggart's house but to do it without Alex, Vinnie, or Farrell—all of whom were guarding the exterior of the building—sensing the three of you. *I* didn't even sense you enter the house, and neither did Luke."

"Like I said earlier, it wasn't hard. The guys were so busy watching out for the cheetahs that they just didn't notice us. And you and your brother were preoccupied with Taggart and his friend."

Tate snorted. *Bullshit*. Vinnie, Alex, and Farrell were too well-trained to not notice three females approaching the house ... unless those three females had once received similar training. "Really? Hmm. I can't help but get the feeling that you have experience with sneaking in and out of buildings, just as I can't help but get the feeling that you have experience with interrogations. Am I right?"

She pursed her lips. "I once had a job where I needed those skills. I wasn't a gun for hire or anything."

"I never thought for one moment that you were," Tate assured her. "You're not going to tell me more?"

Her expression turned grave. "If I tell you, you can't share it with anyone. Not even your dad or your siblings. If you're uncomfortable with keeping a secret from them, I can understand that. But it also means I can't tell you what you want to know."

"If you need something to stay between us, it stays between us. I'm loyal to my family, yes, but *you're* my family, too. More, you're my priority. My loyalty is primarily to you. You can trust me."

"I know that."

Her easy acceptance of his promise warmed him. "So tell me."

She sat up straight and took in a deep breath. "Okay. Me, Aspen, and Bailey once worked for the Movement."

Stunned, Tate simply stared at her for a long moment. "The Movement?"

"Yes. So did Camden, though he mostly worked jobs alone. We were part of the group for eight years. To the outside world, we lived seemingly normal lives."

Nothing she said could have surprised him more ... and yet it fit. Shifters with those three females' traits, strengths, and deep sense of loyalty would make them prime candidates for the Movement. It explained so much—not just the skills she'd shown, but how well she kept it together each time danger came too close.

He gently squeezed her hips. "Thank you for your service. I can easily visualize you working for the Movement. And Aspen and Bailey, for that matter. I'll bet you were good at what you did."

Havana couldn't help but grin. "Oh, we were. And we were proud to be part of the group. We might not have left so soon if members weren't required to retire after eight years. They want people to go out and find their mates."

"Ah, I see. If a shifter is so deeply devoted to such a cause, it might be hard for them to sense their mate or the presence of a mating bond."

"Exactly. Plus, the Movement doesn't want their members spending the rest of their days dealing with prejudiced assholes."

Tate twisted his mouth. "A lot of people believe the group was founded by Clive Vincent, the father of a Mercury Pack margay I know."

"She performs at the Velvet Lounge, right? Plays the electric violin?"

"That's right."

Havana had been there a few times. The club was cool, and the performers were even better. Alex's sister, Mila, often sang there—she was seriously talented.

"Even Clive's daughter is unsure if he heads the Movement," Tate went on. "Since he's in prison, many say he can't possibly be running the group from there. Others believe it's a damn good cover for him."

Sensing that he was fishing for info, Havana shook her head. "I can't give you specifics about the Movement. Not because I don't trust you, but because I pledged an oath that I would never reveal what I knew—I take shit like that seriously, and I would think you'd want that in a mate. They're not just a rebel group. They're a family of sorts. And they once welcomed me into that family. A lot of the strengths I have today, I owe to them. I won't betray them, especially not just to assuage your curiosity."

Tate inclined his head. "Fair enough."

She felt her mouth curve. "There you go gritting your teeth again."

Using his grip on her hips, he pulled her down and nipped her lower lip. "You're supposed to give me my own way all the time."

Havana snorted. Not freaking likely. She was about to make it clear that no such thing would ever happen, but then his tongue swept into her mouth, bold and sure … and all she could think about was having more.

His warm hand clasped her nape as he took complete possession of her mouth. There was nothing slow or easy about his kiss. No, it was so hot and wet and explicitly carnal that her body came to life. There was a lot of tingling and pulsing and throbbing in some *very* interesting places. She broke the kiss, needing to catch her breath.

Tightening his grip on her nape, he yanked her so that their lips touched. "I'll let your mouth go when I'm done with it."

Oh, defiance surged through her system in a hot rush. She stabbed his chest with the tips of her claws—not drawing blood, just warning him. "Careful."

His free hand clutched her ass. "No fighting me today. You're going to give me what I want exactly how I want it."

Havana could only smile. "Aw, Garfield, that's gotta be the cutest damn thing I've ever heard."

Tate cursed as his mate disappeared from his arms and leaped off the sofa. Adrenaline coursed through his blood as he jumped to his feet and pursued her. She was fast, but he caught up to her in the kitchen and managed to tag her with an arm around her waist. Hauling her against him, he ignored her kicks and insults and pressed her front against the wall, caging her there with his body.

She hissed, growled, struggled, writhed. He pinned her wrists above her head and sank his teeth into the crook of her neck in a dominant hold. Her body went rigid. For all of three seconds. Then she went back to squirming and snarling.

Tate didn't react. He just kept her wrists pinned and her flesh gripped between his teeth. But even when he made it clear he wouldn't back down, she didn't settle. Transferring her wrists to one hand, he clawed off her shorts and panties. Oh, she stilled then. To reward her, he licked over his bite. His cock throbbed at the mere sight of it, straining against his fly. Seeing the indentation from his teeth on her skin always heated his blood. It also made his cat growl in a primal satisfaction.

Tate punched his hips forward, pressing his cock against her ass. "Love that this is now my ass, babe." He had all kinds of future plans for it.

She peered at him over her shoulder and snorted. "Yours?"

He put his mouth to her ear. "There's not a single part of you—inside or out—that doesn't belong to me. You're my other half. That ownership is imprinted in every cell of your body. I'm written into your skin, your bones, your soul. You have the same deep, absolute claim to me. And I wouldn't have it any other way."

He clawed off both her tee and bra. "Now … I'm going to release your hands so you can turn around. Then you're going to undo my jeans so I can hoist you up and fuck you against this wall. Understood?" He raked his teeth over her shoulder when she didn't answer. "Understood?"

"I hear you, kitty," she sassed.

He bit her earlobe. "Watch it, baby." He slowly released her hands and edged back enough that she had adequate space to turn. He braced himself for impact as she spun to face him. But she didn't shove him away as he'd half-expected. She snapped open his fly and curled her fingers around his pulsing cock. He groaned. "That's my girl." Then she dropped to her knees.

He hissed as her tongue lashed the head of his dick. "You trying to take control?" She took him into her mouth. And as all that wet heat engulfed him, he found it hard to give a shit that she was trying to top from the bottom.

Havana sucked hard, keeping the suction tight, remembering how he liked it. He was right. This was her way of taking control. Her way of stealing *his* control. And if he was weak enough to give into the pleasure rather than snatch back what she'd stolen, that was on him.

She kept on sucking and licking, losing herself in the act ... which hadn't been part of the plan, but she *liked* him this way—his thighs trembling, his cock throbbing, his hand in her hair to guide her movements. She liked making him feel good. Liked that he was hers to taste.

His eyes bore into her, hooded and flinty. "Fuck but you look good on your knees with my cock in your mouth." His fingertips dug into her scalp. "Take more, baby. Christ, yeah, that's it."

She didn't object when he tangled his hand in her hair and began pumping his dick into her mouth. She just sucked harder, humming and dragging her nails down his thigh.

He growled. "Eyes, Havana," he bit out. "I want you looking right at me while my come is sliding down your throat."

She flicked her gaze up to his, and whatever he saw there made him thrust faster and deeper. He exploded, holding her head still while she swallowed it all. As he loosened his grip on her hair, breathing hard, she inwardly smiled. Oh yeah, she'd obliterated his control and topped—

He dropped to his knees, pushed her flat on her back, grabbed her hips, and pulled her pussy up to his mouth. She arched, her head lolling back. His tongue did all kinds of wicked things. Licked, probed, lashed, thrust, rolled around her clit—winning him lots of sexual points.

She'd had guys eat her out before, but Tate? He didn't simply go down on her. He *dined*. Savored. Purred like the self-indulgent cat he was.

He didn't let her come, though. Which lost him a whole lot of points. He ignored her indignant hiss.

Licking his lips, he dropped her hips to the floor, his eyes crazed. Hmm, he was hard again. She did appreciate his quick recovery time.

He roughly spread her thighs. "You're going to get so fucked."

She went to make a run for it just because.

He covered her body with his. "Oh, no you don't."

Oh yes, she did. She curled her legs around him and kicked like crazy.

He slipped his hand under her knee, bent her leg toward her chest, and plunged his cock deep inside her. And she came. *Hard.*

Gritting his teeth, Tate rode her through her orgasm, pounding into her, relishing the feel of her tight inner muscles spasming and quaking around him. "Yeah, this is where I need to be."

He might have come once already, but it hadn't taken the edge off. He was all fired up from … *everything.* Her taste on his tongue. Her moans and whimpers. Her tits bouncing against his chest. Her scent spiced with arousal. Her slick pussy squeezing his dick. More, the memory of her sucking him off was on replay in his head. Coming down her throat wasn't only hot as hell, it was another way to mark her as his.

Knowing she liked it, he sucked and nipped at her pulse as he kept slamming into her. She clung tight to his shoulders, and her claws slid out just enough to dig into his skin. Lifting his head, he saw the struggle on her face, and he knew she was fighting the urge to leave her brand on him.

"Do it," he snarled. "Mark me."

She squeezed her eyes tightly shut and retracted her claws.

He growled. "*Havana.*"

"Your cat—"

"Needs this. *I* need it." Tate pinched her nipple, making her eyes snap open. "Fucking do it. Mark me. Make sure every female out there knows I'm taken. Make sure none of the women from my past thinks they can—" He groaned as her teeth latched onto the crook of his neck. More, she dragged her claws down his back, roughly drawing blood.

Tate swore. His control gone, he hooked both her legs over his shoulders, and buried himself inside her yet again—deeper this time. So fucking deep it shocked the breath out of her.

He powered into her, feeling his orgasm creep toward him. "I love knowing my come is inside your belly right now." It gave him a primitive satisfaction that his cat shared. "Know what else I love? Being balls-deep in this pussy. So fucking tight. Perfect. Made for me."

Her upper lip curled back. "Yeah well your cock was made for me."

"Every inch of it." Feeling her pussy tighten and flutter, Tate slipped his hand between their bodies to part her folds, exposing her clit to every rough thrust of his cock.

Her eyes went wide. "Shit, shit, shit, I'm gonna …"

He slid his hand around her throat and squeezed. "All over my cock, baby, come all over … *Christ,* yeah." Wave upon wave of pleasure thundered through him. He ground out her name as he shoved his cock deep and spilled himself inside her.

His heart thumping hard in his chest, Tate let her legs slip from his shoulders and draped himself over her. Resting his weight on his forearms, he slowly glided in and out of her, just enjoying the feel of her.

Once he'd finally gotten his breath back, he rolled over, taking her with him so that she was sprawled on top of him. The move pulled a little on the claw marks spanning his back, but he didn't mind that. He liked feeling that twinge of pain; liked the reminder that she'd branded him.

She hummed. "If there's an award out there for eating pussy, you totally deserve to win it."

A low laugh rumbled his chest. "I don't even have a response for that."

She danced her fingers over his shoulder. "How's your cat?"

"He's not upset about the bite, babe, if that's what you're wondering. He's actually pretty damn smug."

Relief filled Havana, and the tightness in her chest eased away. "Good." She poked his shoulder. "You mentioned the women from your past because you knew it would make me think of Ashlynn and that I'd want to brand you as a warning to her."

He shrugged, unrepentant. "I needed you to power past your hesitation and stop fighting yourself. Is your devil unhappy that you marked me?"

"No. Which is a good sign." If Havana had done it just a week ago, her devil would have pitched a fit for sure. "Seems like your plan to win her over is working."

"But she hasn't opened that mental door even a crack yet, has she?"

"She's stubborn that way."

"And highly protective of you."

"That, too."

He smoothed his hand up her back and delved it into her hair. "Stay here tonight."

"Can't. I didn't pack a bag." She snorted as his face morphed into that "why aren't things going my way, I'm confused" frown that never failed to tickle her.

"You have some of your things here," he pointed out.

"But not everything I need."

"So let's go to your place and pick up more of your stuff. I don't want us sleeping in separate beds. I like waking up and seeing you right there."

"Hmm, well, you *are* a pleasant sight to wake to, so I won't argue. Come on then, let's go to my place."

Walking into the living area of her apartment a short time later, Havana saw a highly agitated Camden standing near the bookcase. As she took in the entire scene, she could only sigh.

A black mamba was curled up on the bookcase, a large part of her lower body dangling from the piece of furniture ... and the base of her body wrapped tight around a bearcat's neck. Choking, the bearcat kicked and scratched. Then she sank her teeth into the snake, who hissed loudly.

Havana cursed beneath her breath. "You two have *got* to be kidding me."

Both animals froze. Their gazes snapped to her and then briefly slid away.

"Put her down," Havana told the mamba.

The snake did it fast, no doubt roughly dumping the bearcat on the hardwood floor on purpose just to be a bitch.

Camden scratched his head. "I tried calming them down, Havana. It didn't work. They both went to bite me when I intervened."

Havana scrubbed a hand down her face. "I'm honestly worried they'll kill each other one day."

Coming up behind her, Tate splayed a hand on her back. "I don't think they'll *kill* each other. Well, not on purpose."

The mamba slithered down to the floor and then shifted. Bailey sniffed at Aspen, who'd also shifted and was pulling on her clothes. "You can't blame my snake for the fight this time. She was all the way up there minding her own business. Your bearcat provoked her."

Aspen tossed Bailey's clothes at her. "You missed out the part where your shit-stirring mamba took my bearcat's bamboo shoots up there with her."

"She was hungry."

"She doesn't eat bamboo shoots."

"She wanted to try something different."

"No, the bitch wanted to pick a fight, so she did."

Bailey wagged her finger. "Don't act like your bearcat is all innocent. She stole the batteries out of my vibrator. Again. And I would love to know where they are, because I have a feeling that more of my stuff is in her private stash—like my unicorn voodoo doll."

Aspen leaned toward the mamba. "She didn't touch your stupid vibrator, or your stupid unicorn."

Havana wrinkled her nose at Aspen. "I do hope your bearcat didn't put her hands anywhere near another person's vibrator, but she *is* inappropriate enough to explore someone's underwear drawer. Tell me she didn't snatch any of Bailey's thongs or panties."

"I don't wear thongs," said Bailey, folding her arms. "Don't see why anyone would want to. You're just buying a wedgie."

Tate coughed out a laugh and put a fist to his mouth.

Sighing, Havana pointed from Aspen to Bailey. "You two need to get a handle on your inner animals before they do some permanent damage to each other."

Bailey's brow furrowed. "My mamba would never *really* hurt Aspen or her bearcat. She loves them. She just also has *the best time* driving them to the brink of insanity. Is that so terrible?"

Aspen flexed her fingers. "Just because *you* long ago tumbled over said brink doesn't mean *I* want to."

"But it's more fun on this side," said Bailey.

As her girls continued to argue, Havana turned to Tate and said, "I know, I know, they're crazy."

Tate pulled her close. "On the upside, it means they'll fit perfectly in my pride."

Havana felt her brows lift. "Well, there is that."

CHAPTER EIGHTEEN

Entering his living room the next morning, Tate frowned. "What are you doing here?"

Sitting on the sofa with Bailey, Aspen briefly looked away from the TV and replied, "We wanted to talk with Havana, but we heard you two fucking like bunnies upstairs so figured we'd just wait here."

"You couldn't have just called?" he asked.

"That would have been lazy when she's such a short walk away," said Bailey. "Love your TV, by the way. It's *way* bigger than mine, and the quality of the picture is ace."

"Yep," agreed Aspen. "We *so* need one of these for our movie nights."

Bailey's eyes widened. "Ooh, yeah, that would be cool."

"How did you even get in here?" Tate cut in. "And why didn't one of my enforcers stop you?" *No one* got inside unless he invited them in—his cats knew that.

Aspen scratched her cheek. "Yeah, I don't think they know we're here. And getting inside was easy—the front door was unlocked."

His frown deepened. "No, it wasn't."

Bailey lifted her shoulders. "How else would we have gotten inside?"

Probably with the skills they'd learned when working for the Movement. Which his cat respected, despite the feline not being too keen on people turning up to his lair uninvited.

God, it was too early in the morning to deal with this. Tate sighed. "I need coffee."

"There's some in the pot," said Bailey.

With a grunt, he headed for the kitchen. Havana descended the stairs mere moments later. She briefly spoke with her girls in the living room, but their voices were too muffled for him to make out the words.

Entering the kitchen, Havana took the mug of coffee he held out. "Thanks."

Leaning against the counter with a cup in hand, he gently drew her closer so that she stood between his legs. And just like that, his irritation at her friends slipped away. "You're welcome." He sipped at his coffee. "Do you want to tell me why Aspen and Bailey are here?"

"Apparently, Dieter turned up at my apartment this morning looking for me."

Tate felt his face harden. His cat bared a fang. "Is that so?"

"They said he looked like a kicked puppy, so I'm guessing he intended to apologize for how he acted last time he was there."

"Maybe, but I still don't like it." Tate suspected the man still wanted her, which was why he'd told her guards to contact him if Dieter approached her. "You say he's your friend, but I don't think he's much of one. And yeah, I also don't like that this guy you once cared for is still in your life—I'll own that. But I'd set it aside if he was a good friend to you."

Havana leaned into him. Some women got off on displays of jealousy from their men, but she wasn't one of them. "I get it. I don't like that Ashlynn's around. It also isn't easy for me to know that you've had flings with some of your pride mates, but none of them have tried poaching and—unlike Ashlynn—they've all been perfectly civil, so I don't let it get to me. You don't need to feel threatened by Dieter's presence any more than I need to feel threatened by theirs or Ashlynn's. They're all just parts of our past. That's it."

"In the cases of Dieter and Ashlynn, they're parts that are trying to intrude on our present. He doesn't like that you now have me. And I don't like that he doesn't like it, because it implies that he might want you for himself."

"He has a girlfriend. He's serious about her."

Tate grunted. "Not serious enough that he could be happy for you when he learned you'd found your mate."

"Well, the girls seem to think he intended to apologize for how he behaved before."

"Maybe he does, and maybe he'll prove me wrong. But I don't think so."

She sighed. "Even if he did want me for himself, he wouldn't do anything about it, given that I now have you." It would be plain pointless.

"Don't be so sure of that. There have been many cases where a shifter has found their true mate but chose to forsake them. Koby's a perfect example. So is Bree, for that matter. Okay, so hers was a psychopath, but it still counts."

Havana fisted his tee and pinned his gaze with her own. "I wouldn't forsake you for Dieter or anyone else," she assured him.

"I know that, babe. Just as you know that you and you alone will always be my choice. But that doesn't mean I'm going to be fine that you have someone in your life who might wish they could come between us." Just then, Tate's phone chimed to signal an incoming text message. He whipped out his phone and read it. "Luke says there's no jaguar by the name of Lola in the local jaguar prides."

"It doesn't necessarily mean she's Gideon's kin, though, does it? Or even that she's a loner. I mean, her family could have mated into a wolf pack or bear clan or something. It doesn't seem likely that *she* herself had mated into one, considering she was—and may even still be—involved with Enrique."

"True." Tate took a sip of his drink. "Hopefully River can find her address. That would help."

She blew out a breath. "I have to get to work soon. Call or text me if and when you hear from River."

He kissed her. "Will do, babe." He smoothed the stray strands of her hair away from her face. "I'll miss you."

She smiled. "Of course you will. I'm fucking brilliant."

He chuckled. "You're supposed to say you'll miss me, too."

"You already know I will." She chugged back the rest of her coffee. "Now I need to chomp down some cereal so I'm not late for work."

"Give me one last kiss."

With a roll of her eyes, she did so.

He hummed and then patted her ass. "Let's get you fed."

Stepping out of the deli after lunch, Tate heard his cell ring. He dug it out of his pocket. The muscles in his shoulders bunched. "It's River," he told his brother. Tate then answered, "Tell me you have good news."

"Wish I could," River grumbled. "I looked into Lola. She was fired from the casino not too long ago. She was also evicted from her apartment a week after being fired. I so far haven't been able to locate her."

Tate pinched his lips shut as disappointment flooded him. "Fuck."

"I doubt she's now living on shifter territory, considering she recently resided in a crummy apartment in a very shady area. My guess? She's either a loner or part of Gideon's weird family."

"It would seem so," said Tate, rolling back his shoulders. "Thanks, River. Let me know if you manage to find her."

Ending the call, Tate sighed.

"I take it River didn't have anything good to say," hedged Luke.

"No, he didn't." Tate relayed the short conversation to his brother. "I was hoping Gideon would show up at Taggart's address." But according to the enforcers watching the house, plenty of cars had driven down the road, but none had stopped. "If Gideon or one of his minions *did* go looking for

Taggart and Clementine, they might have decided not to bother searching the house after seeing that the Charger is gone."

"Maybe." Tate exhaled heavily. "I'd like to do another search of the house. I'm not optimistic that we'll find anything that might point toward Gideon's location, but it's worth a shot."

"Then let's do it."

Keeping his promise to Havana that he'd relay any intel he received, Tate sent her a message: *Just spoke to River. No good news to report as yet.* Tate gave her a brief summary of what the cat told him.

Her reply came quickly: *Bummer. Was hoping I could pull out the pom poms later. Like you've said lots of times, Gideon can't hide from us forever. We're getting closer, so don't brood. Later.*

Tate snorted. *Later, babe. And I don't brood.*

She sent him a message with several emojis of a face with a long nose.

Shaking his head, Tate pocketed his phone and took a swig from the soda he'd bought at the deli. He was just about to pass the bakery when the door opened, and five familiar shifters stepped out. Spotting Tate and Luke, the Phoenix Pack wolves turned to face them.

"Oh, hey, how are you guys doing?" asked Taryn, the Alpha female, holding a huge box of baked goods.

"Fine," replied Tate. He and Luke exchanged greetings with her mate, Trey, their Beta Dante, their Head Enforcer Tao, and Trey's grandmother, Greta.

"I heard about all the chaos surrounding your woman," Trey said to Tate. "We've been doing our best to locate Gideon York, but he's proven to be pretty elusive."

"How's Havana?" asked Taryn.

"Good, all things considered," Tate replied.

Giving him a wan smile, Greta patted his arm. "You have my utmost sympathy, boy."

Tate's brow creased. The antisocial, maladjusted woman generally wasn't a person who felt compassion for anyone. "I do?"

Greta rested a hand on his shoulder. "Anyone who's been lumbered with a devil shifter for a mate deserves sympathy."

Trey rounded on her. "*Greta.*"

"Well, it's true," the old woman insisted. "They're a bloodthirsty lot, and they seem to live by the motto that any day is a fine day to kill."

Tate knew that. He also liked it, as did his cat. Which was the only reason he didn't whack his brother over the head for nodding in agreement.

Taryn sighed. "Don't take her bitchiness personally, Tate. She *can't* be nice, she sold her soul to Satan himself long ago. I'm guessing she was granted eternal life in return, because we just can't get her to die. She has the wrinkles, the scaly skin, the fuzzy gray hair, the rickety bones, the musty old lady smell

"... but her heart still beats."

Greta scowled. "Oh, you wish me gone, do you?"

"Every time I blow out my birthday candles. Now let's get going, Bride of Beelzebub." Taryn herded her toward an SUV that was idling at the curb.

Trey sighed. "Yeah, this is my life. See you around."

Tate inclined his head while Luke tipped his chin.

"*I am not senile!*" Greta shouted at Taryn.

"*But you are fucking demented.* Now get in the SUV, Wrinkles." Taryn all but shoved the woman into the vehicle. "I did *not* push you, I was just trying to help."

Exchanging a smile with his brother, Tate took another drink of his soda. Taryn was crazy enough to be a pallas cat.

It was as he and Luke began their drive to Taggart's old address that Tate heard his phone beep again. It was a message from Deke: *A guy called Dieter just showed up at the center to speak privately with your mate.*

Tate felt his nostrils flare. *Son of a motherfucker.* "We're making a pit-stop at the center," he told Luke, glad they were only minutes away from the building.

"Why?" asked Luke. "Everything okay with Havana?"

"Depends just what her ex has to say to her."

"Her ex? What ex?"

"Funny story."

Havana was in the middle of straightening out the filing cabinet in Corbin's office when someone knocked on the already open door. She glanced over her shoulder. Her devil narrowed her eyes.

Looking like a man who'd been kicked in the gut, Dieter slowly walked in, rubbing his nape. "Havana," he greeted softly.

She closed the metal draw of the cabinet and turned to face him. "Hi," she said, her voice just as low.

He cast the two enforcers leaning against the wall a brief look. "Can we talk alone?" he asked her.

She studied his expression. He didn't *look* as though he'd come here to mouth off again. In fact, he had his metaphorical tail tucked between his legs. Deciding to give him the benefit of the doubt, she looked at the enforcers. "It's okay, guys."

Deke and Isaiah left without a word, each shooting Dieter a hard look. They didn't close the door behind them, and she knew they'd rush in if they thought it necessary.

"Your bodyguards, I presume," said Dieter.

She folded her arms. "Yes."

Sighing, he made his way toward her. "You're probably super pissed at me. I don't blame you. I was an asshole last time we spoke. It's just … It was a shock. All of it. The drive-by, how you almost died, that you'd found your mate." His shoulders drooped. "I'm sorry for being an ass. You didn't deserve it."

Havana stared at him. He'd said all the right things and looked appropriately repentant, but there was an *off* note to his tone. She couldn't help but get the feeling that this was leading up to something. Something that she wasn't going to like.

"I heard about the second drive-by," he said. "I also heard that Devereaux saved the day."

She squinted at the edge to his words. "Dieter, if you're going to act like a shithead again—"

"I'm not, I …" He trailed off with a soft curse.

"Why are you here?"

"To apologize. To check that you're okay."

"Apology accepted." Well, sort of. Her devil jutted out her chin, unmoved by his apparent remorse. "And I'm good."

He swallowed. "I'm glad. I've been worried about you." Licking his lips, he took a step closer. "I need to know something," he added, looking more serious than she'd ever seen him. "If I'd offered you more than casual sex at some point in the past, would you have agreed to try it?"

Well that came out of left field. "You never would have offered me that, Dieter. You want to be part of a flock, and no lone shifter can give you that."

"But if I'd shoved that shit aside and asked you to try something serious, would you have done it?"

"Does it really matter? I'm with Tate now."

His face darkened. "It matters to me. Be honest with me, please."

She sighed. "The truth? I'd have agreed to more. I wanted more. But you didn't. We shared a bed off-and-on for a year. You never asked for exclusivity or stuck around long. You flitted from person to person, keeping things simple and shallow."

"Because I was a fucking idiot," he clipped. "I was obsessed with becoming part of a flock. I lost sight of what else was important to me. *You.*"

A snort bubbled up. "You never made me feel important."

"I should've done, because you are."

"Things often seem much more appealing when they're out of our reach."

"This is not me being drawn to forbidden fucking fruit. This is me realizing how badly I messed up. This is me wanting you back."

She almost gaped. Oh, he could *not* be doing this. He could not be pulling this crap. Tate had been right about him, she realized. "You never had me to begin with. You kept me dangling on a string. You'd disappear for months at a time, return to throw scraps at my table so I'd find it hard to forget you, and then you'd be gone again."

"I didn't keep coming back to stop you from forgetting me. I did it because I couldn't fucking help it." He ground his teeth. "You say the pallas cat is your mate. But you're still not bonded to him, so how do you know it for sure?"

"I just do."

"Or maybe you *want* to believe it. Maybe you're done being alone. Maybe you want to finally settle down. I can give you that, Havana."

Her lips parted. "You have got to be kidding me."

"No joke, no lie, I can give you that. He doesn't know you like I do. You and I have history. *Good* history."

"Dieter—"

"No, listen to me." He took another step closer. "I love you, all right. I love you. I should've said it before now. I should have gotten my act together, admitted what was most important to me, and asked you to take a chance on me, on us. I didn't, but I'm doing it right here, right now. If you need time for me to prove to you that I mean every word, I'll give you that time. I will. Whatever you want, Havana, I'll give you whatever you want. I'm in this for the long haul."

She stared at him, hurt. Once, hearing those three little words from him would have delighted her. Now, they only made her sad. Because if he truly meant them, it had taken her finding her mate for Dieter to actually realize he cared for her so deeply.

If the situation were reversed, she wouldn't have made this declaration. She wouldn't have messed with his head this way. She'd have had more respect for the fact that he'd found his true mate. Yet, he apparently couldn't do any of that for her. He expected—*literally* expected it, she could hear it in his voice—her to drop Tate for him. "You need to go."

Dieter frowned. "What?"

"I'm with Tate now. I have no wish to change that. I don't want to hurt you, but I won't lie to you. I don't want what you want."

"Because he's got you convinced that you two are mates. I don't see it, Havana. When I looked at the two of you standing side by side, I didn't see any connection there. You believe him because you *want* to believe him. You want to put down some roots and settle. I get it. Like I said, I can give you that."

"I don't want you to." And it was pretty much *the last* thing her devil wanted. "He and I *are* mates, Dieter. I don't expect you to be happy for me. But I'm asking that you respect that and just drop this."

His eyes flared. "I'd respect it if I believed it, but I don't."

"Lucky for me and Havana, we don't require you to believe it."

Tate almost snorted at how fast the eagle twirled to face him. He'd overheard plenty as he stood outside the office moments ago, and he was finding it an honest to God's struggle not to drop-kick the son of a bitch. His cat had sliced out his claws and was now drumming them on the ground, raring to pounce.

Dieter had tried to move in on Tate's woman. Had claimed that there was no true-mate bond. Had professed to love her and be ready to fully commit to her. Really, it was like Dieter *wanted* to have the shit kicked out of him.

Tate planted his feet and cocked his head. "I figured you'd make this play sooner or later. Havana's not a woman who's easy to let go of, is she?" Tate had learned that the hard way. He'd initially made the mistake of not instantly snapping her up, but not because he hadn't *wanted* to. No, he'd held back to protect her from any hurt that his cat could potentially cause her. Dieter, though, simply hadn't bothered to offer her more until he learned she was taken.

Dieter sneered. "If you think I'm going to cower or apologize, you're wrong. I won't give her up without a fight."

"I won't give her up *period*. You made this move too late. And for that, I thank you. Because I might not have her now if you'd tied her to you. But that has already occurred to you, hasn't it? Things could be so different now if you'd just done this sooner. And that knowledge is eating away at you, isn't it?" The idea gratified his cat.

"She *is* tied to me in her way."

Tate almost rolled his eyes at the pathetic claim. "Can't you just be a friend to her? Someone who'll support and be pleased for her? Do you really not care how hard this is for her? You want her to choose between her friend and her mate. And, weird as it is, you expect her to choose you." *That* Tate really didn't get … unless Dieter had always suspected that Havana cared for him.

"She and I are more than just friends with benefits," the eagle insisted. "Always were."

Yep, Dieter had suspected that she cared for him. Tate's nostrils flared. The motherfucker had known she felt something for him. He'd known that going back to her bed again and again was giving her false hope that their little arrangement could evolve into something else. More, he'd known that he was hurting her by bedding other females and seeking her out when lonely. But he'd selfishly done it all anyway.

"I know her inside and out," Dieter went on. "I know everything there is to know about her. I know what she needs, and I'm ready to give it to her."

"You think you deserve her? Odd. You didn't propose a relationship until after another man entered the picture. You didn't hesitate to sleep with other women. You didn't appreciate what was right in front of you. Instead, you quite simply used her. Used and then tossed her aside again and again."

"I didn't—"

"You also had no problem committing to another woman. Then you heard that Havana had found her mate, and you realized how badly you'd messed up. But rather than accepting that you missed your chance and just wishing her well, you decided to ask her to dump *her mate* for you. You expect her to choose a man who didn't appreciate how special she is, which I think is plain fucking insulting."

"You're not really her mate. You've fooled her into thinking you are, but it isn't true."

Tate's cat snapped his teeth. "You truly believe that Havana is so easily manipulated? That she doesn't know her own mind?" Unlikely. "The only person here trying to manipulate her is *you*. I truly can understand why you'd want her to be yours, but you can't have her." Tate moved toward Havana, but the eagle quickly blocked his path. Tate felt a cold smile curve his mouth. "You think you can stand between me and what's mine?"

"She's not your mate."

"So you stupidly keep saying. But even if she wasn't—which she absolutely is, I assure you—I wouldn't let her go."

"You can't hold someone against their will."

"I won't need to. Despite what you might have told yourself, Havana's not going to leave me for you. If you make her choose, you'll lose her." Which would suit Tate fine, to be honest, because Dieter had never treated her how she deserved to be treated. He'd never appreciated, treasured, or been considerate of her.

"You can see the brand on my neck," Tate said to him. "It should tell you that she considers me hers just as much as I consider her mine. You don't have a prayer of coming between us."

"He's right, Dieter," said Havana, making the guy turn back to her. "Tate and I *are* mates. This little declaration of yours ... you made it too late. I'm not going to leave him for you or anyone else. I wouldn't even if he wasn't my true mate."

Dieter swallowed, his face falling. "You hardly *know* him. I've been part of your life a hell of a lot longer. He might think you belong to him, but notice he didn't once say he cares about you."

"I don't need him to say it. I *feel* that he cares. I never once felt that you did."

Dieter advanced on her, looking ready to grab her.

"That's close enough," Tate warned him, a growl rumbling in his chest—one that came from both him and his cat. "Step away from her."

The eagle rounded on him, his face red. "You think I'm afraid of you?" He let out a derisive snort. "Fuck you." Retracting his fingers like they were claws, he lunged.

Tate snapped out his fist, slamming it into Dieter's jaw. The eagle dropped like a stone, dazed. "It didn't have to go this way." Tate fisted the guy's shirt, dragged him out of the office, and dropped him at Luke's feet. "Get rid of him." Tate then spun on his heel and headed straight to his mate.

Havana went easily into his arms and blew out a breath. "Well that was unpleasant."

He cupped one side of her neck. "You okay?"

"Yes. Your enforcers gave you a heads-up that he was here, huh?"

"They did. My gut told me that Dieter would make this play at some point, so I had a pretty good idea of why he'd come here. I didn't want you dealing with it alone."

"And you wanted to metaphorically pee on your territory."

"You're more than just my territory, baby. You're my everything." He squeezed the side of her neck. "If it turned out that we weren't mates, you'd still be my everything."

Her face went all soft in that way he liked. "Right back at you."

"Good. But we *are* mates. We just need your devil to accept me as you do."

"She's more than halfway there." Havana smoothed her hands up his chest. "I'm sorry that she's taking her sweet time."

"Don't be. This is all on me. I let her down. I let you down. In doing so, I hurt you both. I don't expect her to just forgive and forget all that—she doesn't understand *why* I originally held back. She's just looking out for you. Although it stings that she'd feel you need protecting from me, I know it's my own fault. She'll come around. And when she does, I can officially claim you."

"A claim I will return."

"Yes, you will." He slowly took her mouth in a soft, languid kiss, loving how she strained toward him for more. He pulled back with a sigh of regret. "I've got to go. I have a few things to do."

"Alpha stuff?"

"Alpha stuff. I'll pick you up at the end of your shift."

"Okay. See you then."

CHAPTER NINETEEN

Havana sighed. "I'm not calling you 'Alpha' in bed."

"Why not?" Tate asked, fighting a smile. Teasing his mate had fast become one of his favorite things to do. "You could play the shy submissive devil who can't meet my eyes."

"You are *nuts* if you think that's going to happen."

"It could be fun." He'd never really been a big fan of soaking in a bathtub. He preferred showers. But as he lay in his freestanding tub with his mate situated comfortably between his legs, he felt more relaxed than he had in days. It was a combination of things—the feel of her skin against his, the heat of the water, the lavender scented bath bomb, the relative silence. The fact that she was naked was a bonus.

"You won't even try?" he asked. "Playing the role of shy submissive devil who has disobeyed pride rules and needs to be punished by her Alpha ... yeah, that would work."

"Not happening, Garfield."

Tate nipped the tip of her ear. "Fine, be that way. I'd rather play the 'Alpha Male Claims his Mate' game anyway. We can call it practice."

A claiming between Alphas could be *savage*. The moment the mental path for their true-mate bond cleared, the mating urge would slam into them. It was said to be so all-consuming that it robbed a person of all control and left them with only one thought in their head—to claim their mate. But the mating urge also fed a natural-born alpha female's need to test their male, so there would be no fast, sex-crazed fuck for Havana and Tate. She'd make him work for it, just as she always did.

Until her devil opened that damn door, the mating urge would remain dormant. *Assuming* that was the only thing blocking the bond's frequency, of course. There was no saying for certain that Havana had gotten rid of whatever issues that blocked it before her devil shut him out. But Tate believed they'd worked through them together.

"You're not reluctant to become Alpha female, are you?" He dragged his fingertips up the arm she'd braced over the side of the tub. "I was hoping you'd come around to the idea." His cat tensed as he waited for her answer.

"I can't say I'm excited to lead your pride, but I don't have an issue with it," she said, her eyes closed, her head resting on his chest. "I was hesitant at first, but that was mostly because I worried your pride mates would see you mating a lone shifter as a weakness. But now that I've met each of your pride mates and—with the exception of a few—seen that they're nothing but happy for you, I'm okay with it."

Tate felt his mouth tip up, touched by her concern. "I didn't realize you worried they'd consider my claiming a loner a demonstration of weakness. You should have mentioned it. I could have told you that it was a senseless worry—my pride mates don't have issues with lone shifters. We employ them, we associate with them, and we support Dawn's shelter. In fact, my pride mates often donate blankets, food, furniture, and clothing to the shelter. I don't order them to do it. They do it because they want to."

"I was pretty sure you'd tell me that I was worrying unnecessarily, but I needed to *see* for myself that that was the case."

"So you're good with ruling the pride alongside me now?"

"Yes. Don't think my not being excited means I'll do a half-assed job. I won't shirk my duties, neglect the pride, or leave the main bulk of the responsibilities to you. I'll be your partner, your equal, your sounding board—whatever you need."

"I've never doubted that you'd be a committed Alpha. You already are one. It's just that your clan currently consists only of you, Aspen, and Bailey. Camden sort of lingers on the periphery of it. He gives off the lone wolf vibe."

"I suspect the only thing that keeps him in one place is Aspen."

Tate felt his brow crease. "I don't think so. He cares about you and Bailey in his way."

Havana's nose wrinkled. "I don't know if he cares about us per se. It's more like he cares what *happens* to us. Aspen's the only person he's formed a bond with, from what I can tell. But I don't know if it's a healthy bond. It's just a little too intense. I can't explain it well."

"I know what you mean. Something about him is …. *off*. But I don't get the sense that he's cruel or unfeeling."

"The stuff that happened in his life before he appeared at the center … It's a doozy of a story, Tate. Maybe it all switched off something inside him, or maybe he's always lacked a certain something that I can't quite put my finger on. Corbin said he used to watch Camden very closely when he was a kid, worried he'd go down a dark path. But then Aspen turned up at the center, and Camden connected with her. That seemed to stabilize him somehow."

"They could be true mates."

"Maybe. I don't know if what they feel for each other is actually platonic, though I suspect it isn't." She shrugged. "It's all a bit of a mystery."

"You've never asked Aspen how she feels about him?"

"No. If things are platonic on his part but not hers, she'll avoid voicing what she wants so that she doesn't have to be hurt by it. I haven't raised the subject because if I make her face something she's subconsciously ignoring, she could start hurting over it, and that could come between them."

"Then I guess it's best to leave it be. There's no sense in fixing what isn't broken."

Tate got the impression that Camden liked being a loner, so he wasn't certain the tiger would accept his invitation to join the pride. Tate just hoped the guy didn't try to talk Aspen out of joining. Havana wouldn't truly be happy in the pride if her girls weren't part of it.

He nuzzled her wet hair. "You know, I was thinking …"

"What?"

"Aspen and Bailey would make good enforcers."

Havana twisted her head to look up at him, her face a study in surprise.

"They learned a lot of skills during the years they worked for the Movement," Tate added. "I'd be a fool not to put those skills to good use. Plus, I want you to have your own bodyguards once you take on the position of Alpha female. Who better to guard you than two of the people you trust most?" In actual fact, they were also the people *he'd* trust most to protect his mate. They adored her with the ferocity that shifters were known for. His cat felt equally comfortable with the idea of them guarding her.

Havana bit her lip. "I can't be sure whether or not they'd accept your offer, but I do agree that they'd make good enforcers. Will Luke, Farrell, or any of your existing enforcers have an issue with Aspen and Bailey being part of your ranks?"

"No. They're impressed by what they've seen of your girls so far. Even Luke, despite that Bailey watches him like she's waiting for him to blow a fuse."

"She said there's a darker side to your brother. She believes he has a storm inside him."

"She's very perceptive." Tate sighed. "The past six years have been hard for him."

"Why?"

"Because he never feels close enough to the person he most needs to protect. His mate was twelve when he found her—they recognized each other at first sight. She's part of the local bush dog pack."

Havana's lips parted. "I had no idea he'd found his mate. It explains why I've never seen him with a woman."

"For obvious reasons, he hasn't yet claimed Blair. He visits her, calls her, has people watch over her. But it's not easy for him to not have her close." Personally, Tate would find it a sort of hell. "He intended to claim her on her eighteenth birthday, but her parents nagged him to wait until she's twenty-one. He refused, but he has agreed to hold back until she turns nineteen, which is ten months from now. His cat has been riding him hard ever since her eighteenth birthday—the feline feels that, as an adult female, Blair's ready to be claimed."

"Poor Luke," said Havana, her voice soft. "It can't be easy for Blair either."

"I suspect not. The only saving grace is that bush dogs are one of the few shifter breeds that don't experience the mating urge. Since she isn't able to experience it, Luke hasn't been struck by it either. That's good, or they'd otherwise be a sexual mess."

"Have you met her?"

"Yeah, plenty of times. I like her a lot. So will you. She's pretty mature for her age. Knows how to handle herself—and how to handle Luke, for that matter. She has a steely stare that freaks people out, watches everyone like they're prey. My cat likes it."

"A bush dog will fit well here. They're insane on their best day."

"That they are. Back to the subject of your girls becoming enforcers ... I'm aware there's no guarantee that they'd follow my every directive. But I don't want blind obedience. I want people who can think for themselves." Tate kissed her temple. "Besides, I'm confident that you can keep them out of trouble. For the most part."

"You're obviously forgetting that Bailey *likes* trouble."

"I haven't forgotten. I'm just positive that you'll handle her."

Havana almost snickered. Leading her friend was one thing. Handling Bailey was a whole other ball game, and Havana doubted that anyone would win the mamba at that. "I suppose I should be flattered by your faith in me." She frowned as a porcelain ornament on the window shelf caught her eye. "That's my buddha."

"Is it?"

Her lips thinned at his airy tone. "*Yes.*" It used to sit quite comfortably on *her* bathroom window shelf. She hadn't noticed it was missing, which bugged her.

"Maybe it's just similar to yours."

She snorted. "Like I'm not fully aware that you've been moving my stuff here little by little." She felt him smile against her neck.

"Busted. I just want you to feel at home here. The best way to achieve that is to bring a little of your home here."

"Ooh, nice save."

"Think of it this way. You'll have less things to transport here when you do finally move in with me." He lightly nipped the bite mark on her shoulder. "You practically live here now, so it wouldn't be such a huge thing to just make it official," he added, his voice far too casual.

Shaking her head, she sighed, tired of going over old ground. But of course he hadn't dropped it—typical Alpha male, really. "You just can't help yourself, can you?"

"You know you want to move in with me. Why not just do it?"

"God, you are so damn spoiled."

"I'm not going to feel bad for wanting my mate living with me." He curled his arms around her. "It's where you belong."

"We've already had the conversation of *why* I'm not going to do it yet." She slashed her hand through the air. "I refuse to have it all over again."

"You know, I shouldn't like it when you use that school-teacher tone and take me to task for pushing so hard, but I do."

"I guess that's a good thing, because I'm sensing I'll be doing it *a lot*."

"Probably."

"Kudos to your dad for raising two alphas. *Especially* when said alphas repeatedly tried to kill each other as kids."

"Yeah, we were a trial." He idly danced his fingertips over her stomach. "How many kids do you want?"

As his lips began to trail suckling little kisses down her neck, Havana tilted her head to give him better access. "I'd be good with two. Hopefully one of each gender, but I'm not fussy. I just want them to be happy and healthy."

"Two works for me. But we have to have the boy first, so that he can look out for his sister."

Like Rolando had for her, Havana thought. "It sucks that our kids will never know their maternal relatives, especially my parents and brother. But they'll have your siblings, plus two honorary aunts who'll no doubt spoil them rotten and teach them things they shouldn't."

He kissed her shoulder. "I hate that my mother will never get to hold our kids; that they'll only know of her through whatever stories I tell them." He tucked his face into the crook of Havana's neck. "Gaia would have liked you. No, she'd have fucking loved you."

Havana reached back to hook her hand around his nape. "My mom would have adored you. Rolando and my dad would have thought you were awesome, but they were so gruff and broody they probably wouldn't have showed it."

She and Tate sat like that for a short while, giving comfort and taking it.

"We need to get out of this tub before the water goes cold," she finally said.

He traced her collarbone with one finger. "Not until I've made you come." He dipped his hand under the water and unerringly found her clit, making a gasp fly out of her. "Feel free to scream."

Keeping his mate close to his side, Tate stared down at the two females sitting on Havana's sofa the next morning. "Well?" he prompted.

Aspen tilted her head. "You're not just saying this in the hope that it'll make Havana more comfortable about being part of your pride? You truly want to make us enforcers-slash-her personal bodyguards if we join?"

Tate hiked up a brow. "Can you think of anyone who'll protect her more vigorously than you and Bailey would?"

"No."

"Then there's your answer." Tate cut his gaze to Camden, who sat on the armchair, his expression carefully blank. "I'm open to offering you a place in the pride, Camden. You wouldn't be the only shifter who joined when their relative mated into the pride. These girls are your family. I see that, and I don't wish to take them from you. I couldn't even if I tried. And I believe you'd make a loyal member of my pride." Purely because he'd do nothing to hurt Aspen.

Havana, Bailey, and Aspen watched the tiger closely, looking hopeful.

Camden clasped the arms of the chair, seeming torn. "I don't like being under anyone's rule," he said, but it wasn't a no.

"I have no wish to run your life or take your choices from you. All I'll want is your loyalty and for you to respect my status—the rest will automatically follow."

Camden licked the front of his teeth. His eyes snapped to Aspen and lingered there for a long moment. Sliding his gaze back to Tate, he said, "I wouldn't join your ranks."

Meaning the male didn't believe he could deal with someone directing his movements day after day, Tate understood. "I don't require you to."

"All right. If the girls join, I'll join."

Tate didn't miss the relief that flickered across the bearcat's face. "Good." Tate turned back to Aspen and Bailey. "You two, however, I do wish to have in my ranks. So, what will it be?" He watched as Havana, Aspen, and Bailey each looked from one to the other, having one of those silent conversations again.

Aspen's focus returned to him. "Okay, we accept your offer."

"So long as you understand we're likely to piss you off occasionally," Bailey added.

"That has already occurred to me," said Tate. "Once you've joined my pride—which can happen at any time you wish, even right this moment—"

Havana snorted. "Nice try, Garfield, but stop."

Annoyed that she'd guessed his game, Tate inwardly sighed. Yeah, okay, so he'd thought that maybe if her girls joined *now*, she'd do the same. His cat thought it amusing that they struggled to get anything past their mate.

"As I was saying," Tate went on, "once you've joined, I'll arrange for you two and Camden to move to one of the pride's complexes. This building is strictly for lone shifters. Plus, you should all be surrounded by your pride mates anyway; you need to know and feel that you belong. Your inner animals will need that, too. Do you all want to live in separate apartments?"

Her hands joined together as if in prayer, Bailey turned to Aspen. "Oh, I *love* having a roommate. Please be mine."

"No way," said Aspen. "I'd kill you within a day if we had to share the same living space. Or, more to the point, my bearcat would kill your mamba."

"You'll be sharing an apartment with me anyway," Camden told Aspen.

The bearcat scratched her cheek. "I think it'll be better if we live separately."

The guy scowled. "How do you figure that?"

"You don't see just how uncomfortable your partners are with me living with you," said Aspen. "They're suspicious of me, they feel awkward having me there, and then they do things that make *me* feel uncomfortable in my own home. I know a few of my exes have treated you badly, too. Living with you is a blast, but it isn't something we can realistically keep doing."

"The fuck we can't," clipped Camden. "Ever since we moved out of Corbin's house years ago, we've been roommates in whatever apartment we lived in. Like you said, it's a blast."

"You're not getting tired of ending relationships because your partners have bitched at me? You're not getting tired of my dates giving you shit out of jealousy?"

"No, and no. None of those people were worth our time, or they'd have accepted that you and I are close friends."

"Wouldn't you prefer to live alone so that you can have a regular bachelor pad?" Bailey asked the tiger.

Camden frowned. "No. I like things the way they are. I like having my best friend living with me."

Havana raised a finger. "Which is why Randy—"

"Don't even mention that sack of shit," clipped Camden.

"—and others you've dated have found it hard to accept Aspen," said Havana. "You might have an easier time making your partners get along with your best friend if she isn't living with you."

The tiger's face scrunched up. "I could give less of a fuck if people don't like that she lives with me."

"Your mate would care," Aspen pointed out. "If you meet him or her, they're not going to want me living with you. Come on, Camden, it's not like we'll never see each other—we'll probably be living in the same building."

But the tiger didn't drop it, so the two disputed the matter right up until the moment they walked out the front door with an exasperated Bailey, who was pushing them to hurry so that they didn't miss the movie they planned to go see at the theater.

Alone with Tate, Havana relaxed against him. "Thank you for giving my honorary family a place in the pride. You're getting lucky later for sure."

He smiled. "I'm already lucky. I have my mate right here. And she's naked."

Havana felt her brow furrow. "No, I'm not."

"You are in my head," said Tate. "It's impossible for a man to look at you and *not* wonder what you look like naked. I don't need to wonder. I *know*. And my mind brings up that pretty picture very often. It's kind of distracting, but I'm good with it." He kissed her soft and slow and languid. "I need to use the bathroom. I'll be right back." He patted her ass and strode off.

Just then, Havana's phone rang. She grabbed it from the coffee table. *Cesário*. Damn. She hadn't kept him up to date on all that had occurred, because she suspected he'd be pissed if he knew she'd almost died. Havana didn't want him jumping into the situation and, in doing so, misusing the group's resources. He'd regret it later.

She put her cell to her ear and greeted, "Hey, how are you?"

"You haven't called with any updates," he gruffly complained.

"I *would* have, but I know you find uninformative conversations boring and pointless, and since I don't yet have intel about Gideon to pass on ..."

"You must have *something*."

"We did manage to find out that one of his jaguar-minions is named Enrique—that's all we have on him so far, though. Well, it's possible he's a regular at a local casino, but we can't be sure of that. Still, Tate's enforcers are staking it out."

He grunted. "How will they know if the jaguar shows?"

"We spoke to someone who was able to give us a description of both him and his buddy." There was no need to explain she'd gotten that info out of a man who targeted her with a gun. Twice.

"That's something, I suppose," Cesário muttered. "I didn't call just to moan at you."

"At least you're admitting that you're moaning."

"I wanted to know if you had anything to do with your old Alpha's death."

Both Havana and her devil went utterly still. "What?"

"Someone from our group knows of your old clan. They told me Yasiel was found dead in his cabin a few days ago. Well, *some* of him was found. It looked like whoever mauled him—and I'm guessing it was a shifter—also *ate* some of him. The killer didn't set off any alarms. No one sensed them enter the territory or leave it."

Feeling her chest squeeze tight, she said, "It could have been an inside job."

"It probably was. I just thought I'd ask if you had a hand in it."

"No, I didn't." She looked up as Tate strolled back into the living area. "But if I find out who did, I'll be sure to shake their hand." She had a pretty good idea of whose hand she'd be shaking, actually. Her gut rarely led her wrong. And right then, it was pointing its metaphorical finger at her mate. So was her devil, shocked by the news of Yasiel's demise.

"As will I, Ramos. The fucker reaped what he sowed—it's that simple." Cesário paused when a muffled voice spoke in the background. "I need to run. Don't forget to keep me in the loop about the auctions."

"I won't." Without looking away from Tate, she rung off and returned her cell to the table.

Frowning, he cupped her chin. "Is everything all right, babe?"

"Yeah," she breathed.

"You don't look okay." He slid his hand from her chin to her nape, pulled her closer, and curled his other arm tight around her. "What's wrong?"

"Nothing, I just …" She licked her lips and watched his expression carefully as she explained, "I just spoke with my old boss from the Movement. He told me that Yasiel was murdered." There wasn't even a *flicker* of surprise on Tate's face. "You had something to do with it, didn't you?"

Tate pinned her gaze with his own. "If it wasn't for that bastard," he began, his voice low and deceptively calm, "you wouldn't have lost your family. You wouldn't have been banished from your clan. You wouldn't have been on your own from the age of twelve. So yeah, babe, I had something to do with his death."

"Just how close a hand did you have in it? Were you there?"

"I was there. So was Luke and Alex."

"I take it Alex's wolverine is the one who chomped down some of Yasiel."

Tate shrugged. "Wolverines often eat their prey."

Staring up at him, she swallowed as the matter truly hit her. "You went all the way to Vancouver. You trespassed on Yasiel's territory, knowing there was a risk you'd be seen and captured. And you mauled and killed him right in his cabin with the aid of both Luke and Alex."

"That bastard needed to pay, Havana. He had no business walking this Earth after all he'd done."

Oh, Havana couldn't have agreed more. Her devil was *delighted* to hear that their old Alpha no longer breathed. The animal was also impressed and moved by what Tate had risked and done all in the name of avenging Havana. Especially since he obviously hadn't done it to win points or he'd have told her about it himself. He'd done it because he was quite simply Tate—a man who'd never let someone who'd so gravely wronged his mate live.

This was what her inner devil wanted in a partner—a male who'd protect, treasure, and avenge Havana. And, feeling it was time, the animal let the mental door finally creak open.

And the mating bond snapped into place.

Pain knifed through Havana's head and chest, dazing her. Her vision blurred and darkened for a few seconds, but then it righted, and the pain faded away. She looked at Tate, her lips parted, as peace fluttered through her like a warm breeze. God, she could *feel* him. Could feel his elation, surprise, relief, and—

She sucked in a breath as a blindsiding, elemental, all-consuming arousal *whipped* through her system and made her body surge to life. Her blood heated. Her skin tingled. Her nipples beaded. Her pussy spasmed.

Havana's breaths came hard and fast as the visceral, violent need pressed her to lunge. Taste. Fuck. Bite. Pressed her to claim the male in front of her and brand him as her mate.

That was exactly what she and her devil planned to do.

CHAPTER TWENTY

Tate wasn't sure which of them moved first, but their mouths clashed in a kiss that was hungry and savage. He buried his hands in her hair, keeping her mouth exactly where it was, refusing to release it for even a second.

Shock had slammed into him when their mating bond came to life, but the emotion had been washed away by warm, fuzzy feelings that were quickly overridden by such blinding need he fairly shook with it.

People weren't exaggerating when they said that the mating urge was overpowering. It was like he was in the grip of a fever. One that heated his blood, made his flesh burn, and tightened his body. Possession coursed through him, hot and intense, *demanding* he claim this female for his own; demanding he leave an irrevocable brand on her.

Her arousal echoed along their bond, ramping up his own. *Their bond.* It had finally snapped into place, finally connected them on a metaphysical level. And now he could finally make her his. That thought only made him more desperate to be inside her.

He roughly clawed off her clothes, deliberately scoring the flesh of her chest, back, hips, and thighs. All the while, he kept on eating at her mouth. She tore at his own clothes, ripping them from his body, and he almost groaned in relief as his cock was freed from the confines of his jeans. He was so hard and heavy it actually fucking hurt.

Using his grip on her hair, he yanked her head back and forced her body to arch into his. Ignoring her hiss, he swooped down and latched on to her nipple. He sucked, bit, licked, and plucked at the tight bud with his teeth before moving onto the neglected nipple.

He could smell her need. He knew she was already slick and ready for him. That sent his hunger for her soaring through the roof, making his dick impossibly harder.

He abruptly pulled her upright. "Need to fuck you," he growled, the words deep and guttural.

His cat urgently pushed him to take her now, to solidify their claim on her—he wouldn't be satisfied until it was done. Neither would Tate.

Hungry for the taste of her, Tate devoured her mouth again as he began backing her toward the bedroom. Then suddenly she was out of his arms and standing a few feet away, her eyes holding a challenge. Yeah, he should've known it wouldn't be that easy.

Her heart pounding, Havana raced into the nearest room—the kitchen. Need so raw and carnal beat in her blood, but so did the drive to *test* him. It felt more intense, more primal … as if the mating urge had somehow magnified it.

A hand gripped her arm and spun her around. Tate slammed her against the fridge, sending the breath gushing out of her lungs.

He crushed her body with his own and snarled. "Mine." He bit into the crook of her neck. *Hard.*

Havana shoved and kicked at him, wild and relentless. Her devil urged her on, determined that he prove himself worthy of her surrender. So Havana kept on fighting him, but she might as well have been tickling him for all the good it did.

He paid no attention to her struggles. He just kept her caged there with his body, his cock throbbing against her abdomen, his teeth firmly in her neck, his breath hot on her skin—making it clear who was in charge. Or who he *believed* was in charge.

She let out an indignant hiss. "Get your teeth out of my skin," she gritted out.

Instead, he boldly sank them deeper, drawing blood.

She intensified her struggles ten-fold. She cursed him, cursed his cock, cursed his teeth, everything. But he paid no heed to it. Paid no heed *to her.* "You goddamn—" She stilled with a shocked gasp as one blunt finger plunged deep inside her. "Fuck."

"Oh, we will," he said, lapping at the fresh bite. "But not yet."

She opened her mouth to curse him yet again, but then his hand began to move; the heel of his palm rubbed against her clit with each thrust of his finger. "Oh, God."

"That's it, babe, let me have my way with this pussy."

Oh, it was tempting. Really tempting. Because his hands were freaking magic, and they knew her well. Knew how to make her so frantic and desperate she lost the will to battle him.

Havana gave herself a mental slap when she realized she was trying to ride his hand. She couldn't give in so easily, no matter how good it felt. *Couldn't.*

But since he had a finger buried inside her, she also couldn't exactly scamper.

He put his mouth to her ear. "Can you *hear* how wet you are? I can. I'm not sure what I love more. That I can hear it, or that I can feel all that slickness around my finger."

Sensing an opportunity, she lifted a brow and asked, "Don't you want to taste it?"

He stilled. "Hmm, yes, I do." He withdrew his finger, brought it to his mouth, and sucked it clean. And she used that moment to escape.

Tate swore as she shoved him backwards and made a run for it. Oh no, he wasn't having that. He didn't let the tricky little minx get far—he quickly grabbed her and then roughly bent her over the dining table. "I'm not done playing yet."

He kept her pinned in place with his hand on her nape, but that didn't stop his mate from fighting his hold. He skimmed two fingertips between her slick folds. "Now, one of two things can happen. I can finger-fuck you hard and rough, just how you like it. Or I can keep the thrusts *real* nice and slow. If you want to choose door number one, be. Fucking. Still."

She hissed long and loud and *furious*, but she ceased fighting him. It wasn't a full surrender, though. No, there was still a lot of defiance bunching each muscle of her body. But it was progress.

"Very good," he said. "Now you get what you want." He drove two fingers deep into her pussy, and then he did exactly what he'd said he'd do—he took her hard and rough with his fingers, not stopping until she came all over his hand.

He slowly withdrew his fingers and then held them close to her face. "Look how soaking wet you are right now. Hmm, I think you should lick them clean for me."

She twisted, swiped out, and slashed his chest with her claws deep enough to draw blood. He flinched back in sheer surprise. She took instant advantage of that and fled.

Growling, Tate was hot on her heels as she ran back to the living area. He looped an arm around her waist and hauled her against him. She sank her teeth deep into his arm. He grunted and kept his grip on her tight as he carried her into her bedroom, ignoring her kicks. He tugged on her hair, making her unlock her teeth from his arm with a gasp, and then he threw her on the bed.

She bounced onto her back and readied herself to lunge at him. He didn't give her the chance. He covered her body with his own, pressing her into the mattress. She curled her limbs around him, but only so she could pound her fists and heels on him.

He snapped his hand around her throat and wedged the head of his cock in her pussy. "I'm going to claim you now. I'm going to make you mine and only mine. You want that, don't you? Hmm? You want me to claim you. Say it."

"You want me to claim you," she parroted.

He bit her jaw for being a smartass. "Last chance, baby. Tell me you want me to claim you or get ready for me to play with this body a while longer—just note that I won't stop playing until you *beg* me to take you. You know I mean every word."

Havana froze because, yeah, she *did* know that. Just as she knew that he really could reduce her to begging if he put his mind to it. He never had in the past, because he knew it would take a bite out of her pride, and Tate didn't get off on that. But he was ruthless enough to do it now if she didn't finally surrender control.

His brow hiked up. "Well?"

Havana let her muscles relax. "I want you to claim me." She'd barely gotten out the last word when he slammed home with a growl, making her breath catch in her throat. The feel of his fat, long shaft throbbing inside her, stretching her inner muscles, was exactly what she needed.

Tate briefly closed his eyes, taking a moment to quite simply bask in the fact that he was balls-deep inside his mate. He flexed his hips, sliding his cock even deeper inside all that tight, wet heat. She gasped, tightening her legs around him and digging her fingertips into his back. The prick of her claws made his cock pulse.

Releasing her throat, Tate gave her all of his weight, knowing she could take it. He threaded his fingers through hers and pinned her hands to the bed. He wanted her to feel surrounded by him. Wanted her to feel trapped and helpless beneath him, because a part of her got off on it—something he doubted she'd ever admit out loud.

Tate brushed his lips over hers. "Being in you brings me peace, you know." He very slowly pulled back until only the head of his dick was inside her. "It also makes me want to fuck you so raw you never forget who you belong to." He rammed his cock deep. "That would be me."

Havana clung to his shoulders as he fucked her into the mattress. It wasn't just rough. It was so brutal and wild it was almost callous, much like the cold expression he wore. But there was no cruelty in the eyes that watched her—they were alive with hunger, possession, and raw adoration. She could *feel* those emotions humming along their bond.

She could also feel the friction building inside him, and she knew his orgasm was close. Hell, so was hers. The mating urge was riding them both, giving them no reprieve from the drive to take and fuck and come and claim. She knew it wouldn't ease off until they'd done exactly that.

Havana arched into every savage surge of his hips, moaning each time his cock slammed *so damn deep*. He was strength and power and danger. Which made him a living, breathing aphrodisiac for her devil.

Havana's lips parted as he shifted his angle just a little, finding that delightful sweet spot inside her. Then he was hammering into her once more, and the tension inside her built and built, winding her super tight. "I'm close," she warned him.

"I know," said Tate, feeling her pussy heat and tighten. His own release was creeping up on him fast, but he didn't want to come until after she'd claimed him. "Bite me, baby."

"You first."

He pressed her hands harder into the mattress. "Do it or I slow down."

Her nostrils flared. "You are such a goddamn—"

"*Do it.*" Tate groaned as her teeth sank deep into his throat. He swore, fucking her so hard and fast the headboard slammed against the wall over and over. She sucked and licked the bite before finally releasing him. "My turn," said Tate. He bit her neck hard, tasting blood.

Her orgasm ricocheted up their bond and shot straight to his cock. Like that, his own release violently tore through him—the pleasure so intense it almost hurt. He exploded inside his mate with a snarl of her name.

Tate managed to catch his weight on his forearms, not wanting to crush her. His lungs burning for air, he carefully rolled them onto their sides and held her trembling body close. As he lay there trying to catch his breath, he marveled over the bond connecting them.

Although a couple might feel the tug of the true-mate bond, its development was usually a gradual thing. It often took certain emotional steps for said bond to fully snap into place. But his connection with Havana hummed between them—strong, vibrant, and true. Even their scents had mixed, declaring to the world that they were mated.

It sometimes happened that a bond instantly became whole. That was usually because the couple didn't have any emotional hurdles to jump—their issues were already resolved—but a little something stood in the way of the bond. In his and Havana's case, the bond had simply been waiting for her devil to stop fighting it.

She slid a hand up his chest. "I came so hard I felt it in my gums," she more or less slurred.

Brimming with masculine satisfaction, Tate gently sank his hand into her hair. He pressed a soft kiss to her mouth, feeling more at peace than he'd ever thought it possible to feel. He stared into those beautiful eyes, so fucking glad and proud she was his. He'd almost missed out on this. He'd almost failed to sense who she was to him because of his stupid fucking hang-ups. Thank Christ he'd gotten past that shit.

Tate understood now why his father didn't wish he could mate again. There was no replacing someone who was written into your soul the way Havana was written into Tate's. She lived in every part of him—his mind, his soul, his heart, everywhere.

She brushed her finger over the throbbing bite mark on this throat. He liked that she'd left her claiming brand in such a visible place. "Is your cat okay?" she asked. "He's not freaking out or anything?"

Tate snorted. "He's curled up in a ball of pure male smugness. What about your devil?"

"Oh, she's totally content."

"As are you—I can feel it." He inhaled deeply. "I like that our scents have finally mixed." He wanted their combined scent filling his—no, *their*—house. He glanced around the room. "How long will it take to pack your stuff?"

Her brow furrowed. "You want me to move into your house today?"

"Uh, *yeah*. I want it to be *our* home. I want your things to be mixed with mine. I want it to be clear to one and all that we're now mated. Besides, you're not a loner anymore. That means you can no longer live in this complex. I'm sorry—it's against the rules."

"You don't *sound* sorry."

Because he wasn't. He rubbed his nose against hers. "Come on, baby, move in with me."

She sighed. "If I do, you can't whine if you find Aspen or Bailey hanging out in the living room uninvited. Which you will. Often."

"They'll have apartments of their own."

"Yes, they will. It won't make a blind bit of difference."

"I'll deal with it when and if the time comes. On another note, the pride is going to want to throw a 'Welcome to the Pride/Congrats on Your Mating' party."

"Maybe we could mix it with our mating celebration instead of holding multiple parties."

"Sure, if that's what you want."

"Where does the pride hold mating celebrations?"

"The Tavern. We often invite the Phoenix and Mercury Pack."

Havana bit her lip. "Can we hold off on having the mating ceremony until after the Gideon bullshit is over?" She wasn't surprised when his expression darkened. "I don't want our minds to be on anything other than the celebration." She didn't want to spend the day worrying Gideon would choose then to strike, or that the asshole would do something that would eat into the celebration.

Tate's frown was thoughtful. "I don't *like* the idea of waiting, but it might be the best option. That day will be special for us, and I don't want him taking up any of your mental space during the celebration."

"Then we wait." Doodling a circle on his chest with her fingertip, she said, "I forgot to ask you before, but … why didn't you tell me that you, Luke, and Alex had some fatal fun with Yasiel?"

"I planned to at some point. But you have enough going on right now that's messing with your head. I didn't want to bring him up again and dredge up painful memories for you unless I absolutely had to."

Her heart squeezed. "Thank you. Not just for what you did, but for caring enough to do it." Maybe another woman might have been disturbed that he'd killed for her, but Havana was a big believer in vengeance. Yasiel had taken everything from her. There'd been no justice in him walking the Earth.

Tate's brow creased. "You don't have to thank me. You're mine, Havana. This is what it means to be mine. I will protect and spoil and cosset you to the point of making you crazy. I'm also a man who'd *never* allow a person who hurt you that badly to live. Never."

"If you tell anyone I'll deny it, but you make me all tingly when you dish out these darkly overprotective declarations. And I'm all about the tingles."

His mouth quirked. "Kiss me."

She did, and he quickly took over and made the kiss his own. Not roughly, but decisively—every lick of his tongue was bold and sure.

He gently nipped her lower lip. "I'm not going to make an easy mate. And being Alpha female won't be any easier. But I swear I'll never do anything to make you regret being mine. I'll never take you for granted. Never let you down again. Never do anything but love the shit out of you."

Oh, now her throat was aching. "You love me?"

He smiled. "Fuck, yeah. I didn't think it'd come as a surprise to you."

She gently dragged her nails down the column of his throat, knowing he liked it. "It's a good thing you feel that way, because it just so happens that I love you."

His eyes warmed. "I know. I feel it. And it's even more of a reason for you to move in with me today."

"I said I would," she reminded him.

"Yes, you said it. But I don't see you packing. Or even looking particularly committed to the idea."

"Would you feel better if I stood up and started jumping for joy?"

"Yeah, because then I could watch your tits bounce—that's always fun." He softly slapped her ass. "Come on, let's get your stuff packed. I'll have Luke and Farrell help transport your things to what will from today onwards be *our* house. We can christen at least two of the rooms tonight."

"Oh, now that's a plan I can get behind."

As the furniture had come with the place and wasn't hers to take, it really was a simple matter of tossing all her stuff into her suitcase and duffels. But even with help, it took longer than she'd expected. She'd just packed the last duffel when Bailey, Aspen, and Camden returned.

Sensing that Havana and Tate were fully bonded, they all congratulated them. They weren't surprised to find that Havana was moving out. Bailey, of course, got all dramatic and cried that her and Havana no longer being roommates was an end to an era. But she stopped with a chuckle when Aspen lightly slapped her over the head.

Luke and Farrell arrived only minutes later. The Beta handed over three sets of keys to Tate.

"Keys to your new apartments," said Tate, handing a set to first Aspen, then to Bailey, and then to Camden. "You're living in the same building on the same floor."

The tiger glared at Aspen. "I still say there's no reason we couldn't have remained roommates."

"Color me surprised," said Aspen, her voice dry.

"Once you've packed your things, my enforcers will help you move them," Tate added.

"Cool." Bailey smiled at Havana. "You'll miss living with me. I know you will."

"Actually, I will," said Havana. "You might be mostly insane, but you're endlessly entertaining."

Grinning, the mamba elbowed Aspen. "You hear that? Endlessly entertaining."

"She also called you insane," the bearcat pointed out.

"*Mostly* insane."

"Yeah, I left out the 'mostly,' because you and I both know you're fucking certifiable."

"It's really not so bad." Slumping her shoulders, Bailey put on a weepy, devastated face. "Can't you just love me the way I am, Aspen? Can't you just accept me, warts and—"

"Stop, stop."

The mamba just chuckled.

Looking from one female to the other, Havana sighed. "I'm dreading what damage your animals will do to each other when I'm not around to intervene."

"Don't worry about us." Bailey waved a hand at Havana. "Go shack up with your dude. It's clear he's eager to get gone from here."

Tate put a hand on Havana's back. "I am," he confirmed. "Ready, babe?"

Havana nodded. "Ready."

"Then let's go."

The next morning, Tate folded his arms as he stared down at the females lounging on his sofa watching TV. "Why are you here? Uninvited? Again?"

Aspen's brow creased. "We're Havana's bodyguards, right? We can't guard her if we're not around."

Bailey nodded. "That would be a struggle, even for us."

"You only need to guard her when she's *out* of the house," Tate explained.

"Oh," both females said, but neither moved.

"I'd ask how you got in here," began Tate, "but you'll only tell me you slipped in through an unlocked door or open window when I'd know that to be untrue. Do the enforcers guarding the house know you're here?"

Aspen pursed her lips. "Not that I'm aware."

Yeah, that was what he'd thought. His cats would be furious when they realized the two females had snuck inside undetected a second time.

"I really like the apartment you assigned me, by the way," said Bailey. "It's super swanky."

"And yet, you're not in it," he pointed out.

"Your TV is better."

"It *is* better," Aspen agreed. And then both females went right back to watching it.

Tate sighed. He needed coffee. In the kitchen, he found that there was some in the pot. Well at least the females had the common courtesy to make coffee. Knowing his mate would appear any moment, he poured her a drink and set it on the table. He was just about to fix them both some breakfast when there was a knock at the front door.

Considering how fast news spread around his pride, he knew that all his pride mates would know by now that he was officially mated to Havana. Each member would likely turn up at some point to swear fealty to their new Alpha female. He hadn't thought people would start pledging their loyalty to her this early in the morning.

Having placed his mug on the counter, Tate walked down the hallway and glanced through the door's peephole. Ashlynn stood on his porch, her expression sober. He sighed, and his cat bared a fang. She could be here to swear fealty to Havana, sure—she'd have to if she wanted to stay part of the pride. But he'd thought he'd have to push her to do so or even offer her an ultimatum. He definitely hadn't thought she'd be the first to show.

Distrusting her apparent eagerness, Tate blanked his expression as he opened the door. Her shoulders hunched, Ashlynn tried for a smile. The enforcers who guarded his house were leaning against the porch rails, ready to remove her from the property at Tate's request. It seemed they didn't trust her either.

Ashlynn raised her hands in a gesture of peace. "Don't worry, I'm not here to ask you to have dinner with me or for us to talk. That ship has sailed, I know."

"Do you?" Tate asked, skeptical.

She swallowed. "Yes." Her eyes dropped to the claiming mark on his throat, and pain briefly flashed on her face. "It was clear you'd moved on before I even came home. I just hadn't wanted to see it. You told me over and over that you didn't want us to try again. I should have listened, should have heeded you. I didn't. I just kept pushing, and then I got all bitchy when things didn't go my way." She licked her lips. "I didn't behave fairly to you. For that, I'm sorry."

Tate didn't say "apology accepted" for the simple reason that he wasn't yet certain that she meant it.

"I won't lie and say I'm happy that you and Havana have mated—I'm not quite there yet. But I am glad that *you're* happy. You deserve to be."

"Okay," he said, because there was a ring of truth in her voice. "But I don't think you came here just to say that."

"You're right, I didn't. I came to tell you that, well ..." She paused and lifted her chin. "I've decided to leave the pride. Again. I've already packed my things and booked a flight for later today. I don't feel that I could be happy here."

The words "Bon Voyage" were on the tip of his tongue. While he wouldn't wish the dangers of a lone shifter lifestyle on anyone—not even her—he couldn't say he was disappointed that she planned to leave. Particularly because Havana would feel more comfortable if the woman wasn't around. Plus, he'd never fully trust Ashlynn to be loyal to him, his mate, or the pride. His cat would be glad to see the back of her.

"I don't have to warn you that being a loner isn't easy and comes with a lot of risks—you've already lived that lifestyle once," said Tate. "If you're fine with taking those risks and this is what you want, fair enough."

She looked at him, her face lined with sadness. "You really don't care if I go, do you? Understandable, I guess. I wasn't lying when I said I've accepted that you've moved on. Still, it's hard to know that someone I love—someone who was once open to mating with me—doesn't care one iota about me now." She worried her lower lip. "I really did hugely mess up, didn't I?"

Several times, but Tate saw no point in discussing it.

"I hope one day you'll stop hating me."

"I don't hate you, nor am I holding a grudge. If you hadn't messed up the way you did, I probably wouldn't be mated to Havana right now."

She winced but then nodded. "Right. Good. Still, I'm sorry for everything, Tate. I'd like to apologize to Havana before I leave."

"I doubt she'll think it's necessary."

"You mean she won't care if I'm sorry. I'd still like to apologize."

He was about to repeat that it wasn't necessary, but then his mate came up behind him and said, "I'll hear her out."

Hell, Tate hadn't even heard Havana descend the stairs, let alone sense her creep close. The woman would keep him on his toes for sure. Although he didn't like his mate being so close to this woman he didn't trust, he stepped aside. As Havana sidled up to him, he slid his arm around her waist to cup her hip.

Straightening her shoulders, Ashlynn cleared her throat and forced a smile for Havana. "I'd congratulate you on your mating, but you'd know it to be false, and there's no sense in insulting your intelligence or mine. Still, I hope you appreciate how lucky you are to have found your mate and claimed him. That doesn't always work out as it should. Anyway ... I came to tell Tate that

I'm leaving the pride today. Which I'm sure will come as a relief to you. Before I go, though, I wanted to …" A slyness slid over Ashlynn's face. "Challenge you. I wanted to challenge you."

CHAPTER TWENTY-ONE

Outrage tore through Tate. He growled, and his furious cat sliced out his claws. The enforcers on the porch cursed and shot Ashlynn looks of disgust. Havana? Well she just sighed and scratched the side of her head.

Flexing his fingers, Tate glared at Ashlynn. "Are you fucking kidding me?"

"Don't think I came here under false pretenses," said Ashlynn. "I meant the things I said to you, Tate. I truly did. But I'm not leaving here without paying her back for what she did to me at the Tavern."

"It was *you* who started that shit." Snarling, Tate made a move toward her. But then his mate's arm shot out in front of him, acting as a barrier.

"Where do you want to do this?" Havana asked her, sounding as bored as she looked.

Ashlynn shrugged one shoulder. "We might as well do it on the lawn."

"Works for me," said Havana.

Ashlynn turned and stepped off the porch.

When Havana went to follow, Tate curled his hand around her arm. "Baby—"

"No, Tate, don't ask me to ignore her challenge," said Havana.

"I do not want that bitch touching you again."

Her expression solemn, Havana rested her hand on his chest. "I know it goes against the grain for you to stand back while someone tries to hurt me, but I can't turn down this challenge without looking weak. An Alpha can't afford to appear weak. You know that. And, well, I'll be honest with you—I'm going to enjoy this."

Bailey and Aspen came out of nowhere and appeared at the base of the porch steps—he hadn't even sensed them leave the house. He distantly noted that the mamba was holding the mug of coffee he'd earlier poured for Havana.

"I can take her," Havana assured him.

"Oh, I don't doubt that. But it makes me no less pissed, because I don't want her laying her hands on you. I warned her to leave you be."

"But I don't think you believed she really would. I certainly didn't."

"The bitch won't fight fair," he cautioned.

Havana smiled. "And what in the world made you think *I* would? As Bailey would say, fairness is for losers."

"It totally is," Bailey chimed in.

Able to *feel* his anger through their bond, Havana pressed a quick, comforting kiss to his mouth. She'd have been irritated if she thought Tate felt that she needed him to fight her battles. But it wasn't that at all. He simply didn't want anything remotely negative touching her. Which was sweet for sure. But she'd really have to work on that with him, because she liked a good fight here and there.

"On a side note, I'm gonna want pancakes after this, by the way." With that, Havana turned and strode off the porch. Her inner devil stretched, looking forward to what would come next. So was Havana. Each spike of adrenaline that pumped through her body seemed to ramp up her eagerness.

Bailey held out a mug. "Thought you might want some of this first."

"Thanks." Havana sipped at her coffee, casual as you please—making Ashlynn wait, communicating that she wasn't whatsoever anxious about the challenge.

Just then, Luke and Farrell turned into the cul-de-sac. Spotting Havana and the other three females on the lawn, both men frowned and then jogged over to Tate. Good. They'd hopefully keep him from leaping into the fray.

Havana handed the cup back to Bailey and then turned to face Ashlynn, who stood tall and silent with her feet planted and her hands balled up into tight fists. "Kind of pathetic of you to turn up here early, hoping I'd be sleepy enough that it'd give you an edge in the fight," said Havana. "Aspen predicted you'd do that. Bailey thought you'd turn up later tonight, hoping to ruin my evening with Tate. Me? I thought you'd come at a time when there were more of your pride mates around. You do like to have an audience, after all."

Ashlynn frowned. "Don't act like you saw this coming."

Havana chuckled. "Apparently you don't realize how predictable you are. Come on, you were *never* going to pledge your loyalty to me or spend years of your life answering to me. It was inevitable that you'd choose to leave the pride instead, and I was pretty sure you'd be tempted to try to kick my ass before you left. Not just because I hurt you at the Tavern, but because you've got a lot of anger to burn off."

Havana sensed more than saw her neighbors step out of their houses. She didn't bother to look their way, not worried that any would attempt to intervene on Ashlynn's behalf. "You came here to win Tate back. Your plan was to become his mate and Alpha female. That plan failed, and I now have what you want. I had hoped that you'd have more respect for Tate than to pull this crap, though." Havana sighed. "It says real bad things about you that you'd try to shit all over his happiness."

Ashlynn's frown deepened. "I'm not doing that. Like I already told him, I'm glad that he's happy."

Tutting, Havana wagged her finger. "Come now, don't tell lies. You're not pleased that he found his happily ever after. In fact, I'd say you're pretty ticked off at him."

"You're wrong."

"Nope. This here and now isn't only about you wanting to hurt me. You want to weaken me in the eyes of the pride. You want them to watch their new Alpha female be overpowered right here in her own front yard. And weakening *my* standing with the pride would also weaken Tate's. You like that idea, because you want to punish him for rejecting you, don't you?"

Ashlynn's eyelids flickered.

"And that makes you a pretty hypocritical bitch. I mean, you hated that a woman came between you and *your* true mate. You were angry at Koby for choosing another female over you. You felt that *you* should be his world. Yet, you resent that Tate would find happiness with his true mate. You see what I'm getting at?"

Ashlynn sneered. "I hope you're not feeling too smug that he didn't leave you for me. There was a time when he was more than happy to forsake you."

"And that's why you figured there was a chance he'd walk away from me, huh? Maybe if you'd known that it wasn't so much *me* that he was willing to forsake but the true-mate bond, you'd have given up trying to win him back." Rolling back her shoulders, Havana tilted her head. "You sure you want to do this?"

"Oh, I'm sure." A smirk flirted with the edges of Ashlynn's mouth. "It'll be an utter joy to kick your ass."

She thought she had a prayer of winning this duel? Oh, that was just precious.

Aspen snickered at the feline. "A regular Pollyanna, aren't you? So blindly optimistic it's honestly disturbing. It stops you from seeing the facts. And the fact in this case? You're not going to come out on top. Nope. You're about to go through a world of pain."

"It's kind of exciting," said Havana. And then she started to undress.

Ashlynn's brows snapped together. "What are you doing?"

"Oh, well you see, my devil *really* wanted to get a few licks in last time you and I went head-to-head. I promised her that if you ever challenged me again, I'd let her take care of the matter. So, I'll let you two get acquainted." Naked,

Havana smiled. "I'll be honest, this is *really* going to hurt." Then she gave her animal supremacy.

Tate wasn't surprised to see that her devil's ears were flushed red—it was a sure sign that she was pissed. Focused on Ashlynn, she let her mouth gape open almost impossibly wide, displaying those bone-crushing teeth. She released an ear-splitting, otherworldly screech that could chill a man's blood. Her jaws snapped shut with unbelievable force, like that of a crocodile ... only faster.

Ashlynn stared down at the angry creature like she wasn't sure what to make of it, so Tate could only assume that she hadn't before seen a devil shifter in their animal form up close.

"Hey Ash," Bailey called out. "Did you know that devils will eat *anything*? I mean, seriously, nothing is off the menu for those little critters. Not even teeth or tongues or anything. What I find more disturbing—yet also *morbidly* fascinating—is that they often eat the digestive system of their kills first and then make themselves comfortable inside the cavity of the carcass while they eat everything else."

Aspen nodded. "You gotta respect the downright savagery of it. Oh, I'd watch your fingers, if I were you," she advised Ashlynn. "One bite will sever them."

The devil let out another harsh, high-pitched screech, her black glare still locked on Ashlynn.

"Uh-oh, she's getting antsy," said Bailey. "You really should probably hurry this along," she told Ashlynn.

The feline notched up her chin and huffed at the devil. "Think you're tough, do you? Let's see how you hold up against my cat. We'll let our animals settle this." She shed her clothes and shifted.

Arching her back, the cat hissed and whipped up her tail.

A spine-chilling scream came out of the devil, who then *exploded* into action. She charged fast, her jaws wide open. Both animals reared up on their hind legs as they clashed. And the devil clamped those sheering teeth on the cat's face. *Fucking ow.* The feline yowled in pain and tried tugging herself free of those powerful jaws.

"*Rip her fucking head off!*" yelled Aspen.

"*Make that bitch bleed!*" shouted Bailey.

The devil ferociously tore into the cat like a rabid animal, biting and clawing and sending tiny tufts of gray fur fluttering through the air. Scratches and puncture wounds soon marred the cat's body—particularly her face.

The feline fought back, and she fought hard. She did some damage to the devil, swiping out her claws and carving deep gouges into the animal's fur and flesh. Through the mating bond, Tate felt the echo of every scratch, every bite, every blow. The pain only seemed to spur the devil on. Or maybe the critter simply didn't care about the pain.

Their neighbors gathered around the lawn to get a better view, mindful to give the two animals plenty of space. Tate didn't move from his spot on the top step of the porch. He didn't trust himself to get any closer; didn't trust that he wouldn't wade in. Whether he liked it or not, this wasn't his fight.

Bone *cracked,* and the cat flinched backwards with a yowl. The devil gave her no reprieve. She pitched forward and savagely bit into the cat's face yet again with another of those high-pitched shrieks.

The animals were matched in size and attitude. But the devil was *lightning* fast. A growling, shrieking, screaming tornado of sheer viciousness. Those teeth of hers were lethal, ripping through flesh and snapping bones like they were twigs. One of a pallas cat's biggest defenses was that their hides were very thick, but the devil's sheering teeth effortlessly chomped through her opponent's hide.

For the devil, this wasn't a battle for dominance, Tate realized. It wasn't even a fight, really. No, it was a *beating.*

"Your mate's animal is hardcore," said Luke, his respect clear in his voice.

Pride welled up inside Tate. He felt his mouth curve, despite the knot in his stomach. Havana had been right that Ashlynn wanted to make his mate look weak before the pride. It wasn't working, though. All Ashlynn was doing was proving that Havana made a worthy Alpha female.

Everyone gathered around could see that his mate was powerful, fearless, and vicious enough to protect them and help keep the pride strong. Word of the beating would soon travel among the other members. If any of his cats had been debating challenging Havana for leadership, they'd rethink that after this.

"Are my ears bleeding?" asked Farrell. "I feel like they should be bleeding."

Well there was a fuck of a lot of noise. The cat hissed, snarled, and yowled. The devil barked, growled, and screeched. To add to that, their pride mates—particularly Aspen and Bailey—loudly egged the devil on.

The feline repeatedly tried grabbing her opponent by the throat and grappling her to the ground. But the devil was constantly moving and jerking, making herself a difficult target and coming at the cat from other angles. In sum, she ran rings around the feline.

Although Tate could see that his mate was in no danger of being overpowered by Ashlynn's cat, he wanted nothing more than to put an end to the whole thing. It went against every protective streak he had to just stand there while she was dueling, bleeding, and injured. His cat was much calmer about it; he respected his mate's right to defend herself.

Tate flinched as a particularly sharp pain rushed up their bond, courtesy of a harsh bite to the flank from Ashlynn's feline. "Bitch."

"It's almost over," said Luke. "The cat's got very little 'go' left in her. She's losing, and she knows it."

That wasn't stopping the cat from attacking. Again and again, she and the devil lunged, pounced, and tore strips out of each other. The air was heavy with the cloying scents of blood, pain, and anger.

He could *feel* that his mate was beginning to tire. To look at her, though, you'd never think it. She seemed hyped-up on sheer rage.

A well-aimed swipe from the devil knocked the cat down. Slow to right herself, the feline backed off, panting heavily ... as if needing a moment to orientate herself. She was a fucking mess. Her body was covered in vicious wounds. Many patches of her fur were dark and matted with blood. And her face, fuck, it sported so many grotesque bite wounds that it was hard to look at her.

It was a wonder she could see clearly through the blood all over her face. She had to be in some *serious* pain. Pride, apparently, wouldn't let her admit defeat.

The devil had almost as many injuries, and a lot of them were deep and ugly. Blood stained her muzzle and matted her coat, but she stood tall, braced to fight on.

"It's over, Ashlynn," said Tate. Her cat wouldn't understand the words, but Ashlynn would hear them. "Submit," he advised.

Instead, she weakly bared a fang at him—which earned her a snarl from the devil.

"Ashlynn, the only reason she hasn't burst open your goddamn skull with those jaws is that she's too mean to give you a way out. She wants you to have to skulk out of here on your own two feet, embarrassed and defeated. It's no skin off her nose if you want to keep this up. But you're not going to win, and she's not going to kill you. Cut your losses and submit now."

A low growl came from the cat, but then bones began to snap and pop as she shifted.

The devil let out a put-out sound, apparently disappointed that the battle was now over. She also then shifted.

Her breaths coming in short, soft pants, Havana stood upright. Her wounds protested the movement, but she made sure that her pain didn't show on her face.

Ashlynn had done some damage. The skank wasn't smirking anymore, though. Especially now that scratches crisscrossed over dozens of swelling bites on her face. The rest of her looked no better.

Trembling and breathing heavily, Ashlynn stared at Havana, looking somewhat dazed. That she'd been defeated? That the devil had so badly wounded her?

Havana shrugged one shoulder. "Told you it'd hurt."

Tate descended the porch steps and moved to Havana's side, but his eyes were on Ashlynn. "You challenged my mate."

The skank sneered. "You can't discipline me for it," she said, her voice edged with pain. "I don't answer to you anymore. I'm a lone shifter now."

"Which also means my healer isn't compelled to tend to your injuries."

Ashlynn's face went slack.

"You're banished from here," Tate declared, *all* Alpha. "Grab your shit and *go*. You don't return. Ever. Not even to visit your family. If you want to see them, you invite them to wherever you're staying. But you don't come back here."

She let out a derisive snort. "Like I'd even want to." She stiffly pulled on her clothes and, without a single look at anyone, hobbled across the lawn and through the crowd.

Tate looked at Farrell. "Follow her. Make sure she retrieves her stuff and leaves immediately."

The Head Enforcer nodded and trailed after the feline. A few words from Luke had the crowd dispersing.

Tate turned to Havana, his jaw tight. He looked eager to hold her, but he settled for cupping one side of her face. "Your devil really is a bloodthirsty little thing."

Her devil preened at that. "Was that ever in doubt?"

"No. But it's one thing to know it. It's another thing to witness it."

One of the pride's healers, Helena, approached. "Let's get you fixed up." She rested her hand on Havana's arm, and the healer's energy poured into her. Wounds closed over, bruises faded, and the fractures in her ribs healed.

Havana smiled. "Thanks."

"No problem," said Helena before striding away.

Havana blew out a breath and turned back to Tate. "I kind of need to clean up. Then I want pancakes."

He slid an arm around her shoulders. "I can make that happen."

As they all began to make their way back to the porch, Havana noticed that Bailey hadn't moved and was staring into space. Havana let out a sharp whistle. "Yo, mamba, you okay?"

Her eyes coming back into focus, Bailey nodded. "Yeah, I was just wondering … why do people say 'unsolved mysteries?' I mean, *obviously* they're unsolved, or they wouldn't be mysteries. Don't you think it's weird?"

Havana blinked. "Put that way, yeah, it's weird."

The rest of the day was pretty eventful, but not in a negative way. Members of the pride turned up in clumps to swear fealty to Havana and congratulate both her and Tate on their mating—even Eva, Aimee, and Priscilla. Havana had thought Ashlynn's mother might appeal her daughter's banishment, but Priscilla didn't even bring it up. Either she knew it would be pointless or she felt that it would be better if Ashlynn didn't return here.

Later that night, when Havana and Tate were finally alone, they each grabbed a beer and headed to the patio deck. It was a little cool out, so she snuggled into him on the rattan sofa. "It's nice having a backyard. I haven't had one since I lived with Corbin."

Tate took a swig from his bottle. "Did you talk to him about reducing the number of hours you work at the center?"

"Yep. He was already expecting it, because he knows how many responsibilities come with being an Alpha. And he knows the girls will be working the same hours as me from now on, what with them being my bodyguards and all. It doesn't leave him in the lurch. It means he can hire more loners or give other employees extra hours."

"Hmm," said Tate, a little gruff.

She sighed. "You can't possibly *still* be sulking."

He frowned, affronted. "I'm not sulking, I'm just annoyed." He knocked back some beer. "You should have told me."

"So you keep saying, *but* ... if I'd told you that I suspected Ashlynn would turn up and challenge me, you would have paid her a visit and ordered her to keep her distance."

"Well of course I would have. I don't want anyone laying their hands on you."

"Understandable. However, she'd have then spread the word that you intervened before she could challenge me. She'd have insinuated that you didn't trust I could hold my own. That would have tempted other people to challenge me, like Eva or Aimee or anyone who wasn't completely sold on having a devil shifter for an Alpha female. I didn't want to fight random members of your pride to prove my worth. So I let Ashlynn come for me, I used her to make my point, and now I won't have to beat up anyone else."

After a long moment of silence, he exhaled heavily. "You still should have told me."

She rolled her eyes. "No, I shouldn't have. Let it go. We've come out here to relax. So relax."

Intent on doing just that, Tate inhaled deeply—taking in the scents of flowers, herbs, beer, and the combined scent of both he and his mate. Music filtered out the open window of a nearby house, mingling with the sounds of grass rustling, branches creaking, and pond water rippling. Beneath all that was the soothing, steady beat of his mate's heart—no other sound would ever bring him more comfort.

"Okay, that's just weird," she said.

Tate frowned. "What?"

"You can hear that song playing, right?"

"*Pollyanna*. Yeah."

"Well, Aspen called Ashlynn 'a regular Pollyanna' earlier. Then the

Pollyanna movie was on TV this afternoon. And now *this*."

"Okay," he said carefully, unsure whether to laugh or just shake his head.

"You don't believe in signs, I know. But *I* do. And I'm not sure what the universe is trying to tell me yet, but there's obviously a Pollyanna involved."

Tate went to point out that coincidences happened all the time and it was no big deal, but instead he said, "Right. Well, whatever."

A loud thump came from inside the house.

Tate tensed. "Stay here," he said, even as he knew she wouldn't. He quickly but quietly slipped through the back door and followed the sounds of scuffling. Coming to a halt in the living room, he ground his teeth.

A bearcat had not only emptied the bucket he used to hold the logs for his fire, she'd flipped it over and was sitting on top of it. The bucket was rattling and bopping and hissing. Or, more to the point, whatever she'd trapped inside it was hissing.

He rubbed at his temple. "I don't know how or when you two got back in here, I don't even care. I'm going outside to finish my beer. When I get back inside, you'd both better be gone." Turning, he found his mate standing there, her lips twitching. He grabbed her hand and took her outside.

"They're still adjusting to not having me close-by," she said, leaning into him again on the sofa. "To be fair, I *did* warn you they'd be this way."

He sighed. "Yeah, you did. But I thought they'd be more interested in spending time in their new apartments."

"Imagine if you, Luke, and Farrell joined another pride. Don't you think they'd want to stick close to you until they felt settled; until they were certain *you* felt settled?"

"Well ... okay, yeah, maybe they would."

"The girls will adjust. They need a little time. You can give them that, right?"

He opened his mouth to say a reluctant yes, but then there was an exceptionally loud hiss. A bearcat came barreling out of the house and rushed across the backyard. A mamba gave chase, slithering along the ground remarkably fast, and lunged with a hiss. The bearcat grabbed the snake by her neck and shoved her coffin-shaped head under the pond water.

Watching as the bearcat tried to drown the mamba, Tate took a long swig of his beer. "No, babe. No, I can't give them time."

Havana sighed. "Right now, I can't even argue that you should."

CHAPTER TWENTY-TWO

Having filled yet another page of her notepad, Havana flipped the page and braced the tip of her pen over a fresh one. "Okay ... next family," she said, looking up at Tate. Noticing his face had gone all soft, she frowned. "What?"

Sitting beside her on the sofa with his hand splayed over her thigh, he dipped his head and pressed a kiss to her mouth. "I like that it's so important to you to know about the families within our pride. A lot of Alphas in your position would choose to just pick it up as they went along."

"These people pledged their loyalty to me yesterday, Tate. That's some serious shit. The least I can do is show interest in them." They'd each introduced themselves, of course, and made clear what position if any they held within the pride. But Havana wanted to know more. Nothing too personal. Just things that were necessary for an Alpha to know in order to properly look out for them.

It was also good to be aware if any of them were shit-stirrers, regularly defied authority, or had beef with other members. She'd then know to be prepared for any future issues that may arise.

"Do you mind if I share these notes with Aspen and Bailey?" asked Havana. "Because, as enforcers, it would be good for them to have at least some basic info on everyone in order to watch out for the pride's general well-being."

"Feel free to share anything that is relatively common knowledge within the pride," said Tate. "As for the things I told you were more private matters that members would only trust their Alphas and Betas with, keep those to yourself."

She nodded. "No problem. Now, tell me about the next family."

Tate went to speak, but then his cell phone rang. "Just a sec." He grabbed the phone from the coffee table. "It's Chen, one of the enforcers staking out the casino," he told her.

Havana straightened. "Please let it be good news."

Putting the cell on speakerphone, Tate answered, "Yeah?"

"A man fitting the description of Enrique just walked into the casino," said Chen.

Tate felt his muscles go tight. He scooted forward to sit on the edge of the sofa. "Alone?"

"No," replied Chen. "He has a guy with him who matches the description of the *other* jaguar."

Tate pushed to his feet, every part of his body feeling charged. "The original plan still stands—we follow them when they leave and hope they'll lead us to Gideon. I'll leave here as soon as I can and park a few blocks away from the casino. I can't tail the jaguars in the pride's SUV—it's too noticeable—so I'll need you and JP to take the lead on this and give me directions as to where they're heading. If they leave before I arrive, follow them. Don't wait for me."

"Understood."

Tate rang off and turned to his mate, whose eyes were bright with the same anticipation that pumped through both him and his cat. "We nearly have them."

"As time went on, I was beginning to worry that they wouldn't return to the casino," said Havana, placing the pen and notepad on the coffee table.

"So was I." Tate held up his phone. "I need to call Luke and the others so we can all get going. I don't foresee the jaguars leaving the casino very soon, so there's no reason for us to rush, but I'd rather we were in place just in case."

"And if they don't lead us to Gideon?"

"We'll just have a little talk with them. They must know where he is. If they have any common sense, they'll quite simply tell us." But Tate doubted they'd cough up the information easily, which didn't bother him at all. He had no issue doling out a little pain after all the bastards had done. Particularly since they'd have handed Havana over to Gideon if things had gone down differently. His cat was looking forward to making them pay.

"I'll contact Aspen and Bailey and tell them to get their asses here; they should come with us."

Tate bit back the reflexive urge to suggest that his mate remain here. It would be senseless, since she'd never agree to do so. It would also insult her, because she was more than capable of handling this situation—she'd already proven that. Plus, she was his partner, his equal. She had every right to be there.

Although her girls were often laws onto themselves, he'd been well-aware of that when he instated them as enforcers. He couldn't argue that they'd be useful, given the skills they'd picked up from their years working for the Movement. And he'd feel more comfortable if they were there, because he knew they'd protect his mate with everything in them if necessary.

He gave Havana a quick kiss. "You make your calls. I'll make mine."

Soon, they had Luke, Farrell, Alex, Vinnie, Aspen, and Bailey gathered around the living room. Tate quickly brought them up to speed.

"The jaguars probably plan to hang out at the casino for a few hours at least," hedged Vinnie.

"Probably," said Tate, his arms folded. "But I still want to leave as soon as possible. They could head somewhere pretty far from here when they leave. The closer we are to them when they head out, the better." He looked at Luke. "Depending on where Gideon is and how many he has with him, we may need more people. Tell the other enforcers to be ready in case we have to call on them."

Luke gave a crisp nod and pulled out his phone. "Sure thing."

Tate turned to Havana, impressed she stood so still and quiet when he could sense through their bond just how restless both she and her devil felt.

Havana gave him a hard look. "Don't ask me to remain behind, Tate."

He squeezed her hand. "Not gonna lie, I *did* consider doing so earlier. But I know you'd never go for it, and I know it'd be unfair of me to ask it of you."

Havana's hackles immediately lowered, and her devil ceased snarling. They could accept that he'd always be so overprotective *providing* he didn't expect she or her devil to cater to it. Havana could no more sit out of the action than he could.

Luke ended his call. "We ready?"

"We're ready," said Tate.

Inside the SUV, they didn't take the same seats as last time. Vinnie and Farrell insisted that Havana and the girls take the middle row instead of the back row. Havana quickly realized it was an acknowledgement of her new status.

Then they were on the road. It wasn't long before Luke was parking a short distance away from the casino. Tate checked in with Chen and JP, who confirmed that the jaguars were still inside the building and that there was nothing new to report so far.

Unable to do anything but wait for Enrique and his friend to move, Havana and the others remained in the SUV. Sometimes they talked about general things, sometimes there were long periods of silence. The time seemed to tick by at an exasperatingly slow pace—especially while she was all fired up to act, knowing they were so very close to finally getting their hands on the jaguars and, ultimately, Gideon York.

Finally, Chen called again. Tate put his cell on speakerphone as he answered, "Are our boys now on the move?"

"They are," Chen confirmed. "I'm passing you onto JP so I can concentrate on driving."

"JP, when you catch their license plate number, text it to River," said Tate. "Ask him to look it up."

"No problem," JP responded.

Luke pulled onto the road. "We'll be close but not close enough to spot, so keep me updated on every turn you make." The Beta trailed after their enforcers, following the directions JP gave. Before they knew it, half an hour had gone by.

"Just got a response from River," JP announced. "The license plate number doesn't match the car."

"Well of course it wouldn't be that easy," Havana grumbled.

Luke kept on tailing Chen and JP from a distance, never coming too close lest they be seen.

Tate sat up straighter when JP announced that the jaguars had turned into a housing estate. "Don't follow them," Tate ordered. "Drive past the estate and park nearby."

"There's a wooded area behind it," said Chen. "I'll stop the car there."

"We'll be with you soon." Tate rang off.

It wasn't long before Luke pulled up behind Chen's car. Everyone filed out of both vehicles.

Tate's eyes darted from JP to Chen. "Describe the jaguar's car."

"It was a gray Lexus," said JP, who then reeled off the false license plate number.

Tate turned to Farrell. "Find the Lexus. I want the jaguars' *exact* location."

The Head Enforcer quickly shed his clothes, shifted, and then flew off in his avian form. A mere minute later, he returned. Back in his human form, Farrell said, "The car's parked in the driveway of a house that backs onto the wooded area here. There are no other cars in the driveway, and no other people were visible through the windows, so I'd say they're alone."

Tate licked his front teeth. "Then this is more than likely their home."

"I wondered if the whole estate could have been claimed by Gideon for his 'family,' but the area doesn't reek of various breeds of shifter," said Farrell. "At least that means we don't have to worry that a bunch of shifters are going to descend on us to protect the jaguars."

"No one would descend on us anyway—we'll be in and out of there before anyone can notice us," said Tate. He glanced at the forest. "As their house backs onto the woods, we might as well take this route."

As a group, they traipsed through the wooded area—skirting around trees, stepping over fallen branches, sidestepping shrubs.

Finally, Farrell halted and gestured at a house. "That's the place."

Courtesy of her shifter-enhanced vision, Havana was able to get a good look at the two-story building. There was a light on in a room upstairs. The curtains weren't closed, so she could see a man who fit the description of Enrique's friend moving around in there. More lights were on downstairs, so it was possible that Enrique was somewhere on the lower level.

"None of the windows are open at the back of the house," Tate noted. "Alex, I need you to get us inside."

Havana wasn't surprised that he assigned that job to Alex. No one could keep a wolverine out of anywhere they wanted to be.

Tate ran his gaze along everyone as he said, "Okay, this is how it's gonna go down. Havana, you and your girls deal with the shifter upstairs. Detain him, don't kill him. And Bailey, don't bite him. Luke, Alex—you come with me; we'll subdue our good friend Enrique. I want people outside just in case they make a run for it or receive some visitors. Chen, JP—you two cover the front. If anyone turns up, give us the signal. Farrell, Dad—you cover the rear. When the bastards are secured, I'll call you both inside. Now, is everyone clear on what they're doing and where they should be?"

Each of them answered in the affirmative.

"Good, then let's get the fuck on with this," said Tate. He gave Havana a brief kiss. "Be careful."

"You, too." She, Aspen, and Bailey then melted into the shadows.

As the others took up position, Tate, Luke, and Alex crossed to the back door. The wolverine effortlessly picked the lock, and then the three of them were inside a somewhat small but stylish kitchen. Mostly white, it had an off-putting clinical feel.

Tate stood still, listening for sounds. All he could hear was the crunching of chips, the occasional deep chuckle, and a gameshow playing on the TV—all of which seemed to be coming from the other side of the house. He followed the sounds into the living room and, yeah, there was Enrique.

Sensing he wasn't alone, the jaguar shot his gaze to the doorway. He stilled, a chip halfway to his mouth. "The fuck?" He jumped to his feet, knocking the bowl of chips onto the floor. His eyes slid to the phone on the coffee table.

"Don't," said Tate, his voice pitched low and deep. "This isn't the time to do anything stupid, Enrique."

His nostrils flaring, the jaguar clenched his fists. "Get out of my fucking house," he spat, his voice unnecessarily loud, clearly trying to get his friend's attention.

Tate shook his head. "He's not coming to help you. No one is." Tate

Tate signaled at his brother and Alex, who then quickly subdued the jaguar. "Tie him up. The dining chairs looked pretty sturdy."

Telling himself that the silence upstairs was a *good* thing, Tate headed up there and made a beeline for the back bedroom. Inside, the other jaguar was gagged, out cold, and bound with zip ties.

Havana smiled at Tate and held up a wallet. "According to our boy's ID, his name is Gavin Wheeler. I interrogated a Gavin once. He was *very* chatty."

"I'm not so sure this guy will be," said Tate. "Not if he and Enrique have served Gideon for many years."

"You need to identify which of the jaguars is the weakest. Then you put the majority of your focus onto the strongest of the two. You make him hurt, make him bleed, put him through the kind of pain that will scare the weakest into confessing whatever he knows." When Tate stared at her, she lifted her shoulders. "What?"

His lips twitching, Tate said, "I like how ruthless you are. Now let's get Gavin downstairs."

Soon, both jaguars were securely bound to dining chairs. They'd been injected with shifter-suppressing serum, just as a precaution.

Enrique glared at Tate, his body very still, his dark eyes glinting with defiance. Gavin was breathing hard and fast, sweat beading his forehead.

"I think poor Gavin is struggling to breathe," said Havana, sounding as though she truly cared. "I'll remove the gags. Aspen, I could use your help with that."

Enrique and Gavin eyed them warily. Both males turned to stone when they noticed the black mamba slithering along the floor.

The moment the gags were gone, the jaguars flexed their jaws and licked their lips. They couldn't seem to decide whether to focus on Tate or whether to keep an eye on Havana and Aspen. Apparently, the cats were smart enough to sense that they didn't have harmless young women at their backs.

"Ooh, look at all this hair, Vana. So pretty." Aspen none too gently yanked out Enrique's hair tie, causing his brown hair to tumble free. She speared her fingers through it. "I wish my hair was so thick."

Enrique jerked his head to the side, trying to avoid her hand. He glared at Tate again. "We'll never tell you anything, no matter what you do."

Luke smiled. "Now he's just daring you to do your worst, Tate."

"It would seem so." Taking a seat at the table opposite the duo, Tate glanced from one to the other. Gavin was now trembling, eyeing the mamba slithering over his feet. And Enrique, well, he was grinding his teeth because Aspen and Havana had begun to put intricate, girly braids into his hair. Tate's cat probably would have been amused if he wasn't so preoccupied with thoughts of vengeance.

It was clear that Enrique was the more dominant personality. Gavin possessed none of his friend's bravado. With the right amount of pushing, he'd crumble.

Tate would do just as Havana advised; he'd focus mostly on Enrique and let Gavin witness just what lay ahead for him if he didn't talk. "You can't save your boss from me."

Enrique sneered. "You'll never find him."

"I found you."

Enrique's smirk faltered.

"I'm guessing you both escaped the compound with Gideon years ago. You must both be very loyal to him, considering he allowed you to live. Unlike the rest of your 'kin.' He killed them without blinking."

"He didn't take them with us because he wasn't sure of their loyalty," Enrique defended.

"He didn't take them because he didn't give a sliver of a fuck about them. They'd served their purpose. They'd helped him wipe out his pack. But he needed a few people to aid him in carrying out certain things while he laid low, didn't he? And that's where you both came in. All these years later, you still serve him."

"Yeah, we do. And we won't tell you *shit* about him."

Tate idly stretched his legs out in front of him and folded his arms. "You know, I've heard it said ... that there's nothing more dangerous than an Alpha shifter whose mate has been threatened. It's correct. I suppose the reason for that is twofold, really. One, our primal protectiveness is enhanced by our innate need to shield those under our care, and that primal protectiveness is a live wire when it comes to our mates. Two, our inherent instinct to take charge—not just of others, but of ourselves—pushes us to pursue the things we want, and that means our prey drive is so much more intense.

"Your patriarch became my prey when he targeted my mate. I'll *never* stop hunting him. Never. And I *will* find him, even if it takes years. So you see, you really can't save him from me. But you can save yourselves from a night of pure and utter agony by simply being cooperative. Tell me where he is."

Enrique let out a long breath. "All right, fine. He lives on Hampton Road. Or is it Chancellor Street? Hmm, it could even be Cleaver Avenue. You know, I really can't be sure." His head jerked as he hissed.

"Sorry," said Aspen. "Didn't mean to pull your hair so hard. It was a *total* accident."

Alex sidled up to Tate, his eyes on their captives. "Gideon's worth going through hours of excruciating pain? To him, you're nothing but a couple of easily replaceable employees. Loyal, sure, but still replaceable. Your deaths will be no more than a minor hindrance to him, if that."

"Wrong," Enrique bit out. "You kill us, he'll make you pay."

Noticing that the mamba was now beginning to twine her body around Enrique's leg, Tate flicked up a brow. "And why would he bother to do that? Maybe you were good little minions, but not good enough to avoid getting caught." Tate paused. "I want his location."

"I'd tell you, I would, but it's hard to remember," said Enrique. "My memory isn't what it used to be."

Wicked fast, Havana twisted a hand in his hair and yanked his head back.

She smiled down at him. "Well, hello." She slashed her claws across his face.

Enrique hissed between his teeth, the sound edged with pain.

Music filled the air as Vinnie chose a song from the selection on his cell phone. "Thought it might be good to disguise the screams. We don't want the neighbors coming to investigate, do we?"

"He looks pretty with those braids," said Aspen. "I think he'd look even prettier with some piercings." She stabbed a claw through his earlobe, eliciting another hiss from him. "Whoops! Made that hole a little too big. Don't worry, sweetie, I'll be more careful when piercing your nipple, I swear." Aspen ripped open his tee and pressed the tip of her claw against his nipple.

"Where will we find Gideon?" Havana asked him ever so pleasantly.

"Fuck you," Enrique gritted out. He again bit back a cry as Aspen sliced right through his nipple. He didn't make a sound when she sliced through the left one either. Or when she "pierced" his nose, or his eyebrow. But when she mentioned piercing his cock, the guy's entire body went rigid.

Tate pushed to his feet, slid the small table aside, and stepped forward. "Where do we find Gideon?"

Enrique snarled. "Fuck y—" He grunted as Tate slammed his fist into the guy's jaw. "*Bastard.*"

"So I've been told." Adrenaline pumping through him, Tate hit him again and again. Not in anger, not from a loss of control. No, it was a methodical beating designed to both make Enrique cave and Gavin piss his pants. And his cat enjoyed every moment of it.

Tate occasionally stopped, giving the captives a chance to talk, but they kept silent. So he pummeled Enrique's face until the jaguar's eyes swelled, his nose broke, his lips split, and his cheekbone fractured.

His knuckles a little banged up, Tate again asked, "Where do we find Gideon? It's such a simple question. One of you needs to be smart and answer it."

Enrique spat at him instead. There was a lot of blood mixed with his saliva.

Alex tutted. "That was a very stupid thing to do." He snapped one of Enrique's fingers, causing the cat to *finally* cry out.

Gavin looked away, but Havana gripped his head and forced him to watch as Tate again beat on Enrique, careful where and how hard he hit. He wanted the jaguar to break, not slip into unconsciousness.

"Not telling you shit, Dever—" Enrique screamed as the mamba constricted around his leg, crushing bones.

Havana sighed. "He's not going to talk, Tate. Other than to swear at you, that is."

Tate shrugged. "Then he doesn't need his tongue anymore, does he?"

Gavin's eyes widened in alarm. Enrique's eyes probably would've done the same if they weren't almost completely swollen shut.

Aspen held Enrique's jaw wide open while Luke drew out the man's tongue.

"A few slices from your claw should sever it easily enough," Havana said to Alex, who'd unsheathed his large, curved claws.

Gavin panted heavily, his face losing its color.

Still gripping the cat's head, Havana said, "Gavin, if you want your friend to keep his tongue, you need to tell us where to find Gideon. And if you don't, if Enrique here loses his tongue … well, he can't talk anymore, can he? So the only person we'd be able to question is … you. Yes, we'd have to turn all our attention onto you. I don't think you'd like that Gavin. Nobody would. Save yourself and Enrique. Tell us what we want to know."

Enrique squirmed, trying to speak but unable to while Luke held his tongue out. But the jaguar soon stilled when Tate aimed his claw just right, ready to slice through the appendage.

"No!" Gavin burst out. "Stop! You've hurt him enough!"

"We wouldn't have had to hurt him at all if he'd just answered Tate's question," said Havana. "When you think about it, he did this to himself in a roundabout way. But there's no reason for it to go on any longer. It can all stop right now. *Providing* somebody tells us where Gideon lives."

Tate hummed. "I don't hear anyone talking." He signaled at Alex, who lifted his claw ready to slice right through Enrique's tongue and—

"*We don't know!*" Gavin shouted.

CHAPTER TWENTY-THREE

"What do you mean, you don't know?" asked Tate.

"No one knows where he lives," Gavin swore. "He doesn't trust anyone with the information. He's paranoid that way."

"You're telling me Gideon is still underground? That he keeps himself secluded?"

"No, he isn't in hiding anymore."

Panting, Enrique shook his head. "Gavin, stop talk—" He slumped in his chair as Alex dealt him a knock-out blow to the temple.

Gavin's head whipped around, and he gaped at his friend.

Tate clicked his fingers. "Don't look at him, Gavin. You need to pay attention to me right now. I need you to focus. You can do that, can't you?"

His chest heaving, Gavin raised his eyes to Tate, looking lost and dazed. "You ... He ..."

"I know, he's a bit of a mess right now," said Tate. "But things didn't have to go down this way. All I want is answers. So let's get back to what you were saying before. You said Gideon isn't in hiding anymore."

"N-no," Gavin stuttered. "H-he doesn't go out a lot in public, but he hasn't isolated himself. He changed his appearance. No one who's seen him at the auctions has ever guessed he's Gideon York. Or if they did, they never said."

Tate narrowed his eyes. "He attends the auctions?"

"He hosts them, just like the one tonight."

Tate stilled, his pulse quickening. "There's an auction happening tonight?"

"Yes."

"And Gideon will be there?"

"Yes. He's always the auctioneer."

Anticipation once again pounded through Tate. "Where will it be held?"

"I ..." Gavin snapped his mouth shut, his face strained. "If I tell you, you'll go there and kill him."

"Fuck, yeah, I will. And I'll free all those loners who did nothing to deserve what's happening to them. He deserves what's coming, Gavin. He's had it coming for a long time. How you can't see he's one sick puppy, I don't know. I'll just bet he gets off on the power that comes with taking bids and declaring who is sold to whom."

Gavin frowned, shaking his head. "Gideon isn't like that."

Luke snorted. "Don't kid yourself. Your Alpha is all about wielding that kind of dark power."

"Gideon's not our Alpha. Our group ... it isn't like a pack or clan. We're a family. Gideon is head of our family. Our patriarch."

"So, he's your Alpha," said Luke.

Gavin's mouth tightened. "No. We're not like all of you. We don't want that cult-type life. Gideon guides us. Provides for us. Protects us."

"So, he's your Alpha," Luke repeated.

"No," Gavin bit out. "He just ... gives us direction. Helps us fight our nature. Following his order to shift only twice a year is hard, and disallowing our animals to influence our actions can be even harder. Especially when the animals know we never intend to claim our mates."

Havana shook her head. That had to be a fate worse than death for the guy's inner jaguar—it would never co-exist with its human half, never bind with the other half of its soul, never find the peace that came with a mating bond. Skirting around Gavin so that she could meet his eyes, she asked, "Why fight who you really are? What did your cat ever do to you?"

"It's his fault that my human family wouldn't accept me," replied Gavin. "His pride didn't want me either—they don't want hybrids polluting their gene pool." He snorted. "I never fit in either world."

Havana frowned. "And you think that makes you a special snowflake or something? The reason a lot of shifters become loners is that, like you, they had no one from either world who'd accept them. How are you any different from them? Why is your pain more important than theirs? Where was your empathy for them when your patriarch-who's-basically-an-Alpha asked you to help him sell them?"

Gavin's brow creased, as if he'd never before considered that his plight was similar to that of many loners. "But ... they're all doomed anyway. Loners never live long. That life is too dangerous for them to survive it."

"I'm guessing it was Gideon who fed you that bullshit," said Tate. "But, honestly, I don't care. I have only one question on my mind right now. Where will the auction be held?"

Gavin opened his mouth, but no words came out. He shook his head sadly.

Tate sighed. "Alex."

The wolverine gripped Gavin's pinky finger, which had the jaguar's eyes widening almost comically.

Gavin writhed. "No! No, don't!"

"Where will the auction be held?" Tate asked calmly.

Havana nudged the cat. "Come on, Gavin. I don't think your beloved patriarch would want you to suffer for him. And why stop now? You've already told us plenty. There's no sense in holding onto the location when we'll get it out of you eventually anyway."

"Why endure pain for him?" Tate asked the jaguar. "You say he protects you. I don't see how. He sends off you and Enrique to do much of his dirty work, doesn't he?"

Gavin's mouth bobbed open and closed. "Well ... yes."

"He never takes any of the risks," Tate pointed out. "He leaves you and Enrique to do that. So he's not really much of a protector, is he?"

"I, well, I don't know."

"Sure you do. Wake the fuck up, Gavin. He saw that need you have to belong, he gave you the 'family' you wanted, and then he took it from you. He went into hiding. Did he insist on you and Enrique going into hiding with him? Or did he have you two go out and do things on his behalf, again taking the risks?"

Gavin didn't answer, his expression pensive.

"The loners up for sale tonight ... one of them could just as easily have been you, Gavin. And if it had been you on the auction block, wouldn't you have wanted someone to speak out for you? To at least give the location of the auction so that it could be stopped?"

Gavin squeezed his eyes shut.

"He dirtied your soul by pulling you into his trafficking operation. A lot of lone shifters were probably sentenced to fates worse than death, and you sent them to that auction block. But now is your chance to wash away some of that dirt. You can save the people who are up for auction tonight. You can save yourself from receiving the same beating that Enrique got. So do it. Help us help them. Help yourself. Tell us where the auction will be held."

Gavin swallowed hard and lowered his eyes. "The yacht."

Tate's insides jumped. "Yacht?"

"It belongs to Gideon. He takes the assets and customers on board and then holds the auction at sea," Gavin confessed, his shoulders sagging. "The boat is called the Pollyanna."

Tate looked at his mate, who gave him a look that said, "Told you the universe was giving us another heads-up." Ignoring it, he turned back to the jaguar. "Well done, Gavin. This is almost over. First, tell me everything there is to know about this yacht."

From their shadowy spot near a closed rental office at the dock, Tate and his pride mates closely observed the goings-on near the Pollyanna mega yacht. Gideon was so certain he wasn't trackable that he didn't even have sentries posted around the dock. With the exception of the armed guards stationed on the upper level of the yacht, the only people in sight were the two males manning the entrance, clad in tuxedos.

"I'm getting the sense that those two have been doing this job for a while," said Luke. "They didn't just politely greet the people who boarded. They spoke to them like they'd met them before. Gideon must have a lot of repeat customers."

"What disgusts me is that everyone who boarded was dressed like they're attending a black-tie event," said Havana. "They're here to buy people, and they're acting like it's a regular swanky night out. They didn't even scurry on board while glancing guiltily over their shoulders. No, they all just strolled leisurely toward the boat without a care in the world."

"They won't be feeling so cool and casual when we board," said Alex. "And I don't think we'll find that too difficult. The two men on the dock aren't on high alert. The people patrolling the upper deck are pacing around, their guns at the ready, but none are paying as much attention as they should."

"Everyone seems quite sure that no one will be here who shouldn't be," Tate agreed. "I thought that Gavin was either wrong or lying when he said the security wouldn't be tight. Gideon's apparently too arrogant to accept that the people hunting him might just get close."

Gavin had finally broken after confessing the name of the boat. The rest of the information had just tumbled out of him—where the yacht was docked, how many minions would be on board, the names of the clientele, and even the layout of the boat.

The fiberglass and chrome mega yacht had several levels. According to Gavin, the captives were kept in the crew's quarters, which had been converted into rows of jail cells. The bidders were taken straight up to the spacious and luxurious middle deck, where they'd be given a catalogue of the "assets" to glimpse through. After cocktails, the loners were brought up, one by one, to be viewed and sold.

"I'm hoping the plan is as simple as this—we sneak on board and kill everyone except for the captives," said Havana. "Because, personally, I don't think the bidders should be allowed to wander free any more than Gideon and his employees should."

"Nor do I, babe," said Tate. "His 'guests' are here to buy people—that lost them the right to live. If it wasn't for fuckers like them, there'd be no market for this kind of thing."

Bailey's brows lifted. "Then no one has a problem if I kill any whom I happen across?"

"No," Tate told her.

The mamba smiled. "Groovy. Because I'd have done it anyway."

Tate turned to his pride mates. He'd brought plenty along with him after hearing that Gideon would have a lot of workers on board—some were chefs, waiters, etc., but they were loyal to Gideon and would join him in a fight if necessary.

"This all has to happen very fast. As soon as Gideon realizes his guards are down, he'll know something is wrong." Tate turned to Luke. "Alex and I will take out the men on the dock. You will lead some of our pride onto the upper deck to put the guards out of commission. Once they're down, the rest of us will board except for Farrell, Grant, JP, Chen, and Joaquin—they'll stand on the dock and eliminate anyone who throws themselves overboard and tries swimming to safety."

Tate turned to his mate. "I want you, Aspen and Bailey to head to the lowest quarters, take care of whatever guards might be there, and free the captives. Deke and Isaiah will aid you. Take the captives straight to one of our SUVs. We can't risk them running into the fight, potentially getting caught, and unwittingly making themselves hostages. Sam is waiting near the SUVs, he'll heal any who might have wounds," Tate added, referring to the second healer within his pride.

"I'll get them to safety," Havana vowed.

"I don't doubt that. Dad, I want you to see if you can find any papers or documentation from prior auctions that might show us where other trafficked loners were taken. Alex will go with you. If there's a safe or locked room, he can get you into them."

Vinnie nodded.

Tate cupped his mate's neck and gave it a gentle squeeze, almost smiling at her "Be careful" look. "All right, let's move."

Despite having utter faith in Tate, Havana felt her pulse quickening when he and Alex slipped away and became part of the night. Luke and a small team of cats also melted away, heading in the other direction.

She squinted, straining to catch sight of Tate. Nothing. Her heart began to beat a little faster, and a knot formed in her gut. It was only her past experiences with these sorts of situations that stopped her from restlessly tapping her foot.

She stilled as he and Alex materialized behind the two men on the dock. Both Tate and the wolverine snapped the necks of their targets in an instant. And the knot in her gut blessedly unraveled. Her devil chuffed, impressed by their stealth. No sooner had they hauled off the bodies than Luke signaled that the guards were all down.

Havana glanced at Farrell and the cats who'd be watching the dock. "Call out if you need us." She skimmed her gaze over the others and then tipped her chin toward the yacht. With little to no sound, they hurried toward it. She was thankful for the music she could hear playing on the middle deck, because there was no way to stop the wooden boards of the dock from creaking here and there as they dashed across it.

Tate caught up to her there. "Stay alert."

"You, too," she said.

Everyone swarmed the yacht in an eerie silence and headed in different directions. The scents of saltwater, sea air, and wood polish were heavy, making her devil's nose twitch.

Keeping her tread light so that the soles of her sneakers wouldn't squeak on the deck, Havana led the way as she, Bailey, Aspen, Deke, and Isaiah wandered the ground level in search of the entrance to the crew's quarters. She heard muffled voices coming from a room up ahead that, if the scents filtering out of it were anything to go by, was probably a kitchen.

Latch door.

Recognizing it from Gavin's description, Havana crouched near it and grabbed the handle. According to Gavin, only one shifter stayed down there with the captives. Havana knew they'd need to eliminate him fast so that he wouldn't have a chance to call out for help. She signaled to Bailey, who promptly shifted.

Havana whipped up the hatch door. A man sitting on a stool at the base of the stairs looked up just as the snake dived at him. Before he had the chance to cry out, she'd curled her slender body tight around his neck.

Havana leapt down, grabbed his head, and sharply twisted it—breaking his neck in one smooth movement. She lowered him to the floor just as Aspen and the others descended the stairs, closing the latch door behind them.

Havana turned to the cells, and her chest squeezed. Three young men. An elderly woman. Four teenage girls. A middle-aged man. And, oh God, a little boy—he couldn't be any older than eight. Unlike the others, he hadn't stood or moved to the door of his cell, he sat huddled in the corner.

"Please stay as quiet as you can," she said to the captives. "My name is Havana Ramos, and these are my pride mates. We're here to free you. But we have to do it quickly and without drawing attention."

One of the teenage girls gestured at the dead guard, a glitter of disgust in her eyes. "He said someone will come for us soon to escort us upstairs."

"Well, my pride mates are currently up there, and they'll take care of those assholes, so don't worry about them." Havana snatched the set of keys from the guard's pocket and tossed them to Deke, who then began to free the lone shifters.

She'd half-expected to find them in dirty, tatty clothing. But although they looked tired and undernourished, they were all clean and dressed in decent clothing. Probably so that they'd look presentable for their potential buyers.

One of the girls marched to the dead guard and spat on him. Recognizing her from the description Dawn gave her, Havana asked, "Are you Keziah?"

The girl stilled. "Yes."

"Dawn has been very worried about you. She asked me to do my best to find you."

Keziah's eyes glistened with unshed tears. "I didn't think anyone would even notice I was gone."

Havana looked briefly at the guard. "He hurt you?"

She gave a tight nod. "He wasn't the only one. You'll kill the others, too? Gideon? Earl?"

Her jaw hard, Havana said, "I can assure you that none of the fuckers on this yacht will survive what my pride mates do to them."

"Havana," said Deke. He tipped his chin toward the little boy's cell. "Need some help there."

Havana crossed to the cell. The kid still hadn't moved an inch, and he didn't look inclined to. Poor thing was terrified. She crouched down and kept her voice low as she said, "You're safe now." He didn't appear convinced of that.

Just then, Aspen came over in her bearcat form. Unsurprisingly, the boy's eyes lit up just a little at the adorable sight of her.

"Can she go inside to see you?" asked Havana.

He frowned. "It's not a good place. It's small and cold."

"I see. Then maybe you could come over and pet her. She likes that." Havana tilted her head. "What do you think?"

"It's okay, Robbie," said the elderly woman. "These people aren't here to hurt us."

"The man said others would come for us, Mary," Robbie reminded her. "That they'd buy us and take us away."

Havana shook her head. "We're not those people."

"It really is okay, Robbie," Keziah told him. "They know my friend, Dawn. She asked this lady to find me. Dawn wouldn't have done that if Havana was bad, would she?"

He chewed on his lower lip for a moment. Then, ever so slowly, he unfurled from his position and exited his cell. He stroked the bearcat. "Can we go now?"

"We certainly can," Havana replied, standing upright. She looked at the other loners as she said, "Please don't race ahead of me when we leave the room. Some of my pride mates are on the dock, ready to take down any fleeing bidders. I don't want them to mistake any of you for one of them."

"I want to fight," declared Robbie.

Deke looked down at him. "There's a very important job that needs to be done. A man's job. Mary needs someone to stick close to her to stop her from being scared. One of the other men could do it, of course. Up to you."

Robbie's chest puffed up a little. "I can do it."

"I thought so," said Deke.

Havana ran her gaze along each of the loners. "Stay quiet and follow us, we'll get you to—" A loud cry came from far above them, and then there was a roar. Shit. "Come on, let's move."

Havana stayed close behind Aspen's bearcat as the animal raced up the stairs. The bearcat pushed open the hatch and stepped out.

Two people in uniform skidded to a halt in front of her, their mouths parted in surprise. Their expressions softened. "Aw," they said in unison.

The bearcat leaped on one of the men, swiping out with her claws like a damn housecat, and knocking him flat on his back. More uniformed crew members came dashing around the corner just as Havana and the others reached the ground level. For a moment, everyone just stared at each other. Then claws sliced out, upper lips peeled back, and snarls sounded throughout the large space.

Havana, Deke, and Isaiah stood in front of the loners like a barrier. The crew charged as one, and she found herself facing a slim brunette. Havana whipped up her arm to block the hand that came at her with its claws extended, and then she shoved her own claws right in the bitch's throat.

The ground level became a battlefield. Fists flew. Feet kicked. Claws raked. Teeth bit. It was quite simply mayhem, but her devil damn well loved it.

Aiming to quickly incapacitate her attackers, Havana didn't bother with fancy moves. She punched throats, snapped necks, broke bones, severed arteries, and sliced open stomachs.

Flanking her, Deke and Isaiah were equally pitiless as they fended off the crew and decimated their numbers.

Some of the loners joined the fight, but they quickly began to tire. They thankfully had the help of Aspen's bearcat—the animal jumped on backs, slashed Achilles heels, and sank her teeth into sensitive body parts. Bailey's mamba also helped the loners, using those fangs of hers to inject venom into Gideon's people.

When only three crew members were still standing, Havana used that moment to lead the loners to the exit. As they clambered off the yacht, she nodded at Farrell, ensuring he knew they weren't enemies. It seemed that a few bidders were trying to flee the yacht by climbing overboard, because a number of dead bodies lay at the feet of Farrell and the other Olympus cats.

Deke and Isaiah closely followed the loners, helping to herd them off the yacht and along the dock. Havana waited, expecting Aspen and Bailey to be right behind them. Her heart sank when they didn't appear. She rushed back onto the yacht, along a corridor ... and almost crashed into two males.

One of them looked down at her, and his mouth curved into a slick, insincere smile. "Well, if it isn't Miss Ramos."

She knew that voice. Gideon.

"We finally meet in person." He pointed a gun at her head.

Fuck.

CHAPTER TWENTY-FOUR

Slicing open a male fox's throat, Tate let the body drop to the floor like a rock. He glanced around, searching for the man who'd stood on the manmade podium only minutes ago, speaking in a voice Tate had heard many times recently over the phone. But there was no sign of Gideon now.

Pandemonium had broken out literally the moment Tate and his pride mates raided the middle deck. Some of the clientele and workers had tried to flee, but most had braced themselves to fight. As such, Tate hadn't been able to rush straight for Gideon; he'd found himself facing a pissed-the-fuck-off hyena—who was now very dead.

The air rang with the yipping of jackals, the hissing of a lioness, the laughs of hyenas, and the roar of a black bear. The beasts were deadly, but they were supremely outnumbered. Pallas cats might not have size on their side, but they were incredibly vicious and had more manpower. So it was only a matter of time before the bigger animals had numerous pallas cats crawling all over their bodies, biting and clawing and weakening them.

Some of the bidders were already dead, as were the waiters who'd been serving cocktails to the sick bastards. Their broken bodies littered the floor, staining the wooden planks with blood, guts, and even bits of brain matter. Gideon *should* be among them, purely because he fucking deserved to be.

He'd either escaped via the staircase or he'd tossed himself overboard. If it was the latter, Farrell and the other pallas cats would get the pleasure of killing him.

Tate tensed as a large male abruptly rushed him. Tate dodged the punch that came his way and rammed his fist into the fucker's throat. The male sucked in a choked breath and swung again, clumsy this time. Tate ducked and slammed his fist into the side of the guy's knee, dislocating the bone. The male dropped, crying out in pain. That cry died when Tate snapped his neck.

Luke crossed to him, panting. "I don't see Gideon. You?"

"I'm thinking he went down that staircase over there. I can't see him tossing himself overboard." Seeing that few bidders still stood, Tate trusted that his pride could deal with them. He made a beeline for the staircase and jogged down it. He was stealthily making his way down a corridor, his brother hot on his heels, when he heard Gideon's voice coming from around the corner.

Tate quickened his pace, his blood pumping, but then he stopped dead when an achingly familiar female voice spoke.

"Leaving so soon? Your evening isn't going to plan, huh?" *Havana.*

Tate closed his eyes, and his cat arched his back as his fur stood on end. They'd both hoped their mate would be off the yacht by now.

"You have caused me a *lot* of trouble," said Gideon.

A snort popped out of Havana. "I'd say you created that trouble for yourself. You shouldn't be so surprised to see me. Tate did warn you that we'd find you sooner or later. Not sure why you didn't believe him."

"I would have let you all be if you'd only returned the favor."

"And we'd have let you be if you weren't a twisted asshole who sells people."

Tate slowly peered around the corner. And there was Havana, facing Gideon and another male. She also had a gun aimed at her fucking head. Tate's cat rushed for the surface in panic, trying to force the shift. Tate breathed through it, holding himself very still as he fought to keep his cat contained.

Dread seemed to sink into every bone in Tate's body, but this wasn't the time for him to rush in. If Gideon realized that she had backup so close, he could shoot her out of spite. Tate couldn't risk that. But, fuck, it was hard to just stand there and do nothing.

"How *did* you find me?" Gideon asked her.

"We had a long talk with Enrique and Gavin," she replied. "Two very brainwashed people, I must say."

She looked as cool and composed as she sounded. Tate knew it wasn't forced. He *felt* no panic from her. Only impatience and a sense of battle-readiness. He wondered if, sensing Tate's rage and dread through their bond, she'd guessed that he was nearby.

"Are all your 'kin' that way?" she asked Gideon.

"I didn't brainwash them. Didn't need to. Their hate for shifters was already there. I just … nurtured it a little. Now come on, you and I are going on a little walk. You're my ticket to getting away from here safely."

"I'm not going—"

Gideon shot her in the shoulder, and red-hot pain blasted down the mating bond. If Luke hadn't right then grabbed onto him, Tate would have charged at that motherfucker—common sense be damned. His cat raged and snarled and just about lost his mind.

"You won't help your mate if you rush over there," Luke quietly hissed into his ear. "Right now, Gideon needs her as a hostage. He won't kill her. But he *might* if he realizes he's cornered."

Tate gritted his teeth, reminding himself that his brother was right; that he himself had had the same thought only moments ago. But it was hard to be rational when Havana was injured and in pain. This was *his mate*. His other half. His better half. And hadn't she taken enough fucking bullets lately?

Tate held up a hand. "I'm fine," he ground out, his voice low. "You can let go."

Once his brother released him, Tate poked his head around the corner. Fury blasted through him at the sight of the blood staining the sleeve of her long-sleeved tee.

"There's no way you'll get out of here safely, Gideon," she said, a note of pain in her voice—a pain that pulsed down their bond. "You know that, right?"

"What I know is that you seem to matter very much to the Olympus Alpha male," said Gideon. "I'm guessing that your claiming bite is from him, because I can smell him on you. That must make you his Alpha female. Which means not one of those damn pallas cats will do anything to risk your life."

The male at Gideon's side cleared his throat. "Sir? There's a bearcat by the stairs chewing on a shoe."

Looking further along the corridor, Tate saw Aspen's bearcat sitting there, looking adorable and harmless and utterly indifferent to all that was happening around her.

"Can't say I give a shit, Earl," said Gideon, keeping his gaze on Havana. "Before we leave, I don't suppose there's a chance you didn't free my assets, is there, Miss Ramos?"

Furious, Havana felt her lips thin. "The word you're looking for is 'people,' not assets," she said, putting pressure on her aching wound, not a real fan of blood loss. Her devil was pacing, worried and enraged. Only the knowledge that their mate *had* to be close and quite simply needed an opening kept them from panicking. "As for whether I freed them, why don't you go check?"

"Um, sir, the bearcat's now hitting a *mean* looking snake with that shoe," said Earl.

Gideon's brows snapped together. "What?" He tracked his friend's gaze.

Havana acted fast, whipping up her arm and knocking the gun out of his hand. Several things then happened at once.

The bearcat crashed into Gideon, knocking him down.

The mamba rocketed at Earl and sank her fangs into his throat with a vicious hiss.

Tate and Luke raced around the corner and along the corridor ... just as Gideon grabbed the gun that had fallen to the floor. He fired at Havana, the fucker. But the bearcat chose that moment to throw herself at Havana and knock her down, taking the bullet with a pained growl.

The son of a bitch might have shot at Havana again if Tate hadn't then kicked the gun out of his hand and sent it skidding along the floor to Luke, who promptly picked it up.

Relief flooded Havana at the sight of her mate, alive and uninjured. She pressed hard against the bearcat's wound, unbelievably grateful that it wasn't fatal. "Bailey, take out my cell phone and call Sam."

Having shifted back to her human form, Bailey crouched beside her and did just that.

Gideon looked up at Tate, a cruel smirk shaping his mouth. "So glad you could join us."

"I highly doubt that," said Tate, menace etched into every line of his face. "Baby," he called out without moving his eyes from the wolf, "how are you and Aspen doing?"

"Our injuries aren't fatal, but they hurt like a mother," replied Havana.

"I just called Sam," Bailey informed him. "He's on his way."

"Gideon," began Earl, his voice shaky, "I think ... something's ..."

"You're dying, dude," said Bailey. "And I'm delighted to tell you that it's gonna hurt *a lot.*"

Gideon's eyes dropped to the gun Luke held. He lifted a taunting brow at the Beta. "Well? Aren't you going to shoot me?"

Luke frowned. "Why would I do that?"

Tate cocked his head, staring at the wolf. "You'd thought we'd kill you straight off? Why? I warned you when you called me that you'd die hard. It wasn't an empty promise. You should have heeded it. You didn't. You should have believed me when I swore that I'd find you. You didn't." Tate took a single step toward him. "And you really, *really* shouldn't have shot my mate. She's taken enough bullets because of you. So I think it only fair that she gets to be the first to hurt you. You good with that, baby?"

"Oh yeah," said Havana, taking the gun from Luke. She glared down at Gideon, who finally looked nervous. Yes, it was occurring to him that he didn't have a way out of this.

Gideon's eyes slid to the barrel of the gun as she aimed it at him. He swallowed. "Wouldn't you like to know where the other loners are who were auctioned off?"

"You know where they all are?" asked Tate.

"I chipped them before I sent them off with their new owners," replied Gideon. "Can't risk them fleeing and hiding. I can tell you where they all are."

Just then, Sam boarded the yacht. He quickly healed both Havana and the bearcat before taking a position by the wall.

"Sam here is our healer, as you might have guessed," Tate told Gideon. "I brought him with us for three reasons. One, there was a possibility that the captives might need him. Two, I wanted a healer on hand in case one of our pride was hurt. Three … I needed him to be here while we tortured you, because we don't want you to die *too* quickly, Gideon. There'd be no fun or real justice in that."

Gideon's breathing began to quicken. "We can talk first, surely. I can tell you where the other assets are."

"You can tell us *while* we hurt you," said Havana, who'd fully enjoy every moment of it. "I'd say you'll tell us absolutely anything we want to know in the hope of making the pain stop. But it won't stop. Not until we're done, anyway."

Gideon jerked toward her threateningly.

She smiled. "Oh, you thought I'd reflexively shoot in my defense? That's cute." Her devil all but rolled her eyes. "You know, I don't use guns—I prefer to fight with teeth and claws, like any self-respecting shifter. But for you, I'll make an exception. Call it a little tit for tat." She twisted her mouth as her gaze roamed over his body. "Now, where do I begin?"

"I'd shoot his kneecap first," said Bailey.

Aspen, now back in her human form, hummed. "I'd go for his gut. All the bile in his stomach will make the wound burn like holy hell."

"Both ideas hold some appeal. I'll get to them later." Havana lowered the gun until it was pointed at his crotch. "You raped Keziah, didn't you, Gideon? Probably raped many others, too."

Fear glimmered in his eyes for the first time. "My men might have done."

"Yes, they might have. But so did you and Earl." Havana frowned. "I never did get why a guy would think that taking a female against their will made them a *man*. There's nothing manly about it. The act is cruel. Cowardly. Dickless. And so I don't think you need yours."

His eyes widened, and he shook his head. "No."

Havana pulled the trigger.

Tate massaged conditioner into his mate's hair as the hot water drummed against their skin and pattered the base of the shower stall. Condensation streaked the tiled walls and the frosted glass door. The humid, steamy air was laced with her coconut-scented shampoo and conditioner.

After returning from the dock, they'd headed straight to the bathroom and into the shower. They both needed this. Needed to wash the evening away. Needed a bit of normal. Needed to feel clean again. Needed the tropical smells of her soap and hair products to drown out the scents of anger, fear, blood, and pain that had overwhelmed their senses and filled their lungs.

More, Tate needed to touch her. Hold her. Breathe her in.

As she rinsed the conditioner from her hair, Tate found himself tracing the spot on her shoulder where the bullet had passed through. Too close. He'd come too close to losing her. Again. His chest went tight each and every time he thought about it.

There wasn't even a blemish on her skin, thanks to Sam. But Tate knew it would be a while before he'd be able to look at her shoulder without remembering there'd once been a fucking hole in it.

Havana sighed. "You've got to stop with the brooding. I'm trying to make my mind and body relax. It's kind of hard to do that when I can feel you dwelling and obsessing over what happened."

He frowned. "Firstly, I don't brood." He ignored her snort. "Secondly, it's pretty hard to just *forget* that you were shot. I saw it happen, felt the impact of the bullet, felt your pain."

She placed her hands on his chest. "I don't expect you to forget. I just don't want you to keep thinking about it."

He grunted. "That's easier said than done. Being so close yet so far while the bastard aimed that gun at you ... I almost charged right at him, which would have been the height of stupidity, but rationality left me for a few seconds."

"And you feel guilty about that?" She shook her head. "Tate, you didn't let me down. You felt my pain, but you didn't feel any fear from me, did you?"

No, he hadn't.

"You know why? Because I trusted that you'd *never* let him get me off that boat. I knew you were close—I could feel your panic and powerlessness through the bond. I knew I just needed to give you an opening. And when I did, you rushed right over. Gideon probably would have shot at me again, since the other bullet hit Aspen's bearcat, but then you were there. At no point did you let me down."

She grabbed his bottle of citrus shower gel from the corner shelf. He liked seeing her toiletries mingled with his own. He liked seeing her toothbrush in the holder next to his. Liked that one of the vanity drawers was filled with her cosmetics, that the bathroom often smelled of her body spray, and that her hair products lined the counter right beside her round makeup mirror. It reminded him that they'd blended their worlds.

As she lathered the creamy soap onto his skin, he decided he liked that more. Her touch was soft and sensual, and he knew ... "You're trying to distract me."

"You should just let me. Go with it."

"You find it easy to just put the evening out of your head?"

"No. But I don't see any sense in obsessing over what did and didn't happen. I thought about it. I processed it. And then I decided I wasn't going to give Gideon or his bullshit anymore mental space."

"But—"

"It's over," Havana reminded him, pressing a kiss to his mouth, wishing she could put him at ease somehow. "All of it is over. He's dead now. Dead and mere ashes." As were the bidders and crew members. Her pride mates had tossed the bodies from the dock back onto the yacht and then set the damn thing on fire.

She dabbed another kiss on his mouth. "Let yourself feel some relief and happiness in the fact that the threat that once hung over our heads is now gone. We saved a lot of people today. And we'll soon be able to return home the shifters who were auctioned off in the past."

Between the things Gideon confessed and the documentation that Vinnie found on the yacht, they'd be able to locate and rescue all of the sold loners. They'd also take it upon themselves to subject their "owners" to whatever suffering they'd put the trafficked shifters through. It seemed only fair.

The people they'd rescued from the yacht tonight were now safe at Dawn's shelter. Some of them, such as young Robbie, would be reunited with their family members—people who'd lived the lone shifter lifestyle right alongside them. Dawn would also be sure to get them whatever help, support, or counselling they needed, even if they didn't remain at the shelter.

Tate pressed a kiss to her throat. "There is a lot of relief in knowing the threat to you is gone. And now you and I can simply enjoy being mated without Gideon distracting us. We can even start planning our mating ceremony/welcome to the pride/congrats on your mating party now."

"We can indeed. We could even start celebrating it now," she added, fisting his cock. "Just the two of us."

They kissed, stroked, probed, shaped, and teased until neither could take any more.

Tate backed her against the tiled wall. "Got to be in you now." He hooked one of her legs over his hip, angled her hips just right, and then slid his cock inside her.

CHAPTER TWENTY-FIVE

Two months later

Havana felt her brow crease. "So, her problem with me is simply that I'm a devil shifter?" she asked, speaking over the loud music.

"It's not really a case of shifter-breed prejudice," said Jaime, the Phoenix Pack's Beta female. "Greta's an equal opportunist when it comes to hating people—she detests most of the population pretty much equally."

"Ah." The old woman had been shooting death glares at Havana all evening, and she was getting on her inner devil's last nerve. "She seems to get along well with Ingrid, though."

"Greta thinks pallas cats are much like her," began Dante, Jaime's mate, "so she has a lot more tolerance for them."

The woman sounded like a complete basket case to Havana, but whatever. She sipped from her neon-colored cocktail. As it was tradition for the pride to hold celebratory events at the Tavern, everyone had gathered there for the afterparty of her and Tate's mating ceremony.

Beneath the blasting music was the sounds of laughing, talking, bottles clinking, and dancers cheering. She and Tate were "doing the rounds," speaking with various guests and thanking them for coming—hence why they were currently talking with the Phoenix Pack Betas and two of the pack's wolves, Trick and Frankie.

Looking at Havana, Jaime tilted her head. "You don't give off the 'I'm an Alpha, fear my wrath' vibe, but my wolf can sense how strong your animal is. My beast is stuck between respecting that strength and being a little unnerved by it."

"From what I've observed," began Tate, curling his arm around Havana's waist, "her devil seems to have that effect on a lot of people's inner animals."

Havana felt her lips twitch. "Including yours?"

"My cat's not unnerved by your strength," said Tate. "He finds it a turn-on."

She lifted one shoulder. "I can live with that."

Dante took a swig from his beer bottle. "I'll bet you're both relieved that the whole Gideon business is behind you."

"Very much so," said Havana. Especially since the loners who were sold in past auctions had all been returned home.

"It seemed to take forever to track him down," Tate grumbled.

Adjusting the position of the little boy balanced on his hip, Trick said, "Yeah, but you played it right—you didn't waste time or resources on guesses, you didn't let your emotions get in the way. You remained careful and patient during the hunt, and it paid off. As they often say, slow and steady wins the race."

Frankie's brows drew together. "I can't say I've *ever* seen a slow Olympic runner win a race."

Trick's eyelid twitched. "Oh my God, Frankie, it's just a—"

"Turn of phrase, yada, yada," the she-wolf finished, rolling her eyes. "We've been over this; proverbs are plain dumb."

"Dumb," echoed their son, who then squeezed his father's nose hard with an impish chuckle.

Noticing his aunt trying to get his attention, Tate gently squeezed Havana's hip. "Valentina's waving us over." He turned to the Phoenix wolves. "I appreciate you all coming."

Jaime smiled. "Thank you for inviting us."

"Enjoy the rest of your night," Havana told them.

Leading his mate toward the corner table where Valentina, James, Mila, and Dominic were gathered, Tate was careful to stop Havana from being jostled as they shrugged through the tight crowds.

Valentina gave them air kisses and pretty much ordered them to sit. Exchanging hellos with the other shifters at the table, Tate and Havana took the two empty seats.

"Having a good night so far?" asked James.

"Oh, yeah," said Havana. "Pallas cats are nothing if not entertaining."

James smiled. "True enough. I've noticed that you seem to get along well with Vinnie, Luke, Elle, and Damian."

"I do," she said. "I mean, what's not to like about them?"

Valentina huffed. "Do not get me started on Vinnie. The man is *useless*. Too weak to be pallas cat. You know I *despise* weakness. It is good that Tate took over our pride."

Tate felt his lips twitch, and he noticed James roll his eyes. Vinnie was *anything* but weak. Still, there'd be no convincing Valentina differently, so no one even tried anymore.

James pointed at Havana. "Don't take for granted that you've blended well into Tate's family. I can't boast the same. Valentina's dysfunctional relatives will never accept me." He didn't sound too bothered by that, though.

Valentina rounded on him. "Perhaps if you did not call my mother 'Skeletor'—"

"It's just a pet name," said James.

"—and my father her 'man-slave'—"

"That's just a statement of fact."

"—they would be inclined to accept you. And my family is *not* dysfunctional."

"You think it's normal that your mother once gagged and bound your father to the bed in their spare room because she 'wanted a little peace and quiet'?"

"It was just role play. She freed him after two days."

"Oh, well, then it's okay."

Struggling to hold in a laugh, Dominic smiled at Havana and Tate. "You two look so loved up I'd find it nauseating if I wasn't the same with my mate." He looked at Havana, adding, "Mila was my first, you know. She took my virginity." Everyone snorted, but Dominic ignored them. "She wasn't so keen on having me at first, but who can resist an offer of ten solid inches of warmth, love, and understanding?"

Mila sighed at Havana. "I know what you're asking yourself. And yes, he *is* always this weird."

Dominic peered down at Mila. "But you can't say I don't make a good mate, baby." He slid his gaze back to Havana. "I treat her like my homework. Toss her on the table and spend all night doing her."

Mila lifted a hand. "That's it, you don't get to talk to other people anymore."

As the couple quarreled, Tate looked at Havana and said, "Apparently, he used to spout cheesy lines at every woman he met. Some think it's a mental disorder, but they're not sure."

After talking with his relatives a little longer, Tate and Havana thanked them for coming. They then went back to strolling around the Tavern, mingling and accepting people's well wishes. Soon, they were approaching the bar where Vinnie, Luke, Elle, Alex, and Bree stood.

Vinnie looked from Havana to Tate, his eyes dancing. "The mating ceremony was … interesting."

Havana raised her hands. "I wasn't laughing because I wasn't taking it seriously. I heard Bailey fart, and then she and Aspen got into a whispered dispute about whether farting in public was rude. I could hear it the whole time, and it just set me off. I did apologize to Tate."

"And I do forgive you," Tate told her. He put his mouth to her ear and whispered, "But you'll still pay for that later when we're in bed." He smiled at her little shiver.

Hearing a lot of rhythmic hissing, Tate turned to see a bunch of shifters in their mink form dancing and hissing in tune with the song. His inner cat scrunched up his face.

"I didn't know minks were into Freddie Mercury," said Havana.

"They're certainly into this song, since if what I heard is true, they've been known to hiss *Another One Bites the Dust* during battle," said Tate. And that wasn't weird at all, was it?

The only mink who'd been officially invited to the party had been Casey, a Mercury Pack member. When her friends had heard about the celebration, they'd asked to come along.

It had been a great night so far but, cranky about having to share his mate's attention, his cat wanted to leave. Honestly, Tate would like to take her home and spend the rest of the night celebrating their mating in style. But one of the setbacks of being Alpha was that he couldn't do as other couples often did and escape their party early. He had to "set an example" and be sure to thank all the other Alpha pairs for being present.

Holding a paper plate *piled* with food from the buffet table, Alex said, "Go, Tate, take your mate and have some time alone with her—it's obvious you want to. No one will judge you for it."

Bree snorted at the wolverine. "You're just saying that because if *they* leave early, it won't look so awful if *you* leave early."

Alex appeared genuinely perplexed. "You're clearly forgetting it means nothing to me if people would find me 'awful' for leaving. My opinion matters. Your opinion matters. Anyone else? I could give less of a fuck what they think."

"Now you're being rude," said Bree.

Alex shrugged. "I don't care."

Just then, Jessie and Farrell approached. The female beamed and said, "Congratulations on your mating."

"Aw, thank you." Havana smiled at the tiny baby in the Head Enforcer's arms. "I don't know how he's sleeping through all this noise."

"He seems to sleep better *when* there's noise," said Jessie.

Havana put her hands together as if in prayer. "Can I have a hold?"

"Sure," said Farrell, who then carefully placed the baby in her arms.

Watching his mate cradle the newborn, Tate felt his chest tighten. He wanted that. Wanted them to start their own family one day. Wanted to see her holding *their* child. "How's fatherhood?" he asked Farrell.

The male grinned. "The best. And exhausting, but worth it."

Tate had arranged for Deke to temporarily replace Farrell as one of Tate's bodyguards, wanting the Head Enforcer to have plenty of time to spend at home with his mate and newborn baby boy.

At first, Tate had wanted both Deke and Isaiah to continue shadowing Havana, but she'd fought him on it every step of the way, refusing to have added protection when she simply didn't need it. She had, however, agreed to keep the car with the bulletproof windows. Mostly because she couldn't argue that Vinnie's enemies might strike at him via her or Tate.

The music changed again, but the minks didn't leave the dance floor. Tate twisted his mouth as he watched them. "So, minks like the conga too, huh?"

"As does Bailey, apparently," said Luke.

So it would seem. The female mamba was actually *leading* the line, looking in her element. A little girl with ruby red hair was at the rear, having the time of her life—the daughter of Casey and Eli, the Mercury Pack's Head Enforcer. Her slightly older brother stood off to the side, shaking his head at her.

Elle chuckled. "Bailey is a riot. I just love her. Oh, she's dragging Damian into the conga line. And he's *letting* her. Someone should really warn her that she's dancing with the son of Satan."

Vinnie flicked his daughter an exasperated look. "Elle, you've got to let it go."

The redhead's lips thinned. "He painted satanic symbols on my front door."

"Probably because you painted crucifixes on his bedroom door," said Vinnie.

Elle threw up her arms. "How else can we combat his evil?"

Still cradling the baby, Havana looked at Luke. "Hey, how's your left hand?"

The Beta's brow creased. "My hand?"

"Yeah," she replied. "Is it sore or anything?"

Luke slid Tate a confused glance before shaking his head. "No, it's fine," he told her.

Havana frowned. "Oh. Okay."

Feeling his mouth quirk, Tate leaned into her. "You almost sound disappointed."

"Not disappointed," she said. "Just surprised. The universe warned me that something would happen to his hand. I don't get why he's fine."

"I do. It's because the universe doesn't warn us." But Tate still found it endearing that she believed differently.

"Come on, even *you* have to admit the signs are there. The movie *Cool Hand Luke* popped up as a new title on my streaming service, I saw a novel in the bookstore yesterday with that exact same title, *and* a song called *Left Hand Luke* played on the radio this morning."

"I think it's a coincidence. Nothing more."

She sniffed. "There's no helping you. There really isn't."

At that moment, Aspen sidled over with Camden close behind her. After cooing and awing over the baby, the bearcat said, "Bailey's certainly popular with the minks. You have to admire her ability to blend into whatever social circle she enters. Not that she's always welcome for long, since she can't help but stir shit. Still ..."

Camden looked at Tate. "Not sure if you know, but those two wolves look like they're about to throw down. Well, the youngest doesn't seem all that pissed. But the older one is getting all worked up."

"Yeah, they do that often," said Tate. "Nick, who's the Alpha male of the Mercury Pack, doesn't like that the son of the Phoenix Pack Alphas hangs with Nick's daughter a lot. The two males regularly get into stare-outs, but they never take it further."

Aspen tipped her chin toward Corbin and Dawn. "Those two are *so* cute together."

"Totally," agreed Havana. "I'll be surprised if they don't imprint on each other. Corbin's absolutely gone for her."

Luke smirked at Tate. "Kind of like you're gone for Havana. Or 'whipped' might be a better word. *Kidding*, no need to growl." He clapped Tate on the back. "Happy for you, bro. You might have tried to kill me several times over the years, but I still got nothing but love for you." Luke sighed when Tate didn't speak. "You're supposed to return the sentiment."

"You want me to lie to you?" asked Tate.

Luke rolled his eyes. "I know you love me."

"Funny. You once accused me of hating your guts with a pathological passion."

"You broke my leg in two places! And you did it because I went into your room without knocking first."

"You missed out the part where you peed all over my shoes while you were in there."

"I only did that because you tried to drown me *for the third time*."

Tate shrugged. "They say 'third time's a charm,' so I figured it was worth a shot."

"Come on," Havana cut in, tugging on Tate's shirt. "Let's go thank some more people before you and your brother get into a full-blown argument." She returned the sleeping baby to Farrell.

She and Tate spent over another hour circling the Tavern and dishing out their thanks.

When they'd finally done their rounds and the night was coming to a close, Tate grazed her ear with his lips as he said, "Don't know about you, but I'm ready to get out of here."

"Sounds good to me," she said.

Luke and Deke escorted them home, but Tate dismissed them the moment he and Havana stepped into the house. He then crossed to his mate, who was hanging up her jacket. Once she'd kicked off her shoes, he pulled her flush against him. "It's been hours since I had a taste of that mouth. Open for me."

Her nose wrinkled. "Not really feeling in the mood. Too tired."

He felt one corner of his mouth kick up, knowing she was playing with him. "I'll bet I could get you in the mood."

"I don't think that'll happen."

He backed her into the wall. "I accept your challenge." He dropped to his knees, hiked up her dress, and pressed a kiss to a bite mark he'd left on her inner thigh. He had a very vivid memory of branding her there just before he'd flipped her over and claimed her ass. It was an experience he intended to repeat, but not tonight.

He caught the waistband of her panties and dragged them down her legs. "I've wanted to do that since the moment you pulled them on. I also wanted to do this." He hooked one of her legs over his shoulder, spread her plump folds, and took a long lick.

Havana slammed her palms on the wall behind her as he began to eat her out. He didn't tease. He feasted. Every erotic flick of his tongue, every scrape of his teeth, and every suckle on her clit wrenched moan after moan out of her.

She arched into his mouth, wanting more. He thrust his tongue deeper, giving her what she needed. The tension inside her built and built until she was hanging on the edge of a momentous orgasm. Her knees buckled. Her thighs tremored. Her face flushed.

She slipped her fingers through his hair, scratching his scalp. He growled. The guttural sound rumbled against her flesh and vibrated up her pussy. And she came, her back bowed, her claws slicing out and digging into the wall.

Breathing heavily, she looked down at Tate. Licking his wet lips, he stared up at her, his eyes glittering. Even on his knees, he looked dominant, in charge, and fully in control. The latter made her devil bristle. No, he didn't have that control. Not yet.

Havana slowly pulled back the leg he'd hooked over his shoulder. She rested her foot against his chest ... and shoved him hard enough to give her room to escape. She ran. Her feet pounded on the stairs as she rocketed up them, egged on by her cat, conscious of him pursuing her.

Hands grabbed her hips as Tate pulled her to a halt halfway up the stairs. He covered her body with his, forcing her to her knees. She hissed and writhed and tried bucking him off. But he slipped one arm beneath her and banded it diagonally across her body to grip her shoulder, holding her securely in place. Still, she fought him. He let her, pressing soft kisses and gentle suckling little bites to her nape ... acting for all the world like her struggles simply weren't on his radar.

Havana slapped the stair in front of her. "You motherfucking motherfucker."

"That wasn't very nice." He roughly plunged two fingers inside her, shocking the breath right out of her. "I'm not saying it ain't true, but it wasn't nice." He pulled back his hand, spread his fingers inside her, and drove them deep. "Now you're going to be still while I have my way. That understood?"

"Uh, no." She lunged, meaning to escape again, but his grip on her shoulder kept her exactly where he wanted her. Which pissed her off even as it turned her on. All that strength and power ... yeah, it pushed all her best buttons. Still, she growled and struggled.

"Yeah, fight me, baby."

She did. Even as he fucked her with his fingers, she fought to be free. But it wasn't long before her body betrayed her and got swept away by the feel of his fingers swirling and plunging and scissoring. She kept one hand planted on the stair in front of her while reaching back her other arm to curve her free hand around his nape.

"Yield, baby, and I'll give you what you need."

Havana let her body relax beneath him, as if the fight had drained out of her.

He hummed, sliding his arm out from beneath her to cup her hip. "Good girl."

No, she wasn't a good girl. And forgetting that was his mistake.

Tate swore as she fled. One moment his fingers were buried inside her, the next she was rushing up the rest of the stairs. He followed, hot on her heels. In the bedroom, she dashed around to the opposite side of the bed. They stared at each other, panting, tense, each waiting for the other to move.

He feigned right. She leaped onto the bed, ran across it, and jumped. He caught her midair and, ignoring her punches and kicks, set her on the floor near the wardrobe. He roughly turned her to face the mirrored door, plastered his front against her back, and curled his arm tight around her. "Tricky little bitch, aren't you?" He kicked her legs apart and thrust his rock-hard cock inside her.

"Fuck." The word *popped* out of her as she instinctively shot out her hands, bracing herself against the wardrobe.

Tate clawed off her dress. "Now you'll watch me take you," he growled into her ear, "so you remember you can't keep this pussy from me."

He pounded into her body, sensing her surrender, relishing that she'd yielded control to him.

She was pure liquid heat around him, holding his dick in the snuggest grip. In the most *perfect* grip, because she was tailor-made for him in every way. Other men might have been in her bed, but she hadn't been created for them, hadn't existed purely for them. She was Tate's. Always had been. Always would be.

He hadn't lied when he told her that being inside her brought him peace. It did. It also brought out his most primitive instincts. The instincts to fuck, claim, possess, own. He wanted to crawl so deep inside her he'd never find his way out.

Moaning, she began shoving back her hips to meet his thrusts. He fucked her harder, loving the perfect view he had, thanks to the mirror in front of him—her eyes glazed, her skin flushed, her tits bouncing, her nipples tight.

"You look even more beautiful when you're taking my cock." He slid one hand from her hip to her breast and squeezed it, his grip nothing short of proprietary. "Touch your clit."

"That's sort of your job." Havana gasped as he pinched her nipple, and the pain shot straight to her clit.

"Do it." He dragged his blunt nails up her inner thigh. "Suddenly feeling shy?" He took her hand and used her finger to rub at her clit.

Oh, God. The damn cat knew what she liked, and he used her own finger to give it to her. Shit, she was *so close*. His breath hot on her neck, his fingertips digging into her hips, his cock slicing into her again and again … It was all too much, but her orgasm remained out of reach.

Needing to come, she said what she knew would make his self-control crumble into pieces. "I love you."

He hissed out a curse, and then he was jackhammering into her in that way she loved. She reveled in it, pushed back to meet each thrust, kept on working her clit. He fisted her hair, wrenched her head back, and bit her throat.

Like that, she imploded.

Her release washed over her, so damn intense her knees buckled. His teeth sank deeper into her neck as he rammed into her again and again and again … And then he was spilling himself into her.

Her legs like jelly, she had to lean back against Tate just to say upright.

He nuzzled the fresh bite. "Love you too, baby." Locking eyes with her through the mirror, he wrapped his arms around her. "Always will."

"That's because I'm awesome."

His mouth quirked. "Not telling me anything I don't already know."

She chuckled. "I need to go clean up."

Enjoying holding her while looking his fill, Tate very reluctantly withdrew his softening cock and then released her. As she disappeared into the bathroom, he began shedding his clothes. By the time she'd returned, he was naked and lying on the bed. His heartbeat still hadn't calmed, but the panting had passed.

"Did you enjoy the ceremony?" he asked.

"Yup. And the afterparty." She took fresh panties and a long tee out of the dresser. "You?"

"Well, there was you, our families, food, music, and our pride mates. So, yeah, it was a good night. Thank you for not ending it with a barfight."

Dressed, she smiled. "I'll be honest, it wasn't easy."

"I liked watching you hold Jessie and Farrell's baby," he said as she sprawled over his chest. "I'm looking forward to us having our own, but I'm in no rush." He slid his hand under her tee and slipped it into her panties to palm her ass. "I like having you all to myself. I'm not so good at sharing you. Neither is my cat. He likes having all your attention, so he wasn't happy at the party."

"I know, my devil sensed it. She found it amusing."

"Oh, she did?" Tate lifted his head to nip her lower lip, trying not to smile at the cranky face his cat pulled. "She's often amused at his expense."

"Well, he *is* kind of spoiled. As are you. You both always seem so confused when you're not getting what you want."

"We have what we want: You." He took her mouth in a slow, shallow, lazy kiss, feeling so fucking full. Of her, of joy, of peace.

What he felt for Havana ... fuck, it was so all-consuming and bottomless he could drown in it. She was his world. Filled him up, made him whole, soothed every hurt he'd ever felt. She was imprinted on his soul and embedded so deep inside him he'd never get her out, which was exactly how he wanted it. "You know you're everything to me, don't you?"

"Sure I do. Just as you know you're everything to—"

There was a loud bang downstairs followed by a familiar hiss that was quickly overrode by a bearcat-yowl.

Tate felt his jaw go hard. "They are *not* here. They're not."

Havana sucked in her lips to hide a smile.

"I warned them we wanted to be alone tonight," he said.

"Which, in their crazy minds, was the equivalent of daring them to come here."

"*Will you two stop!*" a voice bellowed. *Luke.*

Tate gritted his teeth. "*He's* not here either. He's just not."

Luke cursed long and loud. "*For God's sake, let the damn mamba go before you—ow, get your teeth out of my fucking hand!*"

Tate narrowed his eyes as amusement and smugness rippled down the mating bond. Unfuckingreal.

Havana gave him a little smirk. "I told you the universe—"

"No. Just no."

ACKNOWLEDGEMENTS

Thank you so much to my unfailingly supportive family for all you do, I love you all. A mega thanks to my son for creating the cover for me - you're so amazingly talented, and I am in total awe of you. Also, thank you to my wonderful PA, Melissa, who I'd be lost without. I also have to thank my wonderful editor, Melody Guy, for all her help and guidance. Last but not least, I'd like to say a gigantic thanks to all my readers - for taking the time to read this book and for taking a chance on the series itself.

Take care

S :)

ABOUT THE AUTHOR

Suzanne Wright lives in England with her husband, two children, and two Bengal cats. When she's not spending time with her family, she's writing, reading, or doing her version of housework—sweeping the house with a look.

TITLES BY SUZANNE WRIGHT

The Deep in Your Veins Series
Here Be Sexist Vampires
The Bite That Binds
Taste of Torment
Consumed
Fractured
Captivated
Touch of Rapture

The Phoenix Pack Series
Feral Sins
Wicked Cravings
Carnal Secrets
Dark Instincts
Savage Urges
Fierce Obsessions
Wild Hunger
Untamed Delights

WHEN HE'S AN ALPHA

The Dark in You Series
Burn
Blaze
Ashes
Embers
Shadows
Omens
Fallen

The Mercury Pack Series
Spiral of Need
Force of Temptation
Lure of Oblivion
Echoes of Fire
Shards of Frost

The Olympus Pride Series
When He's Dark
When He's an Alpha
When He's Sinful (Coming 2022)

Standalones
From Rags
Shiver
The Favor

Printed in Great Britain
by Amazon